NEW GEPT

新制全民英檢

中級 閱讀測驗必考題型

陳頎／著

國際語言中心委員會／監修

 英檢出題方向來自**日常生活**
3大類英檢**最常考**情境融入題型演練

Step 1

● **必考單字片語**

本書精心整理必考的詞彙、片語及常見諺語,搭配豐富例句說明,方便學習者複習及背誦,扎實地強化英文實力。

Step 2

● **10 大必考文法**

深入分析全新中級英檢閱讀測驗常考的 10 大文法,幫助學習者整理各種文法考題的要點,釐清文法觀念之後,就能更進一步培養解題技巧。

Step 3

● **英檢閱讀 3 大題型**

題庫的編排方式完全模擬全新英檢中級考試的 3 種題型:詞彙、段落填空、閱讀理解。重新整理必考題型,提供學習者最逼真的考試臨場感。

Step 4

● **生活場景 3 大主題**

本書歸納最常考的 3 大情境主題,包括:生活休閒、書信應應、記敘論說。完整收錄情境必考題庫,讓學習者在考前精準猜題,掌握生活情境主題的閱讀文章。

Step 5

● **閱讀模擬測驗考題**

學習者熟悉這些上述這些常考題型後,可以再做一回模擬試題,把自己所學習的知識運用到考試中,在考試前事先知道自己的弱點在哪裡,再回頭複習一遍前面所提到的重點。

新制中級閱讀**測驗題型**超完整收錄！
全面**掌握**考試方向

▼ 速見 p.8

強化英語閱讀能力 ≫ 打好詞彙、文法基礎

「實力培養」部分為學習者整理新制英檢中級閱讀答題所需的詞彙、片語、句型、文法，採分類條列及表格方式整理，彙整出考是最常出現的詞彙、片語、文法，加上豐富的例句說明，方便學習者查考及背誦，學習完這些考試重點後還有練習題讓學習者能夠複習。

> **UNIT 1** A~Z 的精選字彙
>
> **Study 1** A 開頭的單字
>
> 1. absorb [əb`sɔrb] (v.) 吸收（液體，氣體等）；汲取（知識等）
> 例 The plants absorb water from the soil.
> （植物從土壤中吸收水分。）

▼ 速見 p.126

第一部分「詞彙」≫ 著重英語詞彙評量

整理出中級閱讀測驗最常出現的英語詞彙，按照主題設計出各類單選題，讓學習者能夠依照自己較弱的主題加強，找出自己不熟悉的單字，再翻回前面的「實力培養」部分對照例句重新將這些單字記住。

> Q1 Goods that _____ in China are exported all over the globe.
> (A) are manufactured (B) are manufacturing
> (C) manufactured (D) have manufactured
>
> Q2 She had never _____ so much wine before, and she started to feel like the world was spinning around her.
> (A) drank (B) drink
> (C) drunk (D) drunken
>
> Q3 The car accident _____ right here several days ago. It

▼ 速見 p.166

第二部分「段落填空」≫ 增加句子選項

依照「生活休閒」、「書信應用」、「論說敘述」三種情境設計出有句子選項的題組，讓學習者能依照不同情境主題學習判斷文章脈絡的能力，也增進找出正確的詞彙、文法的能力，若找到自己不熟悉的文法、句型，也能夠翻回前面的「實力培養」部分複習文法常識。

> **Study 1** The Weekend Cabin
>
> Having a weekend cabin is the dream of many North Americans. Most people in Canada and the United States live in big cities and there is a certain __1__ for them about spending free time in the country. The ultimate fantasy includes buying an older cabin and being able to renovate it and decorate it to your own tastes. Such a desire __2__ comes from an idea that one is re-living the pioneering experience of the original European settlers in North America.

▼ 速見 p.254

第三部分「閱讀理解」≫ 增加多篇文章題組

除了「生活休閒」、「書信應用」、「論說敘述」三種情境的題組，也加上了多篇閱讀的題組，讓學習者除了能夠依照各種情境學習查找文章資訊的能力，也能夠在多篇文章題組中，學習利用有限的時間從上下文裡找出與題目最相關的回答。

> **Study 1** Kwanzaa
>
> When the short days of winter begin, many cultural and religious groups celebrate holidays that incorporate the use of light to symbolize peace, love and togetherness. These celebrations often encourage people to look away from material concerns and spend time reflecting on what it means to be a good person. Jewish people celebrate Chanukah, Christians celebrate Christmas and Muslims Ramadan.
>
> Within the last few decades some African-Americans have

▼ 速見 p.394

擬真模擬試題

最後做一回模擬試題，讓學習者在進考場前先知道自己的實力，事先了解自己的弱點在哪。

> 第一部分：詞彙
> 共 10 題，每題含一個空格。請由試題冊上的四個選項中選出最適合題意的字或詞作答。
>
> Q1 The restaurant is always _____ to choose a supplier in order to provide high-quality fresh foods.
> (A) selective (B) careful
> (C) magnificent (D) acceptable
>
> Q2 Throughout his career, Tom has _____ the respect of his coworkers for his integrity and dedication.

CONTENTS

PART 2　閱讀測驗試題練習

Vocabulary & Phrases

CHAPTER 1
必備單字片語歸納

UNIT 1 A~Z 的精選字彙

Study 1 A 開頭的單字

1. absorb [əb`sɔrb] (v.) 吸收（液體，氣體等）；汲取（知識等）
例 The plants **absorb** water from the soil.
（植物從土壤中吸收水分。）

2. academic [ˌækə`dɛmɪk] (adj.) 學術的
例 His research is very famous in the **academic** world.
（他的研究在學術界非常有名。）

3. achieve [ə`tʃiv] (v.) 達成
例 If you made better use of your time, you would have **achieved** a higher goal.
（如果你更善用你的時間，就可以達成更遠的目標。）

4. athletic [æθ`lɛtɪk] (adj.) 運動的
例 John enjoyed watching **athletic** games on TV on weekends.
（週末時，約翰喜歡在電視上看運動比賽。）

5. associate [ə`soʃɪˌet] (v.) 連繫；聯想 (n.) 夥伴
例 I have never **associated** you with the case.
（我從未把你跟這個案件聯想在一起。）

6. additional [ə`dɪʃənl̩] (adj.) 額外的
例 She gets an **additional** income by working at night.
（她藉由上大夜班來獲得額外的收入。）

7. accustomed [ə`kʌstəmd] (adj.) 習慣的；一貫的
例 I am **accustomed** to staying up late.
（我習慣熬夜。）

精選字彙 A~Z的

的變化 常見字尾

字彙 易混淆

常見片語

片語 易混淆

常見諺語

8. atmosphere [`ætməsˌfɪr] (n.) 氣氛；大氣（the atmosphere）

例 There is a friendly **atmosphere** in this office.
（這間辦公室有友善的氣氛。）

9. aborigine [æbəˋrɪdʒəni] (n.) 原住民

例 She is an **aborigine** on this island.
（她是這島上的原住民。）

10. abundant [əˋbʌndənt] (adj.) 大量的；豐富的

例 Their home is **abundant** in love and laughter.
（他們的家充滿了愛與歡笑。）

11. accuse [əˋkjuz] (v.) 指控；指責

例 To see is to believe. Don't **accuse** others without evidences.
（眼見為憑，沒有證據就不要隨便指控他人。）

Study 2 B 開頭的單字

12. beware [bɪˋwɛr] (v.) 當心

例 Apart from that, you have to **beware** of pickpockets.
（除此之外，你還必須謹防扒手。）

13. budget [`bʌdʒɪt] (n.) 預算 (v.) 把～編入預算

例 The government introduced the new **budget**.
（政府提出新預算。）

14. branch [bræntʃ] (n.) 樹枝；分部

例 The school has a **branch** in Taipei.
（這間學校在台北有一所分校。）

15. breadth [brɛdθ] (n.) 寬度

例 What is the **breadth** of the room?
（這間房間的寬度是多少？）

16. boast [bost] (v.) 自誇 (n.) 自吹，大話

例 He **boasted** of his English ability.
（他自誇他的英文能力。）

17. brook [bruk] (v.) 忍受 (n.) 小溪
例 I will not **brook** anyone interfering with my affairs.
（我無法忍受任何人干涉我的事情。）

18. bury [`bɛrɪ] (v.) 埋葬
例 The dog **buried** the bone in the ground.
（這隻狗把骨頭埋在地下。）

19. beneath [bɪ`niθ] (prep.) 在～之下
例 The earth is **beneath** our feet.
（地球就在我們的腳下。）

20. bargain (v.) [`bɑrgɪn] 討價還價 (n.) 協議；買賣
例 Are you a **bargain** hunter?
（你是一個殺價高手嗎？）

Study 3　C 開頭的單字

21. circulation [ˌsɝkjə`leʃən] (n.) 循環；發行量
例 The newspaper has a large **circulation**.
（這報紙的發行量很大。）

22. composition [ˌkɑmpə`zɪʃən] (n.) 創作；構成
例 His latest **composition** is good for my taste.
（他最新的作品很符合我的胃口。）

23. conclusion [kən`kluʒən] (n.) 結論
例 What **conclusions** did you reach?
（你們達成了什麼結論？）

24. costume [`kɑstjum] (n.) 服裝；戲裝
例 They wore historical **costumes** for the parade.
（他們為了這場遊行而穿著古裝。）

25. complicated [`kɑmpləˌketɪd] (adj.) 複雜的
例 He is good at solving **complicated** math problems.
（他擅長解出複雜的數學問題。）

精選字彙
A~Z的

常見字尾
的變化

易混淆
字彙

常見片語

易混淆
片語

常見諺語

26. crawl [krɔl] (v.) 爬行 (n.) 爬行；自由式游泳（the crawl）

例 A baby **crawls** before it can walk.

（嬰兒在能夠走路之前會先爬行。）

27. churchgoer [`tʃɝtʃ͵goɚ] (n.) 經常上教堂做禮拜的人

例 A person who goes to church services regularly is called a **churchgoer**.

（一個定期到教堂做禮拜的人被稱作「churchgoer」。）

28. contractor [`kɑntræktɚ] (n.) 承包商

例 We are the building **contractors**.

（我們是建築承包商。）

29. courtesy [`kɝtəsɪ] (n.) 禮貌

例 He did not have the **courtesy** to reply to my question.

（他很沒禮貌地回答我的問題。）

30. correspond [͵kɔrɪ`spɑnd] (v.) 相符；通信

例 She **corresponds** regularly with her pen pal.

（她定期地與她的筆友通信。）

Study 4　D 開頭的單字

31. devise [dɪ`vaɪz] (v.) 設計；發明

例 Who **devised** the phone?

（誰發明了電話？）

32. decoration [͵dɛkə`reʃən] (n.) 裝飾（品）

例 What kind of **decoration** will be on the Christmas tree this year?

（今年的聖誕樹上會有哪種裝飾品？）

33. dreadful [`drɛdfəl] (adj.) 可怕的；糟糕的

例 The weather today is really **dreadful**.

（今天的天氣真的很糟。）

34. despite [dɪ`spaɪt] (prep.) 不管，儘管

例 **Despite** danger, he still wants to do that case.

（不顧危險，他還是要做那個案件。）

35. disastrous [dɪz`æstrəs] (adj.) 災難性的

例 It is really a **disastrous** accident.

（那真是一場災禍。）

36. deformed [dɪ`fɔrmd] (adj.) 畸形的；變形的

例 He was born with a **deformed** hand.

（他生來就有一隻畸形的手。）

37. definition [ˌdɛfə`nɪʃən] (n.) 定義

例 I think the **definition** is incorrect.

（我認為這個定義不正確。）

38. deceive [dɪ`siv] (v.) 欺騙

例 I know he is **deceiving** me.

（我知道他在欺騙我。）

39. declare [dɪ`klɛr] (v.) 宣布；宣稱

例 The man **declares** he is going to marry Sue.

（這個男人宣布他將與蘇結婚。）

40. drought [draʊt] (n.) 旱災

例 There was a **drought** last year.

（去年有場旱災。）

Study 5　E 開頭的單字

41. effect [ɪ`fɛkt] (n.) 效果；影響

例 One of the **effects** of bad weather is poor crops.

（惡劣天氣的其中一項影響是作物歉收。）

42. element [`ɛləmənt] (n.) 要素
例 Do you have the **elements** of a good personality?
（你具有健全人格的要素嗎？）

43. envy [`ɛnvɪ] (v.) 忌妒
例 John passed GEPT test. We all **envy** his big success.
（約翰通過了全民英檢的考試，我們全都很忌妒他的成功。）

44. etiquette [`ɛtɪkɛt] (n.) 禮儀
例 It's against **etiquette** to open a door without knocking first.
（開門前不先敲門是違反禮儀的。）

45. exaggeration [ɪgˌzædʒəˋreʃən] (n.) 誇大
例 The story is full of **exaggeration**.
（這篇故事充滿誇大不實。）

46. editor [`ɛdɪtɚ] (n.) 編輯
例 The **editor** made some interesting statements yesterday.
（這位編輯昨天做了一些有趣的敘述。）

47. evaporate [ɪˋvæpəˌret] (v.) 蒸發
例 Heat **evaporates** water.
（熱能使水蒸發。）

48. evidence [`ɛvədəns] (n.) 證據 (v.) 證明
例 Can you show me the **evidence** for your statement?
（你能為你的陳述提出證據嗎？）

49. encompass [ɪnˋkʌmpəs] (v.) 包含
例 The course **encompasses** all of the English literature since 1990.
（這門課程包含 1990 年之後所有的英國文學。）

50. enthusiastic [ɪnˌθjuzɪˋæstɪk] (adj.) 熱情的
例 He is a very **enthusiastic** person.
（他是一個十分有熱情的人。）

精選字彙 A～Z的
的變化 常見字尾
字彙 易混淆
常見片語
片語 易混淆
常見諺語

51. ferocious [fə`roʃəs] (adj.) 兇猛的
例 The tigers are **ferocious**.
（這些老虎是兇猛的。）

52. flutter [`flʌtɚ] (v.) （使）飄動；拍（翅）
例 The butterfly **fluttered** from flower to flower.
（蝴蝶在花朵間翩然飛舞。）

53. fray [fre] (v.) 磨損
例 The shirt was **frayed** at the collar.
（這件襯衫的衣領磨損了。）

54. far-fetched [`far`fɛtʃt] (adj.) 牽強的
例 The story is really **far-fetched** as if he was telling a lie.
（這個故事真的太牽強了，彷彿他在說謊一樣。）

55. fabric [`fæbrɪk] (n.) 布；織物
例 My shorts are made of cotton **fabric**.
（我的短褲是由棉布料製成的。）

56. flexible [`flɛksəbl] (adj.) 可變動的；有彈性的
例 I am **flexible** to accept new changes.
（我有接受新改變的彈性。）

57. fearlessly [`fɪrlɪslɪ] (adv.) 無懼地
例 They fought **fearlessly** against the enemy.
（他們無懼地對抗敵軍。）

58. faded [`fedɪd] (adj.) 褪色的
例 I wear a pair of **faded** blue jeans.
（我穿著一條褪色的藍色牛仔褲。）

59. foreseeable [for`siəbl̩] (adj.) 可預見的
例 The problem can be solved in the **foreseeable** future.
（這個問題在可預見的未來能夠被解決。）

精選字彙 A～Z 的

常見字尾 的變化

易混淆 字彙

常見片語

易混淆 片語

常見諺語

61. glowing [`gloɪŋ] (adj.) 熱烈讚揚的；發光的
例 She gave a **glowing** description of the art.
（她對於這件藝術品給予了熱烈的讚賞。）

62. generic [dʒɪ`nɛrɪk] (adj.) 普通的
例 This is only a **generic** art.
（這只是一件很普通的藝術品。）

63. graciously [`greʃəslɪ] (adv.) 親切地
例 She asked me **graciously** if I needed a blanket.
（她親切地問我，是否需要一條毯子。）

64. glide [glaɪd] (v.) 滑動，滑行 (n.) 滑動，滑行
例 The skater **glided** over the ice.
（這位溜冰者在冰上滑行。）

65. gobble [`gɑbl] (v.) 狼吞虎嚥
例 Don't **gobble**. Eat more slowly.
（別狼吞虎嚥，吃慢一點。）

66. glance [glæns] (v.) 匆匆一看 (n.) 一瞥
例 She **glanced** through today's paper.
（她粗略看過今日的報紙。）

67. grind [graɪnd] (v.) 磨碎 (n.) 研磨；苦差事
例 The barista is **grinding** coffee beans.
（這位咖啡廳店員正在研磨咖啡豆。）

68. guarantee [͵gærən`ti] (v.) 保證 (n.) 保證書
例 Some firms **guarantee** their workers a job.
（有些公司保障員工工作）。

69. gutter [`gʌtɚ] (n.) （道路邊的）排水溝；貧民區
例 He was raised in the **gutter**.
（他是在貧民區長大的。）

70. gardener [`gɑrdənɚ] (n.) 園丁
例 The **gardener** is planting the trees.
（這名園丁正在植樹。）

Study 8　H 開頭的單字

71. harmonious [hɑr`monɪəs] (adj.) 和諧的
例 I have a **harmonious** relationship with colleagues.
（我與同事們有和諧的關係。）

72. humble [`hʌmbl̩] (adj.) 謙卑的
例 Intelligent people are always **humble**.
（智者總是謙卑。）

73. hew [hju] (v.) 砍
例 They **hewed** down the tree.
（他們把這棵樹砍倒了。）

74. humanity [hju`mænətɪ] (n.) 人類；人性
例 He convicted the crimes that were against **humanity**.
（他犯下了違反人性的罪。）

75. hateful [`hetfəl] (adj.) 可恨的
例 War is **hateful** to us.
（戰爭對我們來說是可恨的。）

Study 9　I 開頭的單字

76. identification [aɪˌdɛntəfə`keʃən] (n.) 身分證明；辨認
例 What is your **identification** card's number?
（你的身分證字號是幾號？）

77. inspect [ɪn`spɛkt] (v.) 檢查
例 My boss **inspects** my work every day.
（我的老闆每天檢查我的工作。）

78. intimate [`ɪntəmɪt] (adj.) 親密的 (n.) 密友
例 They became **intimate** friends after that party.
（在那次派對之後，他們成為親密的朋友。）

79. insult [ɪn`sʌlt] (v.) 侮辱 (n.) 侮辱，羞辱
例 She **insulted** her boyfriend by telling him that he was stingy.
（她跟她男友說他很小氣來羞辱他。）

80. inhale [ɪn`hel] (v.) 吸入
例 I **inhaled** fresh air in the mountains.
（我在山中吸收新鮮空氣。）

81. innocent [`ɪnəsn̩t] (adj.) 無罪的
例 I believe that he is **innocent**.
（我相信他是無罪的。）

82. infect [ɪn`fɛkt] (v.) 感染
例 Lots of people were **infected** with SARS last year.
（去年有很多人感染了 SARS。）

83. interfere [ˌɪntɚ`fɪr] (v.) 妨礙；插手
例 The noise is **interfering** with my work.
（這個噪音在妨礙我的工作。）

84. instruction [ɪn`strʌkʃən] (n.) 教導；指示
例 Please follow the **instructions**.
（請遵照這些指示。）

85. inflation [ɪn`fleʃən] (n.) 通貨膨脹；膨脹
例 The government made this policy to control **inflation**.
（政府制定這項政策以控制通貨膨脹。）

Study 10 J 開頭的單字

86. journey [`dʒɝnɪ] (n.) 旅行；旅程
例 He made a **journey** around the world.
（他完成了一趟世界的旅程。）

A~Z的
精選字彙

常見字尾
的變化

易混淆
字彙

常見片語

易混淆
片語

常見諺語

87. juicy [`dʒusɪ] (adj.) 多汁的

例 The fruit is sweet and **juicy**.

（這個水果香甜多汁。）

88. junk [dʒʌŋk] (n.) 垃圾

例 Don't make so much **junk**.

（別製造這麼多的垃圾。）

89. jewelry [`dʒuəlrɪ] (n.) 【美】珠寶；首飾

例 She never wears **jewelry**.

（她從不戴珠寶。）

90. jeer [dʒɪr] (v.) 嘲笑

例 They are **jeering** my mistake.

（他們在嘲笑我的錯誤。）

Study 11 K 開頭的單字

91. knowledge [`nɑlɪdʒ] (n.) 知識

例 **Knowledge** is power.

（知識就是力量。）

92. kingdom [`kɪŋdəm] (n.) 王國

例 He is the king in this **kingdom**.

（他是這個王國的國王。）

93. kettle [`kɛtl̩] (n.) 水壺

例 The **kettle** is boiling.

（這個水壺的水燒開了。）

94. knowledgeable [`nɑlɪdʒəbl̩] (adj.) 有知識的；博學的

例 He is a **knowledgeable** person.

（他是位博學多聞的人。）

95.　knot [nɑt] (v.) 打結
例　**I knotted** the tie.
（我將領帶打結了。）

Study 12　L 開頭的單字

96.　laboratory [ˋlæbrəˏtorɪ] (n.) 實驗室（＝lab）
例　This **laboratory** is full of poisonous gas.
（這間實驗室充滿有毒氣體。）

97.　litter [ˋlɪtɚ] (v.) 亂丟東西 (n.) 垃圾
例　No **littering**.
（禁止亂丟垃圾。）

98.　lousy [ˋlaʊzɪ] (adj.) 很糟的
例　The show is really **lousy**.
（這場表演實在很糟糕。）

99.　leisurely [ˋliʒɚlɪ] (adj.) 從容不迫的，悠閒的 (adv.) 從容不迫地
例　We walked **leisurely**, looking at all flowers on the ground.
（我們從容地走著，看著地上全部的花。）

100.　limousine [ˋlɪməˏzin] (n.) 大型豪華轎車
例　Joe drove a **limousine** to pick his girlfriend up.
（喬開了大型豪華轎車去接他的女友。）

Study 13　M 開頭的單字

101.　millionaire [ˏmɪljənˋɛr] (n.) 百萬富翁
例　He is far from being a **millionaire**.
（他絕不是百萬富翁。）

102.　machinery [məˋʃinərɪ] (n.)（大型的）機器；機械
例　**Machinery** uses lots of electricity.
（機器耗費大量電力。）

103. membership [`mɛmbɚˌʃɪp] (n.) 會員資格

例 He has **membership** in that tennis club.
（他有那間網球俱樂部的會員資格。）

104. model [`madl] (n.) 模型

例 Can you follow the conversation **model** and practice it again?
（你可以跟著這個會話模式，並再練習一遍嗎？）

105. military [`mɪləˌtɛrɪ] (adj.) 軍事的 (n.) 軍人；軍隊

例 I was trained in this **military** school.
（我在這間軍事學校受訓。）

Study 14　N 開頭的單字

106. neighborhood [`nebɚˌhʊd] (n.) 臨近的地區

例 Is there a bookstore in the **neighborhood**?
（這附近的區域有一間書店嗎？）

107. nuisance [`njusn̩s] (n.) 討厭的人（或事物）

例 Never make a **nuisance** of yourself.
（絕對不要讓你成為討厭的人。）

108. novelist [`navl̩ɪst] (n.) 小說家

例 The **novelist** has published her new novel.
（這名小說家已經出版了她的新小說。）

109. notify [`notəˌfaɪ] (v.) 通知；告知

例 Please **notify** your staff we will have a meeting later.
（請告知你的部屬，我們等一下要開會。）

110. neutral [`njutrəl] (adj.) 中立的

例 The country is **neutral** between the two fighting counties.
（這個國家在另外兩個交戰國之間保持中立。）

精選字彙 A～Z的

常見字尾的變化

易混淆字彙

常見片語

易混淆片語

常見諺語

Study 15　O 開頭的單字

111. overcome [ˌovɚ`kʌm] (v.) 戰勝；克服

例　You have to **overcome** your problems.

（你必須克服你的問題。）

112. observation [ˌɑbzɚ`veʃən] (n.) 觀察

例　His **observation** is very detailed.

（他的觀察十分入微。）

113. obtain [əb`ten] (v.) 獲得

例　I want to **obtain** the latest information.

（我想要獲得最新的資訊。）

114. ordinary [`ɔrdn̩ˌɛrɪ] (adj.) 普通的；一般的

例　This is only an **ordinary** product.

（這只是一個普通的產品。）

115. occasion [ə`keʒən] (n.) 場合；時刻

例　I am going to attend a special **occasion**.

（我將去參加一個特別的場合。）

Study 16　P 開頭的單字

116. paralysis [pə`ræləsɪs] (n.) 麻痺；癱瘓

例　He can't move because of **paralysis**.

（他因為癱瘓而無法移動。）

117. pension [`pɛnʃən] (n.) 退休金

例　He retired with a big **pension**.

（他退休時有一大筆退休金。）

118. partial [`pɑrʃəl] (adj.) 部份的

例　I got **partial** money. The rest belongs to him.

（我得到一部份的錢，剩下的則屬於他。）

119. primitive [`prɪmətɪv] (adj.) 原始的；簡陋的

例 The facilities are very **primitive** here.

（這裡的設備很簡陋。）

120. provoke [prə`vok] (v.) 激怒

例 Her complaints **provoked** him.

（她的抱怨激怒了他。）

Study 17　Q 開頭的單字

121. quote [kwot] (v.) 引用 (n.) 引文

例 She **quoted** a sentence from the article.

（她引用了這篇文章中的一句話。）

122. qualification [ˌkwɑləfə`keʃən] (n.) 資格

例 I have **qualifications** for this position.

（我有資格勝任這個職位。）

123. questionable [`kwɛstʃənəbl̩] (adj.) 有問題的；可疑的

例 It is **questionable** whether he will come or not.

（他是否會來是令人疑惑的。）

124. quiver [`kwɪvɚ] (v.) 顫抖

例 I **quivered** because of fear.

（我因為恐懼而顫抖。）

125. quarrel [`kwɔrəl] (n.) 吵架 (v.) 爭吵

例 They had a **quarrel** about money and love.

（他們因為金錢和感情糾紛而爭吵。）

精選字彙 A～Z 的
的變化 常見字尾
字彙 易混淆
常見片語
片語 易混淆
常見諺語

Study 18　R 開頭的單字

126. recite [rɪ`saɪt] (v.) 背誦
例　I could **recite** the paragraph.
（我可以背誦這個段落。）

127. recognize [`rɛkəg͵naɪz] (v.) 認出
例　When I first met her, I **recognized** that she was my high school classmate.
（我第一次遇到她時，就認出她是我高中同學。）

128. reunite [͵rijuˈnaɪt] (v.) 再聯合；再統一；重聚
例　He **reunited** with his family after he returned to his country.
（他回國之後與家人團聚。）

129. recognize [`rɛkəg͵naɪz] (v.) 認出
例　I didn't **recognize** her when I met her on the street.
（當我在街上遇到她時，我沒有認出她。）

130. regulation [͵rɛgjəˈleʃən] (n.) 規則
例　I am not sure about the **regulations**.
（我不清楚這些規則。）

131. represent [͵rɛprɪˈzɛnt] (v.) 代表
例　He **represented** his class at the meeting.
（他在會議中代表他的班級。）

Study 19　S 開頭的單字

132. superiority [sə͵pɪrɪˈɔrətɪ] (n.) 優越，優勢
例　He has a strong sense of **superiority**.
（他有一股強烈的優越感。）

133. stagger [`stægɚ] (v.) 蹣跚
例　The old man **staggers** in the street.
（這個老人在街上蹣跚而行。）

134. swell [swɛl] (v.) 腫脹；情緒高漲 (n.) 腫脹
例 His pride **swelled** quickly.
（他的自豪感快速高漲）

135. select [sə`lɛkt] (v.) 挑選
例 I **selected** some dresses while he was doing the shopping for his suit.
（當他在買西裝的同時，我挑了一些洋裝。）

136. sophomore [`safmor] (n.) 大學、高中的二年級生
例 He is a **sophomore** in this college.
（他是這所大學二年級的學生。）

Study 20　T 開頭的單字

137. thrust [θrʌst] (v.) 猛推；擠；塞
例 I **thrust** my money in my wallet.
（我把我的錢塞進皮夾裡。）

138. tolerant [`talərənt] (adj.) 寬容的
例 He is **tolerant** to this murderer.
（他對這個殺人犯很寬容。）

139. twinkle [`twɪŋkl̩] (v.) 閃爍 (n.) 閃爍
例 I have a **twinkle** in my eyes.
（我眼中有閃爍著亮光。）

140. transformation [ˌtrænsfɚ`meʃən] (n.) 變化
例 Can you predict the **transformation**?
（你可以預測出這段變化嗎？）

141. temptation [tɛmp`teʃən] (n.) 誘惑
例 I couldn't resist the **temptation** to open the case.
（我禁不起打開這個箱子的誘惑。）

精選字彙 A～Z的

的變化 常見字尾

字彙 易混淆

常見片語

片語 易混淆

常見諺語

Study 21 U 開頭的單字

142. undertake [ˌʌndɚˋtek] (v.) 從事
例 I have to **undertake** this work.
（我必須要從事這份工作。）

143. urgent [ˋɝdʒənt] (adj.) 緊急的
例 I got an **urgent** call from my mother.
（我接到了一通我媽媽打來的緊急來電。）

144. unfamiliar [ˌʌnfəˋmɪljɚ] (adj.) 不熟悉的
例 I am **unfamiliar** with his case.
（我對他的案子並不熟悉。）

145. undivided [ˌʌndəˋvaɪdɪd] (adj.) 專心的；未分的
例 She always gives **undivided** attention to her job.
（她總是能專心在她的工作上。）

146. unconscious [ʌnˋkɑnʃəs] (adj.) 昏迷的；無意識的
例 He has been **unconscious** for a few days.
（他已經昏迷不醒數天了。）

Study 22 V 開頭的單字

147. vacant [ˋvekənt] (adj.) 空的
例 There is no **vacant** tables for us.
（我們沒有空的桌子可用。）

148. variety [vəˋraɪətɪ] (n.) 多樣化；變化
例 People like to have a life that is full of **variety**.
（人們喜歡擁有充滿變化的生活。）

149. vivid [ˋvɪvɪd] (adj.)（描述、記憶等）生動的；（顏色）鮮豔的
例 Dreams sometimes are **vivid**.
（有時候有些夢境很生動。）

150. visible [`vɪzəbl] (adj.) 看得見的
例 The future is sometimes **visible**.
（未來有時是可看見的。）

151. virtual [`vɝtʃʊəl] (adj.) 實質上的；【電腦】虛擬的
例 The role in this film is **virtual**.
（這部電影裡的這個角色是虛構的。）

Study 23 W 開頭的單字

152. wail [wel] (v.) 嚎啕大哭
例 There's no use **wailing** over the mistake.
（為了這個錯誤大哭是沒有用的。）

153. well-mannered [`wɛl`mænɚd] (adj.) 行為端正的；有禮貌的
例 The gentleman is very **well-mannered**.
（這位紳士很有禮貌。）

154. wrinkle [`rɪŋkl̩] (v.) 起皺 (n.) 皺紋
例 He likes to **wrinkle** his forehead.
（他喜歡皺起他的額頭。）

155. wary [`wɛrɪ] (adj.) 謹慎的；警惕的
例 He is the **wariest** person that I have ever seen.
（他是我見過最謹慎的人。）

156. worthwhile [`wɝθ`hwaɪl] (adj.) 值得的
例 It is **worthwhile** for us students to study hard.
（對我們學生來說，用功讀書是一件很值得的。）

Study 24　X 開頭的單字

157. x-ray (n.) X 光 (v.) 用 X 光線檢查

例　We used **x-rays** to examine his body.
（我們用 X 光檢查他的身體。）

Study 25　Y 開頭的單字

158. yell (v.) 大叫 (n.) 叫喊

例　Don't **yell** at me just because you are unhappy today.
（不要只是因為你今天不高興就對我大叫。）

159. yield [jild] (v.) 出產；屈服

例　We will **yield** to the enemy.
（我們會向敵人屈服。）

Study 26　Z 開頭的單字

160. zeal [zil] (n.) 熱忱

例　He has a great **zeal** for helping others.
（他對幫助他人有極大的熱忱。）

161. zone (n.) 地帶 (v.) 把～分成區

例　Here's a no-smoking **zone**.
（這裡是個禁菸區。）

精選字彙 A～Z 的

的變化 常見字尾

字彙 易混淆

常見片語

片語 易混淆

常見諺語

Q1 Peter and Susan have a _____ relationship with their colleagues. They always hang out together in the weekend.

(A) harmony

(B) harmful

(C) harmonious

(D) harmonic

Q2 The plot was predictable, the actors were terrible, and the special effects looked really fake. The whole movie was _____ .

(A) lousy

(B) interesting

(C) entertaining

(D) long

Q3 The old lady was really _____ toward the thief. She didn't call the police when she caught him.

(A) hateful

(B) tolerant

(C) mean

(D) serious

Q4 After three women were attacked in the same neighborhood, police began warning people in the _____ not to walk alone at night.

(A) community

(B) street

(C) building

(D) place

Q5 My parents have removed _____ in this house because they want to give the house a makeover.

(A) the furnitures

(B) furnitures

(C) the furniture

(D) a furniture

Q6 Jenny is a very _____ person. She always has lots of energy to do what she wants.

(A) enthusiastic

(B) flexible

(C) polite

(D) ordinary

精選字彙 A~Z的

的變化 常見字尾

字彙 易混淆

常見片語

片語 易混淆

常見諺語

Q7 We felt very _____ when we reached the destination.

(A) exhaustion   (B) exhaust

(C) exhausting   (D) exhausted

Q8 Canned foods aren't affected by _____, we still can buy them at the same price.

(A) regulation   (B) quarrel

(C) temptation   (D) inflation

Q9 It is difficult to _____ under water.

(A) breath   (B) breathe

(C) breadth   (D) bread

Q10 The cartoon is really _____. Many children like it very much.

(A) primitive   (B) wary

(C) vivid   (D) urgent

Q11 The swimmer _____ from the pool.

(A) emerged   (B) immerged

(C) emigrated   (D) immigrated

Q12 He has the _____ of a good constitution.

(A) disadvantage   (B) advantage

(C) addition   (D) attention

Q13 All the doctors in this hospital have medical _____.

(A) occasions   (B) quotations

(C) qualifications   (D) instructions

Q14 These paintings are all painted by Chinese _____.

（A）fire fighters   （B）photographers

（C）artists   （D）musicians

Q15 The word "take" has many different _____.

（A）mistakes   （B）ways

（C）description   （D）meanings

解答： 1. C   2. A   3. B   4. A   5. C
6. A   7. D   8. D   9. B   10. C
11. A   12. B   13. C   14. C   15. D

常見字尾的變化

　　有些單字我們可以從字首及字尾來判斷他的詞性。以下列舉常見的字尾，並以詞性來做分類。

- 名詞常見字尾：-ance / -ence / -ation / -ian / -ism / -ist / -ment / -ness / -ship / -or / -er
- 動詞常見字尾：-en / -ify / -ize
- 形容詞常見字尾：-able / -ible / -al / -ful/ -ish / -ive / -ous
- 副詞常見字尾：-ly / -ward / -wise

常見字尾						
名詞		動詞		形容詞		副詞
-ance	attendance	-en	redden	-able	lovable	-ly	suddenly
-ence	existence	-ify	modify	-ible	accessible	-ward	afterward
-ation	conversation	-ize	memorize	-al	final	-wise	likewise
-ian	politician			-ful	helpful		
-ism	terrorism			-ish	childish		
-ist	journalist			-ive	native		
-ment	argument			-ous	studious		
-ness	sickness						
-ship	relationship						
-or	doctor						
-er	robber						

參考例字				
名詞		動詞	形容詞	副詞
事物	人			
application（申請）	applicant	apply	applicable	
competition（競爭）	competitor	compete	competitive	competitively
criticism（批評）	critic	criticize	critical	critically
economy（經濟）	economist	economize	economical	economically
finale（最終）	finalist	finalize	final	finally
interpretation（翻譯）	interpreter	interpret	interpretive	
maintenance（維持）	maintainer	maintain	maintainable	
management（管理）	manager	manage	managerial	
mechanism（機器）	mechanic	mechanize	mechanical	mechanically
nation（國家）	nationalist	nationalize	national	nationally
negotiation（談判）	negotiator	negotiate	negotiable	
politics（政治）	politician	politicize	political	politically
production（產品）	producer	produce	productive	productively

精選字彙 A～Z的
的變化 常見字尾
字彙 易混淆
常見片語
片語 易混淆
常見諺語

UNIT 2 常見字尾變化的練習

Q1 The _____ predicted that the government would increase the budget to build the dam.
（A）economy
（B）economist
（C）economical
（D）economize

Q2 We need the _____ of this speech. The lecturer didn't speak English.
（A）interpretation
（B）interpret
（C）interpreter
（D）interpretive

Q3 Do you _____ for the position in that big corporation? I hear that the job is really competitive.
（A）applicable （B）applicant （C）application （D）apply

Q4 Many people from worldwide enjoy watching the broadcast of the _____ Basketball Association.
（A）Nation （B）Nationalize （C）National （D）Nationalist

Q5 Do you tell the _____ about the contract? We need to discuss it in the meeting.
（A）manage
（B）manager
（C）management
（D）managerial

Q6 Many audiences agree with the _____'s comments, after they watch the movie.
（A）criticism （B）critical （C）critically （D）critic

Q7 Does everybody prepare for the _____ exam?
（A）finale （B）finalize （C）final （D）finally

Q8 Has Jason finished the report I asked him to _____?
（A）modification
（B）modify
（C）modified
（D）modifying

解答： 1. B　2. A　3. D　4. C
5. B　6. D　7. C　8. B

ascent [ə`sɛnt] （n.）上升；（身分、地位等）提升

例　His **ascent** as a manager was due to his hard work.
（他晉升為經理，是因為工作認真。）

assent [ə`sɛnt] （n.）同意

例　His parents gave **assent** to his plan to study medical research.
（他的父母同意他研讀醫學研究的計畫。）

assay [ə`se] （v.）嘗試；檢驗

例　Let's **assay** the qualities of the western part of the country first to see what it has to offer.
（讓我們先檢驗這個國家的西部，看看它能提供什麼。）

essay [ɛ`se] （v.）嘗試（n.）短文

例　She **essayed** to express her own opinion in her university term paper.
（她嘗試在她的大學學期報告中發表她自己的意見。）

attend to 注意；照顧

例　Please **attend to** the baby so it won't be hurt or lost.
（請注意這個小嬰兒，這樣他才不會受傷或走失。）

tend to 傾向於

例　People who eat a lot of fatty foods **tend to** be overweight.
（吃太多高脂肪食品的人有過重的傾向。）

aisle [aɪl] （n.）走道

例　Don't block the **aisle** of the plane with your luggage.
（不要把你的行李擋在飛機走道上）

isle [aɪl]（n.）島嶼

例 I want a cabin on an **isle** in the Pacific where there won't be too many neighbors.

（我想一棟在太平洋小島上的小屋，在那裡沒有太多的鄰居。）

allusion [ə`luʒən]（n.）間接提及

例 She only made an **allusion** to his dirty clothes because she was too polite to say anything directly.

（她只間接提到他的一些髒衣服，因為她太禮貌以至於不把話說直。）

illusion [ɪ`luʒən]（n.）錯覺；幻想

例 The magician performed many amazing **illusions**.

（這名魔術師表演了許多令人驚奇的幻象。）

adapt [ə`dæpt]（v.）使適應

例 You must have the ability to **adapt** yourself if you want to live in a foreign country.

（假如你想要住在國外，你必須要有能力讓自己適應。）

adopt [ə`dɑpt]（v.）採用；領養

例 My friends, who are unable to have a baby of their own, have decided to **adopt** a child.

（我的一對無法生育的朋友，決定要領養一個小孩。）

adept [`ædɛpt]（adj.）熟練的

例 She was **adept** at cooking and always made delicious meals.

（她對烹飪很在行，總是煮得出可口的菜餚。）

adapted to 適應

例 People from northern are **adapted to** living in very cold climate, but not for people from Southern.

（來自北方的人們適應了嚴寒的氣候，但對南方的人就不行。）

精選字彙 A～Z的

的變化 常見字尾

字彙 易混淆

常見片語

片語 易混淆

常見諺語

adapted for 改編成

例 This material was written for advanced level English learners, but it can be **adapted for** beginners.

（這個教材是為進階程度的英文學習者編寫的，但它可以被改編成給初學者看的。）

adapted from 從～改編

例 The play was **adapted from** a short story.

（這齣劇改編自一則短篇故事。）

addition [əˋdɪʃən]（n.）附加

例 I bought a new hat in **addition** to my new coat.

（除了我的新外套，我還買了一頂新帽子。）

edition [ɪˋdɪʃən]（n.）版本；（發行物的）版

例 I always buy the morning **edition** of the newspaper on my way to work.

（我總是在上班的途中買一份早報。）

advantage [ədˋvæntɪdʒ]（n.）優勢；好處

例 Travelers who can speak the local language have an **advantage** over those who don't.

（會說當地語言的旅行者比那些不會說的人佔優勢。）

benefit [ˋbɛnəfɪt]（v.）有益於（n.）利益

例 Reading books to small children **benefits** their language skills.

（唸書給小孩聽有益於他們的語言技巧發展。）

affect [əˋfɛkt]（v.）影響

例 Going on a diet **affects** your health.

（減肥影響你的健康。）

effect [ɪˋfɛkt]（n.）結果；效果；影響

例 Poor health is the **effect** of eating too much junk food.

（健康不佳是吃太多垃圾食物的結果。）

anarchy [`ænə-kɪ]（n.）無政府狀態；混亂

例　When the elections failed to create a majority leader, **anarchy** occurred.

（當選舉無法產生一個多數選出的總統，無政府狀態就發生了。）

architect [`ɑrkə͵tɛkt]（n.）建築師

例　The government hired an **architect** to design a new city hall building.

（政府僱用了一位建築師來設計一棟新的市政大樓。）

astrology [ə`strɑlədʒɪ]（n.）占星術

例　He really believes in **astrology** and never goes out before reading his sign in the newspaper.

（他十分相信占星術，而且在報紙上閱讀他的星座運勢前絕不出門。）

astronaut [`æstrə͵nɔt]（n.）太空人

例　The **astronaut**'s mission was to fly the spaceship to Mars to take pictures.

（這名太空人的任務是駕駛太空船到火星拍照。）

astronomy [əs`trɑnəmɪ]（n.）天文學

例　He was interested in planets and stars, so he studied in **astronomy**.

（他對行星和恆星有興趣，所以他研究了天文學。）

audible [`ɔdəbl̩]（adj.）可聽見的

例　In the library your voice must not be **audible** to the other people that are reading books.

（在圖書館裡，你的聲音不可以吵到其他在看書的人。）

audience [`ɔdɪəns]（n.）聽眾；觀眾

例　The **audience** clapped when the movie star appeared.

（當這位電影明星出現時，觀眾都拍手。）

精選字彙 A~Z的

常見字尾的變化

字彙 易混淆

常見片語

片語 易混淆

常見諺語

audit [`ɔdɪt]（v.）審核；查帳

例　The government had some questions about his income so they **audited** his tax return.

（政府對他的收入有些疑問，因此他們調查他的稅務申報。）

audition [ɔ`dɪʃən]（n.）試演

例　Actors have to perform at an **audition** to earn a part in a play.

（為了贏得戲中的角色，演員必須在舞台上試演一段）

auditor [`ɔdɪtɚ]（n.）聽者；旁聽生；查帳員

例　The **auditor** needed to see all the receipts and my previous tax return.

（這位查帳員需要看所有的收據以及我先前的繳稅單。）

auditorium [ˌɔdə`torɪəm]（n.）禮堂；觀眾席

例　Everyone sat in the **auditorium** to listen to the musical concert.

（每個人坐在禮堂裡聽這場音樂會。）

caption [`kæpʃən]（n.）標題

例　The **caption** explained what was happening in the picture.

（這個標題解釋了這張圖片發生的事。）

captious [`kæpʃəs]（adj.）吹毛求疵的

例　I didn't like talking to him because his **captious** attitude made me feel annoyed.

（我不喜歡和他說話，因為他吹毛求疵的態度令我惱怒。）

captivate [`kæptəˌvet]（v.）使迷惑

例　She didn't move for the entire concert because she was **captivated** by the singer's beautiful songs.

（她在整場的音樂會都沒有動，因為她被歌手的美妙的歌曲給迷住了。）

capture [`kæptʃɚ]（v.）捕獲；贏得

例　The spider **captures** a fly in its web.

（這隻蜘蛛將蒼蠅捉入牠的網內。）

captain [ˈkæptɪn]（n.）船長；機長
例 The ship's **captain** ordered the crew to return to the harbor when the weather became really rough.
（當天氣變得十分惡劣時，這艘船的船長命令船員回港。）

recession [rɪˈsɛʃən]（n.）後退；衰退
例 There are fewer new job opportunity when the economy is in a **recession**.
（在經濟衰退時期，新的工作機會比較少。）

secession [sɪˈsɛʃən]（n.）脫離，退出
例 The rest of the United Nations membership worried that the **secession** of the USA would weaken the power of the organization.
（剩下的聯合國會員國擔心美國的退出將減弱這個組織的力量。）

decide [dɪˈsaɪd]（v.）決定
例 He **decided** to eat at the restaurant right in front of him, so he walked in.
（他決定在他對面的那家餐廳用餐，因此他走進去了。）

secede [sɪˈsid]（v.）脫離；退出
例 A group of poor countries was dissatisfied with the decisions being made at the United Nations and decided to **secede**.
（一些貧窮國家因為不滿聯合國作出的決議，而決定退出。）

homicide [ˈhɑməˌsaɪd]（n.）謀殺（行為）
例 She killed her boss and was charged with **homicide**.
（她殺了她的老闆，因而被控殺人罪。）

suicide [ˈsuəˌsaɪd]（n.）自殺
例 The businessman lost all his money and was so depressed that he committed **suicide** by jumping off a bridge.
（這個商人失去了他所有的錢而十分沮喪，以致於他跳橋自殺。）

A～Z的精選字彙

常見字尾的變化

易混淆字彙

常見片語

易混淆片語

常見諺語

cosmetic [kɑz`mɛtɪk]（n.）化粧品

例　She looked in the mirror to apply her lipstick and other **cosmetics**.

（她看著鏡子來上唇膏和其他化妝品。）

cosmic [`kɑzmɪk]（adj.）宇宙的

例　Astronauts are interested in all things **cosmic**, such as planets and stars.

（太空人對所有宇宙的事物都有興趣，像是行星和恆星。）

accurate [`ækjərɪt]（adj.）準確的、精準的

例　She spoke **accurate** English and never made any grammar mistake.

（她說正確的英文且從未犯過文法的錯誤。）

cure [kjʊr]（v.）治療；治癒

例　People go to doctors to **cure** their illnesses.

（人們去看醫生以治療他們的疾病。）

manicure [`mænɪ͵kjʊr]（n.）修指甲；指甲護理

例　She went to a beauty salon for a **manicure** because she would like to have well cared for hands.

（她去了一家美容院做指甲護理，因為她想要好好呵護她的手。）

secure [sɪ`kjʊr]（adj.）無慮的；安全的

例　She felt **secure** after receiving a letter from her son who studied abroad.

（收到了一封來自國外念書的兒子來信之後，她才覺得放心。）

UNIT 3 易混淆字彙的練習

精選字彙 A～Z的

常見字尾的變化

字彙 易混淆

常見片語

片語 易混淆

常見諺語

Q1 The test requires students to give the _____ answers.

（A）accurate　　（B）access　　（C）cure　　　　（D）secure

Q2 Students need to hand in their _____ at the end of this semester.

（A）essays

（B）assays

（C）cosmetics

（D）benefits

Q3 Many people _____ to join this charity activity.

（A）recite

（B）pesticide

（C）decide

（D）beside

Q4 Please note that children need to stay in a _____ environment.

（A）manicure

（B）rescue

（C）dangerous

（D）secure

Q5 When he was young, he wanted to be an _____.

（A）astronomy

（B）astrology

（C）astronaut

（D）astrolabe

Q6 Many audiences sit in the _____ to listen to the speech.

（A）audit

（B）auditorium

（C）auditor

（D）audition

Q7 The bird _____ the worm and ate it.

（A）captivated

（B）captioned

（C）capped

（D）captured

Q8 The coke was placed in the beverage _____.

（A）isle

（B）aisle

（C）island

（D）aid

解答： 1. A　2. A　3. C　4. D
　　　5. C　6. B　7. D　8. B

UNIT 4 常見片語

Study 1 「in ~ of」與「under ~ of」的形式

1. in appreciation of（為了感謝）
   例 We gave Mr. Chen a trophy **in appreciation of** his service to our company.
   （為了感謝陳先生對我們公司的服務，我們贈與他一份獎品。）

2. in case of（在～的情況下）
   例 **In case of** fire, use wet towel to cover your mouth and nose.
   （在火災的情況下，用濕毛巾遮住你的口與鼻。）

3. in defense of（為了維護）
   例 The group of young men argued with them **in defense of** their ideals.
   （為了維護他們的理想，這群年輕人與他們爭論。）

4. in honor of（向～表示敬意）
   例 The officials hold a dinner party **in honor of** the teacher.
   （官員們舉辦晚宴來表示對這位老師的敬意。）

5. in place of（代替）
   例 We had a set of new machines **in place of** the old ones.
   （我們採購了一批新機器以代替舊的機器。）

6. in praise of（為了讚揚）
   例 The president gave a speech **in praise of** his minister's performance.
   （總統發表演說來讚許他的部長的表現。）

7. in recognition of（褒獎）

例 The company gave a lot of bonuses **in recognition of** its entire staff's contribution.

（這家公司發了一大筆獎金以獎勵全體員工的貢獻。）

8. in the name of（以～的名義）

例 He opened a bank account **in the name of** his son.

（他用他兒子的名義開了一個銀行帳戶。）

9. under the excuse of（以～作為藉口）

例 He refused to see his girlfriend **under the excuse of** illness.

（他用生病當作藉口來拒絕見他的女友。）

10. under the guise of（假～之名）

例 The officials abused their authority **under the guise of** freedom.

（這些官員假自由之名濫用職權。）

Study 2　形容詞片語（Adj.＋Prep.）

11. according to（根據）

例 Please take the medicine **according to** the instructions.

（請根據指示服藥。）

12. accustomed to（習慣於）

例 I am **accustomed to** getting up early.

（我習慣早起。）

13. angry about（對～生氣）

例 I'm very **angry about** your dishonesty.

（我對你的不誠實感到非常生氣。）

14. aware of（意識到）

例 I am **aware of** the serious situation.

（我意識到這個嚴重的局勢。）

精選字彙 A～Z 的

的變化 常見字尾

字彙 易混淆

常見片語

片語 易混淆

常見諺語

15. bad at（不擅長）

例 She is **bad at** dancing.

（她不擅長跳舞。）

16. crowded with（擠滿；滿是）

例 That is a day **crowded with** activity.

（那是一個忙得不可開交的日子。）

17. devoted to（致力於）

例 Mother Teresa was **devoted to** help poor people.

（德蕾莎修女致力於幫助窮人。）

18. famous for（有名的）同義：noted for

例 The city is **famous for** its silk.

（這座城市以出產絲綢而聞名。）

19. fed up with（對～厭煩）

例 I am **fed up with** it. Please stop talking about that.

（我真是受夠了。請不要再說那件事了。）

20. full of（充滿）

例 The pool is **full of** water.

（這個池子裡充滿了水。）

21. good at（擅長）

例 Is he **good at** painting?

（他擅長繪畫嗎？）

22. hungry for（渴望於）

例 The prisoners are **hungry for** freedom.

（這些囚犯渴望自由。）

23. impressed with（對～印象深刻）

例 We were deeply **impressed with / by** your efficiency.

（我們對你的效率印象深刻。）

24. interested in（對～有興趣）

例 I'm not **interested in** this topic.

（我對這個主題不感興趣。）

25. kind of（種類；有一點兒；仁慈）

例 There are all **kinds of** animals in the zoo.

（動物園裡有各式各樣的動物。）

例 The movie is **kind of** moving.

（這部電影有點兒感人。）

例 That's very **kind of** you.

（多謝你的好意。）

26. lots of（＝a lot of，很多，後面接複數可數或不可數名詞。）

例 There are **a lot of** people in the railway station.

（這個火車站裡有許多人。）

27. plenty of（許多的，比 a lot of 少，後面接複數可數名詞或不可數名詞。）

例 The doctor advised me to get **plenty of** exercise.

（醫生建議我要做很多運動。）

28. powered of（以～為動力）

例 The toy rabbit is **powered of** batteries.

（這個玩具兔是以電池驅動的。）

29. proud of（為～而驕傲）

例 She is **proud of** her accomplishments.

（她為自己的成就感到自豪。）

30. responsible for（為～負責）

例 They all desire you to be **responsible for** the project.

（他們全都想讓你負責這項計畫。）

31. shame on（感到可恥）

例 **Shame on** you!

（你真可恥！）

32. short of（短缺）

例 We're very **short of** help.
（我們非常缺少幫手。）

例 If I take a long walk, I'll get **short of** breath.
（如果我長途步行，就會氣喘呼呼的。）

33. surprised at（驚訝的）同義：astonished at

例 I am **surprised at** your behavior.
（我對你的行為感到震驚。）

34. tired of（厭煩）

例 I'm **tired of** it, the same old story.
（我很厭煩這老套的故事。）

35. tired out（非常疲倦）

例 I was **tired out** by driving on the highway for hours.
（在高速公路上開車數個小時讓我非常疲倦。）

例 I must have **tired** myself **out**.
（我一定是過於勞累了。）

36. worried about（對～擔心）

例 I'm **worried about** getting lost in a strange city.
（我擔心在陌生的城市中迷路。）

Study 3 動詞片語（Verb＋Prep.）

37. apologize to someone for something（因某事而向某人道歉）

例 He **apologized to** her **for** not going to her party.
（他因為沒有出席她舉行的宴會而向她道歉。）

38. apply for something（申請某個東西）

例 He has **applied for** a post in England.
（他已申請在英國任職。）

39. approve of（贊成）
例 Her father will never **approve of** her marriage to Tom.
（她父親絕不會贊成她和湯姆結婚。）

40. believe in（＝trust，信賴）
例 We **believe in** him.
（我們信任他。）

41. call on（拜訪；號召；請求）
例 I **called on** my relatives yesterday.
（我昨天拜訪了我的親戚。）

例 The teacher **calls on** his students to take notes in class.
（這位老師要求學生在課堂上記筆記。）

42. clear up（清理）
例 Would you please **clear up** the table?
（可否請你把桌子清乾淨？）

43. complain about / of（抱怨）
例 I have nothing to **complain of**.
（我沒什麼可抱怨的。）

44. congratulate someone on something（向某人恭喜某事）
例 I **congratulate** you **on** your great discovery.
（我恭喜你的偉大發現。）

45. consist of（由～組成）
例 Water **consists of** hydrogen and oxygen.
（水由氫和氧組成。）

46. depend on（依賴）
例 You can **depend on** him.
（你可以依賴他。）

精選字彙 A～Z的

的變化 常見字尾

字彙 易混淆

常見片語

片語 易混淆

常見諺語

47. die of（死於疾病）; die from（死於事故）

例 He **died of** a stroke.
（他因中風而死。）

例 He **died from** a traffic accident.
（他死於一場交通事故。）

48. discuss something with someone（和某人討論某事）

例 They **discussed** the education plans **with** Shirley.
（他們與雪莉討論了教育計畫。）

49. escape from（從～逃脫）

例 They **escaped from** the big fire.
（他們自大火中逃脫。）

50. forgive someone for something（原諒某人某事）

例 I **forgave** Mary **for** her mistakes.
（我原諒了瑪麗的錯誤。）

51. get in / get out of（上車 / 下車，用於小型車）

例 **Get in**, please.
（請上車。）

例 **Get out of** my car.
（滾出我的車子。）

52. get on / get off（上車 / 下車，用於大型車）

例 Yes, Please **get on**.
（是的，請上車吧！）

例 You should **get off** at the square and transfer to Bus No.17.
（你應該要在廣場下車，再轉乘 17 路公車。）

53. go by（經過）

例 Time **went by** slowly.
（時光慢慢流逝。）

54. graduate from（畢業）
例 I **graduated from** college last year.
（我去年從大學畢業。）

55. have a look at（＝glance at，看一眼）
例 He **had a look at** the envelope and recognized his uncle's handwriting.
（他瞥了一眼那個信封，並認出他叔叔的筆跡。）

56. hear about（聽說）
例 I've just **heard about** his illness.
（我剛聽說了他生病的事。）

57. hear from（得到～的消息）
例 I haven't **heard from** Alice since she telephoned last month.
（自從上個月愛莉絲來過電話後，我就沒有得到她的音信了。）

58. insist on（＝persist in，堅持）
例 He **persisted in** the study of law.
（他堅持學習法律。）
例 I **insisted on** my opinion.
（我堅持我的意見。）

59. introduce someone to someone（介紹某人給某人認識）
例 I **introduced** my brother **to** Mary's sister. We hope they'll date each other.
（我介紹了我哥給瑪麗的姐姐認識。我們希望他們可以和對方約會。）

60. invite someone to do something（邀請某人做某事）
例 Kevin **invited** me **to** join the party.
（凱文邀請了我來參加派對。）

61. leave for（去、前往）
例 I **left for** Taipei last week to have an interview.
（上週我去台北參加一場面試。）

精選字彙 A～Z 的

的變化 常見字尾

字彙 易混淆

常見片語

片語 易混淆

常見諺語

62. listen to（聽）

例 We are **listening to** a report.

（我們正在聽一份報告。）

63. look after（照顧）

例 Who will **look after** your children while you go out to work?

（你出去上班時，誰會照顧你的孩子？）

64. look at（注視）

例 **Look at** the map, please.

（請看著這張地圖。）

65. look for（找尋）同義：look up from

例 She is **looking for** her lost child.

（她正在尋找她失蹤的孩子。）

66. look forward to＋V-ing / N（期待）

例 They are **looking forward to** her visit.

（他們正期待著她的來訪。）

67. look up（查閱）

例 If you don't know a word, you can **look** it **up** in a dictionary.

（如果你有不認識的字，你可以查字典。）

68. look up to（尊敬）

例 The students all **looked up to** the old philosophy teacher.

（學生們都很尊敬那位年邁的哲學教授。）

69. prefer A to B（喜歡 A 而不喜歡 B）

例 I **prefer** the quiet countryside **to** the noisy cities.

（我喜歡安靜的鄉村勝過喧鬧的城市。）

70. put off（延遲）

例 The students **put off** their homework.

（這些學生遲交了他們的作業。）

71. run out of（從～跑出來；用盡）

例 Have you **run out of** petrol?

（你們把汽油用完了嗎？）

例 He **ran out of** the room with an umbrella.

（他帶著一把雨傘從房間裡跑了出來。）

72. shout at（對～喊叫）

例 Don't **shout at** me!

（別對著我喊叫！）

73. spend on（花費）

例 I **spent** $100 **on** the bike.

（我花了一百美元買下那輛自行車。）

74. suffer from（受～之苦）

例 She often **suffers from** stomachache.

（她時常受胃痛所苦。）

75. suspect sb of sth / suspect sb of doing sth（懷疑某人做了某事）

例 Who do the police **suspect** (**of** the crime)?

（警方懷疑這是誰犯的案？）

例 What made you **suspect** her **of** having taken the money?

（是什麼讓你懷疑她拿了那筆錢？）

76. take care of（照顧）

例 Please **take care of** the baby for me for a while.

（請替我照顧一下這個嬰兒。）

77. take off / touch down（飛機起飛 / 飛機降落）

例 The plane will **take off** soon.

（飛機馬上就要起飛了。）

例 The plane will **touch down** soon.

（飛機馬上就要降落了。）

精選字彙 A～Z的

常見字尾的變化

易混淆字彙

常見片語

易混淆片語

常見諺語

78. take out（取出；扣除）/ take away（拿走，帶走）

例　**Take** your hands **out** of your packets.
（把你的手從口袋裡拿出來。）

例　I'm afraid it's not possible for you to **take** it **away**.
（恐怕你無法把它帶走。）

79. turn on（打開）/ turn off（關起來）

例　Will you **turn on** the radio?
（你會打開這台收音機嗎？）

例　Please **turn off** the light.
（請把這盞燈關了。）

80. wait for（等待）

例　I have been **waiting for** the bus a long time.
（我已經等公車很久了。）

UNIT 3　常見片語的練習

Q1 **After the student finish all the courses, he will _____ college.**

（A）escape from　　　　（B）graduate from
（C）get on　　　　　　（D）depend on

Q2 **Henry is a good brother. He often _____ his little sister.**

（A）take a look at　　　（B）clear up
（C）take care of　　　　（D）complain about

Q3 **The station is _____ many passengers. Many people are heading to Taipei.**

（A）tired of　　　　　（B）aware of
（C）kind of　　　　　　（D）crowded with

Q4 _____ this report, the company will build the new highway in 2022.

(A) According to　　　　　　(B) In the name of

(C) In case of　　　　　　　(D) Under the excuse of

Q5 The boss has bought many sets of new computers _____ the old ones.

(A) in praise of　　　　　　(B) in place of

(C) in defense of　　　　　(D) in recognition of

Q6 Could you _____ your friends to me? I want to get to know them.

(A) hear　　　　　　　　　(B) look

(C) forgive　　　　　　　　(D) introduce

Q7 Her mother was really _____ her because she got a college degree.

(A) angry about　　　　　　(B) proud of

(C) tired of　　　　　　　　(D) worried about

Q8 Could Mary _____ my pet dog when I travel to New York this weekend?

(A) listen to　　　　　　　(B) run out of

(C) look after　　　　　　　(D) turn off

精選字彙 A～Z的

常見字尾 的變化

字彙 易混淆

常見片語

片語 易混淆

常見諺語

解答： 1. B　2. C　3. D　4. A
5. B　6. D　7. B　8. C

act on（產生作用）

例　The drug doesn't **act on** the negative feedback.

（這個藥不會產生副作用。）

act out（把～付諸行動）

例　You should **act out** your plans.

（你應該把你的計畫付諸行動。）

act up（出問題；調皮）

例　My computer has been **acting up** again.

（我的電腦又出問題了。）

beat down（殺價）

例　I **beat down** the price, for it is really too expensive.

（我殺價，因為它實在太貴了。）

beat off（擊退；趕走）

例　I **beat off** this annoying guy, whereas he doesn't quit staying here.

（我趕走這個討厭鬼，但他不放棄待在這裡。）

beat up（痛打一頓）

例　I **beat up** my naughty kid.

（我把我那頑皮的小孩痛打一頓。）

break away（逃脫）

例　The robber **broke away** from the police.

（這名搶匪從警方手中逃脫。）

break down（發生故障）

例 Your car **broke down** on the street.

（你的車在街上拋錨了。）

break off（中斷）

例 The peace talks **broke off** without any reason.

（這場和平會談沒來由地中斷了。）

check in（辦理登記手續）

例 We **checked in** into the hotel the day before yesterday.

（我們前天在飯店登記入房。）

check over（檢查）

例 Can you **check over** my homework?

（你可以檢查我的作業嗎？）

check up（核對）

例 Please **check up** this form.

（請核對這個表格。）

come down（倒塌）

例 The building has **come down** because of the earthquake.

（這棟建築物已經因為地震而倒塌了。）

come down to（歸結為）

例 It **comes down to** why you did that.

（歸結到底的是你為何這樣做。）

come down on（嚴懲）

例 The police **come down on** anyone who abuse drugs.

（警方嚴懲任何濫用藥物的人。）

die for（渴望）

例 I'm **dying for** a cup of coffee.

（我非常想要一杯咖啡。）

die out（滅絕）

例 Dinosaurs **died out** millions of years ago.

（恐龍在數百萬年前就滅絕了。）

die of（因某種疾病而死亡）

例 My brother **died of** cancer the day before yesterday.

（前天我弟弟因癌症而過世。）

die from（因意外或事故而死亡）

例 His daughter **died from** a car accident.

（他的女兒死於一場車禍。）

drop by（順道拜訪）

例 I **dropped by** my old friend on my way home.

（在我回家的途中，我順道拜訪了我的老朋友。）

drop out（退出；退學）

例 You shouldn't **drop out** the game.

（你不應該退出比賽。）

drop off（下車；打瞌睡；減少）

例 Please **drop** me **off** at next stop.

（請讓我在下一站下車。）

face off（對抗）

例 The two teams will **face off** next month.

（這兩隊將在下個月進行對抗。）

face up to（接受，正視困境）

例 You should **face up to** your problems.

（你應該正視你的問題。）

face down（壓倒）

例 He **faced down** all his opponents.

（他壓倒他所有的對手。）

get over（從～恢復過來）

例　I need one month to **get over** my illness.

（我需要一個月的時間從病痛中痊癒。）

get through（通過）

例　It's easy to **get through** this game.

（通過這個比賽是很容易的。）

get down（使沮喪）

例　Don't let the thing **get** you **down**.

（別因為這件事使你氣餒。）

kick about（討論）

例　We are **kicking about** your plans.

（我們正在討論你的計畫。）

kick out（解僱）

例　You shouldn't **kick** him **out**; he did not do anything wrong.

（你不應該解僱他，他沒有做錯任何事。）

kick back（付回扣；放鬆）

例　After they finished the job, they **kicked back** and ate some snack.

（他們完成這項工作後，就放鬆、吃一些零食。）

UNIT 4　易混淆片語的練習

Q1 **Competition can _____ the price.**

（A）beat off　　　　　　（B）beat down

（C）beat up　　　　　　（D）beat out

Q2 **The medicine will take some time to _____ the cells.**

（A）act out　　　　　　（B）act up

（C）act on　　　　　　（D）act for

精選字彙　A～Z的

的變化　常見字尾

字彙　易混淆

常見片語

片語　易混淆

常見諺語

Q3 Jamie _____ his parents' house to have dinner with them.

(A) drop by   (B) drop out

(C) drop off   (D) drop into

Q4 Amy and her husband just _____ at the luxurious hotel.

(A) checked up   (B) checked over

(C) checked out   (D) checked in

Q5 All the students in the class _____ the examinations. The teacher was really happy.

(A) got through   (B) got over

(C) got down   (D) got up

Q6 She is _____ a cup of ice-cream.

(A) dying of   (B) dying for

(C) dying from   (D) dying out

Q7 Annie needs some time to _____ the shock.

(A) get through   (B) get over

(C) get down   (D) get up

Q8 People should _____ their problems.

(A) face off   (B) face up to

(C) face down   (D) face in

Study **1** 人生哲理篇

1. A bad penny always comes back.（惡有惡報。）
2. A contented mind is a perpetual feast.（知足常樂。）
3. A stitch in time saves nine.（防微杜漸。）
4. Actions speak louder than words.（事實勝於雄辯。）
5. Advice when most needed is least heeded.（忠言逆耳。）
6. After a storm comes a calm.（雨過天晴。）
7. All good things come to an end.（天下無不散的筵席。）
8. All roads lead to Rome.（條條大道通羅馬。）
9. Bad news travels fast.（壞事傳千里。）
10. Better bend than break.（大丈夫能屈能伸。）
11. Don't count your chickens before they are hatched.
    （不要打如意算盤。）
12. Easy come, easy go.（來得快，去得快。）
13. Even Homer sometimes nods.（智者千慮必有一失。）
14. Every dog has his day.（風水輪流轉。）
15. Extremes meet.（兩極相逢。）
16. History repeats itself.（歷史會重演。）
17. Honesty is the best policy.（誠實為上策。）
18. In wine there is truth.（酒後吐真言。）
19. It is never too late to mend.（亡羊補牢猶未晚也。）
20. It is no use crying over spilt milk.（覆水難收。）
21. It never rains but it pours.（禍不單行。）
22. Look before you leap.（三思而後行。）
23. Lookers-on see most of the game.（旁觀者清。）
24. Make hay while the sun shines.（未雨綢繆。）

精選字彙 A～Z 的

常見字尾的變化

易混淆字彙

常見片語

易混淆片語

常見諺語

25. No man can serve two masters.（一人不能事二主。）

26. No news is good news.（沒有消息就是好消息。）

27. Nothing comes of nothing.（事出必有因。）

28. Once bitten, twice shy.（一朝被蛇咬，十年怕草繩。）

29. Out of sight, out of mind.（眼不見，心不念。）

30. Prevention is better than cure.（預防勝於治療。）

31. Seeing is believing.（百聞不如一見。）（眼見為憑。）

32. Still water runs deep.（靜水流深。）（大智若愚。）

33. Strike while the iron is hot.（打鐵趁熱。）

34. Take the rough with the smooth.（逆來順受。）

35. Talk of the devil and he is sure to appear.（說曹操曹操就到。）

36. The child is father of the man.（江山易改，本性難移。）

37. The darkest hour is that before the dawn.（否極泰來。）

38. The tongue is not steel, yet it cuts.（舌頭不是鋼鐵卻能傷人。）

39. There is no rose without a thorn.（朵朵玫瑰皆有刺。）

40. There is no smoke without fire.（無風不起浪）。

41. Two heads are better than one.（集思廣益。）

42. Walls have ears.（隔牆有耳。）

43. Where there is life, there is hope.（留得青山在，不怕沒柴燒。）

44. Words cut more than swords.（舌劍利於刀劍。）

45. You cannot burn the candle at both ends.（蠟燭不能兩頭燒）

46. You cannot sell the cow and drink the milk.（魚與熊掌不可兼得。）

47. You can't make something out of nothing.（巧婦難為無米之炊。）

Study 2　時間金錢篇

48. A heavy purse makes a light heart.（錢包重，心輕鬆。）

49. A light purse makes a heavy heart.（錢包輕，心沉重。）

50. Health is better than wealth.（健康勝於財富。）

51. Money makes the mare go.（有錢能使鬼推磨。）

52. There is no grief which time does not lessen and soften.
（時間能減緩所有傷痛。）

53. Time and tide waits for no man.（歲月不饒人。）
54. Time flies.（時光飛逝）
55. Time is money.（時間就是金錢。）
56. Truth is the daughter of time.（日久見真章。）

Study 3　人際禮俗篇

57. A friend in need is a friend indeed.（患難見真情。）
58. All that glitters is not gold.（虛有其表。）
59. Barking dogs seldom bite.（會叫的狗不會咬人。）
60. Beauty is but skin deep.（美麗只是膚淺的。）
61. Beauty is in the eye of the beholder.（情人眼裏出西施。）
62. Birds of a feather flock together.（物以類聚。）
63. Blood is thicker than water.（血濃於水。）
64. Courtesy costs nothing.（禮多人不怪。）
65. Diamond cut diamond.（兩虎相爭必有一傷。）
66. Do as you would be done by others.（己所不欲，勿施於人。）
67. Do in Rome as the Romans do.（入境隨俗。）
68. Everybody's business is nobody's business.（眾人之事乏人管。）
69. He who has many friends has no friend.（相交滿天下，知己無一人。）
70. Like father, like son.（有其父必有其子。）
71. Love is blind.（愛情是盲目的。）
72. Love is forgiving even if you can't forget.（愛就算是不能忘懷，也要原諒。）
73. One man's meat may be another man's poison.（人各有所好。）

Study 4　教育學習篇

74. A Jack of all trades is master of none.（樣樣都會，樣樣都不精通。）
75. A little learning is a dangerous thing.（一知半解最危險。）

精選字彙 A～Z的
的變化 常見字尾
字彙 易混淆
常見片語
片語 易混淆
常見諺語

76. An idle youth, a needy age. （少壯不努力，老大徒傷悲。）

77. As you sow, so shall you reap. （種瓜得瓜，種豆得豆。）

78. Better be the head of an ass than the tail of a horse.
（寧為驢頭不為馬尾。）

79. It's never too late to learn. （學習永遠不嫌晚。）

80. Books, like friends, should be few and well chosen.
（讀書如擇友，宜少且宜精。）

81. Constant dripping wears away the stone. （滴水穿石。）

82. Easier said than done. （說來容易做來難。）

83. Everything must have a beginning. （萬丈高樓平地起。）

84. Genius is one percent inspiration and 99 percent perspiration.
（天才是百分之一的靈感，加上百分之九十九分的努力。）

85. Heaven helps those who help themselves. （天助自助者。）

86. Idle folk have the least leisure. （懶漢無閒暇。）

87. It is easy to be wise after the event. （經一事，長一智。）

88. Knowledge is power. （知識就是力量。）

89. Live and learn. （活到學到老。）

90. Never put off till tomorrow what you can do today.
（今日事今日畢。）

91. No pains, no gains. （沒有付出就沒有收穫。）

92. Nothing is impossible to a willing mind.
（天下無難事，只怕有心人。）

93. Nothing venture, nothing have. （不入虎穴，焉得虎子。）

94. Practice makes perfect. （熟能生巧。）

95. Rome was not built in a day. （羅馬不是一天造成的。）

96. Slow and steady wins the race. （穩健紮實必能致勝。）

97. Spare the rod and spoil the child. （孩子不打不成器。）。

98. Well begun is half done. （好的開始是成功的一半。）

99. Where there is a will there is a way. （有志者事竟成。）

100. You cannot teach an old dog new tricks. （老狗學不會新把戲。）

Grammer

CHAPTER 2
必備句型文法分析

UNIT 1 名詞與冠詞

Study 1 名詞的種類

名詞分為：**普通名詞**是指一般的人事物，如：boy, table, shoes 等。**集合名詞**則是指 people, family 等代表這一類的全體，這類名詞沒有複數型。**專有名詞**指的是一般人名、地名或機構名稱，如：America, Charles, Taipei 等。**物質名詞**指的是與物質或材料有關的名詞，包括如：fire, salt, silver 等。**抽象名詞**則是指沒有形體的名詞，如：knowledge, health 等。

Study 2 普通名詞的單複數

	規則	單數 Singular	複數 Plural
1	大部份的名詞複數型均加 **-s**。	book boy	book**s** boy**s**
2	字尾為 -ss, -sh, -ch, -x 的名詞複數型要加 **-es**。	class dish watch box	class**es** dish**es** watch**es** box**es**
3	-y 結尾的名詞，若 -y 前的字母是子音，複數型則要去掉 -y，加上 **-ies**；若 -y 前的字母是母音，複數型則直接加上 **-s**。	city toy	cit**ies** toy**s**
4	-o 結尾的名詞，若 -o 前的字母是子音，複數型直接加上 **-es**；若 -o 前的字母是母音，複數型則直接加上 **-s**。	potato tomato radio	potato**es** tomato**es** radio**s**
5	字尾為 f 或 fe 的名詞複數型要去掉 -f 或 -fe，再加上 **-ves**。	wife wolf knife	wi**ves** wol**ves** kni**ves**
6	名詞複數型不規則變化。	child man woman foot mouse tooth	child**ren** m**e**n wom**e**n f**ee**t m**ice** t**ee**th

Study 3 冠詞的種類

　　冠詞分為 a, an, the 三類，而冠詞的目的在區別為不特定名詞與特定名詞，其中 the 可以同時用於單數與複數：

不特定（指一本書）	I read **a** book that was very good. （我讀了一本很好的書。）
特定（指特定的一本書）	The title of **the** book was *Harry Potter*. （這本書的書名是哈利波特。）
不特定（指一些書）	I read **some** books that were very good. （我讀了一些很好的書。）
特定（指特定的一些書）	The author of **the** books is Tim. （這些書的作者是提姆。）
不特定（指一些小說）	I read **some** novels that was very good. （我讀了一些很好的小說。）
特定（指特定的一些小說）	The theme of **the** novels was love and peace. （這些小說的主題是愛與和平。）
不特定（指一位新的祕書）	Our boss needs to hire **a** new secretary. （我們的老闆需要僱用一位新祕書。）
特定（指一家特定的公司）	The name of **the** company is ASA. （這家公司的名稱是 ASA。）
特定（指特定的一些問題）	Please answer **the** questions on this form. （請回答這張表格上的這些問題。）

Study 4 冠詞的用途

（1）用於「計量」或表示「每一」的表達：

　　　a half (one half)

　　　an apple a day (one apple per day)

例　Eliza has **an** apple **a** day.（伊萊莎一天吃一顆蘋果。）

（2）用於「唯一」或「指定」的表達：

例　**The** sun went behind some clouds.（太陽退到雲層後面。）

例　Please close **the** window.（請把這扇窗關上。）

例　We can see **the** stars tonight.（今晚我們可以看到這些星星。）

（3）用於「時間」或「位置」的表達：

　　　時間：the morning, the past, the future...

例　Elaine will come back in **the** near future.

　　　（伊蓮近期將會回來。）

名詞與冠詞
代名詞
形容詞與副詞
動詞
介系詞
句型與附加問句
比較級與最高級
時態與被動語態
條件句與假設語氣
關係詞與三大子句

位置：the front, the bottom, the beginning, the end...

例　**The** front of the hotel is the driveway.（飯店的前面是車道。）

（4）用於「序數」前，而不用於基數前的表達：

序數：the First World War, the tenth day...

基數：World War II, day ten, Volume Four...

例　**The** 2nd World War took place in 1938.
（二次世界大戰發生在 1938 年。）

（5）用於「世紀」或「年代」，而不用於某一年的表達：

世紀或年代：in the 1990s, in the twenty-first century...

單指某一年：in 1981, in 2009...

例　In **the** 1970s, there were many famous writers.
（在 1970 年代有很多有名的作家。）

（6）用於「最高級」的表達：

不規則：the worst mistake

規則：the most interesting idea

例　This is **the** best movie that I have seen before.
（這是我看過最棒的電影。）

（7）用於「種族」或「國籍」的表達：

例　**The** Chinese are proud of their ancestors' invention.
（中國人為他們祖先的發明感到自豪。）

（8）用於「被限定」名詞的表達：

例　**The** rice that I bought yesterday is in the bag.
（我昨天買的那些米在這個袋子裡。）

例　**The** letter that I gave you yesterday is important.
（我昨天給你的那封信很重要。）

（9）用於「學術領域」的表達：（用於後面接 of 的情況，不會單獨出現）

the art of Japan, the history of the 20th century...

例　Heather studied **the** art of Japan in college.
（希瑟在大學研究日本的藝術。）

UNIT 1　名詞與冠詞的練習

代名詞

形容詞 與副詞

動詞

介系詞

句型與 附加問句

比較級與 最高級

時態與 被動語態

條件句與 假設語氣

關係詞與 三大子句

Q1 There are some _____ on the table. Could you pass them to the classmates?

（A）book（B）books

（C）bookes（D）bookies

Q2 They want to move _____ in this room to the other room because the other room need more of them.

（A）the chairs（B）chairs

（C）the chair（D）chair

Q3 Many _____ wrote their homework before going to the class.

（A）child（B）children

（C）childs（D）childish

Q4 Peter is _____ first student that gave me his report.

（A）a（B）some

（C）one of（D）the

Q5 Amy was born in _____, so she is 20 years old.

（A）1990（B）the 1990s

（C）the 1990（D）1990s

Q6 Please put these _____ in the drawer.

（A）knifs（B）knives

（C）knife（D）the knife

Q7 Jenny have studied _____ history of Germany since she entered the university.

（A）a（B）some（C）the（D）those

Q8 He read _____ book yesterday.

（A）two（B）some（C）a（D）these

解答： 1. B　2. A　3. B　4. D
5. A　6. B　7. C　8. C

UNIT 2 代名詞

Study 1 代名詞的種類

　　代名詞分為人稱代名詞、指示代名詞、不定代名詞。人稱代名詞，主要的功能為代替先前提過的人或物，又分為主詞、受詞、所有格、所有格代名詞、反身代名詞、疑問代名詞等六大類用法；指示代名詞是用來代表某個特定或指定的名詞；不定代名詞則用來代替不確定或不特定的名詞。

Study 2 人稱代名詞的六大類用法

（1）主詞用法
　　例 **You** have those luggage.（你有那些行李。）
　　例 **I** have those luggage.（我有那些行李。）
　　例 **He** has those luggage.（他有那些行李。）

（2）受詞用法
　　例 He gives **you** those luggage.（他給你那些行李。）
　　例 He gives **me** those luggage.（他給我那些行李。）
　　例 He gives **him** those luggage.（他給他那些行李。）

（3）所有格用法
　　例 Those are **your** luggage.（那些是你的行李。）
　　例 Those are **my** luggage.（那些是我的行李。）
　　例 Those are **his** luggage.（那些是他的行李。）

（4）所有格代名詞用法
　　例 Those luggage is **yours**.（那些行李是你的。）
　　例 Those luggage is **mine**.（那些行李是我的。）
　　例 Those luggage is **his**.（那些行李是他的。）

（5）反身代名詞用法
- 表同位

例 Henry hit **himself**.（亨利打了他自己。）

例 I made **myself** a new knife.（我替自己做了一把新的刀子。）

- 表強調

例 Even John **himself** became suspicious.

（甚至約翰自己都變得疑神疑鬼的。）

例 Mary made the blouse **herself**.（瑪麗自己做了那件襯衫。）

（6）疑問代名詞用法
- who（誰）

例 **Who** is the tall man?（那個高個子的男人是誰？）

- which（哪一個）

例 **Which** shall I select?（我應該選擇哪一個？）

- what（什麼）

例 **What** should I do?（我應該要做什麼？）

- whom（who 的受格，誰）

例 I know who you love, and **whom** you want to marry.

（我知道你愛誰，想跟誰結婚。）

- whose（who 或 which 的所有格，誰的）

例 **Whose** shoes are these?（這些是誰的鞋子？）

＊人稱代名詞用法一覽表

主格	所有格	受格	所有格代名詞	反身代名詞
I（我）	my	me	mine	myself
you（你）	your	you	yours	yourself
he（他）	his	him	his	himself
she（她）	her	her	hers	herself
it（它）	its	it	X	itself
they（他們）	their	them	theirs	themselves
we（我們）	our	us	ours	ourselves
you（你們）	your	you	yours	yourselves

Study 3　指示代名詞的用法

指示代名詞是用來代表某特定或指定的名詞，例如：this, that, these, those。

例　It is my book. **This** is yours.
（它是我的書，這本是你的。）
（this＝this book，指特定的「書」。）

例　The weather in Taiwan is much hotter than **that** in Russia.
（在台灣的天氣比在俄羅斯的更加炎熱。）
（that＝the weather，指特定地區的「天氣」。）

Study 4　不定代名詞的用法

不定代名詞用來代替不確定或不特定的名詞，常見的不定代名詞有 some, one, both, few, each, another, all, many 等。

例　I have a black cat, and he has a white **one**.
（我有一隻黑貓，而他有一隻白貓。）
（one 用來取代前面提過的 cat。）

例　I have three pens. **One** is red, **another** is blue, and **the other** is black.
（我有三枝筆，一枝是紅色，另一枝是藍色，還有一枝是黑色。）
（One, another, the other 各自代表前面提過的三枝筆。）

名詞與冠詞

代名詞

形容詞與副詞

動詞

介系詞

句型與附加問句

比較級與最高級

時態與被動語態

條件句與假設語氣

關係詞與三大子句

Q1 There are some pencils on the desk. These are mines, and those are _____.
（A）him 　　（B）he 　　（C）his 　　（D）himself

Q2 _____ is the woman with pink shirt? She keeps looking at you.
（A）Whose 　　　　（B）Who
（C）What 　　　　（D）Which

Q3 This is her book. She will read _____ this evening.
（A）it 　　（B）its 　　（C）them 　　（D）their

Q4 She bought _____ some new shirts, so she could wear them in the interview.
（A）her 　　　　（B）him
（C）herself 　　　　（D）his

Q5 Don't take it. That is _____ laptop.
（A）himself 　　　　（B）Peter
（C）his 　　　　（D）hers

Q6 The temperature in the classroom is higher than _____ in the auditorium.
（A）it 　　（B）that 　　（C）those 　　（D）these

Q7 There are so many pants in my closet. _____ should I wear?
（A）What 　　（B）Whose 　　（C）Who 　　（D）Which

Q8 Annie has three cats. One is white, another is black, and _____ is orange.
（A）other 　　　　（B）that
（C）the other 　　　　（D）this

解答：　1. C　2. B　3. A　4. C
　　　　5. C　6. B　7. D　8. C

UNIT 3 形容詞與副詞

Study 1 性狀形容詞

　　性狀形容詞主要的目的在形容某一名詞的狀態，分為六種：

（1）指性質：good, beautiful, tall, fast...
（2）指感覺：thirsty, sad, angry, uncomfortable...
（3）指形狀大小：small, large, square, round...
（4）指材質：wood, wool, leather, silver...
（5）指顏色：red, purple, orange, blue...
（6）指國籍：Spanish, Chinese, American, Russian...

Study 2 指示形容詞

　　指示形容詞用來指定某一名詞，包括有：this, that, these, those。

例　I have two beautiful vases, and **that** vase is my favorite.
　　（我有兩個漂亮的花瓶，而那個花瓶是我的最愛。）
　　（用 that 來形容所指的 vase 花瓶。）

Study 3 數量形容詞

　　數量形容詞的目的在形容「數量多少」，包括：one, two, many, much, lots of, plenty of, a few, a little, some 等。

例　I have **two** beautiful vases, and that vase is my favorite.
　　（我有兩個漂亮的花瓶，而那個花瓶是我的最愛。）
　　（用 two 來形容 vase 花瓶。）

名詞與冠詞
代名詞
形容詞與副詞
動詞
介系詞
句型與附加問句
比較級與最高級
時態與被動語態
條件句與假設語氣
關係詞與三大子句

Study 4　形容詞的位置

例　William is **handsome**. （威廉很英俊。）
（形容詞 handsome 作為 William 的補語。）

例　William is a **handsome** guy. （威廉是個英俊的傢伙。）
（形容詞 handsome 作為名詞 guy 的修飾語。）

Study 5　副詞的作用

　　副詞可以修飾動詞、形容詞、其他副詞，也可用來修飾整個句子。

* 修飾動詞

例　I run **slowly**. （我慢慢地跑。）

* 修飾副詞

例　I run **very** slowly. （我跑得非常地慢。）

* 修飾形容詞

例　I am **pretty** handsome. （我非常地英俊。）

* 修飾整個句子

例　**Amazingly**, the little boy solved the problem.
（令人驚訝地，那個小男孩解決了那個問題。）

　　Suddenly, the student opened the door and ran out.
（突然，那個學生開門跑了出去。）

　　Fortunately, I found my lost keys.
（幸運地，我找到了我遺失的鑰匙。）

　　Tragically, no passengers survived in the crash.
（悲慘地，沒有乘客在那次的撞擊事故中生還。）

　　Carefully, I looked after this injured boy.
（謹慎地，我照顧這個受傷的小男孩。）

　　Thankfully, I appreciated his assistance.
（感激地，我謝謝他的協助。）

　　Sincerely, I must say I am sorry to him.
（由衷地，我必須說我對他感到抱歉。）

Frankly, he is not the right person for this position.
（坦白說，他不是這個職位的合適人選。）
Happily, the family enjoyed their dinner together.
（高興地，那家人一起享用他們的晚餐。）
Doubtfully, he asks for my address but doesn't tell me why.
（可疑地，他問我的地址又不告訴我為什麼。）

Study 6　副詞的種類

（1）情狀副詞：slowly, happily, fast, terribly, suddenly...
（2）時間副詞：early, before, since, soon, ago, yet, once a year...
（3）頻率副詞：sometimes, always, usually, rarely, hardly, seldom...
（4）程度副詞：very, pretty, enough, too...
（5）地方副詞：in the park, at school, in Taiwan, in the classroom...

頻率副詞（以%代表發生的頻率）		時間副詞	
always 100%	occasionally 30%	annually	once a year
usually 90%	seldom 20%	monthly	once a month
often 80%	rarely 20%	weekly	once a week
sometimes 50%	never 0%	daily	every day

Study 7　副詞的位置

（1）情狀副詞的位置

主詞	動詞	冠詞	副詞	副詞	形容詞	名詞
Iverson	is	a			good	driver.
Iverson	drives		very	**carefully.**		
Iverson	drives		very	**well.**		

（2）時間副詞的位置

時間副詞	主詞	動詞		時間副詞
	I	study	for the GEPT	**every day.**
Every day	I	study	for the GEPT.	

（3）頻率副詞的位置

主詞	助動詞	頻率副詞＋動詞	
They	can	**always** work	until six.
They		**usually** start	at eight.
They		are **never**	on time.
They	should	**always** be noted	on the memo.

（4）例句：

- The mail is **seldom** distributed before 8:00 in the morning.
  （郵件很少在早上 8 點前送達。）
- The president of the company **always** enjoys talking with each new employee.
  （這家公司的總裁總是喜歡與每位新進員工談話。）
- The housekeeper services the rooms **every day**.
  （這位管家每天都整理房間。）
- The department of human resources provides a new directory of employee telephone numbers **every four weeks**.
  （人力資源部每四週提供一份新的員工通訊錄。）

UNIT 3　形容詞與副詞的練習

Q1　I can speak Japanese _____. I have many Japanese friends.

（A）bad　　　　　　　　（B）fluently
（C）fluent　　　　　　　（D）poorly

Q2　This blanket is Patrick's _____ blanket. He can't sleep without it.

（A）favor　　　　　　　（B）favorably
（C）favorite　　　　　　（D）favorites

名詞與冠詞

代名詞

形容詞與副詞

動詞

介系詞

句型與附加問句

比較級與最高級

時態與被動語態

條件語氣與假設語氣

關係詞與三大子句

Q3 He _____ goes to the class, so the teacher will not give him good grades.

(A) seldom   (B) usually

(C) always   (D) often

Q4 Britta has two dolls, and _____ doll with blue dress is her favorite.

(A) these   (B) a

(C) that   (D) those

Q5 _____, the teacher called my name and asked me a question.

(A) Sudden   (B) Suddenly

(C) Suddenness   (D) Suspicious

Q6 Ian can cook Italian cuisine very _____. Many friends compliment about his cooking.

(A) good   (B) the best

(C) well   (D) better

Q7 The desserts of this café are _____ delicious. They're often sold out when they come out.

(A) many   (B) very

(C) various   (D) vary

Q8 The housekeeper cleans all the rooms _____, so this house is always clean.

(A) twice a year   (B) once a month

(C) weekly   (D) every day

解答： 1. B   2. C   3. A   4. C
5. B   6. C   7. B   8. D

74

名詞與冠詞

代名詞

形容詞與副詞

動詞

介系詞

句型與附加問句

比較級與最高級

時態與被動語態

條件句與假設語氣

關係詞與三大子句

UNIT 4　動詞

Study 1　動詞與主詞的一致性

　　動詞的單複數必須和主詞一致，單數的主詞使用單數動詞，複數的主動則使用複數動詞。遇到以下七種主詞的形式時要特別注意，仔細判斷：

（1）主詞由連接詞連接：and, along with, in addition to, as well as

例 Tony **and** his partner **are** good friends.

（東尼與他的的夥伴是好友。）

（用 are 複數動詞，因為主詞是兩個人。）

例 Mr. Lin, **along with** his family, **lives** in Taipei.

（林先生，與他的父母一起，住在台北。）

（用 lives 單數動詞，因為主詞是 Mr. Lin。）

例 The chairman, **in addition to** his assistant, **is** coming.

（主席，還有他的助理，來了。）

（用 is 單數動詞，因為主詞是 the chairman 一個人。）

例 Ms. Lee, **as well as** her children, **lives** in Taipei.

（李小姐，與她的孩子們，住在台北。）

（用 lives 單數動詞，因為主詞是 Ms. Lee 一個人。）

（2）主詞為「不規則複數型」或「集合名詞」時

例 The **people enjoy** music.（人們欣賞音樂。）

例 The **children are** playing.（孩子們在玩耍。）

例 His **family is** famous in the village.

（他的家庭在村裡很有名。）

（用 lives 單數動詞，因為把 his family 當「一個整體」來看。）

例 The **family are** waiting outside the room.

（這家人正在房外等著。）

（用 are 複數動詞，因為把 the family 當「家庭的每個個體」來看。）

例 The **police** finally **arrest** the robber.

（警方最終逮捕這名搶匪。）

（用 arrest 複數動詞，因為 the police 代表「一群警察」。）

（3）主詞的字尾是 -s 的單數型

例 **Economics is** my major.（經濟學是我的主修。）

例 The good **news is** that nobody was hurt.

（好消息是沒有人受傷。）

例 **Mathematics is** not easy for me.（數學對我來說不容易。）

例 **Physics is** her favorite subject.（物理是她最愛的學科。）

（4）There 所引導的句子

例 There **was a meeting** in the conference room.

（這間會議室裡有一場會議。）

例 There **were two customers** in the store.

（這間商店裡有兩位顧客。）

例 There **is a little ink** left in the bottle.

（這個瓶子裡只剩一點墨汁。）

例 There **are many people** coming this week.

（這個禮拜很多人會來。）

（5）主詞為「名詞＋介系詞＋名詞」的形式

例 The **plan** for the July meetings **has** changed.

（七月的會議計畫已經改變了。）

例 The **apples** on the table **are** delicious.

（桌上的蘋果很可口。）

例 The **author** of the books **is** Amy.（這些書的作者是艾美。）

（6）主詞包含 "every" 或 "each" 一類的詞彙

例 **Every one** of the workers **is** called by his name.

（每一個工人的名字都被叫到。）

例 **Everything was** fine last month.（上個月一切都好。）

例 **One** of my friends **lives** in the US.

（我的一個朋友住在美國。）

例 **Each** of the four divisions **has** its own office.

（四個部門各自有自己的辦公室。）

（7）主詞為金錢、時間、容量

  例 **Two hundred dollars is** enough for a kid.

  （兩百塊對一個小孩子來說是足夠了。）

  例 **Three months is** called a quarter.（三個月稱為一季。）

UNIT 4 動詞的練習

名詞與冠詞

代名詞

形容詞與副詞

動詞

介系詞

句型與附加問句

比較級與最高級

時態與被動語態

條件句與假設語氣

關係詞與三大子句

Q1 There _____ some delicious desserts on the table.

（A）have　　（B）is　　（C）are　　（D）has

Q2 The news coming from different parts of the world _____ often utterly terrible recently.

（A）are　　（B）were　　（C）do　　（D）is

Q3 These fruits _____ quite good. Let's pick some.

（A）are smelled　　　　　（B）are smelling

（C）smell　　　　　　　（D）smells

Q4 Many festivals _____ in summer, so people have many choices to spend their vacations.

（A）take place　　　　　（B）takes place

（C）are taken place　　　（D）taken place

Q5 Baseball and football _____ very popular in our country.

（A）is　　（B）are　　（C）was　　（D）will

Q6 Each student _____ to hand in their homework today, or they will not get their grades.

（A）have　　（B）give　　（C）has　　（D）gives

Q7 The writer of the book _____ not want to reveal her real name, so she uses a pen name.

（A）does　　（B）do　　（C）did　　（D）has

解答： 1. C　2. D　3. C　4. A
      5. B　6. C　7. A

UNIT 5 介系詞

Study 1 介系詞的種類

　　介系詞的分類大致為三類，即「表示時間」，如：in, on, at, since, within/in, by, till (until), before, after；「表示地點」，如：in, inside, on, at, above/below, over/under, near, next to, underneath, beneath, alongside, beside, between, opposite；「表示動作或方向」，如：towards, away from, up, down。

Study 2 表示時間的介系詞

時間線上的某一點（One point in time）		
介系詞	文法	範例
on	**on＋day (date)** 例 on Monday 　 on Sunday 　 on birthday 　 on 9th Feb	1. 若同時有多個時間出現在一個句子當中，排列順序應由小到大。 　例 I left **at** 7:00 **in** the morning **on** Friday. 2. 一般而言，in, on, at 的時間由大到小為： 　in＞on＞at。 3. 例句： • I was born **in** 1990. • I was born **in** summer in 1990. • I was born **in** July in summer in 1990. • I was born **on** 7th July in summer in 1990. • I was born **on** Monday, 7th July in summer in 1990. • I was born **in** the morning of Monday, 7th July in summer in 1990. • I was born **at** 7:00 in the morning of Monday, 7th July in summer in 1990. 　（我在 1990 年夏天的七月七日星期一早上七點出生。）
at	**at＋time** 例 at 9:30 　 at the moment 　 at present	
in	**in＋year** 例 in 2010 **in＋season** 例 in spring **in＋month** 例 in February **in＋time** 例 in the afternoon	

一段延續的時間（Extended time）		
介系詞	文法	範例
since	**since＋**一段時間**＋ago** **since＋**過去某一個時間點 **since＋**過去式子句	1. since 例句： • I have studied English **since <u>10 years ago</u>**. • I have studied English **since <u>1993</u>**. • I have studied English since **<u>I was an elementary school student</u>**.
for	**for＋**一段時間	2. since 和 for 皆為用於現在完成式的介系詞： 例 I have studied English **for <u>10 years</u>**. ＝I have studied English **since <u>10 years ago</u>**.
from ~ to / till / until	**from ~ to** 用於肯定句 **till, until** 用於否定句	• I work very hard **from** 9:00 AM **to** 5:00 PM every day. • I won't be back **until (/till)** 9:00 PM.
during	**during＋**一段期間	What did you do **during** your Chinese New Year vacation?
by in within	**by＋**一段時間 **in＋**一段期間 **within＋**一段期間	表示在某個時間之前將會發生的動作，必須使用未來式。 例 I will come back **by <u>5 o'clock</u>** （五點之前）. 例 I will come back **in <u>5 minutes</u>** （五分鐘之後）. 例 I will come back **within <u>5 minutes</u>** （五分鐘之內）.

Study 3　表示地方的介系詞

在基準點上	在基準點上方或下方	在基準點附近
in or inside （地方比較大）	over	near（在附近）
	above	next to（在附近） ＝alongside ＝beside ＝by
on	under	
	underneath	
at （地方比較小）	beneath	between
	below	opposite

圖示法：

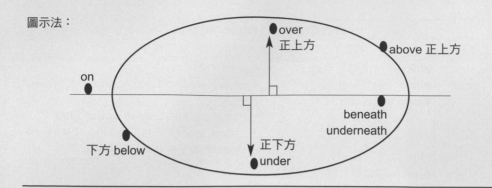

Study 4 表示方向的介系詞

（1）to / form（去／從）
　　例 He always walks **to** school **from** his home.
　　（他總是從他家走到學校。）

（2）toward(s)（朝向）
　　例 The pilgrims headed **toward** Mecca.
　　（朝聖者朝向麥加前進。）

（3）away form（從～離開）
　　例 They moved **away from** their old community.
　　（他們從他們的舊社區離開。）

（4）in(to) / out of（進去／從～出來）
　　例 He **ran into** the house quickly. After some minutes, he ran
　　out of the house with an umbrella.
　　（他很快地跑進房子裡。幾分鐘後，他帶著一把雨傘從房子跑了
　　出來。）

（5）up / down（上／下）
　　例 He climbed **up** the stairs. / He climbed **down** the tree.
　　（他爬上樓。／他從樹上爬下來。）

（6）around（環繞）
　　例 The ship sailed **around** the island.
　　（這艘船繞著島嶼航行。）

（7）through（通過）

例 You can drive **through** that town in an hour.

（你可以在一小時後開車通過那個小鎮。）

（8）past / by（從旁邊經過）

例 He walked **past (/ by)** his alma mater without stopping.

（他經過他的母校而沒有停下來。）

（9）as far as (up to)（到某個地方為止）

例 We'll walk **as far as (/ up to)** that old schoolhouse.

（我們將走到那個舊校舍為止。）

（10）across（橫越）

例 He sailed across the Pacific Ocean.

（他航行橫渡了太平洋。）

（11）over（從上方橫越）

例 The birds flied over the mountain.

（那群鳥飛越了山嶺。）

UNIT 4　介系詞的練習

Q1 ＿＿＿＿＿＿ the age of twenty-two, Tim moved to the big city.

（A）In　　　　　　　　（B）On

（C）At　　　　　　　　（D）During

Q2 Jason has worked in this company ＿＿＿＿＿＿ 10 years ago.

（A）for　　　　　　　　（B）since

（C）in　　　　　　　　　（D）around

Q3 Their anniversary is ＿＿＿＿＿＿ January. They plan to have a romantic dinner then.

（A）at　　　　　　　　（B）in

（C）on　　　　　　　　（D）by

Q4 **My brother will come back _____ 10 o'clock, so he won't have dinner with us.**
　（A）for　　　　　　　　　（B）at
　（C）by　　　　　　　　　（D）of

Q5 **Peter just lives _____ the corner. We can go to his place.**
　（A）at　　　　　　　　　（B）in
　（C）on　　　　　　　　　（D）around

Q6 **Our train will arrive at Taipei station _____ noon.**
　（A）into　　　　　　　　（B）at
　（C）from　　　　　　　　（D）on

Q7 **Joseph walked _____ of the house and went to the bus stop.**
　（A）in　　　　　　　　　（B）away
　（C）out　　　　　　　　（D）to

Q8 **It only took ten minutes for the boat to sail _____ the river.**
　（A）across　　　　　　　（B）around
　（C）to　　　　　　　　　（D）in

解答： 1. C　2. B　3. B　4. C
　　　 5. D　6. B　7. C　8. A

名詞與冠詞

代名詞

形容詞與副詞

動詞

介系詞

句型與附加問句

比較級與最高級

時態與被動語態

條件句與假設語氣

關係詞與三大子句

UNIT 6　句型與附加問句

Study 1　基本符號說明

S＝subject 主詞

V＝verb 動詞
- Vt＝transitive verb 及物動詞
- Vi＝intransitive verb 不及物動詞

O＝object 受詞
- DO＝direct object 直接受詞
- IO＝indirect object 間接受詞

C＝complement 補語
- SC＝subject complement 主詞補語
- OC＝object complement 受詞補語

Study 2　五大基本句型

英文的基本句型有五種，如下所述：

（1）**S＋Vi**

例 A bird flies.（一隻鳥飛起來。）

例 Money talks.（有錢的說話大聲。）

例 I quitted.（我辭職了。）

例 Babies cry.（小嬰兒們在哭。）

> 第一類句型的動詞為「不及物動詞」，動詞之後不加受詞。
>
> 參考動詞（完全不及物動詞）：
>
> cry, run, walk, happen, rise, come, fight, bloom, jump, fly, occur

（2）**S＋V＋SC**

　　例 Allan is a handsome guy.（亞倫是個帥哥。）

　　例 The medicine tastes very bitter.（這個藥嚐起來很苦。）

　　例 I am a student.（我是一個學生。）

　　例 Time is money.（時間就是金錢。）

> 第二類句型的動詞為「**be** 動詞」及「連綴動詞」，動詞之後加主
> 詞補語。
>
> 參考動詞（be動詞與連綴動詞）：
>
> is, are, am, was, were, look, become, get, sound, taste, keep

（3）**S＋Vt＋O**

　　例 A cat catches a mouse.（貓捉老鼠。）

　　例 I have a dog.（我有一隻狗。）

　　例 You can't eat your cake.（你不可以吃你的蛋糕。）

　　例 He plays baseball every weekend.（他每個週末打棒球。）

> 第三類句型的動詞為「及物動詞」，動詞之後加受詞。
>
> 參考動詞（完全及物動詞）：
>
> cook, hit, like, dislike, carry, do, look at, long for, put on, give up

（4）**S＋V＋IO＋DO**

　　＝S＋V＋DO＋to／for＋IO

　　例 I'll give you another book.＝I'll give another book to you.
　　　（我將給你另一本書。）

　　例 He lent me some money.＝He lent some money to me.
　　　（他借我一些錢。）

　　例 He told me that he would go to Thailand in June.
　　　（他告訴我六月會去泰國。）

　　例 I give you $500.＝I give $500 to you.
　　　（我給你五百元。）

> 第四類句型的動詞為「授與動詞」，動詞之後加兩個受詞。
>
> 參考動詞（授與動詞）：
>
> give, tell, show, teach, send, post, owe, buy, lend, do, mail

（5）**S＋V＋O＋OC**

例 She made me happy.（她讓我快樂。）

例 His friends kept him laughing.（他的朋友讓他一直笑。）

例 We call this fruit a watermelon.（我們稱這個水果叫西瓜。）

例 She made me so mad.（她讓我十分生氣。）

> 第五類句型的動詞為「使役動詞」，動詞之後加受詞再加受詞補語。
> 參考動詞（不完全及物動詞）：
> make, let, allow, have, name, prove, declare, watch

Study 3　英文句型的三大規則

（1）一個主詞一個動詞

例 Cindy has tea in the morning.
（辛蒂在早上喝茶。）

（2）句意完整

例 Diana has tea in the morning before she goes to work.
（戴安娜早上在上班前喝茶。）

（3）主詞與動詞的一致性

例 **The front desk**（單數）is always busy.
（櫃台總是很忙。）

例 **The apples on the table**（複數）are delicious.
（桌上的蘋果很可口。）

例 **The writer of the books**（單數）is Bill.
（這些書的作者是比爾。）

例 **Ms. Wang and her friend**（複數）are coming.
（王小姐和她的朋友要來了。）

例 **The man in the red and green tie**（單數）is my best friend.
（打著紅色、綠色領帶的男人是我最好的朋友。）

名詞與冠詞

代名詞

形容詞與副詞

動詞

介系詞

句型與附加問句

比較級與最高級

時態與被動語態

條件句與假設語氣

關係詞與三大子句

主要子句與從屬子句

英文句型中常會見到將主要子句和從屬子句合併成一個句子，例如：Charles has tea in the morning before he goes to work.，其中的主要子句是 "Charles has tea in the morning"，而從屬子句是 "before he goes to work"。

例句：（單底線代表主要子句，雙底線則代表從屬子句）

* When it rains, we will bring an umbrella with us.

  （當天空下雨，我們會帶著雨傘。）

* After Tim got home, he made a call.

  （提姆回家後，他打了一通電話。）

* If Jeff comes early, we will have time to talk.

  （假如傑夫早回來，我們就會有時間講話。）

* You can tell me how you feel.

  （你可以告訴我你的感覺。）

* I don't know what your name is.

  （我不知道你的名字是什麼。）

Study 5 附加問句

（1）附加問句的問與答

肯定的直述句要用否定的附加問句	預期肯定答案
It **is** raining, **isn't** it?	Yes, it **is**.
You **are** Spanish, **aren't** you?	Yes, I **am**.
She **lives** in London, **doesn't** she?	Yes, she **does**.
He **went** to the disco, **didn't** he?	Yes, he **did**.
You **have** a car, **don't** you ?	Yes, we **do**.

否定的直述句要用肯定的附加問句	預期否定答案
It **isn't** raining, **is** it?	No, it **isn't**.
You **aren't** Spanish, **are** you?	No, I'm **not**.
She **doesn't** live in London, **does** she?	No, she **doesn't**.
He **didn't** go to the disco, **did** he?	No, he **didn't**.
You **don't** have a car, **do** you?	No, we **don't**.

（2）附加問句的語調

1. 附加問句的語意依我們說話的語氣而不同。如果語調下降，你並不是真的在問一個問題；相反地，你只是要對方同意你的看法：

例 "It's a beautiful day, **isn't it**?"（天氣很好，不是嗎？）
"Yes, lovely."（是呀，天氣很宜人。）

例 "Darcy doesn't look well today, **does he**?"
（達希今天看起來不太好，是嗎？）
"No, he looks very tired."（不好，他看起來很疲倦。）

例 "She's very pretty. She's got pretty eyes, **hasn't she**?"
（她很漂亮，她有一雙漂亮的眼睛，不是嗎？）
"Yes, she has."（是呀，她有一雙漂亮的眼睛。）

2. 另外，我們常用否定句＋肯定附加問句表示詢問，或請求別人做事情。附加問句結尾處的語調上揚，例句如下：

例 "You haven't got a pencil, **have you**?"
（你還沒有拿到一枝鉛筆，是嗎？）

例 "You couldn't give me a hand, **could you**?"
（你不能幫我的忙，是嗎？）
"It depends what it is."（要看是幫什麼忙。）

例 "You don't know where Mary is, **do you**?"
（你不知道瑪麗在哪裡，是嗎？）

（3）附加問句練習

請寫出下列句子的附加問句：

1. You like to arrange flowers, _____?
2. You are not a student, _____?
3. You can ride a bike, _____?
4. You never go to the movies, _____?
5. You like English, _____?
6. You went shopping last night, _____?
7. You live in Taipei, _____?
8. You are over 170 cm, _____?
9. You are over the age of 30, _____?

名詞與冠詞

代名詞

形容詞與副詞

動詞

介系詞

句型與附加問句

比較級與最高級

時態與被動語態

條件句與假設語氣

關係詞與三大子句

10. This is your first time studying in the AAA school, _____?

解答：

1. You like to arrange flowers, **don't you**?
2. You are not a student, **are you**?
3. You can ride a bike, **can't you**?
4. You never go to the movies, **do you**?
5. You like English, **don't you**?
6. You went shopping last night, **didn't you**?
7. You live in Taipei, **don't you**?
8. You are over 170 cm, **aren't you**?
9. You are over the age of 30, **aren't you**?
10. This is your first time studying in the AAA school, **isn't it**?

名詞與冠詞
代名詞
形容詞與副詞
動詞
介系詞
句型與附加問句
比較級與最高級
時態與被動語態
條件句與假設語氣
關係詞與三大子句

UNIT 7　比較級與最高級

形容詞與副詞有「比較級」與「最高級」的變化，是敘述某人或某事「較」或是「最」如何。這也是是英檢的常考題。以下的表格是形容詞與副詞比較級與最高級的變化分類。

Study 1　形容詞與副詞比較級的變化

兩個音節以下				三個音節以上	不規則變化
原級＋**-er**	字尾為 -e 直接＋**-r**	重複字尾 ＋**-er**	去字尾 -y ＋**-ier**	more＋原形	
long→ long**er**	wise→ wis**er**	hot→ hot**ter**	busy→ bus**ier**	important→ **more** important	good, well→ **better**
short→ short**er**	safe→ saf**er**	big→ big**ger**	lazy→ laz**ier**	interesting→ **more** interesting	bad→ **worse**
tall→ tall**er**	wide→ wid**er**	fat→ fat**ter**	crazy→ craz**ier**	comfortable→ **more** comfortable	many, much→ **more**
clever→ clever**er**	fine→ fin**er**	thin→ thin**ner**	healthy→ health**ier**	expensive→ **more** expensive	little→ **less**

Study 2　形容詞與副詞最高級的變化

兩個音節以下				三個音節以上	不規則變化
原級＋**-est**	字尾為 -e 直接＋**-st**	重複字尾 ＋**-est**	字尾去 -y ＋**-iest**	most＋三音節	
long→ the long**est**	wise→ the wis**est**	hot→ the hot**test**	busy→ the busi**est**	important→ the **most** important	good, well→ the **best**
short→ the short**est**	safe→ the saf**est**	big→ the big**gest**	lazy→ the lazi**est**	interesting→ the **most** interesting	bad→ the **worst**
tall→ the tall**est**	wide→ the wid**est**	fat→ the fat**test**	crazy→ the crazi**est**	comfortable→ the **most** comfortable	many, much→ the **most**
clever→ the clever**est**	fine→ the fin**est**	thin→ the thin**nest**	healthy→ the healthi**est**	expensive→ the **most** expensive	little→ the **least**

Study 3　比較級與最高級句型

比較級基本句型	最高級基本句型
A＋be動詞＋比較級 **than**＋B	A＋be動詞＋**the** 最高級＋B＋in＋場所（或 of all）
例 Mr. Adams is **fatter than** Mr. Church. 例 I am **less strong than** you.	例 Charles is **the most handsome** teacher in this school

例　Jane is a good singer. She sings **better than** Patty. And the director thinks she is **the best** singer in the choir.

（珍是一位好歌手，她唱得比蓓蒂好，而且指揮認為她是合唱團中唱得最好的。）

例　My history essay received a bad grade. It was **worse than** Charlie's grade. But it certainly wasn't **the worst** grade in the class.

（我的歷史論文得到了很差的成績，比查理的成績還差，不過它肯定不是班上最差的。）

例　John ran well in the marathon. He ran **better than** Jimmy. But John didn't run **the best** in his group.

（約翰的馬拉松跑得很好，他跑得比吉姆好，不過他不是他的組中跑得最好的。）

例　Gambling is a bad habit. Smoking is **a worse habit**. Drinking wine too much is **the worst habit** of all.

（賭博是不良嗜好，吸菸是更糟的習慣，而酗酒是所有不良嗜好當中最壞的。）

例　After our team lost the game, everybody felt bad. The soccer coach felt **worse than** the fans did. But the soccer players felt **the worst** of all.

（我們的隊輸了比賽之後，每個人都覺得很難過，足球教練比球迷更難過，不過，球員是所有人當中最難過的。）

例 I like to ski frequently. I ski **more frequently** than Peter. However, Tom skis **the most frequently** of all.

（我喜歡常常去滑雪，我比彼得更常滑雪。然而，湯姆是所有人當中最常去滑雪的。）

例 His bag is light. My big is **lighter than** his. But Mary's is **the lightest** of all.

（他的袋子很輕，我的袋子比他的更輕，不過，瑪麗的袋子是我們之中最輕的。）

UNIT 4 比較級與最高級的練習

Q1 **Bella is the _____ girl in this group.**

（A）tall   （B）taller

（C）tallest   （D）most tall

Q2 **Many students think that science is _____ than art.**

（A）interest   （B）more interesting

（C）intersetinger   （D）the most interesting

Q3 **Adam is _____ than anyone in his class. He doesn't have to worry about his homework.**

（A）smart   （B）more smart

（C）the smartest   （D）smarter

Q4 **Britta arrived at the classroom _____ than I did because she lived just beside the campus.**

（A）early   （B）earlyer

（C）more early   （D）earlier

Q5 **She ran slower _____ her friends, so she was left behind.**

（A）then   （B）to

（C）than   （D）more

名詞與冠詞

代名詞

形容詞與副詞

動詞

介系詞

句型與附加問句

比較級與最高級

時態與被動語態

條件句與假設語氣

關係詞與三大子句

Q6 The _____ he studies, the _____ his grade is.

(A) harder; better   (B) hard; good

(C) more hard; more good   (D) much hard; much good

Q7 He is _____ stronger than his brother, so he looks skinnier beside his brother.

(A) much   (B) less

(C) the most   (D) more

Q8 Drinking too much alcohol is _____ than eating too much drunk food.

(A) badder   (B) bad

(C) worst   (D) worse

名詞與冠詞

代名詞

形容詞與副詞

動詞

介系詞

句型與附加問句

比較級與最高級

時態與被動語態

條件句與假設語氣

關係詞與三大子句

UNIT 8 時態與被動語態

Study 1 十二大時態總表

Simple Present 現在簡單式 **V**	Simple Past 過去簡單式 **V-ed**	Simple Future 未來簡單式 **will＋VR** **be going to＋VR**
Present Continuous 現在進行式 **is / are / am＋V-ing**	Past Continuous 過去進行式 **was / were＋V-ing**	Future Continuous 未來進行式 **will be＋V-ing**
Present Perfect 現在完成式 **have / has＋V-p.p.**	Past Perfect 過去完成式 **had＋V-p.p.**	Future Perfect 未來完成式 **will have＋V-p.p.**
Present Perfect Continuous 現在完成進行式 **have / has＋been＋V-ing**	Past Perfect Continuous 過去完成進行式 **had＋been＋V-ing**	Future Perfect Continuous 未來完成進行式 **will have been＋V-ing**

Study 2 十二時態句型分析（使用動詞：eat）

請看以下的例句，顏色標記為動詞時態的變化，而底線則是時間。

時態	使用動詞 eat 舉例說明
現在式	I **eat** meat every day.
過去式	I **ate** meat yesterday.
未來式	I **will eat** meat tomorrow.
現在進行式	I **am eating** meat now.
過去進行式	I **was eating** meat when he came last night.
未來進行式	I **will be eating** meat when he comes tomorrow night.
現在完成式	I **have eaten** meat already.
過去完成式	I **had eaten** meat before he came last night.
未來完成式	I **will have eaten** meat before he comes tomorrow night.
現在完成進行式	I **have been eating** meat for a while.
過去完成進行式	I **had been eating** meat for a while when he came last night.
未來完成進行式	I **will have been eating** meat for a while when he comes tomorrow night.

不定式	過去式	過去分詞	中文字義
arise	arose	arisen	上升；產生
awake	awoke	awaken	喚醒；覺醒
be	were	been	是；正在
bear	bore	born	承擔；承受
beat	beat	beaten	打，擊；承受
become	became	become	變成
begin	began	begun	開始
behold	beheld	beheld	看，注視
bend	bent	bent	彎曲
bet	bet	bet	打賭；斷言
bind	bound	bound	綑綁
bite	bit	bitten	叮咬
bleed	bled	bled	流血
break	broke	broken	打破；弄壞
bring	brought	brought	帶來
build	built	built	建築，建造
burst	burst	burst	爆炸，爆破
buy	bought	bought	購買
cast	cast	cast	扔，投擲
catch	caught	caught	抓住；捉住；撞見
choose	chose	chosen	選擇
come	came	come	到來
cost	cost	cost	花費
cut	cut	cut	裁切
deal	dealt	dealt	做生意；買賣
dig	dug	dug	挖掘
do	did	done	做
draw	drew	drawn	畫圖
drink	drank	drunk	喝
drive	drove	driven	駕駛
dwell	dwelt	dwelt	居住
eat	ate	eaten	吃

fall	fell	fallen	落下
feed	fed	fed	餵食
feel	felt	felt	感覺
fight	fought	fought	打架；爭吵
find	found	found	找到
fly	flew	flown	飛
forget	forgot	forgotten	忘記
forgive	forgave	forgiven	原諒
freeze	froze	frozen	凍結；僵住
get	got	got	得到
give	gave	given	給予
go	went	gone	去
grow	grew	grown	生長；增多
have	had	had	擁有
hear	heard	heard	聽到；聽說
hit	hit	hit	打；打擊
hold	held	held	握著；持有；舉辦
hurt	hurt	hurt	使受傷；疼痛
keep	kept	kept	保持；保留
know	knew	known	知道；認識
lay	laid	laid	放置；下蛋
lead	led	led	領導；領先
leave	left	left	離開；留下
lend	lent	lent	借出
let	let	let	讓；允許
lie	lay	lain	躺；撒謊
lose	lost	lost	失去；迷失；輸掉
make	made	made	使得；製造
mean	meant	meant	表示～的意思
meet	met	met	遇見；見面
mistake	mistook	mistaken	誤解；誤認
overcome	overcame	overcome	克服
pay	paid	paid	支付
prove	proved	proved, proven	證明
put	put	put	放

read [i]	read [ɛ]	read [ɛ]	閱讀
ride	rode	ridden	騎乘
ring	rang	rung	按鈴；打電話
rise	rose	risen	上升；上漲
run	ran	run	跑
say	said	said	說
see	saw	seen	看
seek	sought	sought	尋找
sell	sold	sold	賣
send	sent	sent	寄送；發送
set	set	set	放置；設定
shake	shook	shaken	搖動，震動；發抖
shut	shut	shut	關上；停止營業
sing	sang	sung	唱
sit	sat	sat	坐
sleep	slept	slept	睡覺
speak	spoke	spoken	說（語言）
spend	spent	spent	花費
spread	spread	spread	展開；擴散
stand	stood	stood	站
steal	stole	stolen	偷
swear	swore	sworn	發誓；咒罵
sweep	swept	swept	打掃
swim	swam	swum	游泳
take	took	taken	拿，取
teach	taught	taught	教導
tear	torn	torn	撕開
tell	told	told	告訴
think	thought	thought	想，思考
throw	threw	thrown	投擲
understand	understood	understood	懂，明白
undo	undid	undone	解開；打開
upset	upset	upset	打翻；打亂
wake	woke	waken	醒來
wear	wore	worn	穿戴

weep	wept	wept	哭泣，流淚
win	won	won	獲勝
write	wrote	written	寫

Study 4 十二大時態的使用時機

時態	使用時機與例句
Simple Present 現在簡單式	• 與現在有關的事實 例 There are 50 states in the US. • 習慣（habit） 例 I study every day except Sunday. 例 I rarely go to the movies on weekends. • 不變的真理 例 The earth is round.
Simple Past 過去簡單式	• 與過去有關的事實 例 I went to a movie yesterday. • 過去的習慣 例 I used to smoke a lot, but now I don't. （「used to＋VR」表示過去經常）
Simple Future 未來簡單式	• 與未來有關的事實或想法 例 I will be an English teacher in the future. • 表示預定的計畫 例 I am going to see a movie this afternoon. • 表示馬上要去做的事 例 I am about to get on the train in 5 minutes.
Present Continuous 現在進行式	• 現在正在進行（發生）的動作 例 I am studying right now. • 表示預定的計畫（限用於表示「來」、「去」的動詞） 例 I am leaving Taipei tomorrow.
Past Continuous 過去進行式	• 過去某個特定時間點正在發生的事 例 I was sleeping when you came last night.
Future Continuous 未來進行式	• 未來某個特定時間點正在發生的事 例 I will be sleeping when you come tomorrow.

名詞與冠詞

代名詞

形容詞與副詞

動詞

介系詞

句型與附加問句

比較級與最高級

時態與被動語態

條件句與假設語氣

關係詞與三大子句

Present perfect 現在完成式	• 從過去一直「持續」到現在的動作或行為 例 It has rained for 3 days. 　＝It has rained since 3 days ago. 例 It has rained since yesterday. • 已經完成（already），尚未完成（yet），以及剛剛完成 （just）的動作 例 I have already done my work. 例 I haven't done my work yet. 例 I have just done my work. • 有關人生的經驗 例 Have you (ever) seen that man before? 例 I have seen that man twice. 例 I have never seen that man before.
Past Perfect 過去完成式	• 在一個過去時間點前，一直「持續」的動作或行為 例 It had already rained for 3 days before yesterday. • 在一個過去時間點前，已經完成（already），尚未完成 （yet）或剛剛完成（just）的動作 例 I had already done my work before yesterday. 例 I hadn't done my work yet before yesterday. 例 I had just done my work before yesterday. • 在一個過去時間點前，有關人生的經驗 例 Had you seen that movie before he did? 例 I had seen that movie twice before he did. 例 I had not seen that movie before he did.
Future Perfect 未來完成式	• 在一個未來時間點前，一直「持續」的動作或行為 例 It will have rained for 3 days by tomorrow. • 在一個未來時間點前，已經完成（already）的動作 例 I will have already done my work by tomorrow. • 在一個未來時間點前，有關人生的經驗 例 Will have you seen that movie by the end of this year?
Present Perfect Continuous 現在完成進行式	• 從過去一直「持續」到現在的動作，且會繼續進行下去 例 I have been learning English before 10 years.
Past Perfect Continuous 過去完成進行式	• 從過去一直「持續」到過去的動作，且會繼續進行下去 例 I had been learning English for 10 years before last 　year.
Future Perfect Continuous 未來完成進行式	• 從過去一直「持續」到未來的動作，且會繼續進行下去 例 I will have been learning English for 10 years by next 　year.

Study 5 判斷句子的時態

請練習判斷下列句子的時態，並且將正確的時態名稱填入空格中：

現在簡單式	現在進行式	現在完成式	現在完成進行式
過去簡單式	過去進行式	過去完成式	過去完成進行式
未來簡單式	未來進行式	未來完成式	未來完成進行式

_____ 1. The USA is bigger than the UK.

_____ 2. Have you ever heard of such a funny thing?

_____ 3. Peter went to Paris two years ago.

_____ 4. His father was born in 1968.

_____ 5. Did you eat breakfast?

_____ 6. How long have you been cooking breakfast?

_____ 7. Were you cooking breakfast at 8 last night?

_____ 8. What are you playing?

_____ 9. John got off the bus while it was moving.

_____ 10. What will Tracy be doing while they are doing their homework?

_____ 11. They have had a terrible accident.

_____ 12. I hope it will have stopped raining before we have to leave.

_____ 13. When we see you again, we will have bought the new house.

_____ 14. We haven't seen him since last year.

_____ 15. It was raining when we had the picnic.

_____ 16. I am studying English and math.

_____ 17. I have a dog and a cat.

_____ 18. Were you going to my party?

_____ 19. I have been doing my housework.

_____ 20. What elementary school did you go to?

_____ 21. What were you doing at 10:00 pm last night?

_____ 22. Will you be listening to the radio at 2:00 pm tomorrow?

_____ 23. Will you go shopping at SOGO when it has a big sale?

_____ 24. How long had you watched TV before you went to bed last night?

_____ 25. How long ago did you play computer games?

解答：

1. 現在簡單式	2. 現在完成式	3. 過去簡單式
4. 過去簡單式	5. 過去簡單式	6. 現在完成進行式
7. 過去進行式	8. 現在進行式	9. 過去簡單式
10. 未來進行式	11. 現在完成式	12. 未來完成式
13. 未來完成式	14. 現在完成式	15. 過去進行式
16. 現在進行式	17. 現在簡單式	18. 過去進行式
19. 現在完成進行式	20. 過去簡單式	21. 過去進行式
22. 未來進行式	23. 未來簡單式	24. 過去完成式
25. 過去簡單式		

名詞與冠詞

代名詞

形容詞與副詞

動詞

介系詞

句型與附加問句

比較級與最高級

時態與被動語態

條件句與假設語氣

關係詞與三大子句

Study 6 改寫時態

請將下列句子改寫為指定的時態：

1. I studied English.（改成現在進行式）

_____

2. What do you do?（改成過去簡單式）

_____

3. Do you like your dogs?（改成未來簡單式）

_____

4. Will you see a movie?（改成未來進行式）

_____

5. I have a dog.（改成現在完成式）

_____

6. Where are you?（改成現在完成式）

_____

7. I have done my homework.（改成現在完成進行式）

_____

8. Did you go to the party?（改成過去進行式）

_____

9. When will you go to America?（改成過去簡單式）

_____

10. I am taking a shower while he comes.
    （將主要子句改成過去進行式）

_____

解答：

1. I am studying English.（我正在讀英文。）
2. What did you do?（你做了什麼？）
3. Will you like your dogs?（你將會喜歡你的狗嗎？）
4. Will you be seeing a movie?（你將會在看電影嗎？）
5. I have had a dog.（我已經有一隻狗了。）
6. Where have you been?（你去哪裡了？）

7. I have been doing my homework. (我已經在做功課了。)

8. Were you going to the party? (你去參加派對了嗎?)

9. When did you go to America? (你何時去了美國?)

10. I was taking a shower while he came. (他來的時候,我在洗澡。)

Study 7　八個被動語態時態的總表

Present Tense 現在式	Past Tense 過去式	Future Tense 未來式
現在被動式 am / is / are＋V-p.p.	過去被動式 was / were＋V-p.p.	未來被動式 will＋be＋V-p.p.
現在進行被動式 am / is / are being＋V-p.p.	過去進行被動式 was / were being＋V-p.p.	未來進行式 ※無被動式
現在完成被動式 have / has＋been＋V-p.p.	過去完成被動式 had＋been＋V-p.p.	未來完成被動式 will have＋been＋V-p.p.
現在完成進行式 ※無被動式	過去完成進行式 ※無被動式	未來完成進行式 ※無被動式

Study 8　八個被動語態句型分析(使用動詞:eat)

現在被動式	Meat **is eaten** by me *every day*.
過去被動式	Meat **was eaten** by me *yesterday*.
未來被動式	Meat **will be eaten** by me *tomorrow*.
現在進行被動式	Meat **is being eaten** by me *now*.
過去進行被動式	Meat **was being eaten** by me *when he came yesterday*.
現在完成被動式	Meat **has been eaten** by me *already*.
過去完成被動式	Meat **had been eaten** by me *when he came yesterday*.
未來完成被動式	Meat **will have been eaten** by me *when he comes tomorrow morning*.

冠詞　名詞與

代名詞

形容詞與副詞

動詞

介系詞

句型與附加問句

比較級與最高級

時態與被動語態

條件句與假設語氣

關係詞與三大子句

Study 9　主動語態與被動語態的轉換

請將下列句子由被動語態改成主動語態，或由主動語態改成被動語態：

1. The cake has been eaten by my mother.

   _____

2. The work will be finished by me.

   _____

3. Are mice eaten by cats?

   _____

4. Was the house built by your father?

   _____

5. Is English being taught by Charles?

   _____

6. The lesson is being taught by the teacher.

   _____

7. Is that cute dog loved by you?

   _____

8. Was the room cleaned yesterday?

   _____

9. The apple will be eaten by me tomorrow.

   _____

10. The work has been done already.

    _____

11. I like these flowers.

    _____

12. She built the house.

    _____

13. They cleaned their rooms yesterday.

    _____

14. I have studied English for 10 years.

    _____

15. Do you finish your homework?

          _____

解答：

1. My mother has eaten the cake.
2. I will finish the work.
3. Do cats eat mice?
4. Did your father build the house?
5. Is Charles teaching English?
6. The teacher is teaching the lesson.
7. Do you love that cute dog?
8. Did someone clean the room yesterday?
9. I will eat the apple tomorrow.
10. Someone has done the work already.
11. These flowers are liked by me.
12. The house was built by her.
13. Their rooms were cleaned by them yesterday.
14. English has been studied by me for 10 years.
15. Is your homework finished by you?

名詞與 冠詞

代名詞

形容詞 與副詞

動詞

介系詞

句型與 附加問句

比較級與 最高級

時態與 被動語態

條件句與 假設語氣

關係詞與 三大子句

UNIT 9 條件句與假設語氣

Study 1 條件句的變化

句型	例句
if 的例句	**If I have your agreement**, I will do it immediately. （假如我有你的許可，我就會馬上做。）
介系詞或介系詞片語	**With your agreement**, I will do it immediately. **In case of having your agreement**, I will do it immediately.
其他的連接詞或連接詞片語	**Provided I have your agreement**, I will do it immediately. **In case I have your agreement**, I will do it immediately.
省略 if（將動詞移到句首）	**Have I your agreement**, I will do it immediately.
不定詞構句（To＋VR 開頭）	**To have your agreement**, I will do it immediately.
分詞構句（V-ing開頭）	**Having your agreement**, I will do it immediately.

Study 2 假設語氣的種類

假設語氣共有四種假設：

（1）可能實現的假設

公式：**If＋S＋現在式 V..., S＋will＋VR...**

例 If I have time, I will do my housework.

（如果有時間，我會做功課。）

（2）與現在事實相反的假設

公式：**If＋S＋過去式 V..., S＋would / could / should / might ＋VR...**

例 If I had time, I would do my housework.

＝In fact, I don't have time, so I won't do my housework.

（如果有時間，我會做功課。

＝事實上，我沒有時間，所以我沒做功課。）

（3）與過去事實相反的假設

公式：**If＋S＋had＋V-p.p. ..., S＋would / could / should / might＋have＋V-p.p. ...**

例 If I had had time last night, I would have done my housework.

＝In fact, I didn't have time last night, so I didn't do my housework.

（如果昨晚我有時間，我早該做了功課。

＝事實上，昨晚我沒有時間，所以我沒做功課。）

（4）與未來事實相反或實現機率極小的假設

公式：**If＋S＋were to / should＋VR ..., S＋would / could / should / might＋VR ....**

例 If I were to have time tomorrow, I would do my housework.

＝In fact, I won't have time tomorrow, so I won't do my housework.

（如果我明天有時間，我就會做功課。

＝事實上，我明天不會有時間，所以我不會去做功課。）

Study 3 改寫條件句與假設語氣

請將下列條件句與假設語氣改寫成指定的句型：

1. If you sleep with a mirror under your pillow, you will dream of what your future husband looks like.（請改寫成不定詞構句）

———————————————————————————

2. If your eyebrows grow together or your arms are hairy, you will be very rich.（請改寫成分詞構句）

———————————————————————————

3. If you have a bike, you can get there by 7:00.（以介系詞 with 開頭）

———————————————————————————

4. If he had known your address, he would have written to you.（改寫成省略 if 的倒裝句）

_____

5. If Bill applies, he will probably get the job.（以 Provided 開頭改寫）

_____

解答：

1. **To sleep with a mirror under your pillow**, you will dream of what your future husband looks like.
   （如果把鏡子放在枕頭下面睡覺，你會夢見未來丈夫的長相。）

2. **Your eyebrows growing together or your arms being hairy**, you will be very rich.
   （如果你的眉毛相連或有很多手毛，你會變得非常富有。）

3. **With a bike**, you can get there by 7:00.
   （如果有腳踏車，你就可以在七點之前到達。）

4. **Had he known your address**, he would have written to you.
   （如果他知道你的地址，他就會寫信給你。）

5. **Provided Bill applies**, he will probably get the job.
   （如果比爾去應徵，他可能會得到這份工作。）

名詞與冠詞

代名詞

形容詞與副詞

動詞

介系詞

句型與附加問句

比較級與最高級

時態與被動語態

條件句與假設語氣

關係詞與三大子句

UNIT 10 關係詞與三大子句

關係詞可分為「關係代名詞」及「關係副詞」；子句則可以依其用途分為「名詞子句」、「形容詞子句」、「副詞子句」三大種類。關係詞和子句的用法是英檢最常考的題型之一。

Study 1 關係代名詞

關係代名詞包括：who, whom, which, that，如下表所示：

先行詞	主格	所有格	受格
人	who	whose	whom
事物	which	of which / whose	which
人或事物	that	X	that

關係代名詞的目的主要在連接主要子句與形容詞子句。而關係詞的使用種類則視所形容的先行詞而定。例如：將 "The girl is my best friend." 及 "The girl lives upstairs." 兩句合併，就會變成 "The girl who lives upstairs is my best friend."。"who lives upstairs" 是形容詞子句，用來形容 the girl 這個先行詞。

以下分析舉例關係代名詞的各種用法：

1. 用 who 來作主格的情形（可以用 that 來代替）
例 The man is friendly. The man lives next to me.
（那個男子很友善。那個男子住在我的隔壁。）
→ The man **who lives next to me** is friendly.
→ The man **that lives next to me** is friendly.
（住在我隔壁的那個男子很友善。）

2. 用 whom 來作受格的情形（可以用 that 來代替；並可完全省略）
例 The man was friendly. I met the man.
（那個男人很友善。我遇見那個男子。）

→ The man **whom I met** was friendly.

→ The man **that I met** was friendly.

→ The man **I met** was friendly.

（我遇見的那個男子很友善。）

3. 用 whose 來作所有格的情形（不可以用 that 來代替；不可省略）

例　The man was friendly. The man's father is a doctor.

（那個男人很友善。那個男子的父親是個醫生。）

→ The man **whose father is a doctor** was friendly.

（那個父親是醫生的男子很友善。）

例　The book was popular. The book's cover is red.

（那本書很受歡迎。那本書的封面是紅色的。）

→ The book **whose cover is red** was popular.

（那本封面是紅色的書很受歡迎。）

4. 用 which 來作主格的情形（可以用 that 來代替）

例　The river is polluted. It flows through Taipei.

（那條河被污染了。它流經台北。）

→ The river **which flows through Taipei** is polluted.

→ The river **that flows through Taipei** is polluted.

（流經台北的那條河被污染了。）

5. 用 which 來作受格的情形（可以用 that 來代替；並可完全省略）

例　The books were expensive. I bought them.

（那些書很貴，我買了它們。）

→ The books **which I bought** were expensive.

→ The books **that I bought** were expensive.

→ The books **I bought** were expensive.

（我買下的那些書很貴。）

6. 若形容詞子句中有動詞片語（動詞＋介系詞）時，介系詞可移至關係代名詞前，但不可以省略關係代名詞，也不可以使用 that 來替代。

名詞與冠詞

代名詞

形容詞與副詞

動詞

介系詞

句型與附加問句

比較級與最高級

時態與被動語態

條件句與假設語氣

關係詞與三大子句

- 有關「人」的例句：

例 The man was industrious. I talked to him.
（那個男子很勤勞。我跟他交談。）
→ The man **whom I talked to** was industrious.
→ The man **that I talked to** was industrious.
→ The man **I talked to** was industrious.
→ The man **to whom I talked** was industrious.
（那個跟我交談的男子很勤勞。）

- 有關「物」的例句：

例 The sofa is comfortable. I'm sitting in it.
（這座沙發很舒服。我正坐在上面。）
→ The sofa **which I'm sitting in** is comfortable.
→ The sofa **that I'm sitting in** is comfortable.
→ The sofa **I'm sitting in** is comfortable.
→ The sofa **in which I'm sitting** is comfortable.
（我正坐著的沙發很舒服。）

7. 省略作為受詞的關係代名詞

例 He is the man **(whom / that) I met on vacation**.
（他就是我在假期中遇見的男子。）

例 These are the photos **(which / that) I took**.
（這些是我拍的照片。）

例 The energetic man **(whom / that) we met on vacation** works for our government.
（我在假期中遇見的那個精力充沛的男子替我們的政府工作。）

例 The agency **(which / that) we bought our tickets from** is bankrupt.
（我們購買票券的那個代理商破產了。）

例 She is the most beautiful girl **(that) I have ever seen**.
（她是我見過最美的女孩。）

Study 2 關係副詞

關係副詞包括 where, when, why, how, whoever, whomever, whatever，以下舉例分析關係副詞的各種用法：

1. Where 表示地點

例 This is **the house**. I was born **in the house**.
（這就是那間房子。我在那間房子裡出生。）

→ This is the house **which** I was born in.

→ This is the house **in which** I was born.

→ This is the house **where** I was born.
（這就是我出生的那間房子。）

2. When 表示時間

例 This is **the year**. The Olympic Games are held **in the year**.
（這就是那一年。奧運會在這年舉辦。）

→ This is the year **which** the Olympic Games are held in.

→ This is the year **in which** the Olympic Games are held.

→ This is the year **when** the Olympic Games are held.
（這就是奧運會舉辦的那一年。）

3. Why 表示原因

例 Give me one good **reason**. You did it **for that reason**.
（給我一個好的理由。你那樣做是為了那個理由。）

→ Give me one good reason **which** you did that for.

→ Give me one good reason **for which** you did that.

→ Give me one good reason **why** you did that.
（給我一個你為何那樣做的好理由。）

4. How 表示方法

例 Tell me the good **way**. You did that **by that way**.
（告訴我那個好方法。你那樣做是依照那個方法。）

→ Tell me one good way **which** you did that by.

→ Tell me one good way **by which** you did that.

→ Tell me one good way **how** you did that.
（告訴我，你如何那樣做的好方法。）

名詞與冠詞

代名詞

形容詞與副詞

動詞

介系詞

句型與附加問句

比較級與最高級

時態與被動語態

條件句與假設語氣

關係詞與三大子句

5. **Whoever＝anyone who**

例 **Anyone who** comes first may take it.

（任何先來的人就可以拿到它。）

→ **Whoever** comes first may take it.

（誰先來就可以拿到它。）

6. **Whomever＝anyone whom**

例 You may invite **anyone whom** you like.

（你可以邀請任何你喜歡的人。）

→ You may invite **whomever** you like.

（你可以邀請任何你喜歡的人。）

7. **Whatever＝anything that**

例 **Anything that** I have is yours.

（任何我擁有的東西都是你的。）

→ **Whatever** I have is yours.

（不管我擁有的什麼東西都是你的。）

Study 3　關係代名詞 that 的使用

1. 一定要使用 that 的情形：

- 先行詞有最高級形容詞

例 He's **the best** student that I've ever seen.

（他是我見過最好的學生。）

- 先行詞同時有人與物

例 **The man and his dog** that are walking along the street are my friends.

（沿著街道行走的男子和他的狗是我的朋友。）

- 先行詞有序數

例 He's **the first** boy that came this morning.

（他是今天早上第一個到的男孩。）

- 不與疑問詞重複

例 **Who** is the girl that is standing over there?

（站在那裡的那個女孩是誰？）

- 先行詞有 nothing, anything, everything, something 等詞彙

例 He has **nothing** that he can say.

（他無話可說。）

- 先行詞有 the very, the same, the only 等詞彙

例 He's **the very** man that the police wanted.

（他就是警察之前在通緝的那個人。）

例 We study in **the same** school that has more than 300 students.

（我們在同一所擁有超過三百名學生的學校就讀。）

例 **The only** one that came here on time got a present.

（唯一準時到這裡的那個人得到了一份禮物。）

2. 不能使用 that 的情形：

- 非限定用法（關係詞前面有逗號）

例 My brother Jim, **who** lives in London is a doctor.

（我住在倫敦的哥哥吉姆是個醫生。）

- 關係詞之前有介系詞

例 The person **to whom** my father talked yesterday is my teacher.

（昨晚和我的父親交談的人是我的老師。）

- 關係詞為所有格的形式

例 The car **whose** door is broken is my sister's.

（那部車門毀損的車子是我妹妹的。）

Study 4 形容詞子句

（1）形容詞子句的分類

1. 形容「人」的子句

例 He paid the money to the man **who (/ that) had done the work**.

（他付了錢給那個之前完成工作的男子。）

名詞與冠詞

代名詞

形容詞與副詞

動詞

介系詞

句型與附加問句

比較級與最高級

時態與被動語態

條件句與假設語氣

關係詞與三大子句

例 He paid the man **whom (/ that) he had hired**.
（他付了錢給他之前僱用的男子。）

例 He paid the man **from whom he had borrowed the money**.
（他付錢給之前借他錢的那個男子。）

例 This is the girl **whose picture you saw**.
（這就是你看到她的照片的那個女孩。）

例 The man **whose car was stolen** called the police.
（那個車子被偷的男子報了警。）

例 I know a girl **whose brother is a movie star**.
（我認識一個哥哥是電影明星的女孩。）

例 The people **whose house we bought** are moving to Hawaii.
（我們買他們房子的屋主要搬到夏威夷。）

例 The woman **whom I work for** pays me a fair salary.
（那位我替她工作的女子給我不錯的薪水。）

例 The man **whom I told you about** is over there.
（我向你提過的男子在那裡。）

例 The person **whom you should talk to about your problem** is sitting at that chair.
（你應該向他談論你的問題的人坐在那個椅子上。）

2. 形容「物」的子句

例 Here is a book **which (/ that) describes animals**.
（這裡有一本描述動物的書。）

例 The chair **which (/ that) he broke** is being repaired.
（他弄壞的那張椅子正在被修理。）

例 She was wearing a coat **for which she had paid $2,000**.
（她穿著那件花了兩千元買來的外套。）

例 The book **whose cover is red** is the best-seller.
（那本紅色封面的書是暢銷書。）

例 The movie **that we went to** was interesting.
（我們看的那部電影很有趣。）

例 I want to tell you about the party **that I went to last night**.
（我想告訴你關於我昨晚參加的派對。）

例 We enjoyed the music **which we listened to after dinner**.
（我們享受晚餐後聆聽的音樂。）

例 His father works in an office **which is about ten miles from his home**.
（她的父親在離家十哩遠的辦公室工作。）

例 George's father has an old car **which he bought ten years ago**.
（喬治的爸爸有一部十年前買的老爺車。）

例 I am reading the book **which you gave me**.
（我正在讀你給我的那本書。）

（2）形容詞子句由關係代名詞所引導
請將下列句子中的形容詞子句劃底線，並圈出關係代名詞：

1. John is the smartest student that I have ever taught.
2. This is the house where I was born.
3. The boy whose parents died in the accident was sent to an orphanage.
4. I must thank the boy who found my bag.
5. Can you remember the day when we first met?
6. The reason why he came back to this town was quite obvious.
7. The foreigner whom we saw yesterday was reading a book.
8. The boy and his cat that were taken care of by their baby-sitter went to the park yesterday.
9. The young man is a manager whom we can trust.
10. I mean the lady to whom you have talked.
11. This is the girl whom I met at the meeting.
12. This is the girl whose sister is in your class.
13. What is the building whose roof we see over there?
14. His aunt, who lives in China, came to visit him recently.
15. Michael, who is a very handsome teacher, works in different schools.

解答：

1. John is the smartest student that I have ever taught.
   （約翰是我所教過最聰明的學生。）

2. This is the house where I was born.
   （這是我出生的房子。）

3. The boy whose parents died in the accident was sent to an orphanage.
   （父母在意外中喪命的男孩被送往孤兒院。）

4. I must thank the boy who found my bag.
   （我必須感謝那個找到我包包的男孩。）

5. Can you remember the day when we first met?
   （你可能記得我們初次相遇的那天嗎？）

6. The reason why he came back to this town was quite obvious.
   （他回到這個鎮上的理由非常明顯。）

7. The foreigner whom we saw yesterday was reading a book.
   （昨天我們看到的那個外國人正在讀一本書。）

8. The boy and his cat that were taken care of by their baby-sitter went to the park yesterday.
   （由保姆照顧的那個男孩和他的貓昨天去了公園。）

9. The young man is a manager whom we can trust.
   （那個年輕人是一位我們能夠信任的經理人。）

10. I mean the lady to whom you have talked.
    （我是指和你交談過的那位女士。）

11. This is the girl whom I met at the meeting.
    （這是我在會議中遇見的那個女孩。）

12. This is the girl whose sister is in your class.
    （這是她姐姐在你班上的那個女孩。）

13. What is the building whose roof we see over there?
    （我們在那裡看見屋頂的那棟建築物是什麼？）

14. His aunt, who lives in China, came to visit him recently.
    （他住在中國的阿姨最近來拜訪他。）

15. Michael, who is a very handsome teacher, works in different schools.
（麥克，一位非常英俊的老師，在幾所不同的學校教書。）

Study 5　副詞子句

副詞子句（Adv. Clause）的用法共有九大類，包括「表時間」、「表地點」、「表狀態」、「表原因」、「表條件」、「表讓步／對比」、「表目的」、「表結果」、「表比較」。

（1）表示「時間」的副詞子句

例 I had done my homework **before my mother came home**.
（在我母親回家前，我已經做完功課。）

例 **As soon as I met her**, I had a crush on her.
（當我一見到她時，我就對她有好感了。）

例 **The first time I entered this classroom**, I found something wrong.
（當我一進入房間時，我就發現有事情不對勁。）

例 I won't let you go **until I get your money**.
（我不會讓你走，直到我拿到你的錢。）

（2）表示「地點」的副詞子句

例 They sat down **wherever they could find empty seats**.
（他們在能找到的任何空位上坐下來。）

例 **Where there is poverty**, there we find discontent and unrest.
（有貧困的地方，我們就會在那裡找到不滿與不安。）

例 **Where there is a will**, there is a way.
（有志者事竟成。）

例 I enjoy my meals **wherever I find a good restaurant**.
（任何我找到好餐廳的地方，我都可以享受我的大餐。）

名詞與冠詞
代名詞
形容詞與副詞
動詞
介系詞
句型與附加問句
比較級與最高級
時態與被動語態
條件句與假設語氣
關係詞與三大子句

（3）表示「狀態」的副詞子句

例 This steak is cooked **just the way I like it**.
（這份牛排剛好按我喜歡的方法烹調。）

例 I feel **as if I'm floating on air**.
（我感覺我好像漂浮在空中。）

例 The meal is served **just the way I love**.
（這頓飯剛好按照我喜愛的方式供應。）

例 He saw me **as if I was a ghost**.
（他看我好像我是鬼一樣。）

（4）表示「原因」的副詞子句

例 They had to move **because the building was to be torn down**.
（她們必須要搬家，因為這棟大樓要被拆除了。）

例 Jim's trying to find a place of his own **since he wants to feel independent**.
（吉姆試著在找一個自己的家，因為他想感覺獨立。）

例 I didn't go to school **due to the fact that I was sick**.
（我沒有上學，因為我生病了。）

例 **Because everyone is out**, I feel so lonely.
（因為每個人都出去了，所以我覺得很寂寞。）

（5）表示「條件」的副詞子句

例 **Unless it rains**, we'll go to the beach this weekend.
（除非下雨，我們這個週末將要去海灘。）

例 **Supposing your house burns down**, do you have enough insurance to cover your loss?
（假如你的房子燒掉了，你有足夠的保險來彌補損失嗎?）

例 You will be punished **if you don't do your homework**.
（假如你不寫作業，你將會被懲罰。）

例 **In the event that you get a bad grade in English**, you won't be able to go out.
（如果你得到很差的英文成績，你之後就不能出去。）

（6）表示「讓步／對比」的副詞子句

例 **While I disapprove of what you say**, I will defend to the death your right to say it.

（雖然我不贊同你所說的，但我會誓死維護你說話的權利。）

例 **However far it is**, I intend to drive there tonight.

（不論有多遠，我今晚都要開車到那裡。）

例 I failed my exam **even though I did my best**.

（即使我盡了全力，我還是考很差。）

例 **Although he is very young**, he is brave enough to do that thing.

（雖然他很年輕，他有足夠的勇氣做那件事。）

（7）表示「目的」的副詞子句

例 I arrived early **in order that I wouldn't miss anything**.

（為了不要錯過任何事，我早到了。）

例 They must have worn gloves **in order that they wouldn't leave any fingerprints**.

（為了不留下任何指紋印，他們一定帶了手套。）

例 I study English very hard **in order that I can get good grades in English**.

（為了可以得到好的英文成績，我非常用功地讀英文。）

例 **In order that I can improve my English ability**, I decide to go aboard to study.

（為了提升我的英文能力，我決定出國唸書。）

（8）表示「結果」的副詞子句

例 This is such an ugly chair **that I'm going to give it away**.

（這一把椅子醜到我要把它丟了。）

例 We arrived **so early that we got good seats**.

（我們非常早到，以至於我們得到了好的座位。）

例 She is **such** a pretty girl **that everyone loves her**.

（她是一個如此漂亮的女孩，以至於每個人都喜歡她。）

名詞與冠詞

代名詞

形容詞與副詞

動詞

介系詞

句型與附加問句

比較級與最高級

時態與被動語態

條件句與假設語氣

關係詞與三大子句

例 I am **so** sad **that I can't speak a word**.
（我太過傷心，以至於無法說出一個字。）

（9）表示「比較」的副詞子句

例 The new machine is **more** efficient **than the old one was**.
（這台新機器比舊機器要有效率。）

例 Take **as much** money **as you need**.
（拿你所需要的錢。）

例 The population of Taipei is three times **as much as that of Tainan**.
（台北的人口是台南的三倍。）

例 She is **more** intelligent **than her brother is**.
（她比她哥哥更聰明。）

Study 6　名詞子句

名詞子句可以代替名詞做為主詞、受詞、補語及形容詞補語。

請將下列句子改寫成名詞子句：

1. Does Charles go to the beach?
   I don't know _____

2. Where did Steve go?
   I don't know _____

3. Is Karen at home?
   Do you know _____

4. Where is Karen?
   Do you know _____

5. How is Gina feeling today?
   I wonder _____

6. Is Gina feeling better today?
   I wonder _____

7. Does the bus stop here?
   Do you know _____

8. Can Jerry speak French?
   I don't know _____

9. Is Jane married?
   Sam wants to know _____

10. Where do you live?
    Please tell me _____

11. Whose pen is this?
    Do you know _____

12. What did you say?
    _____ wasn't true.

13. Why did they leave the country?
    _____ is a secret.

14. What are we doing in class?
    _____ is hard.

15. How old is he?
    _____ is the question.

16. The world is round.
    I believe _____

解答：

1. I don't know **if Charles goes to the beach**.
   （我不知道查理斯是不是去海邊。）

2. I don't know **where Steve went**.
   （我不知道史帝夫去哪裡了。）

3. Do you know **if Karen is at home**?
   （你知不知道凱倫是否在家？）

4. Do you know **where Karen is**?
   （你知道凱倫在哪裡嗎？）

5. I wonder **how Gina is feeling today**.
   （我想知道吉娜今天感覺如何。）

6. I wonder **if Gina is feeling better today**.
   （我想知道吉娜今天是否感覺比較好了。）

冠詞與名詞

代名詞

形容詞與副詞

動詞

介系詞

句型與附加問句

比較級與最高級

時態與被動語態

條件句與假設語氣

關係詞與三大子句

7. Do you know **if the bus stops here**?

（你知道公車是否會在這一站停靠嗎？）

8. I don't know **if Jerry can speak French**.

（我不知道傑瑞是否會說法語。）

9. Sam wants to know **if Jane is married**.

（山姆想要知道珍是否結婚了。）

10. Please tell me **where you live**.

（請告訴我你住在哪裡。）

11. Do you know **whose pen this is**?

（你知道這是誰的筆嗎？）

12. **What you said** wasn't true.

（你說的話不是真的。）

13. **Why they left the country** is a secret.

（他們離開那個國家的原因是個祕密。）

14. **What we are doing in class** is hard.

（我們在課堂上學習的東西很難。）

15. **How old he is** is the question.

（他的歲數有爭議。）

16. I believe **that the world is round**.

（我相信這個世界是圓的。）

Study 7　綜合比較三種子句句型

子句的三大種類包括：形容詞子句、副詞子句、名詞子句，請判斷下列句子顏色的部分是屬於哪一種子句的用法，並將正確答案填在題號前的空格中：

_____ 1. That he was sick seemed doubtful.

_____ 2. Whether he goes or stays makes no difference to me.

_____ 3. We know what you want.

_____ 4. He said that he had never come to London before.

_____ 5. The only reason is that I want a house.

_____ 6. What I said is what I meant.

_____ 7. I'm sure that he was wrong.

_____ 8. He seemed certain whose house we were in.

_____ 9. He went home when the sun set.

_____ 10. As soon as the shower passed, a beautiful rainbow appeared in the sky.

_____ 11. Where there is a will, there is a way.

_____ 12. Wherever they went, they found poverty.

_____ 13. The boy must be punished because he told a lie.

_____ 14. He cancelled the meeting since he was not here.

_____ 15. If you are gentle, animals will like you.

_____ 16. The boy who won the first prize is my brother.

_____ 17. The dictionary which cost me two hundred dollars has been lost.

_____ 18. I will introduce a man whom you have never seen before.

_____ 19. I need a book which can teach me how to write.

_____ 20. He is the person who knows how to guide you.

_____ 21. Is this the car whose air conditioner was stolen?

_____ 22. Yesterday I ran into an old friend whom I hadn't seen for years.

_____ 23. The women whom we met at the meeting last night are all from Japan.

_____ 24. I am reading a book which was written by Linda.

_____ 25. The book whose cover is red is expensive.

解答：

1. 名詞子句	2. 名詞子句	3. 名詞子句	4. 名詞子句
5. 名詞子句	6. 名詞子句	7. 名詞子句	8. 名詞子句
9. 副詞子句	10. 副詞子句	11. 副詞子句	12. 副詞子句
13. 副詞子句	14. 副詞子句	15. 副詞子句	16. 形容詞子句
17. 形容詞子句	18. 形容詞子句	19. 形容詞子句	20. 形容詞子句
21. 形容詞子句	22. 形容詞子句	23. 形容詞子句	24. 形容詞子句
25. 形容詞子句			

名詞與冠詞

代名詞

形容詞與副詞

動詞

介系詞

句型與附加問句

比較級與最高級

時態與被動語態

條件句與假設語氣

關係詞與三大子句

Words & Construction

CHAPTER 3
詞彙

|常|考|詞|彙|題|型|

UNIT 1 字形字義辨析 1

本單元是英檢中級閱讀測驗中「詞彙」的重點題型，考題內容包括：辨別外觀相似的單字、辨別意義相似的單字、辨別同音異義字、辨別詞性、分辨容易混淆的詞彙的用法。

作答說明 本部分每一個題目都有一個空格。請就試題冊上 A、B、C、D 四個選項選出最合適題意的字或詞，填入空格中。

Q1 Goods that _____ in China are exported all over the globe.

（A）are manufactured （B）are manufacturing

（C）manufactured （D）have manufactured

Q2 She had never _____ so much wine before, and she started to feel like the world was spinning around her.

（A）drank （B）drink

（C）drunk （D）drunken

Q3 The car accident _____ right here several days ago. It killed 4 people in the end.

（A）occurred （B）was occurred

（C）has occurred （D）was occurring

Q4 When all the students _____, the professor started his lecture.

（A）were seated （B）were set

（C）were lied （D）were stressed

Q5 A fire _____ in our neighborhood late last night.

（A）broke away   （B）broke down

（C）broke out   （D）broke up

Q6 More crimes _____ in summer, so the police are very busy at this time.

（A）take out   （B）take place

（C）take off   （D）take care

Q7 The train from Paris _____ at 9:00 A.M. next Monday.

（A）infects   （B）frays

（C）arrives   （D）evaporates

Q8 The car _____ a bit rough these days. You should have it checked.

（A）sings   （B）chants

（C）echoes   （D）sounds

Q9 The soup _____ funny. What's in it?

（A）tests   （B）tastes

（C）teases   （D）takes

Q10 Your feet are getting _____. Why don't you put on socks to keep them warm?

（A）old   （B）cold

（C）sold   （D）told

Q11 Why are you looking _____ me like that?

（A）of   （B）to

（C）at   （D）on

Q12 Does this bag belong _____ you?

（A）of   （B）to

（C）by   （D）for

Q13 **Are you going to apologize _____ me for your mistake?**
（A）for （B）at
（C）to （D）on

Q14 **Hello, may I speak _____ Clair, please?**
（A）at （B）for
（C）with （D）to

Q15 **How can you study while listening _____ the music?**
（A）at （B）on
（C）to （D）of

Q16 **What happened _____ the car you just bought the other day?**
（A）to （B）with
（C）at （D）on

Q17 **I'm looking _____ my son. He's about 120 cm, in a red T-shirt and blue shorts.**
（A）about （B）for
（C）to （D）with

Q18 **Take care _____ the children while I'm away, will you?**
（A）with （B）into
（C）for （D）of

Q19 **His father died _____ heart attack at the age of 56.**
（A）of （B）for
（C）with （D）at

Q20 **The naughty boy made faces _____ the passers-by.**
（A）to （B）against
（C）at （D）on

Q21 We got _____ in the downtown when we first visited it.

（A）loose   （B）lose

（C）lost   （D）loss

Q22 You need to have your hair _____. It's too long.

（A）trim   （B）trimming

（C）trimmed   （D）treated

Q23 I ought to get my computer _____, or I can't do my report.

（A）repeat   （B）repeated

（C）repair   （D）repaired

Q24 Don't look out the window. Concentrate _____ the lesson.

（A）on   （B）to

（C）at   （D）in

Q25 He doesn't have a job. He _____ on his parents for money.

（A）describes   （B）decides

（C）depends   （D）departs

Q26 Michael was trying unsuccessfully to hide himself _____ being found by the other playmates.

（A）to   （B）for

（C）from   （D）against

Q27 Steve _____ money from his parents to buy a car because he didn't have enough money.

（A）lent   （B）gave

（C）borrowed   （D）sent

Q28 It's no use blaming anyone _____ the mistakes now.

（A）to   （B）about

（C）with   （D）for

Q29 **A thief broke into the house and stole the money**
_____ the safe.

（A）of（B）to

（C）into（D）from

Q30 **The father bought a bicycle _____ his daughter's six-**
year-old birthday.

（A）for（B）to

（C）with（D）about

UNIT 2 字形字義辨析 2

本單元是英檢中級閱讀測驗中「詞彙」的重點題型，考題內容包括：辨別外觀相似的單字、辨別意義相似的單字、辨別同音異義字、辨別詞性、分辨容易混淆的詞彙的用法。

作答說明 本部分每一個題目都有一個空格。請就試題冊上 A、B、C、D 四個選項選出最合適題意的字或詞，填入空格中。

Q1 The child threw a _____ tantrum, before he got what he wanted.
（A）timid
（B）temporary
（C）tolerant
（D）tropical

Q2 She sued her husband for alimony so that she could continue living the lifestyle to which she had become _____.
（A）accumulated
（B）accosted
（C）accustomed
（D）accredited

Q3 Childhood is a time when we should have fun and let our _____ run wild.
（A）concrete
（B）concern
（C）creativity
（D）compound

Q4 He was respected by the people with whom he studied because he _____ worked so hard.

（A）previously　　　　　（B）obviously

（C）orderly　　　　　　（D）overnight

Q5 Last night I spoke to a man whose _____ greatly angered me.

（A）opponents　　　　　（B）orchestras

（C）opinions　　　　　　（D）organs

Q6 Not only was he the most boring man she'd ever met, _____ he was also the most annoying.

（A）and　　　　　　　　（B）but

（C）then　　　　　　　　（D）who

Q7 He left the spare keys with his neighbor _____ he lost his own set.

（A）in case of　　　　　（B）instead of

（C）in case　　　　　　（D）due to

Q8 He decided to stay home for the holiday because he had _____ the money nor the energy to travel.

（A）either　　　　　　　（B）both

（C）also　　　　　　　　（D）neither

Q9 He is a very kind brother. For _____, he always brings home a gift for me when he goes on vacation.

（A）ever　　　　　　　　（B）instance

（C）everyone　　　　　　（D）instant

Q10 If you are a university professor, it is important for you to _____ many articles and books in order to be seen as an expert.

（A）be published　　　　（B）publish

（C）be publishing　　　　（D）publication

Q11 **We were all very surprised to hear that she got married to him because she hadn't shown much _____ in him before.**

（A）illustration （B）imagination

（C）independence （D）interest

Q12 **I wish I were independently _____ so that I could live anywhere in the world and not worry about having to find a job.**

（A）widespread （B）wealthy

（C）wildly （D）worthless

Q13 **It is such a good _____ that you should not miss it.**

（A）caption （B）chance

（C）check （D）colony

Q14 **I'm sorry to have kept you _____ here. I was stuck in the traffic jam.**

（A）warning （B）washing

（C）working （D）waiting

Q15 **This is a nice hat. I _____ to whom it belongs.**

（A）worry （B）wonder

（C）wrap （D）withdraw

Q16 **Young as he is, he is _____ and kind to people.**

（A）regional （B）respectful

（C）rival （D）rural

Q17 **Driving motor vehicles at very high speeds is extremely _____.**

（A）dangerous （B）delicate

（C）disappointed （D）dynamic

Q18 We'd better _____ now, or we will be late for school.

(A) hint   (B) horrify

(C) hesitate   (D) hurry

Q19 Where he went yesterday is _____. He didn't want to let others know his location.

(A) meaningful   (B) doubtful

(C) lawful   (D) plentiful

Q20 I would like to try it, as long as you agree to do me a _____.

(A) faith   (B) fiction

(C) flame   (D) favor

Q21 _____ are not the only places where animals live. Some of them may live under the soil.

(A) Caves   (B) Cargoes

(C) Cafes   (D) Cabins

Q22 She learns English hard with a view to going _____ for her master's degree.

(A) otherwise   (B) outdoors

(C) overseas   (D) overhead

Q23 It is _____ over spilt milk.

(A) no use to cry   (B) no use crying

(C) useless to crying   (D) useless crying

Q24 Never have I heard of such a _____ thing. I really can't believe it.

(A) realistic   (B) ridiculous

(C) reasonable   (D) reliable

Q25 _____ fame and wealth are important to him.

(A) Either   (B) Both

(C) Neither   (D) Each

Q26 Yesterday it not only rained _____ snowed.

（A）and （B）or

（C）also （D）but also

Q27 Many girls feel that physics is _____ than English.

（A）hard （B）harder

（C）hardest （D）the hardest

Q28 There's a swimming pool _____ to my office. I always go swimming there after a hard day working.

（A）distant （B）far

（C）near （D）close

Q29 Gary can speak French as well _____ English.

（A）and （B）than

（C）to （D）as

Q30 I forgot to set my alarm clock last night _____ that I got up late this morning.

（A）because （B）so

（C）since （D）but

UNIT 3 字形字義辨析 3

本單元是英檢中級閱讀測驗中「詞彙」的重點題型，考題內容包括：辨別外觀相似的單字、辨別意義相似的單字、辨別同音異義字、辨別詞性、分辨容易混淆的詞彙的用法。

作答說明 本部分每一個題目都有一個空格。請就試題冊上 A、B、C、D 四個選項選出最合適題意的字或詞，填入空格中。

Q1 James can't find his favorite brand in this store so we need to go to _____ store.

（A）the other （B）another

（C）other （D）some

Q2 It is my _____ to get up early and have a big breakfast. I do it every day.

（A）hobby （B）habit

（C）hobbit （D）habits

Q3 If you try to enter the _____ of a wild animal, it may attack you.

（A）personal space （B）territory

（C）door （D）house

Q4 He was such a friendly _____ that he brought homemade cookies to every new person who moved into the neighborhood.

(A) nightmare

(B) nutrient

(C) nun

(D) neighbor

Q5 Some of the cars _____ the speed limit, so the police stopped them.

(A) over

(B) exceeded

(C) conceded

(D) accessed

Q6 I dislike this one. Can you show me _____?

(A) other

(B) another

(C) any

(D) else

Q7 The _____ thing to do is to admit your fault and correct it.

(A) decent

(B) dismay

(C) dissent

(D) descent

Q8 The dog likes to eat _____.

(A) cooking fish

(B) boiling egg

(C) frozen meat

(D) frying potatoes

Q9 Some of my father's friends are _____ in this serious case.

(A) imitated

(B) involved

(C) infected

(D) instructed

Q10 I am sorry I can't find _____ of the books you lent me.

(A) one

(B) very

(C) similar

(D) equal

Q11 _____, spring is the season when flowers are in full bloom.

(A) Instead
(B) Elsewhere
(C) Generally
(D) Otherwise

Q12 We shall _____ mountain climbing tomorrow.

(A) assay
(B) ascent
(C) assent
(D) access

Q13 He is a person who is always _____. No wonder everyone dislikes talking with him.

(A) caption
(B) captious
(C) captivate
(D) capture

Q14 As our ship steamed out to sea the coast slowly _____.

(A) precedent
(B) proceeded
(C) receded
(D) recessed

Q15 The South had no right to _____.

(A) secede
(B) cent
(C) centigrade
(D) percent

Q16 He always makes _____ remarks.

(A) incision
(B) incisive
(C) herbicide
(D) intensive

Q17 The result was _____ to expectation.

(A) contraindicate
(B) controversy
(C) counterfeit
(D) contrary

Q18 Your suggestions will be _____ in the plan.

(A) corpus
(B) corpse
(C) cosmos
(D) incorporated

Q19 I can't _____ Mary. The line is busy now.

(A) reach
(B) touch
(C) yell
(D) attempt

Q20 **This is an _____ novel.**

（A）best-seller （B）interesting

（C）fun （D）great

Q21 **Sammy gets an _____ income by taking a part-time job at night.**

（A）absolute （B）impatient

（C）additional （D）mild

Q22 **The weather today is really _____. You'd better take an umbrella when you go out.**

（A）dreadful （B）delightful

（C）destructive （D）distant

Q23 **The story about the politician is full of _____. He actually has lots of scandals.**

（A）etiquette （B）effect

（C）evaporation （D）exaggeration

Q24 **According to the company's safety regulations, the machines in the factory need to be _____ monthly.**

（A）illustrated （B）inspected

（C）input （D）interpreted

Q25 **There are four people in my family, _____ my parents, my brother, and I.**

（A）such as （B）involve

（C）including （D）include

Q26 **Mr. Collins is a good _____, and his _____ is just around the corner.**

（A）bake；bakery （B）baker；bakeware

（C）baker；bake （D）baker；bakery

Q27 **I go to work _____. It's only a 15-minute walk.**

（A）on feet （B）on foot

（C）with foot （D）by foot

Q28 Do you know your _____ card's number?

（A）demonstration　　　　（B）destruction

（C）investment　　　　　（D）identification

Q29 _____ is heavier than _____.

（A）Water; oil　　　　　（B）a water; an oil

（C）The water; the oil　　（D）some water; some oil

Q30 Martin _____ on going with us, and we couldn't refuse him.

（A）disagreed　　　　　（B）insisted

（C）loosened　　　　　　（D）obtained

ANSWER 解答篇

UNIT 1 字形字義辨析 1

Q1 Goods that ____A____ in China are exported all over the globe.

（在中國製造的貨品被出口到全世界。）

► （A）are manufactured   （B）are manufacturing

（C）manufactured   （D）have manufactured

▶解析 「are＋V-p.p.」是現在式的被動語態，表示「被製造」。

Q2 She had never ____C____ so much wine before, and she started to feel like the world was spinning around her.

（她以前從來沒有喝過這麼多的酒，而且她開始覺得整個世界在她的周圍旋轉。）

（A）drank   （B）drink

► （C）drunk   （D）drunken

▶解析 「had＋V-p.p.」是過去完成式，表示過去的時間已完成的動作，因此空格要放上 V-p.p.。

Q3 The car accident ____A____ right here several days ago. It killed 4 people in the end.

（幾天前在這裡發生的車禍，最後奪走了四條人命。）

► （A）occurred   （B）was occurred

（C）has occurred   （D）was occurring

▶解析 occur 的意思為「發生」，使用主動語態。而句中的 several days ago 代表這是在過去發生的事，所以要使用簡單過去式。

Q4 When all the students ____*A*____, the professor started his lecture.

（當所有學生都入座時，教授開始了他的講課。）

▶（A）were seated   （B）were set

（C）were lied   （D）were stressed

▶解析 句意是指教授等學生都坐下後才開始講課，因此只有（A）were seated 這個選項才是正確的，其他選項都不符合句意，是錯誤的選項。

Q5 A fire ____*C*____ in our neighborhood late last night.

（昨天深夜的時候在我們的鄰近地區發生了一場火災。）

（A）broke away（逃脫）   （B）broke down（停止運轉）

▶（C）broke out（突然發生）   （D）broke up（發生）

▶解析 句意是指昨天鄰區突然發生了火災，因此只有（C）broke out（突然發生）才符合句意，其他三個選項皆不符合句意。

Q6 More crimes ____*B*____ in summer, so the police are very busy at this time.

（夏天發生的犯罪案件比較多，所以警察在這段時間會很忙。）

（A）take out（取出）   ▶（B）take place（發生）

（C）take off（脫去衣物）   （D）take care（照顧）

▶解析 句意是夏天發生的犯罪案件比較多，因此（B）take place（發生）才符合句意，其他三個選項皆不符合句意。

Q7 The train from Paris ____*C*____ at 9:00 A.M. next Monday.

（從巴黎來的火車在下週一九點抵達。）

（A）infects（v. 傳染）   （B）frays（v. 磨損邊緣）

▶（C）arrives（v. 抵達）   （D）evaporates（v. 蒸發）

▶解析 句意是火車會在下週一九點抵達，因此（C）arrives 才符合句意，其他三個選項皆不符合句意。

Q8 The car _____*D*_____ a bit rough these days. You should have it checked.

（這台車這幾天聽起來有點刺耳，你應該開去檢查看看。）

（A）sings（唱歌）　　　　　　（B）chants（反覆地說）

（C）echoes（回音）　　► （D）sounds（聽起來）

▶解析　rough是形容詞，因此只有連綴動詞（D）sound 後面才可以加形容詞。

Q9 The soup _____*B*_____ funny. What's in it?

（這湯嚐起來怪怪的，裡面有什麼？）

（A）tests（測驗）　　► （B）tastes（嚐起來）

（C）teases（取笑）　　　　　（D）takes（拿取）

▶解析　funny 是形容詞，因此只有連綴動詞（B）taste 後面才可以加形容詞。

Q10 Your feet are getting _____*B*_____. Why don't you put on socks to keep them warm?

（你的腳變冷了，你為何不穿上襪子讓腳保暖呢？）

（A）old（adj. 老的）　　► （B）cold（adj. 冷的）

（C）sold（sell 的過去式）　　（D）told（tell 的過去式）

▶解析　連綴動詞 "get" 後面要加形容詞，而後面的句子指出「何不穿上襪子保暖呢？」因此只有（B）cold 才是正確答案。

Q11 Why are you looking _____*C*_____ me like that?

（你為什麼那樣看著我？）

（A）of　　　　　　　　　　（B）to

► （C）at　　　　　　　　　　（D）on

▶解析　"look at sb / sth" 是固定的用法，意為「看著某人／物」。其他類似意義的單字，後面通常也接介系詞 at＋名詞，例如："gaze at sb / sth"，意為「盯著某人／物」；"glare at sb / sth"，意為「瞪著某人／物」。

Q12 Does this bag belong _____*B*_____ you?

（這是你的袋子嗎？）

（A）of   ▶（B）to

（C）by   （D）for

▶解析   "belong to sb" 是固定的用法，意為「屬於某人」。注意此片語不可以使用被動語態，因此 is belonged to 為錯誤用法！

Q13 Are you going to apologize _____*C*_____ me for your mistake?

（你要為你的錯誤跟我道歉嗎？）

（A）for   （B）at

▶（C）to   （D）on

▶解析   "apologize to sb" 是固定的用法，意為「向某人道歉」；"apologize for sth" 意為「為某事道歉」。和片語 "say sorry" 意思相同、用法相同：say sorry to sb for sth，意為「為某事向某人道歉」。

Q14 Hello, may I speak _____*D*_____ Clair, please?

（喂，可以請克萊兒聽電話嗎？）

（A）at   （B）for

（C）with   ▶（D）to

▶解析   "speak to sb" 是固定的用法，意為「對某人說話」；"speak with sb" 意為「與某人說話」，則表示一種「狀態」，例如：I was speaking with Clair when you called.（你打電話來的時候，我正在和克萊兒說話。）

Q15 How can you study while listening _____*C*_____ the music?

（你怎麼有辦法一邊聽音樂一邊看書？）

（A）at   （B）on

▶（C）to   （D）of

▶解析   "listen＋介系詞 to＋sth / sb" 為固定用法，絕對不可以使用其他介系詞，相似意義的動詞 hear 的意思是「聽見」，為及物動詞，後面不接介系詞，直接接名詞，例如：Can you hear the music?（你聽得到音樂嗎？）

Q16 **What happened** _____*A*_____ **the car you just bought the other day?**

（你前幾天剛買的車怎麼了？）

► （A）to　　　　　　　　　（B）with

（C）at　　　　　　　　　（D）on

▶ **解析** "What happened to sth/sb…?" 為慣用句型，意為「某物／某人發生什麼事了？」要注意事情已經發生了，所以 happen 一定要用過去語態。

Q17 **I'm looking** _____*B*_____ **my son. He's about 120 cm, in a red T-shirt and blue shorts.**

（我在找我兒子，他大概有 120 公分高，穿著一件紅色T恤和藍色短褲。）

（A）about　　　　　　　► （B）for

（C）to　　　　　　　　　（D）with

▶ **解析** "look for sth / sb" 是固定的用法，意為「尋找某物／人」。

Q18 **Take care** _____*D*_____ **the children while I'm away, will you?**

（我不在的時候照顧一下這些孩子，好嗎？）

（A）with　　　　　　　　（B）into

（C）for　　　　　　　► （D）of

▶ **解析** "take care of sb / sth" 是固定的用法，意為「照顧某人／物」，意義相同的片語為 "look after sb / sth"。離別時常說 "Look after yourself." ＝ "Take care of yourself." ＝ "Take care."（好好照顧自己。）

Q19 **His father died** _____*A*_____ **heart attach at the age of 56.**

（他父親在五十六歲那年因心臟病發作過逝。）

► （A）of　　　　　　　　（B）for

（C）with　　　　　　　　（D）at

▶ **解析** "die of" 是固定的用法，意為「死於某種疾病」。類似的片語有 "die from"，意為「死於某種外在因素」。

Q20 The naughty boy made faces _____*C*_____ the passers-by.

（那個調皮的男孩子對路過的人扮鬼臉。）

（A）to　　　　　　　　　　（B）against

► （C）at　　　　　　　　　　（D）on

▶解析　　"make a face / faces" 是固定的用法，意為「做鬼臉」。"make a＋形容詞＋face＋at＋sb" 則是「對某人做出…的鬼臉」。

Q21 We got _____*C*_____ in the downtown when we first visited it.

（我們第一次到訪市區時迷路了。）

（A）loose（adj. 鬆垮的）　　（B）lose（v. 失去）

► （C）lost（V-p.p.當 adj. 迷失的）　（D）loss（n. 損失）

▶解析　　連綴動詞的後面必須接形容詞，（C）lost 在這裡是以過去分詞做形容詞使用，"get lost" 意為「迷路」。

Q22 You need to have your hair _____*C*_____. It's too long.

（你需要去把頭髮修一修，實在太長了。）

（A）trim（v. 修剪）

（B）trimming（現在分詞當 adj.）

► （C）trimmed（過去分詞當 adj.）

（D）treated（過去分詞當 adj.，對待）

▶解析　　"get / have＋受詞＋過去分詞當形容詞" 是「由別人來做某事」，通常自己是無法處理的事情（剪頭髮通常是由別人幫忙剪）。

Q23 I ought to get my computer _____*D*_____, or I can't do my report.

（我得去把電腦修好，否則我沒辦法寫我的報告。）

（A）repeat（v. 重複）　　（B）repeated（V-p.p.當 adj.）

（C）repair（v. 修理）　　► （D）repaired（V-p.p.當adj.）

▶解析　　通常會請專業維修人員把電腦修好，而不是自己修理，所以使用 "get/have＋受詞＋過去分詞當形容詞" 的句型，表示「由別人來做某事」。

Q24 Don't look out the window. Concentrate ___*A*___ the lesson.

（不要看窗外，專心聽課。）

▶（A）on   （B）to

  （C）at   （D）in

▶️解析 "concentrate on sth / doing sth" 為動詞的固定用法，意為「專心在（做）某事上」，不可使用其他的介系詞。

Q25 He doesn't have a job. He ___*C*___ on his parents for money.

（他沒有工作，他靠父母提供金錢的協助。）

  （A）describes（v. 描述）   （B）decides（v. 決定）

▶（C）depends（v. 依賴）   （D）departs（v. 出發）

▶️解析 "depend on sb / sth" 為動詞的固定用法，意為「依賴某人或某事」，不可使用其他的介系詞。形容詞 dependent 的意思與用法與動詞相同，例如："He is dependent on his parents."（他依賴他的父母。）

Q26 Michael was trying unsuccessfully to hide himself ___*C*___ being found by the other playmates.

（麥可沒有成功把自己躲好，而被其他玩伴找到了。）

  （A）to   （B）for

▶（C）from   （D）against

▶️解析 "hide sb / sth＋from sb / V-ing" 是動詞固定的用法，"from" 有「以免、隔絕」的意思。請注意「將自己藏起來」的用法，要使用「反身代名詞所有格」himself, herself, myself, yourself, themselves 等。

Q27 Steve ___*C*___ money from his parents to buy a car because he didn't have enough money.

（史蒂夫向他的父母借錢來買車，因為他沒有足夠的錢。）

  （A）lent   （B）gave

▶（C）borrowed   （D）sent

▶ **解析** "borrow＋sth＋from＋sb" 意思是「向某人借某物」。
"lend＋sth＋to＋sb" 意思則是「將某物借給某人」。

Q28 **It's no use blaming anyone _____D_____ the mistakes now.**
（現在把錯怪到任何人上是沒用的。）

（A）to   （B）about
（C）with   ▶（D）for

▶ **解析** "blame＋sb＋for＋sth／Ving" 為固定用法，意為「責怪某人
（做了）某事」。如果要把某件事怪罪在某人頭上，句型則是 "blame
＋sth＋on＋sb"，例如："Don't blame the mistakes on me." （不要
把這個錯誤怪到我頭上來。）

Q29 **A thief broke into the house and stole the money _____D_____ the safe.**
（一名小偷闖入屋內，從保險箱內偷走了錢。）

（A）of   （B）to
（C）into   ▶（D）from

▶ **解析** "steal sth＋from sb／somewhere" 是動詞的固定用法，意為
「將某物從某人（某地）那裡偷走」，"from" 有「來自於」、「從某
處」的意思。

Q30 **The father bought a bicycle _____A_____ his daughter's six-year-old birthday.**
（這個父親買了一台腳踏車給他女兒當六歲生日的禮物。）

▶（A）for   （B）to
（C）with   （D）about

▶ **解析** "buy＋sth＋for＋sb／sth" 意為「買了某物作為某種用途」
或「為某人買了某物」。介系詞 for 有「為了…」和「作為…」的意
思。

UNIT 2 字音字形辨析 2

Q1 **The child threw a _____B_____ tantrum, before he got what he wanted.**

（這個小孩在他得到他想要的東西前，短暫的發脾氣。）

（A）timid（adj. 膽小的）　　　►（B）temporary（adj. 暫時的）

（C）tolerant（adj. 容忍的）　　　（D）tropical（adj. 熱帶的）

▶解析　"throw / have a tantrum" 代表「發脾氣」的意思。此處只有（B）temporary 才符合題意。

Q2 **She sued her ex-husband for alimony so that she could continue living the lifestyle to which she had become _____C_____.**

（她控告前夫來要求贍養費，如此她可以繼續過自己習慣的生活方式。）

（A）accumulated（V-p.p. 累積的）

（B）accosted（V-p.p. 搭訕的）

►（C）accustomed（V-p.p. 習慣的）

（D）accredited（V-p.p. 公認的）

▶解析　"be accustomed to" 為固定片語，表示「有…的習慣」。

Q3 **Childhood is a time when we should have fun and let our _____C_____ run wild.**

（童年是一段我們應當歡樂而且讓我們的創造力奔馳的時光。）

（A）concrete（n. 混凝土）　　　（B）concern（n. 關心的事）

►（C）creativity（n. 創造力）　　　（D）compound（n. 化合物）

▶解析　此題要看能與 and 前面的名詞 fun 搭配的名詞，只有（C）creativity 才符合句意。

Q4 He was respected by the people with whom he studied because he ___*B*___ worked so hard.

（他被跟他一起學習的人所尊重，因為他很明顯做得很努力。）

（A）previously（adv. 先前地）

▶（B）obviously（adv. 明顯地）

（C）orderly（adv. 按順序地）

（D）overnight（adv. 通宵）

▶️解析　此提要根據句意來判斷適合放在句中的副詞，只有（B）obviously 才符合句意。

Q5 Last night I spoke to a man whose ___*C*___ greatly angered me.

（昨晚我跟一名男子說話，他的意見真的讓我很生氣。）

（A）opponents（n. 對手）　　　（B）orchestras（n. 管弦樂隊）

▶（C）opinions（n. 意見）　　　（D）organs（n. 器官）

▶️解析　此題要根據句意來判斷適合放在句中的名詞，只有（C）opinions 才符合句意。

Q6 Not only was he the most boring man she'd ever met, ___*B*___ he was also the most annoying.

（他不只是她所遇過最無聊的男人，而且他也是最煩人的。）

（A）and　　　　　　　　　▶（B）but

（C）then　　　　　　　　　（D）who

▶️解析　"not only… but (also)…" 表示「不但…而且…」。

Q7 He left the spare keys with his neighbor ___*C*___ he lost his own set.

（他給他鄰居備用鑰匙，以防止他遺失自己的鑰匙。）

（A）in case of（假如碰上）　　（B）instead of（代替）

▶（C）in case（以防）　　　　　（D）due to（由於）

▶️解析　"in case" 意為「以防」，後面接完整子句。"In case of" 後面必須加名詞。

Q8 He decided to stay home for the holiday because he had ___*D*___ the money nor the energy to travel.

（他決定這個假期待在家裡，因為他既沒有錢也沒有力氣去旅行。）

（A）either　　　　　　　　（B）both

（C）also　　　　　　► （D）neither

▶解析　"neither... nor..." 意為「既不…也不…」。此題看到 "nor" 即可選出 "neither"。

Q9 He is a very kind brother. For ___*B*___, he always brings home a gift for me when he goes on vacation.

（他是個非常慷慨的兄弟。例如，當他去渡假的時候他總是會帶禮物回來給我。）

（A）ever　　　　　　► （B）instance

（C）everyone　　　　　　（D）instant

▶解析　此題為轉折詞 "for instance" 表舉例。第一句先提出一項事實，後面一句則接 "for instance" 再舉出例子。

Q10 If you are a university professor, it is important for you to ___*B*___ many articles and books in order to be seen as an expert.

（如果你是大學教授，發表很多文章、出版很多書讓你看起來像是個專家是很一件重要的事。）

（A）be published　　　► （B）publish

（C）be publishing　　　　（D）publication

▶解析　此題為由虛主詞引導的不定詞句型 "It's＋adj.＋to＋VR＋…"。

Q11 We were all very surprised to hear that she got married to him because she hadn't shown much ___*D*___ in him before.

（聽到她跟他結婚的消息我們都非常驚訝，因為之前她並沒有表示對他有許多的興趣。）

（A）illustration（n. 說明）　　（B）imagination（n. 想像力）

（C）independence（n. 獨立）　► （D）interest（n. 興趣）

解析 此題要根據句意來判斷適合放在句中的名詞，只有（D）interest 才符合句意。

Q12 **I wish I were independently ____B____ so that I could live anywhere in the world and not worry about having to find a job.**

（我希望我有自主的財富，如此一來我可以住在世界任何的角落而且不必擔心必須要去找工作。）

（A）widespread（adj. 普遍的）　▶（B）wealthy（adj. 富裕的）

（C）wildly（adv. 野生地）　　　（D）worthless（adj. 無價值的）

解析 此題要根據句意來判斷適合放在句中的名詞，只有（B）wealthy 才符合句意。

Q13 **It is such a good ____B____ that you should not miss it.**

（這是如此好的機會，你不應該錯過。）

（A）caption（n. 標題）　　　▶（B）chance（n. 機會）

（C）check（n. 檢查）　　　　（D）colony（n. 殖民地）

解析 此題要根據句意來判斷適合放在句中的名詞，只有（B）chance 才符合句意。

Q14 **I'm sorry to have kept you ____D____ here. I was stuck in the traffic jam.**

（我很抱歉讓你在這裡久等。我被困在車陣中。）

（A）warning（V-ing 警告）　　（B）washing（V-ing 清洗）

（C）working（V-ing 工作）　▶（D）waiting（V-ing 等待）

解析 "keep＋sb＋V-ing" 表示「使某人持續地做某事」。而選項中只有（D）waiting 才符合句意。

Q15 **This is a nice hat. I ____B____ to whom it belongs.**

（這是一頂好帽子，我想知道這是誰的。）

（A）worry（v. 擔心）　　　▶（B）wonder（v. 想知道）

（C）wrap（v. 包；裹）　　　（D）withdraw（v. 抽回）

解析 此題要根據句意來判斷適合放在句中的動詞，只有（B）wonder 才符合句意。

Q16 Young as he is, he is _____*B*_____ and kind to people.

（雖然他很年輕，他卻受人尊重，並且待人親切。）

（A）regional（adj. 地區的） ▶（B）respectful（adj. 尊重的）

（C）rival（adj. 競爭的） （D）rural（adj. 農村的）

▶ 解析 此題要根據句意來判斷適合放在句中的形容詞，只有（B）respectful 才符合句意。

Q17 Driving motor vehicles at very high speeds is extremely _____*A*_____ .

（開快車是非常危險的。）

▶（A）dangerous（adj. 危險的）

（B）delicate（adj. 雅致的）

（C）disappointed（adj. 失望的）

（D）dynamic（adj. 動力的）

▶ 解析 此題要根據句意來判斷適合放在句中的形容詞，只有（A）dangerous 才符合句意。

Q18 We'd better _____*D*_____ now, or we will be late for school.

（我們現在最好快一點，否則上學會遲到。）

（A）hint（v. 暗示） （B）horrify（v. 使恐懼）

（C）hesitate（v. 猶豫） ▶（D）hurry（v. 趕緊）

▶ 解析 此題要根據句意來判斷適合放在句中的動詞，只有（D）hurry 才符合句意。"had better＋VR…"表示「最好…」的意思。

Q19 Where he went yesterday is _____*B*_____. He didn't want to let others know his location.

（他昨天行跡可疑。他不想讓其他人知道他的位置。）

（A）meaningful（adj. 有意義的）

▶（B）doubtful（adj. 可疑的）

（C）lawful（adj. 合法的）

（D）plentiful（adj. 豐富的）

▶ 解析 此題要根據句意來判斷適合放在句中的形容詞，前句提到「他昨天去的地點」，後一句提到「他不想讓他人知道自己的位置」，因此只有（B）doubtful 才符合句意。

Q20 I would like to try it, as long as you agree to do me a
_____*D*_____ .

（只要你答應幫忙，我願意嘗試。）

（A）faith（n. 信念）　　　　　（B）fiction（n. 小說）

（C）flame（n. 火焰）　　► （D）favor（n. 幫助）

▶ 解析　"do＋sb＋a favor" 意為「幫某人一個忙」，因此正確答案為（D）favor。

Q21 _____*A*_____ are not the only places where animals live. Some of them may live under the soil.

（洞穴並不是動物唯一的居所，有些動物也會住在土壤下面。）

► （A）Caves（n. 洞穴）　　　　（B）Cargoes（n. 貨物）

（C）Cafes（n. 咖啡廳）　　　（D）Cabins（n. 客艙）

▶ 解析　此題要根據句意來判斷適合放在句中的名詞，後一句提到「有些動物住在土壤下」，因此（B）caves 才符合句意。

Q22 She learns English hard with a view to going _____*C*_____ for her master's degree.

（為了要出國深造碩士學位，她努力學習英文。）

（A）otherwise（adv. 否則）　　（B）outdoors（adv. 戶外地）

► （C）overseas（adv. 在海外）　　（D）overhead（adv. 在頭頂上）

▶ 解析　此題要根據句意來判斷適合放在句中的副詞，前面提到「她努力學英文」，可以得知是「為了出國身造」，因此只有（C）overseas 才符合句意。

Q23 It is _____*B*_____ over spilt milk.

（覆水難收。）（對著打翻的牛奶哭泣是沒有用的。）

（A）no use to cry　　　　► （B）no use crying

（C）useless to crying　　　（D）useless crying

▶ 解析　"It is no use＋V-ing" 表示「無用的」，因此（B）no use crying 是正確答案。

Q24 Never have I heard of such a ____*B*____ thing. I really can't believe it.

（我從來沒聽過這麼荒唐的事，我真是不敢相信。）

（A）realistic（adj. 現實的）　　▶（B）ridiculous（adj. 荒唐的）

（C）reasonable（adj. 合理的）　　（D）reliable（adj. 可靠的）

▶解析　此題要根據句意來判斷適合放在句中的形容詞，前面提到「從來沒有聽到這種事」，後面則說「我真不敢相信」，因此只有（B）ridiculous 才符合句意。

Q25 ____*B*____ fame and wealth are important to him.

（名譽和財富兩者對他來說都很重要。）

（A）Either　　　　　　　　　　▶（B）Both

（C）Neither　　　　　　　　　　（D）Each

▶解析　對等相關連接詞 "both... and..."，意為「兩者皆是」，用以連接前後兩個詞性相同的詞語，因此正確答案是（B）Both。

Q26 Yesterday it not only rained ____*D*____ snowed.

（昨天不但下雨還下雪。）

（A）and　　　　　　　　　　　（B）or

（C）also　　　　　　　　　　▶（D）but also

▶解析　對等相關連接詞 "not only... but also..."，意為「不只…而且…」，用以連接前後兩個詞性相同的詞語，因此正確答案是（D）but also。

Q27 Many girls feel that physics is ____*B*____ than English.

（很多女生覺得物理學比英文難。）

（A）hard　　　　　　　　　　▶（B）harder

（C）hardest　　　　　　　　　（D）the hardest

▶解析　基本的比較句型 "A＋be動詞＋形容詞比較級＋than＋B"，意為「A比B…」，因此（B）harder 是正確答案。

Q28 There's a swimming pool _____ *D* _____ to my office. I always go swimming there after a hard day working.

（有一座游泳池在我的辦公室附近，我總會在辛苦工作一天之後去那裡游泳。）

（A）distant（adj. 遠的）　　　　（B）far（adj. 遠的）

（C）near（adj. 近的）　　　▶（D）close（adj. 近的）

▶解析　"be close＋to＋sth / sb" 為固定句型，意為「在…附近」，意義相近於 "be near＋sth / sb"，因此正確答案是（D）close。

Q29 Gary can speak French as well _____ *D* _____ English.

（蓋瑞既會說法語，也會說英語。）

（A）and　　　　　　　　　　（B）than

（C）to　　　　　　　　▶（D）as

▶解析　"A＋as well as＋B" 的句型，意為「既是 B 也是 A」，這種句型強調的重點在 A 的部分，而不是在 B 的部分，而正確答案是（D）as。

Q30 I forgot to set my alarm clock last night _____ *B* _____ that I got up late this morning.

（我昨晚忘了設定鬧鐘，所以今天早上起床晚了。）

（A）because　　　　　　　▶（B）so

（C）since　　　　　　　　　（D）but

▶解析　以下三組表示結果的從屬連接詞都是固定的句型，意為「因為… 所以…」："表原因的子句＋so that＋表結果的子句"、"so＋形容詞 / 副詞＋that＋表結果的子句"、"such＋名詞＋that＋表結果的子句"。

UNIT 3 字形字義辨析 3

Q1 James can't find his favorite brand in this store so we need to go to ___*B*___ store.

（詹姆士在這個店裡面不能找到他最喜歡的品牌，所以我們必須到另一家店去。）

（A）the other（另一家）　　▶（B）another（adj. 另一）

（C）other（adj. 其他的）　　（D）some（adj. 一些）

▶ 解析　並未指定某家特定的店，所以使用 another；若有指定，則使用 the other。

Q2 It is my ___*B*___ to get up early and have a big breakfast. I do it every day.

（早起然後吃一頓豐盛的早餐是我的習慣。我每天早上都這樣。）

（A）hobby（n. 嗜好）

▶（B）habit（n. 習慣）

（C）hobbit（【小說角色】n. 哈比人）

（D）habits（n. 習慣）

▶ 解析　"It is my habit to＋VR" 是慣用句型，而 habit 不需加 s。

Q3 If you try to enter the ___*B*___ of a wild animal, it may attack you.

（如果你試圖進入野生動物的領域，牠可能會攻擊你。）

（A）personal space（n. 私人空間）

▶（B）territory（n. 領域）

（C）door（n. 門）

（D）house（n. 房子）

▶ 解析　依照題意，應選擇（B）territory，其他選項皆不符合句意。

Q4 He was such a friendly _____*D*_____ that he brought homemade cookies to every new person who moved into the neighborhood.

（他是一個這麼友善的鄰居。他送給每個新搬來這附近住的人他自己家裡做的餅乾。）

（A）nightmare（n. 惡夢）　　　（B）nutrient（n. 營養物）

（C）nun（n. 尼姑）　　　▶（D）neighbor（n. 鄰居）

▶解析　此題要根據句意來判斷適合放在句中的名詞，後面提到「他帶自製的餅乾給社區的新住戶」，前面則說「他很友善」，因此只有（D）neighbor 才符合句意。"such...that ..." 是慣用的句型，表示「如此…以致於…」。

Q5 Some of the cars _____*B*_____ the speed limit, so the police stopped them.

（有些車子超速了，所以警察把他們攔下來。）

（A）over（prep. 越過）　　　▶（B）exceeded（v. 超過）

（C）conceded（v. 承認）　　　（D）accessed（v. 接近）

▶解析　"exceed the speed" 意為「超速」，在這裡要接動詞，所以不能選（A）over。

Q6 I dislike this one. Can you show me _____*B*_____?

（我不喜歡這個，你能讓我看另一個嗎？）

（A）other（pron. 其他）　　　▶（B）another（pron. 另一個）

（C）any（pron. 任何）　　　（D）else（adv. 其他）

▶解析　此為 "another" 的代名詞用法，表示不特定的另一個。

Q7 The _____*A*_____ thing to do is to admit your fault and correct it.

（要做正當的事是承認你的錯誤並且改正它。）

▶（A）decent（adj. 正當的）　　　（B）dismay（v. / n. 氣餒）

（C）dissent（n. 異議；v. 不同意）　　　（D）descent（n. 下降）

▶解析　空格的部分修飾後面的名詞 "thing"，因此要選形容詞，只有（A）decent 是形容詞且符合句意，各選項外觀十分相似，務必要看仔細。

Q8 **The dog likes to eat** _____*C*_____ **.**

（那隻狗喜歡吃冷凍肉品。）

（A）cooking fish （B）boiling egg

▶（C）frozen meat （D）frying potatoes

▶️解析 過去分詞表被動的狀態，"frozen" 指「冷凍的」，在這裡當形容詞用修飾 meat。

Q9 **Some of my father's friends are** _____*B*_____ **in this serious case.**

（一些我爸爸的朋友涉入這件重大案件。）

（A）imitated（p.p. 被模仿） ▶（B）involved（p.p. 被牽連）

（C）infected（p.p. 被感染） （D）instructed（p.p. 被指導）

▶️解析 此題要根據句意來判斷適合放在句中的過去分詞，句意是指「一些朋友被牽連到這件案件」，因此正確答案是（B）involved。

Q10 **I am sorry I can't find** _____*A*_____ **of the books you lent me.**

（我很抱歉，我找不到你借給我的其中一本書。）

▶（A）one（pron. 一個） （B）very（adv. 非常）

（C）similar（adj. 相似的） （D）equal（adj. 等同的）

▶️解析 "one" 能夠表示其中之一，是代名詞的用法。

Q11 _____*C*_____ **, spring is the season when flowers are in full bloom.**

（一般而言，春天是花朵盛開的季節。）

（A）Instead（adv. 反而） （B）Elsewhere（adv. 在別處）

▶（C）Generally（adv. 通常） （D）Otherwise（adv. 否則）

▶️解析 此題要根據句意來判斷適合放在句中的副詞，句意是指「花朵通常在春天盛開」，因此正確答案是（C）Generally。

Q12 **We shall** _____*A*_____ **mountain climbing tomorrow.**

（我們明天將會嘗試登山。）

▶（A）assay（v. 嘗試） （B）ascent（n. 登高）

（C）assent（v. 同意）　　　　　　（D）access（v. 進入；使用）

▶️解析　此題要根據句意來判斷適合放在句中的動詞，句意是指「明天應該嘗試登山」，因此正確答案是（A）assay。

Q13 **He is a person who is always ___B___. No wonder everyone dislikes talking with him.**

（他是一個總是吹毛求疵的人，難怪每個人都不喜歡跟他說話。）

（A）caption（n. 標題）

▶（B）captious（adj. 吹毛求疵的）

（C）captivate（v. 使著迷）

（D）capture（v. 擄獲）

▶️解析　此題要根據句意來判斷適合放在句中的形容詞，後面提到「每個人都不喜歡跟他講話」，可見空格處為負面的人格特質，因此正確答案是（B）captious。

Q14 **As our ship steamed out to sea, the coast slowly ___C___.**

（當我們的船駛入海洋時，海岸漸漸地遠去了。）

（A）precedent（n. 慣例）　　　（B）proceeded（v. 進行）

▶（C）receded（v. 遠去；退後）　（D）recessed（v. 暫停）

▶️解析　按題意的邏輯，船隻入海時，海岸應該是漸漸遠去，因此正確答案是（C）receded。

Q15 **The South had no right to ___A___.**

（南半球的國家沒有權退出。）

▶（A）secede（v. 從～退出）　　（B）cent（n. 一分幣值的硬幣）

（C）centigrade（adj. 攝氏的）　（D）percent（n. 百分之一）

▶️解析　"to" 後面接原形動詞，因此唯一正確的答案是（A）secede。

Q16 **He always makes ___B___ remarks.**

（他總是會做出犀利的評論。）

（A）incision（n. 切入）　　　▶（B）incisive（adj. 敏銳的）

（C）herbicide（n. 除草劑）　　（D）intensive（adj. 密集的）

▶ 解析　此題的空格處是形容詞，修飾 "remarks"（評論），依題意應選擇（B）incisive。

Q17 The result was ＿＿*D*＿＿ to expectation.

（這個結果和預期的相反。）

（A）contraindicate（n. 禁忌）　　（B）controversy（n. 爭論）

（C）counterfeit（adj. 仿冒的）　▶（D）contrary（adj. 相反的）

▶ 解析　"be contrary to" 表示「和…相反」，因此正確答案是（D）contrary。

Q18 Your suggestions will be ＿＿*D*＿＿ in the plan.

（你的建議將會被納入這個計畫中。）

（A）corpus（n. 文集）

（B）corpse（n. 屍體）

（C）cosmos（n. 宇宙）

▶（D）incorporated（adj. 合併的）

▶ 解析　"will be＋V-p.p." 是未來式被動語態用法，空格處應選擇過去分詞作為答案，因此正確答案是（D）incorporated。

Q19 I can't ＿＿*A*＿＿ Mary. The line is busy now.

（我聯繫不到瑪麗，電話忙線中）

▶（A）reach（v. 聯繫）　　　　（B）touch（v. 觸摸）

（C）yell（v. 吼叫）　　　　　（D）attempt（v. 企圖）

▶ 解析　"reach＋sb" 有「與某人取得聯繫」的意思，意義類似於 "get contact with＋sb" 和 "contact＋sb"。

Q20 This is an ＿＿*B*＿＿ novel.

（這是一本有趣的小說。）

（A）best-seller（adj. 暢銷的）　▶（B）interesting（adj. 有趣的）

（C）fun（adj. 好玩的）　　　　（D）great（adj. 很棒的）

▶ 解析　不定冠詞 an 後面要加母音開頭的字，所以只有（B）interesting 符合文法。

Q21 Sammy gets an _____C_____ income by taking a part-time job at night.

（薩米透過在晚上做兼職工作來獲得一份額外的薪水。）

（A）absolute（adj. 絕對的）　　（B）impatient（adj. 不耐煩的）

► （C）additional（adj. 額外的）　　（D）mild（adj. 溫和的）

▶解析　此題要根據句意來判斷適合放在句中的形容詞，後面提到「在晚上做兼職工作」，可見薩米藉此獲得額外的收入，因此正確答案是（C）additional。

Q22 The weather today is really _____A_____. You'd better take an umbrella when you go out.

（今天的天氣真糟糕，你出門時最好帶把傘。）

► （A）dreadful（adj.【口】糟糕的）

（B）delightful（adj. 令人愉快的）

（C）destructive（adj. 破壞的）

（D）distant（adj. 遠的）

▶解析　此題要根據句意來判斷適合放在句中的形容詞，後面提到「出門最好帶把傘」，可以得知今天天氣很糟糕，因此只有（A）dreadful才符合句意。

Q23 The story about the politician is full of _____D_____. He actually has lots of scandals.

（關於這名政客的報導充滿了誇大之詞，他其實有許多醜聞。）

（A）etiquette（n. 禮節）

（B）effect（n. 結果）

（C）evaporation（n. 蒸發）

► （D）exaggeration（n. 誇大之詞）

▶解析　此題要根據句意來判斷適合放在句中的名詞，後面提到「政客有許多醜聞」，可見報導有許多誇大之處，因此正確答案是（D）exaggeration。

Q24 According to the company's safety regulations, the machines in the factory need to be _____*B*_____ monthly.

（根據公司的安全規定，工廠中的機器需要每月檢查一次。）

（A）illustrated（V-p.p. 被說明的）

▶（B）inspected（V-p.p. 被檢查的）

（C）input（V-p.p. 被輸入的）

（D）interpreted（V-p.p. 被口譯的）

▶ 解析　此題要根據句意來判斷適合放在句中的過去分詞，句意是「根據公司的安全規定，工廠的機器要每月檢查」，因此正確答案是（B）inspected。

Q25 There are four people in my family, _____*C*_____ my parents, my brother and I.

（我家有四個人，包括我父母、我哥哥、和我。）

（A）such as（像是）　　　　　（B）involve（v. 包含）

▶（C）including（prep. 包括）　　（D）include（v. 包括）

▶ 解析　這個句子已經有一個動詞 are 了，因此選項 B 和 D 都不正確。選項 A 的作用是在舉例說明，也是錯誤的。可以得知正確答案是（C）including。

Q26 Mr. Collins is a good _____*D*_____, and his _____*D*_____ is just around the corner.

（柯林斯先生是一個麵包師父，他的麵包店就在轉角那裡。）

（A）bake；bakery　　　　　（B）baker；bakeware

（C）baker；bake　　　　▶（D）baker；bakery

▶ 解析　"bake" 名詞和動詞的意思都是「烘烤」。"bakery" 是名詞，意思是「麵包店」。"baker" 是名詞，意為「麵包師父」。"bakeware" 是名詞，指「耐熱的烘焙器具」。

Q27 I go to work _____*B*_____. It's only a 15-minute walk.

（我走路上班，只不過是 15 分鐘的路程。）

（A）on feet　　　　　　▶（B）on foot

（C）with foot　　　　　（D）by foot

▶️ 解析　一般的交通方式是使用「by＋交通工具」的句型，但是「走路」固定的用法是 "on foot"，不可以使用 by 或其他的介系詞，也不可以使用複數的 feet。

Q28 **Do you know your　*D*　card's number?**
（你知道你的身分證號碼嗎？）
（A）demonstration（n. 示範）
（B）destruction（n. 破壞）
（C）investment（n. 投資）
▶（D）identification（n. 身分證明）

　▶️ 解析　此題要根據句意來判斷適合放在句中的名詞，句意是詢問是否知道身分證號碼，因此正確答案是（D）identification。

Q29 　*A*　**is heavier than　*A*　.**
（水比油重。）
▶（A）Water; oil　　　　　　（B）a water; an oil
（C）The water; the oil　　　（D）some water; some oil

　▶️ 解析　"water"（水），"oil"（油）都是「物質名詞」，屬於不可數名詞，前面不可加任何冠詞，因此正確答案是（A）。

Q30 **Martin　*B*　on going with us, and we couldn't refuse him.**
（馬丁堅持要和我們一起去，我們拒絕不了他。）
（A）disagreed（v. 不同意）　▶（B）insisted（v. 堅持）
（C）loosened（v. 鬆開）　　　（D）obtained（v. 獲得）

　▶️ 解析　此題要根據句意來判斷適合放在句中的動詞，（A）disagreed 是及物動詞，後面不須加介系詞，而其他選項則不符合句意，因此正確答案是（B）insisted。

全|民|英|檢|最|常|考|字|彙|片|語|整|理|

Cloze Tests

CHAPTER 4
段落填空

|最|常|考|生|活|情|境|題|型|

UNIT 1 生活休閒類

作答說明 本部分每個題目包括若干段落，每個段落各含5個空格。請就試題冊上A、B、C、D四個選項中，選出最合適題意的選項填入空格。

Study 1 The Weekend Cabin

Having a weekend cabin is the dream of many North Americans. Most people in Canada and the United States live in big cities and there is a certain __1__ for them about spending free time in the country. The ultimate fantasy includes buying an older cabin and being able to renovate it and decorate it to your own tastes. Such a desire __2__ comes from an idea that one is re-living the pioneering experience of the original European settlers in North America.

The goal of all this renovation is to create a place in which every corner is a cozy retreat. The centerpiece of such a dream cabin is always a big stone fireplace with comfortable chairs __3__. Some people also like to add features such as a hot tub or a sauna to make the weekend cabin a little more like a spa. The trick is to keep the rustic feel of a cabin in the woods while being able to enjoy all the conveniences of modern living.

The trouble is that few people have the time, money or skills to make their weekend cabin dream a reality. It's not uncommon to find a family cabin that has been "under __4__" for years because the owners only have a few weekends each summer to spend working on their property. __5__ one can find a cabin that is already renovated and ready for enjoyment, the only stress-free way to enjoy cabin-living is to rent a cabin. That way someone else can do the work and you can be at your leisure during your vacation.

Q1 _____ 　（A）romantic 　　　　（B）romancing
　　　　　　 （C）romance 　　　　 （D）romances

Q2 _____ 　（A）probably 　　　　（B）probability
　　　　　　 （C）probable 　　　　 （D）improbable

Q3 _____ 　（A）nearly 　　　　　（B）nearby
　　　　　　 （C）near to 　　　　　（D）near

Q4 _____ 　（A）construct 　　　　（B）restrict
　　　　　　 （C）restriction 　　　　（D）construction

Q5 _____ 　（A）Unless 　　　　　（B）Until
　　　　　　 （C）When 　　　　　　（D）If

Study 2　Zhihnan Temple

For a chance to __1__ through a Taoist temple over a hundred years old, you should visit Zhihnan Temple. To reach the temple you __2__ to travel outside the city to the hills of Muzha. Then you walk up 200 or more stone steps. Don't worry, though, the views from the top are __3__ the effort.

However, it is not recommended that couples to visit the temple together. Legend has it that the god to whom the temple is dedicated suffered from an __4__ love and is very bitter. Out of jealousy he may try to cause trouble for happy couples he sees __5__ the temple.

Q1 _____ 　（A）wander 　　　　　（B）wandering
　　　　　　 （C）wonder 　　　　　（D）wind

Q2 _____ (A) can   (B) go
         (C) have   (D) has

Q3 _____ (A) worthy   (B) worth
         (C) worthless   (D) weary

Q4 _____ (A) unrequited   (B) requited
         (C) unwanted   (D) wanted

Q5 _____ (A) on   (B) over
         (C) in   (D) out

Study 3 My best friend

I love dogs, because dogs are human beings' best friends. Dogs have a long-time relationship with human beings. Dogs are diligent, loyal and useful animals. They are human beings' companions, servants and helpers. When we are ___1___ them, they are always by us.

Dogs are faithful to their masters. When their masters are attacked, they bark at their masters' attacker loudly, and even attack him. Dogs are ___2___ snobbish; they never ___3___ their masters because they're poor or sick. Some dogs even ___4___ tombs of their deceased masters until they die of starvation. So, we love them all the more for their loyalty.

Dogs are also useful animals. Basically, all dogs can watch our houses. They can also help in hunting; they can track down fugitives. They can detect drugs. They can ___5___ out whether there are survivors under the ruins. Frankly, dogs are really human beings' good helpers.

Q1 _____ (A) in desire of   (B) in need of
         (C) need   (D) needed

Q2 _____ (A) in all ways (B) by all means
(C) in no way (D) not at all

Q3 _____ (A) dessert (B) desert
(C) decent (D) detergent

Q4 _____ (A) guard (B) guide
(C) garage (D) gardening

Q5 _____ (A) sniff (B) snore
(C) smoke (D) smell

Study 4 Job interview

You have to look your best for an interview. The __1__ you make when walking into a room is __2__ important. Try to __3__ whether the company has dress codes. Then you should dress __4__ their regulations. Then, I believe, the __5__ make good comments on you.

Q1 _____ (A) impressionism (B) imprison
(C) impoliteness (D) impression

Q2 _____ (A) extremely (B) suddenly
(C) tragically (D) fortunately

Q3 _____ (A) find out (B) research
(C) look up to (D) now that

Q4 _____ (A) in according to (B) in addition to
(C) in need of (D) in accordance with

Q5 _____ (A) employee (B) interviewer
(C) interviewee (D) staff

Happy Travel
Xizang Road #25 1st Floor, Taipei City

Choosing Happy Travel means opting for trouble-free trips. We specialize in travel to the south of Taiwan. Indeed, for over thirty years, we have been organizing unforgettable holidays for our ___1___ patrons.

March Discounts
Two-day trips to the south of Taiwan
Tainan / $2500
Kaohsiung / $3000
Kenting / $4500
Taitung / $3500

Visit our web site to see more special offers on accommodations. There you will also find lots of useful travel ___2___ and up-to-date resources ___3___ can help you plan next trips. Our friendly and ___4___ and answer your questions.
We are looking forward ___5___ your calls! Call us NOW!

Q1 _____ （A）depressed （B）irritable
（C）contented （D）cozy

Q2 _____ （A）advice （B）device
（C）revision （D）invitation

Q3 _____ （A）that （B）whose
（C）who （D）it

Q4 _____ （A）difficult customers are ready to complain
（B）knowledgeable staff is always willing to give help
（C）wonderful scenery is too beautiful to describe
（D）various trips are ready to provide some feedback

Q5 _____ （A）to have （B）to having
（C）have （D）having

Study 6 Call for volunteers

Call for Volunteers in Zhonghe District

Volunteers are needed for the New Taipei City Water Festival, to be held on April 18th to April 21st in Zhonghe District. Accepted volunteers will complete four shifts ___**1**___ the event (please see the attachment). ___**2**___ that entitles you to enjoy the free food and drinks at the festival when you are on duty.

Volunteers will be assigned to one of these areas:
- Parking Lot: Direct ___**3**___ in and out of the parking lot.
- Main Gate: Sell and Stamp tickets and hand out festival information brochures.
- Information Booth: Provide information and directions to festival guests.
- Waste management: Help guests place trash in the ___**4**___ containers.

If you are interested and can have fun ___**5**___ it, please tell us. We want to hear from you. There will be a big interview for these suitable candidates. Apply for a volunteer position, and you will know how happy you can be when dedicating to this lively district.

Q1 _____ （A）by （B）as
（C）until （D）during

Q2 _____
(A) On behalf of the organizers, we will remind you of problems
(B) In exchange of your hours of volunteering, we will give you a badge
(C) According to some customs, people should wear a special brooch
(D) In charge of the people in the event, we will ask you to follow rules

Q3 _____
(A) passengers (B) vehicles
(C) protesters (D) wheels

Q4 _____
(A) appropriate (B) convenient
(C) attractive (D) precise

Q5 _____
(A) done (B) did
(C) do (D) doing

UNIT 2 書信應用類

Study 1 A note from Mom

Judy,

I needed to go out and pick __**1**__ a few things, but I'll be home again before dinner. Do your homework and help __**2**__ to a small snack. (Don't __**3**__ your appetite for dinner.)

I put a __**4**__ of clothes in the dryer. Please check on it when you're finished with your homework and __**5**__ the clothes if they are dry.

Mom

Q1 _____ （A）out （B）up
（C）at （D）over

Q2 _____ （A）you （B）yours
（C）yourself （D）yourselves

Q3 _____ （A）spoil （B）spill
（C）spare （D）split

Q4 _____ （A）layer （B）piece
（C）article （D）load

Q5 _____ （A）find （B）fold
（C）foal （D）folding

A message

To Whom It May ___**1**___,

    This is a letter to inform you that my mailing address has ___**2**___. Please update your files accordingly and arrange to have all my ___**3**___ statements and other notices sent to the new address.

    My new address, effective immediately, is:

3rd Floor, #134 WenLin Road

Shihlin District, Taipei City 111

    Thank you for taking care ___**4**___ this request. I can be contacted at 5555-8341 ___**5**___ there are any questions.

Sincerely,

John T. Moneybags

Q1 _____ (A) Concern   (B) Concerning

                    (C) Concerns   (D) Concerned

Q2 _____ (A) change   (B) changing

                    (C) changes   (D) changed

Q3 _____ (A) month   (B) monthly

                    (C) regular   (D) usual

Q4 _____ (A) of   (B) with

                    (C) by   (D) for

Q5 _____ (A) when   (B) so

                    (C) because   (D) if

Study 3　A business e-mail

To: <group: sales team>
From: georget@company.com.tw

I'm sending this as ____1____ reminder of our departmental meeting scheduled for 9am next Thursday. Here is a ____2____ agenda.

9:00 am	Introduction of new staff members
9:15 am	Review the minutes of the ____3____ meeting
9:30 am	Quarterly reports
10:00 am	Strategic planning: ABC Company contract bid
11:00 am	Business-like arising
11:30 am	Adjourn

Please ____4____ me by 5:00 pm on Tuesday if you have ____5____ agenda items, as I will be distributing the confirmed agenda on Wednesday afternoon.
Best regards,
George

Q1 _____
(A) an
(B) the
(C) one
(D) a

Q2 _____
(A) draft
(B) drafting
(C) drafty
(D) daft

Q3 _____
(A) precise
(B) predict
(C) previous
(D) prepare

Q4 _____
(A) consider
(B) compromise
(C) contract
(D) contact

Q5 _____
(A) additional
(B) addition
(C) in addition to
(D) in addition

A NOTE FROM JUDY

Mom,

Mrs. Wong called while you were out. She said that she ___1___ to drop her mother-in-law ___2___ at the doctor's office tomorrow morning, so she can't walk with you to the yoga class as planned. ___3___ she said she would meet you there.

She also ___4___ me to remind you to bring the cookbook that you promised to ___5___ to her.

Judy

Q1 _____ （A）has   （B）have
                （C）had   （D）will have

Q2 _____ （A）in   （B）off
                （C）down   （D）over

Q3 _____ （A）Instead   （B）Insist
                （C）Instant   （D）Instance

Q4 _____ （A）wants   （B）want
                （C）wanting   （D）wanted

Q5 _____ （A）borrow   （B）borrowing
                （C）lend   （D）lending

Study 5 **AN E-MAIL FROM NADIA**

To: bob.eager@hotmail.com
From: nadia.chance@home.com

Bob,

I know we had planned to go out to dinner tonight, but I'm afraid that something has just come ___1___ and I have to cancel.

My cousin's cat ___2___ by a dog today and she's very upset

about it because the cat was a gift from her ex-boyfriend with whom she's still in love. She called me in tears a few minutes ago and asked if I would stay with her tonight ___**3**___ she recovers from the shock of Fluffy's frightening ___**4**___.

I'm really sorry about this, especially because this is the third time I've cancelled on you this month. I'm not sure when I'll be available, but I'll ___**5**___ call you.

Thanks for understanding,

Nadia

Q1 _____ （A）under （B）over
　　　　　 （C）up （D）to

Q2 _____ （A）was bitten （B）bit
　　　　　 （C）had bitten （D）was biting

Q3 _____ （A）when （B）during
　　　　　 （C）until （D）since

Q4 _____ （A）expense （B）experiment
　　　　　 （C）expiration （D）experience

Q5 _____ （A）definitely （B）define
　　　　　 （C）definitively （D）infinitely

Study 6 DEAR NICE NEIGHBORS

Dear nice neighbors;

You probably don't know that your roosters crow too loudly, and it really ___**1**___ us. We're ___**2**___ calling 911. Please change this situation as ___**3**___ as possible.

___**4**___ thanks for your kindness.

___**5**___ yours,

Your neighbors.

Q1 _____ (A) pleases (B) disturbs
(C) unhappy (D) imply

Q2 _____ (A) thinking of (B) dreaming
(C) combining (D) considerate

Q3 _____ (A) seem (B) soon
(C) sooner (D) more soon

Q4 _____ (A) Marry (B) Many
(C) Much (D) May

Q5 _____ (A) Sincere (B) Sincerely
(C) Faithful (D) May

Study 7 Business Email

TO: All staff members
FROM: Daniel Lord
SUBJECT: excellent sales numbers

I just talked with our president, Mr. White. He was very happy
with the ___**1**___ our team achieved last quarter, ___**2**___ means our
sales tactics are working. Therefore, to motivate our staff to keep
on doing the great work, ___**3**___ as a reward. Not only that, all of
us will get a ___**4**___ bonus by the end of this month. How does this
sound? I know how I am going to use this extra money. I believe
you ___**5**___ too. Let's continue to work hard together to have a
new record quarter.
Marketing Manager
Daniel Lord

Q1 _____ (A) grades (B) levels
(C) figures (D) alphabets

Q2 _____ （A）which （B）that
（C）in which （D）with whom

Q3 _____ （A）each of our team members will get a three-day vacation
（B）participants will follow all the rules made by the team
（C）money can be earned through hard work
（D）planners should pay attention to all detailed regulations

Q4 _____ （A）significant （B）miserable
（C）digital （D）elegant

Q5 _____ （A）do （B）can
（C）did （D）are

Study 8 An E-mail from mom

To: Tiffany<Tiffany2003@pchome.com.tw>
From: Nina<nina0936@yahoo.com.tw>
Re: Preparations

Dear,

I have to work late today, and I'm not sure ___**1**___. I know we'll have a birthday party for you, so I've asked your brother to pick up the birthday cake at Happy Bakery, which is your favorite, isn't it? Make sure he's put it in the ___**2**___. I bought some juice and fruit yesterday, but I still need some condiments, ___**3**___, please go to Jason Market to buy them when you are free. Remember to check the ___**4**___ because last time we bought something that isn't fresh. Oh, I almost forget to tell you that I also invited your uncles and aunts, and they all want to celebrate their ___**5**___ 15-year-old birthday.

Love you,
Mom

Q1 _____
（A）when am I going to come back
（B）what time I will get home from work
（C）how I can multi-task at the same time
（D）how many parties I have attended

新題型

Q2 _____
（A）oven（B）refrigerator
（C）furnace（D）calculator

Q3 _____
（A）however（B）therefore
（C）additionally（D）by contrast

Q4 _____
（A）ornaments（B）copyright
（C）expiration date（D）state-of-the-art

Q5 _____
（A）sister-in-law's（B）cousin's
（C）niece's（D）nephew's

休閒類
生活書信
應用類
論說類
記敘類
解答篇

UNIT 3 記敘論說類

Study 1 Independence

One of my reasons for ___**1**___ to Taiwan was to experience living in a different culture and to be exposed to new ways of thinking about life. A difference I have noticed ___**2**___ Taiwanese women around my age who are also single and me is our understanding of independence. Although I would say that I have a good relationship with my parents, I have not lived with either of them since I was 17. And yet, a ___**3**___ of the single Taiwanese women in their late 20's or early 30's still live at home with their parents.

In North America, people might think that there is something wrong with a single woman of 30 who still lives at home. Here in Taiwan, ___**4**___, it is expected that women stay at home until they marry unless their only option for work is to move to a different town. Even in that case, the preference is for the woman to live with her family. I think part of the reason for this is financial: it's expensive to live on your own. Aside from that, I think it would also be considered strange for a single woman to live alone in Taiwan when she has family nearby. They say that it would imply that she has some problems with her family.

Despite this, I wouldn't say that any of them are lacking in independence or in the ability to care for themselves. In fact, many of them shoulder huge responsibilities at home including contributing financially to the household, maintaining the home or caring for children and elderly relatives. In North America, we would say that the __5__ of someone's independence is his or her ability to live away from family and survive. Yet many of us struggle for years to become financially independent and end up in dangerous or unsafe living environments to do this. Maybe there is something to be said for developing an independent identity within the family unit instead of having to cut yourself off from your family and rebuild your own life.

Q1 _____ （A）come   （B）to come
             （C）coming   （D）came

Q2 _____ （A）between   （B）in between
             （C）from   （D）in

Q3 _____ （A）major   （B）majority
             （C）majorette   （D）minority

Q4 _____ （A）and   （B）but
             （C）in addition to （D）however

Q5 _____ （A）measurement   （B）measuring
             （C）measure   （D）measures

Study 2 How to Improve Your Writing

Many people study English for years and become __1__ in daily life. They can survive talking to the occasional foreigner or get around with relative ease when they travel in English speaking countries. Nevertheless, there are still many people struggling to write clearly in English. This is where gaps in grammar comprehension and spelling __2__ glaringly obvious.

One great way to improve writing skills doesn't even involve holding a pen. It is enormously helpful just to read in English. This will help you become more familiar with common grammar structures and increase your vocabulary. It will also expose you to the spelling of ___**3**___ that you have heard but have not seen spelled out. Writing is always easier when you have a model to draw on.

The other thing that it is essential to do is to write! Practice makes perfect, ___**4**___ they say. Create for yourself a regular time for writing by taking a class, picking up a writing workbook, or trying to exchange English e-mail with friends. Practice explaining things or describing a scene. Then give your work to someone and ask for his or her opinion. Don't be afraid of ___**5**___. Having other people point out your weak areas is necessary if you want to correct problems. So if you want to write well, read and write as much as you can.

Q1 _____ (A) function   (B) functioning
                 (C) functions   (D) functional

Q2 _____ (A) became   (B) to become
                 (C) become   (D) have become

Q3 _____ (A) the word   (B) words
                 (C) the vocabulary   (D) vocabularies

Q4 _____ (A) as   (B) as if
                 (C) when   (D) that

Q5 _____ (A) critics   (B) critiques
                 (C) criticism   (D) critters

Study 3 Dogs in the City

Some people are just crazy about their dogs. They ___**1**___ to their dogs as family members and buy presents for them on special

____**2**____. Some people even keep pictures of their dogs on their desks at work.

Unfortunately, many people who live in the city are inadvertently cruel to their dogs because they do not provide their beloved pets ____**3**____ enough space to roam around. They buy their dogs as when they are tiny, adorable puppies and don't realize that as these dogs grow they will need more space than the average Taiwanese apartment ____**4**____ allow. Often one can see horribly overfed and under-exercised dogs waddling ____**5**____ on the sidewalk or hear bored dogs barking all day long inside tiny apartments. People who really love dogs should make sure that they have the space to care for their dogs properly.

Q1 _____ (A) prefer   (B) refer
               (C) call   (D) say

Q2 _____ (A) occasionally   (B) occasioned
               (C) occasions   (D) occasion

Q3 _____ (A) for   (B) not
               (C) at   (D) with

Q4 _____ (A) will   (B) won't
               (C) would   (D) willing

Q5 _____ (A) pathetic   (B) pathetically
               (C) sympathetically (D) pathos

Study 4 Foreigners in Taipei

Traveling to foreign countries ____**1**____ a willingness to try things that are different. I believe this based on my current experiences as a foreigner working in Taipei and on the kinds of foreigners I meet from Western countries here. I would describe one kind as having successfully adapted and the others as not having successfully adapted __**2**__ based on their willingness to try new things and, ultimately, their willing to be changed by the experience of living abroad.

The unsuccessful group wishes to duplicate their lives from home to Taipei, make a lot of money and then leave. This is of course impossible __**3**__ of the cultural, linguistic and culinary differences between the West and the East. As a result, they spend a lot of the money they intended to save __**4**__ Western luxuries, and they spend a great deal of their time being frustrated and unhappy.

The successful group is eager to try the unknown and acknowledges that living in a different country involves adopting a new __**5**__. These people may have their frustrations or may develop dislikes about the new culture, but it is with the understanding that things here are "different," not "wrong." The successful group is often much more satisfied with their lives in Taipei, and I try hard to be part of this group.

Q1 _____ （A）requires   （B）required
                （C）requirement   （D）requiring

Q2 _____ （A）simple   （B）sample
                （C）simply   （D）sampled

Q3 _____ （A）since   （B）because
                （C）when   （D）in effect

Q4 _____ （A）in   （B）by
                （C）with   （D）on

Q5 _____ （A）living   （B）identity
                （C）lifestyle   （D）being

Study 5 The importance of English

English is an international language, for it is ___**1**___ used in the world. Over 800 million people are now users of English, and another 130 million ___**2**___ English in the classroom as a second or foreign language. English is important not only because it is a language of commerce, science and technology, ___**3**___ because it is an international language of communication. ___**4**___ many new words are now becoming a part of the English vocabulary that English may be called "an ___**5**___ language." That's what I realize about the importance of English.

Q1 _____ (A) wide   (B) widely
              (C) width   (D) wide

Q2 _____ (A) is learned   (B) is learning
              (C) are learning   (D) be learned

Q3 _____ (A) but only   (B) only also
              (C) also   (D) but also

Q4 _____ (A) Such   (B) So
              (C) So that   (D) Such as

Q5 _____ (A) exploring   (B) experience
              (C) export   (D) expert

Study 6 Tips on learning English writing

Here are some tips on how to improve your writing. First, check that your writing makes sense! Here are some questions for you:

1. Is it correctly ___**1**___?
2. Is your information presented clearly, ___**2**___ a logical order?

3. Have you put in all the information your reader needs?

4. Have you put in any unnecessary information?

5. Can you replace any words with more ___**3**___ vocabulary?

6. Have you checked the spelling and ___**4**___?

7. Have you ___**5**___ any grammatical mistakes?

Next time, when you write a composition, do not forget these points. Try them.

Q1 _____ （A）organization　　　　（B）organized
　　　　　　　（C）organize　　　　　　（D）organizing

Q2 _____ （A）in　　　　　　　　　（B）for
　　　　　　　（C）from　　　　　　　　（D）off

Q3 _____ （A）precise　　　　　　　（B）predict
　　　　　　　（C）present　　　　　　　（D）prepared

Q4 _____ （A）punctuation　　　　　（B）punctual
　　　　　　　（C）punch　　　　　　　（D）bunch

Q5 _____ （A）correct　　　　　　　（B）replace
　　　　　　　（C）retest　　　　　　　（D）value

Study 7　Diversification

There are some reasons for business diversification. Business' growth and diversification may be achieved both ___**1**___ and externally. For some activities, internal development may be advantageous. For others, careful analysis may reveal sound business reasons for external diversification.

___**2**___ that influence external growth and diversification through mergers and acquisitions include the following:

1. Some goals and objectives may be achieved more speedily through an external acquisition.

2. The cost of building an organization internally may ___**3**___ the cost of an acquisition.
3. There may be ___**4**___ risks, lower costs, or shorter time requirement involved in achieving a sizable market share.
4. There may be tax advantages.
5. There may be opportunities to complement the capabilities of other units.

However, there are other things to be considered. Guidance may be obtained by answers to the following questions: Is there strength in the general management functions? Do the firm's financial planning and control effectiveness have broad application? Is the firm clear on both its strengths and its limitations? And in a world of continuing change, does management understand the company's missions ___**5**___ is defined in terms of customer needs and wants, or in terms of problems to be solved? Please think about these questions.

Q1 _____ (A) international (B) intend
(C) interactively (D) internally

Q2 _____ (A) Factors (B) Factories
(C) Face (D) Finally

Q3 _____ (A) exceed (B) export
(C) expert (D) especially

Q4 _____ (A) less (B) fewer
(C) more (D) the most

Q5 _____ (A) which (B) where
(C) when (D) who

Study 8 Students and tests

Students are afraid of tests. ___**1**___ a test or an examination is approaching, they start to ___**2**___ nervous. On the eve of their tests, they usually worry that they will fail ___**3**___ their tests, so they burn the midnight oil in the hope that they will be able to get better grades. ___**4**___, tests are part of students' lives. Why should they be afraid? As students, they ought to study hard and prepare for their future careers. So I think that a test is only used to test whether a student is ___**5**___.

Q1 _____ （A）Whatever （B）Whenever
　　　　　（C）Whichever （D）However

Q2 _____ （A）getting （B）get become
　　　　　（C）becoming （D）become

Q3 _____ （A）to （B）in
　　　　　（C）out （D）off

Q4 _____ （A）With （B）However
　　　　　（C）Nevertheless （D）As a matter of fact

Q5 _____ （A）fully prepared （B）totally wanted
　　　　　（C）absolutely （D）extremely scared

Study 9 How to overcome test anxiety

Some people think high grades are not only obtained by burning the midnight oil on the eve of a test. ___**1**___, the most effective way to learn is to ask your teacher to explain what you don't understand, to practice what you learn, and to ___**2**___ what you acquire.

When you know that a test is ___**3**___, you ought to relax.

When you relax, you ___**4**___ develop your abilities and potential. You will find that it is very easy for you to answer all the questions on your test because relaxation can help you remember better. So nervousness during an examination can have a negative ___**5**___.

Q1 _____ (A) In addition to   (B) Additional
              (C) Added   (D) In addition

Q2 _____ (A) put to use   (B) pull over
              (C) put out   (D) put on

Q3 _____ (A) in the way   (B) approaching
              (C) appreciating   (D) application

Q4 _____ (A) will be able to   (B) can be able to
              (C) may well be   (D) could be able to

Q5 _____ (A) affect   (B) affective
              (C) effect   (D) enable

Study 10 Advertisement

The most important purpose of advertising is to ___**1**___ customers of some products or services. The second purpose is to ___**2**___ products. The second purpose is utterly important to ___**3**___. ___**4**___ advertisements, consumers think they really need something and will then buy it. After ___**5**___ the product, sometimes the consumers will complain to themselves, "Why do I need this?"

Q1 _____ (A) information   (B) inform
              (C) be informed   (D) be acknowledged

Q2 _____ (A) buy   (B) send
              (C) rent   (D) sell

Q3 _____ （A）manufacturers   （B）customers
             （C）consumers   （D）constructors

Q4 _____ （A）Because   （B）Now that
             （C）Due to   （D）As

Q5 _____ （A）bought   （B）buy
             （C）buying   （D）buyed

Study 11 Immigration

There are a good number of immigrants all over the world. Immigrants move to other countries __1__ different reasons. Wars, political and economic problems, or natural __2__, like floods and earthquakes are all possible reasons. Of course, some people move to marry or to find better living conditions. When immigrants arrive in a new country, they often live in urban or suburban areas. __3__, many city neighborhoods change a lot. __4__, in San Francisco and Los Angeles, China towns are full of Chinese stores and restaurants. If you walk in China towns, you will just feel like walking in China, not the United States. Also, in Miami, you can find many Cuban stores and bakeries in some specific areas. People __5__ there can easily buy some special Cuban food and cuisines.

Q1 _____ （A）for   （B）by
             （C）to   （D）on

Q2 _____ （A）disasters   （B）warts
             （C）vacancies   （D）emergencies

Q3 _____ （A）In accordance with traditions
             （B）When it comes to immigration
新題型   （C）As a result of immigration
             （D）In addition to living conditions

Q4 _____ (A) On the contrary   (B) To sum up
            (C) Despite the fact that (D) For instance

Q5 _____ (A) live   (B) to live
            (C) living   (D) who living

Study 12 Inventions of Television and Computer

Television and computer are two important inventions that have a deep __**1**__ on human beings all over the world. Television was invented in 1926 by John Logie Baird, a Scottish inventor. It was made of a box, knitting needles, a bicycle lamp, and a cake tin. Twenty years later, the first computer was built in 1946 by two American engineers. Later in 1972, the "microchip" was used, and small home computers were first __**2**__ for personal use. That's __**3**__ different from the original one which was large enough to take an entire room. That's very hard to believe, __**4**__? Both of these inventions are imperative in the history. __**5**__. That is to say, there must be more new inventions in this modern world in the near future.

Q1 _____ (A) affection   (B) security
            (C) influence   (D) submission

Q2 _____ (A) product   (B) production
            (C) produced   (D) productivity

Q3 _____ (A) comfortably   (B) repetitively
            (C) extremely   (D) authentically

Q4 _____ (A) doesn't it   (B) does it
            (C) is it   (D) isn't it

Q5 新題型 _____ （A）People say that the more we have, the more we want.

（B）It is true that invention is not an easy thing.

（C）Without a doubt, more people will put forth more advice.

（D）What we want to invest is more and more over-whelming.

生活類

書信類

記敘類

休閒類

應用類

論說類

解答篇

最|常|考|生|活|情|境|類|型|

ANSWER 解答篇

UNIT 1 Study 1 假日小屋

    Having a weekend cabin is the dream of many North Americans. Most people in Canada and the United States live in big cities, and there is a certain <u>romance</u> [1] for them about spending free time in the country. The ultimate fantasy includes buying an older cabin and being able to renovate it and decorate it to your own tastes. Such a desire <u>probably</u> [2] comes from an idea that one is re-living the pioneering experience of the original European settlers in North America.

    The goal of all this renovation is to create a place in which every corner is a cozy retreat. The centerpiece of such a dream cabin is always a big stone fireplace with comfortable chairs <u>nearby</u> [3]. Some people also like to add features such as a hot tub or a sauna to make the weekend cabin a little more like a spa. The trick is to keep the rustic feel of a cabin in the woods while being able to enjoy all the conveniences of modern living.

    The trouble is that few people have the time, money or skills to make their weekend cabin dream a reality. It's not uncommon to find a family cabin that has been "under <u>construction</u> [4]" for years because the owners only have a few weekends each summer to spend working on their property. <u>Unless</u> [5] one can find a cabin that is already renovated and

194

生活類
休閒類
書信類
應用類
記敘類
論說類
解答篇

ready for enjoyment, the only stress-free way to enjoy cabin-living is to rent a cabin. That way someone else can do the work and you can be at your leisure during your vacation.

中文翻譯

　　擁有一個週末小屋是許多北美人的夢想。大部分在加拿大及美國的人都住在大城市，所以對於在鄉村度過他們的休閒時光對他們有某種**浪漫的情調**。最極致的夢想包含買一棟比較舊的休閒小屋，而且能夠依自己的喜好來重新裝潢跟修飾。這樣的欲求**大概是**源於想要重新體驗歐洲早期移民在北美開拓的經歷。

　　整個重新裝潢小屋的目標是要去創造一個地方，在那裡每個角落都是舒適的靜居處。這樣一棟夢想小屋最重要的東西總是一個大的石造壁爐以及**爐邊**幾張非常舒服的椅子。有些人也喜歡加上像是熱水浴或三溫暖房的特色，使整個週末小屋更像是一間水療館。訣竅就在於保留林間小屋的鄉村風情，同時也能夠享受所有現代化生活所帶來的便利。

　　問題在於，很少人有時間、金錢或能力去實現他們的週末小屋夢。長年在**建造**中的家庭式休閒小屋並不罕見，因為這些小屋的主人每年夏天只有幾個週末的時間來維修屋子。**除非**有人能夠找到一個已經裝潢好了而且隨時可以讓人享受假日氣氛的小屋，否則唯一讓人沒有壓力地享受渡假生活的方法，就是去租一間渡假小屋。如此一來可以讓其他人來做維持的房子的工作，而你可以悠閒地渡過假日時光。

Q1 ___C___
(A) romantic（adj. 浪漫的）
(B) romancing（romance 的動名詞）
► (C) romance（n. 浪漫）
(D) romances（複數型）

解析 前文有不定冠詞 "a"，空格處需要的是一個單數名詞，因此正確答案是（C）romance。

Q2 ___A___
► (A) probably（adv. 或許）
(B) probability（n. 可能性）
(C) probable（adj. 很可能發生的）
(D) improbable（adj. 未必會發生的）

▶️解析 空格處應為副詞來修飾動詞 "comes"，因此正確答案是（A）probably。

Q3 　*B*　（A）nearly（adv. 幾乎）
　　▶（B）nearby（adj. 附近的）
　　（C）near to（prep. 距離近）
　　（D）near（adv. 近）

▶️解析 此處句型為 "with＋N＋adj."，因此正確答案是（B）nearby。

Q4 　*D*　（A）construct（v. 建造）
　　（B）restrict（v. 限制；約束）
　　（C）restriction（n. 限制；約束）
　　▶（D）construction（n. 建造）

▶️解析 "under construction" 表示「在建造中」，因此正確答案是（D）construction。

Q5 　*A*　▶（A）Unless（conj. 除非）
　　（B）Until（conj. 直到）
　　（C）When（conj. 當）
　　（D）If（conj. 如果）

▶️解析 此處依前後文意判斷，答案為 "unless"，表示「除非」，因此正確答案是（A）Unless。

UNIT 1 [Study] 2 指南宮

For a chance to <u>wander</u> [1] through a Taoist temple over a hundred years old, you should visit Zhihnan Temple. To reach the temple you <u>have</u> [2] to travel outside the city to the hills of Muzha. Then you walk up 200 or more stone steps. Don't worry, though, the views from the top are <u>worth</u> [3] the effort.

However, it is not recommended that couples to visit the temple together. Legend has it that the god to whom the temple is dedicated suffered from an <u>unrequited</u> [4] love and is very bitter. Out of jealousy he may try to cause trouble for happy couples he sees <u>in</u> [5] the temple.

中文翻譯

　　有機會漫步在有百年以上歷史的一間道教廟宇，你應該要造訪指南宮。想要到達這間廟宇，你必須要走出市區到木柵的山區，然後你必須要攀登兩百級以上的石階。不過別擔心，山頂上的風景值得你費這番功夫。

　　然而，並不建議情侶偕伴探訪這間寺廟。傳說這間廟宇供奉的神祇飽受單相思的愛情之苦，所以相當忿忿不平。出於嫉妒，祂可能會試圖讓祂在廟中看到的情侶情海生波。

Q1 ___A___ ▶（A）wander（v. 漫遊）
　　　（B）wandering（wander 的動名詞）
　　　（C）wonder（v. 想知道）
　　　（D）wind（n. 風）

　▶解析　"to" 後面要接原形動詞，所以（A）wander 是正確答案。

Q2 ___C___ （A）can（aux. 能；會）
　　　（B）go（v. 走）
　▶（C）have（v. 使；讓）
　　　（D）has（v. 使；讓）

　▶解析　"have to" 表示「必須」，而空格前面是第二人稱代名詞 you，因此正確答案是（C）have。

Q3 ___B___ （A）worthy（adj. 有價值的）
　▶（B）worth（adj. 有～的價值）
　　　（C）worthless（adj. 無價值的）
　　　（D）weary（adj. 疲倦的）

　▶解析　"be＋worth＋N＝be worthy of＋N"，意思是「值得」，因此正確答案是（B）worth。

Q4 _A_ ▶（A）unrequited（adj. 沒有回報的；單相思的）
（B）requited（adj. 回饋的）
（C）unwanted（adj. 不需要的）
（D）wanted（adj. 被徵求的）

▶解析　"unrequited love" 意指「單相思的愛」，因此正確答案是（A）unrequited。

Q5 _C_ （A）on（prep. 在～上面）
（B）over（prep. 跨越）
▶（C）in（prep. 在～裡面）
（D）out（prep. 在～外面）

▶解析　"in" 表示「在內部，在裡面」，因此正確答案是（C）in。

UNIT 1 [Study] 3　我最好的朋友

I love dogs, because dogs are human beings' best friends. Dogs have a long-time relationship with human beings. Dogs are diligent, loyal and useful animals. They are human beings' companions, servants and helpers. When we are in need of [1] them, they are always by us.

Dogs are faithful to their masters. When their masters are attacked, they bark at their masters' attacker loudly, and even attack him. Dogs are in no way [2] snobbish; they never desert [3] their masters because they're poor or sick. Some dogs even guard [4] tombs of their deceased masters until they die of starvation. So, we love them all the more for their loyalty.

Dogs are also useful animals. Basically, all dogs can watch our houses. They can also help in hunting; they can track down fugitives. They can detect drugs. They can sniff [5] out whether there are survivors under the ruins. Frankly, dogs are really human beings' good helpers.

中文翻譯

　　我喜歡狗，因為狗是人類最好的朋友。狗和人類有著深遠的關係，狗是勤奮、忠心又有用的動物，牠們是人類的夥伴、僕人兼幫手。當我們需要牠們時，牠總會在我們身邊。

　　狗對牠們的主人十分忠心，如果主人遭到襲擊，牠們會對攻擊者大聲吠叫，甚至還會攻擊對方。狗絕不是勢力眼的動物，牠們從不會在主人貧困或生病時離棄他們，有些狗甚至會守護亡主的墳墓，直到牠們自己餓死為止。因此，我們因為狗的忠誠而更愛牠們。

　　狗也是有用的動物，基本上，所有的狗都能看家。牠們還會幫忙狩獵、追蹤逃犯。牠們也會緝毒、在斷垣殘壁下嗅出是否還有倖存者的氣息。誠然，狗真的是人類最好的助手。

Q1 ___*B*___　（A）in desire of（想要）

▶（B）in need of（需要）

　（C）need（v. 需要）

　（D）needed（need 的過去式 / 過去分詞）

▶解析　 "be in need of＋N"，表示「需要某事物」，因此正確答案是（B）in need of。

Q2 ___*C*___　（A）in all ways（通過各種方法）

　（B）by all means（一定）

▶（C）in no way（絕不）

　（D）not at all（一點也不）

▶解析　 "in no way＝by no means"，表示「絕不」，因此正確答案是（C）in no way。

Q3 ___*B*___　（A）dessert（n. 點心）

▶（B）desert（n. 沙漠 / v. 遺棄）

　（C）decent（adj. 正派的）

　（D）detergent（adj. 使潔淨的）

解析 "desert" 作動詞用時，意為「遺棄」，因此正確答案是（B）desert。

Q4 *A* ▶ （A）guard（v. 守衛）

（B）guide（v. 引導）

（C）garage（n. 車庫）

（D）gardening（n. 園藝）

解析 "guard" 作動詞用，意為「守衛」，因此正確答案是（A）guard。

Q5 *A* ▶ （A）sniff（v. 嗅）

（B）snore（v. 打鼾）

（C）smoke（v. 抽菸）

（D）smell（v. 聞）

解析 "sniff" 特別是指用力聞的時候鼻子吸氣而發出聲音，比 "smell" 更適合用在此處，因此正確答案是（A）sniff。

UNIT 1 Study 4 工作面試

You have to look your best for an interview. The <u>impression</u> [1] you make when walking into a room is <u>extremely</u> [2] important. Try to <u>find out</u> [3] whether the company has dress codes. Then you should dress <u>accordance with</u> [4] their regulations. Then, I believe, the <u>interviewer</u> [5] make good comments on you.

面試時你的外表必須是最佳狀態。你走進房間時給人的印象是非常重要的，你應該試著找出這家公司是否有著裝規範。接著你應該依據他們的規範打扮自己。這麼一來，我相信面試人員會給你很好的評價。

Q1 ___*D*___ （A）impressionism（n. 印象主義）

（B）imprison（v. 監禁）

（C）impoliteness（n. 無禮）

▶（D）impression（n. 印象）

▶️解析　"make a＋adj.＋impression"意為「留下…的印象」，因此正確答案是（D）impression。

Q2 ___*A*___ ▶（A）extremely（adv. 非常地）

（B）suddenly（adv. 突然）

（C）tragically（adv. 悲慘地）

（D）fortunately（adv. 不幸地）

▶️解析　"extremely＝really＝very"表示「非常地」，因此正確答案是（A）extremely。

Q3 ___*A*___ ▶（A）find out（找出）

（B）research（v. 研究）

（C）look up to（尊敬）

（D）now that（既然）

▶️解析　依前後文意判斷空格處為（A）find out

Q4 ___*D*___ （A）in according to（根據）

（B）in addition to（除此之外）

（C）in need of（需要）

▶（D）in accordance with（根據）

▶️解析　"in accordance with＝according to"意為「根據」，因此正確答案是（D）in accordance with。

Q5 ___*B*___ （A）employee（n. 受僱者）

▶（B）interviewer（n. 面試人員）

（C）interviewee（n. 受面試者）

（D）staff（n. 員工）

▶️解析　根據前後文判斷空格處是「雇主、面試人員」一類的詞彙，因此正確答案是（B）interviewer。

Happy Travel
Xizang Road #25 1st Floor, Taipei City

Choosing Happy Travel means opting for trouble-free trips. We specialize in travel to the south of Taiwan. Indeed, for over thirty years, we have been organizing unforgettable holidays for our <u>contented</u> [1] patrons.

March Discounts
Two-day trips to the south of Taiwan
Tainan / $2500
Kaohsiung / $3000
Kenting / $4500
Taitung / $3500

Visit our web site to see more special offers on accommodations. There you will also find lots of useful travel <u>advice</u> [2] and up-to-date resources <u>that</u> [3] can help you plan next trips. Our friendly and <u>knowledgeable staff is always willing to give help</u> [4] and answer your questions.

We are looking forward <u>to having</u> [5] your calls! Call us NOW!

快樂旅遊
台北市西藏路二十五號一樓

選擇快樂旅遊也就是選擇沒有麻煩的旅遊。我們專攻在台灣南部的旅遊。的確，超過三十年來，我們一直安排令人難以忘懷的旅遊給我們感到滿意的老顧客。

三月折扣價

南臺灣兩日遊

台南／2500元

高雄／3000元

墾丁／4500元

台東／3500元

　　上我們的網站來看看更多住宿的特別報價。在網站上你也將會找到很有用的旅遊建議以及可以幫助你籌劃下次旅行的最新資源。我們友善又知識豐富的員工一直都願意提供協助以及回答您的問題。

　　我們期待接到您的來電。現在就打給我們吧！

Q1 ___C___ （A）depressed（V-p.p. 沮喪的）

（B）irritable（adj. 易怒的）

▶（C）contented（V-p.p. 滿意的）

（D）cozy（adj. 舒適的）

▶解析　本句是說「的確，超過三十年來，我們一直安排令人難以忘懷的旅遊給我們『感到滿意的』老顧客」，因此答案為（C）contented。

Q2 ___A___ ▶（A）advice（n. 建議）

（B）device（n. 裝置）

（C）revision（n. 修改）

（D）invitation（n. 邀請）

▶解析　本句是說「在網站上你將會找到很有用的旅遊『建議』以及最新可以幫助你籌劃下次旅遊的資源」，因此答案為（A）advice。

Q3 ___A___ ▶（A）that

（B）whose

（C）who

（D）it

203

▶️解析 "Up-to-date resources that can help you plan next trips." 其中 that 是關係代名詞，引導形容詞子句來形容 resources，而形容事物的關係代名詞要用 that 或 which，因此答案為（A）that。

Q4 __B__ （A）difficult customers are ready to complain
（難搞的顧客準備客訴）

▶（B）knowledgeable staff is always willing to give help（知識豐富的員工一直都願意提供協助）

（C）wonderful scenery is too beautiful to describe（美好的景色美到而無法描述）

（D）various trips are ready to provide some feedback（多樣化的旅行準備好提供一些回饋）

▶️解析 根據前後文可以知道，本句是說「我們友善又知識豐富的員工永遠願意提供協助以及回答您的問題」，因此答案為（B）。

Q5 __B__ （A）to have
▶（B）to having
（C）have
（D）having

▶️解析 本句是說我們期待接到您的來電。"look forward to"是「期待」的意思，其中 to 是介系詞，後接動名詞 V-ing，因此答案為（B）to having。

Call for Volunteers in Zhonghe District

Volunteers are needed for the New Taipei City Water Festival, to be held on April 18th to April 21st in Zhonghe District. Accepted volunteers will complete four shifts during [1] the event (please see the attachment). In exchange of your hours of volunteering, we will give you a badge [2] that entitles you to enjoy the free food and drinks at the festival when you are on duty.

Volunteers will be assigned to one of these areas:

- Parking Lot: Direct vehicles [3] in and out of the parking lot.
- Main Gate: Sell and Stamp tickets and hand out festival information brochures.
- Information Booth: Provide information and directions to festival guests.
- Waste management: Help guests place trash in the appropriate [4] containers.

If you are interested and can have fun doing [5] it, please tell us. We want to hear from you. There will be a big interview for these suitable candidates. Apply for a volunteer position, and you will know how happy you can be when dedicating to this lively district.

中和區徵求志工

新北市潑水節徵求志工，活動將於四月十八日到四月二十一日在中和區舉辦。獲選的志工將要在活動期間完成四個輪班（請見附件）。為了交換志工所提供的服務時數，我們將會給予志工們一個徽章，這個徽章將讓您有權在值勤期間，享受慶典中的免費食物與飲料。

志工將會被指派在這些地點的其中一站：

- 停車場：指揮**車輛**進出停車場。
- 大門口：販售、蓋門票章並發放節慶活動的資訊手冊。
- 詢問台：提供資訊與指示給節慶活動的貴賓。
- 廢棄物處理：協助貴賓放置垃圾在**適當**的垃圾筒中。

如果您有興趣，並可以從**做**這件事中獲得樂趣，請告訴我們，我們想要聽到您的回饋。我們將會針對合適的人選進行一場大型的面談。來申請這份志工工作吧，您會知道，當您全心貢獻給這個活潑的社區，您會多麼愉快。

Q1 *D*　（A）by（prep. 透過）

（B）as（prep. 作為）

（C）until（prep. 直到～時）

▶（D）during（prep. 在～期間）

▶**解析**　本句是說「獲選的志工將要在活動期間完成四個輪班」，因此答案為（D）during。

Q2 *B*　（A）On behalf of the organizers, we will remind you of problems（代替主辦單位，我們將會提醒您一些問題）

▶（B）In exchange of your hours of volunteering, we will give you a badge（為了交換志工所提供的服務時數，我們將會給予志工們一個徽章）

（C）According to some customs, people should wear a special brooch（根據一些習俗，人們應該戴上一個特別的別針）

（D）In charge of the people in the event, we will ask you to follow rules（為了管理活動中的人群，我們將要求您遵守規則）

▶**解析**　根據前後文可以知道，本句是說「為了交換志工所提供的服務時數，我們將會給予志工們一個徽章，這個徽章將讓你有資格在值勤期間，讓你享受慶典中的免費食物與飲料」，因此答案為（B）。

Q3 ___*B*___ （A）passengers（n. 乘客）
► （B）vehicles（n. 車輛）
（C）protesters（n. 抗議者）
（D）wheels（n. 輪子）

▶ 解析 本句是說「指揮車輛進出停車場」，因此答案為（B）vehicles。

Q4 ___*A*___ ► （A）appropriate（adj. 適當的）
（B）convenient（adj. 方便的）
（C）attractive（adj. 吸引的）
（D）precise（adj. 精確的）

▶ 解析 本句是說「協助貴賓放置垃圾在適當的垃圾筒中」，因此答案為（A）appropriate。

Q5 ___*D*___ （A）done
（B）did
（C）do
► （D）doing

▶ 解析 "If you are interested and can have fun doing it"，其中 "have fun" 後接動詞時要用動名詞 V-ing，因此答案為（D）doing。

Judy,

    I needed to go out and pick <u>up</u> [1] a few things, but I'll be home again before dinner. Do your homework and help <u>yourself</u> [2] to a small snack. (Don't <u>spoil</u> [3] your appetite for dinner.)

    I put a <u>load</u> [4] of clothes in the dryer. Please check on it when you're finished with your homework and <u>fold</u> [5] the clothes if they are dry.

Mom

茱蒂：

    我必須趕緊出門去**拿**一些東西，但是我將會在晚餐以前再回到家。做你的功課，還有**你自己拿小零食來吃**。（不要讓你晚餐的食慾被零食給**搞糟**了。）

    我放了**一堆**衣服在烘乾機裡面。當你寫完功課的時候請幫我確認一下，如果衣服已經乾了的話，請順便把它們**摺**好。

媽媽

Q1   *B*   （A）out

             ▶（B）up

             （C）at

             （D）over

             ▶解析   "pick up" 是動詞片語，意為「拿起；拾起」，因此正確答案是（B）up。

Q2   *C*   （A）you

             （B）yours

             ▶（C）yourself

             （D）yourselves

解析 "help yourself to＋N" 意為「自行拿取某物」，因此正確答案是（C）yourself。

Q3 ___A___ ▶（A）spoil（v. 搞糟）

（B）spill（v. 濺出）

（C）spare（v. 分出）

（D）split（spill 的過去式和過去分詞）

解析 此句是說「不要搞糟晚餐的食慾」，意指不要吃太多零食，因此正確答案是（A）spoil。

Q4 ___D___ （A）layer（n. 一層）

（B）piece（n. 一片）

（C）article（n. 一件）

▶（D）load（n. 一車；一船；一堆）

解析 "a load of" 意為「一堆的」，比其他選項適合用來形容衣服，因此正確答案是（D）load。

Q5 ___B___ （A）find（v. 找）

▶（B）fold（v. 摺疊）

（C）foal（v. 產駒）

（D）folding（adj. 摺疊式的）

解析 由連接詞 "and" 連接前面的原形動詞 "check" 和後面的空格，可知空格處也是原形動詞，這裡是指「摺衣服」，因此正確答案是（B）fold。

UNIT 2 Study 2 一則訊息

To Whom It May Concern [1],

 This is a letter to inform you that my mailing address has changed [2]. Please update your files accordingly and arrange to have all my monthly [3] statements and other notices sent to the new address.

My new address, effective immediately, is:

3rd Floor, #134 WenLin Road
Shihlin District, Taipei City 111

Thank you for taking care of⁴ this request. I can be contacted at 5555-8341, if⁵ there are any questions.
Sincerely,
John T. Moneybags

致相關人士：

　　這是一封提醒您我的郵寄地址已經更改的信件。請據此更新您的文件，然後安排所有我所有的月結帳單跟其他事項郵寄到我的新地址。

　　我的新地址：111 台北市士林區文林路134號3樓，立即生效。

　　謝謝您處理這項請求。如果有任何問題，可以撥打5555-8341與我聯繫。

謹啟
John T. Moneybags

Q1 ___A___ ▶（A）Concern（v. / n. 關心）
　　　　　（B）Concerning（concern 的動名詞）
　　　　　（C）Concerns（concern 的複數）
　　　　　（D）Concerned（concern 的過去式和過去分詞）

▶解析　助動詞 "may" 之後要接原形動詞，因此正確答案是（A）Concern。

Q2 ___D___ （A）change（v. / n. 改變）
　　　　　（B）changing（change 的動名詞）
　　　　　（C）changes（change 的第三人稱單數）
　　　　▶（D）changed（change 的過去式和過去分詞）

▶解析　"has＋V-p.p." 是現在完成式，表示「已經」，因此正確答案是（D）changed。

Q3 ___B___ （A）month（n. 月）
▶（B）monthly（adj. 每月的）
（C）regular（adj. 有規律的）
（D）usual（adj. 通常的）

▶ 解析　"monthly statement" 指「月結帳單」，因此正確答案是（B）monthly。

Q4 ___A___ ▶（A）of
（B）with
（C）by
（D）for

▶ 解析　"take care of" 表示「處理」，因此正確答案是（A）of。

Q5 ___D___ （A）when（conj. 當）
（B）so（conj. 所以）
（C）because（conj. 因為）
▶（D）if（conj. 如果）

▶ 解析　此句是說「如果有任何問題，請撥打電話」，因此正確答案是（D）if。

UNIT 2 | Study | 3　一封商業電子郵件

To: <group: sales team>
From: georget@company.com.tw

I'm sending this as a [1] reminder of our departmental meeting scheduled for 9am next Thursday. Here is a **draft** [2] agenda.

9:00 am　Introduction of new staff members
9:15 am　Review the minutes of the **previous** [3] meeting

9:30 am   Quarterly reports
10:00 am   Strategic planning: ABC Company contract bid
11:00 am   Business-like arising
11:30 am   Adjourn

Please <u>contact</u> 4 me by 5:00 pm on Tuesday if you have <u>additional</u> 5 agenda items, as I will be distributing the confirmed agenda on Wednesday afternoon.
Best regards,
George

收件人：〈群組：業務組〉

寄件人：georget@company.com.tw

　　我寄這封信作為安排在下週四早上九點的部門會議的一則提醒，以下是議程草稿：

上午 9:00　　　　介紹新進員工

上午 9:15　　　　複習上次的會議紀錄

上午 9:30　　　　當季報告

上午 10:00　　　 策略計畫：ABC 公司的契約投標

上午 11:00　　　 工作效率的提升

上午 11:30　　　 會議結束

　　假如各位還有額外的議程事項，請在星期二下午五點以前聯絡我，我會在星期三下午傳送一份確定的議程表。

謹啟

George

Q1　　_D_　　（A）an

　　　　　　　（B）the

　　　　　　　（C）one

▶（D）a

▶解析　　"a reminder" 意為「一則提醒」，因此正確答案是（D）a。

Q2　*A*　▶（A）draft（n. 草稿）

　　　　（B）drafting（n. 製圖）

　　　　（C）drafty（adj. 通風良好的）

　　　　（D）daft（adj. 愚笨的）

　　　▶解析　"a draft agenda" 指「議程草稿」，因此正確答案是（A）draft。

Q3　*C*　（A）precise（adj. 準確的）

　　　　（B）predict（v. 預測）

　　▶（C）previous（adj. 先前的）

　　　　（D）prepare（v. 準備）

　　　▶解析　"previous meeting minutes" 意為「前一次的會議記錄」，因此正確答案是（C）previous。

Q4　*D*　（A）consider（v. 考慮）

　　　　（B）compromise（v. 妥協）

　　　　（C）contract（n. 合約）

　　▶（D）contact（v. 聯絡）

　　　▶解析　"contact＋sb"，意為「與…聯絡」，因此正確答案是（D）contact。

Q5　*A*　▶（A）additional（adj. 額外的）

　　　　（B）addition（n. 附加）

　　　　（C）in addition to（除此之外）

　　　　（D）in addition（另外）

　　　▶解析　"additional agenda" 指的是「除了已擬出的議程之外的其他議程」，因此正確答案是（A）additional。

Mom,

　　Mrs. Wong called while you were out. She said that she <u>will have</u> [1] to drop her mother-in-law <u>off</u> [2] at the doctor's office tomorrow morning, so she can't walk with you to the yoga class as planned. <u>Instead</u> [3] she said she would meet you there.

　　She also <u>wanted</u> [4] me to remind you to bring the cookbook that you promised to <u>lend</u> [5] to her.
Judy

媽：

　　在妳出門的時候王太太來過電話，她說她明天早上**將必須要**送她婆婆去診所，所以她不能依約和妳一起走路去上瑜珈課，**反而**她說她會和妳在課堂上碰面。

　　她還**要**我提醒妳，要記得帶妳答應要**借給**她的那本烹飪書。

Judy

Q1　　_D_　　（A）has
　　　　　　　（B）have
　　　　　　　（C）had
►　　　　　　 （D）will have

　　🔊解析　這句的時間是 "tomorrow morning"，表示動作是明天早上將要發生， "have to" 表「必須」，「未來式」為 "will have to" 表「將必須」，因此正確答案是（D）will have。

214

Q2 __B__ （A）in
▶（B）off
（C）down
（D）over

▶解析　"drop＋sb＋off" 意為「接送某人」，或「讓某人下車」，因此正確答案是（B）off。

Q3 __A__ ▶（A）Instead（adv. 反而）
（B）Insist（v. 堅持）
（C）Instant（adj. 立即的）
（D）Instance（n. 例子）

▶解析　"instead" 意為「反而」，是轉折詞的用法，因此正確答案是（A）Instead。

Q4 __D__ （A）wants
（B）want
（C）wanting
▶（D）wanted

▶解析　此題的空格處要配合前後的時態，可見句子是在描述過去的事情，因此正確答案是（D）wanted。

Q5 __C__ （A）borrow
（B）borrowing
▶（C）lend
（D）lending

▶解析　"promise＋to＋VR"，表示「保證或答應做某事」。"lend sb sth" ＝ "lend sth to sb"，意為「借某物給某人」。

215

To: bob.eager@hotmail.com
From: nadia.chance@home.com

Bob,

I know we had planned to go out to dinner tonight, but I'm afraid that something has just come <u>up</u> [1] and I have to cancel.

My cousin's cat <u>was bitten</u> [2] by a dog today and she's very upset about it because the cat was a gift from her ex-boyfriend with whom she's still in love. She called me in tears a few minutes ago and asked if I would stay with her tonight <u>until</u> [3] she recovers from the shock of Fluffy's frightening <u>experience</u> [4].

I'm really sorry about this, especially because this is the third time I've cancelled on you this month. I'm not sure when I'll be available, but I'll <u>definitely</u> [5] call you.

Thanks for understanding,
Nadia

收件人：bob.eager@hotmail.com
寄件人：nadia.chance@home.com

Bob：

　　我知道我們已經約好今天晚上要出去吃晚餐，但是我恐怕有些事情發生，我必須要取消這次約會。

　　我的堂妹的貓今天被一隻狗咬了，她很沮喪，因為那隻貓是她仍深愛的前男友送她的。幾分鐘前她哭著打電話給我，問我是否能在今天晚上陪她，直到她能夠從毛毛（那隻貓的名字）可怕經歷的衝擊當中平復過來。

　　對此我真的很抱歉，尤其因為這是這個月第三次我取消了我們的約定，我不確定我什麼時候會有空,但是我一定會打電話給你。

謝謝你的諒解,

Nadia

Q1 ___C___ （A）under
（B）over
► （C）up
（D）to

▶解析 "come up" 是動詞片語,意為「發生」,因此正確答案是（C）up。

Q2 ___A___ ►（A）was bitten
（B）bit
（C）had bitten
（D）was biting

▶解析 此句是指「堂妹的貓被狗咬了」,因此要用 "was＋V-p.p." 過去式被動語態,正確答案為（A）was bitten。

Q3 ___C___ （A）when（conj. 當）
（B）during（prep. 在～期間）
► （C）until（conj. 直到）
（D）since（conj. 自從）

▶解析 本題要依照前後文意來判斷答案,句意是指「堂妹要 Nadia 陪她直到她平復為止」,因此正確答案是（C）until。

Q4 ___D___ （A）expense（n. 費用）
（B）experiment（n. 實驗）
（C）expiration（n. 終結;死亡）
► （D）experience（n. 經歷）

▶解析 "experience" 意為「經歷」,其他選項的拼字也很相似,要仔細看清楚才不會答錯。

Q5 ___*A*___ ► （A）definitely（adv. 明確地；肯定地）

（B）define（v. 定義）

（C）definitively（adv. 決定性地）

（D）infinitely（adv. 無限地）

▶ 解析　"definitely" 意為「肯定地」，強調用副詞修飾的動詞 "call" ，因此正確答案是（A）definitely。

UNIT 2 [Study] 6　親愛的芳鄰

Dear nice neighbors,

　　You probably don't know that your roosters crow too loudly, and it really <u>disturbs</u> ¹ us. We're <u>thinking of</u> ² calling 911. Please change this situation as <u>soon</u> ³ as possible.

　　<u>Many</u> ⁴ thanks for your kindness.

<u>Sincerely</u> ⁵ yours,

Your neighbors.

中文翻譯

親愛的芳鄰：

　　您也許不知道您那幾隻公雞叫得太大聲了，而且真的打擾了我們。我們正考慮要報警，請你盡快改善這種情形。

　　十分感謝您的善心。

誠摯地

您的鄰居

Q1 ___*B*___ （A）pleases（v. 取悅）

► （B）disturbs（v. 打擾）

（C）unhappy（adj. 不開心的）

（D）imply（v. 暗示）

▶解析　"disturb＋sb" 意為「困擾了某人」，此句表示「公雞打擾到鄰居」，因此正確答案是（B）disturbs。

Q2　*A*　▶（A）thinking of（考慮）
　　　　　（B）dreaming（夢想）
　　　　　（C）combining（結合）
　　　　　（D）considerate（adj. 體貼的）

▶解析　"think of＋V-ing"，指「考慮要做某事」，此句表示「正考慮報警公雞很吵的事情」，因此正確答案是（A）thinking of。

Q3　*B*　　（A）seem（v. 似乎）
　　　▶（B）soon（adj. 快的）
　　　　　（C）sooner（adj. 快一點的）
　　　　　（D）more soon（soon 的比較級是 sooner）

▶解析　"as＋形容詞原級＋as possible" 意為「盡可能…」，此句表示「請盡快改善此情形」，因此正確答案是（B）soon。

Q4　*B*　　（A）Marry（v. 嫁娶）
　　　▶（B）Many（adj. 很多的，用在可數名詞）
　　　　　（C）Much（adj. 很多的，用在不可數名詞）
　　　　　（D）May（aux. 可能）

▶解析　"many thanks" 表示「十分感謝」，因此正確答案是（B）Many。

Q5　*B*　　（A）Sincere（adj. 真誠的）
　　　▶（B）Sincerely（adv. 真誠地）
　　　　　（C）Faithful（adj. 忠實的）
　　　　　（D）Best regards（最好的祝福）

▶解析　"sincerely yours" 是信件的結尾語，意為「您誠摯地」，因此正確答案是（B）Sincerely。

TO: All staff members
FROM: Daniel Lord
SUBJECT: excellent sales numbers

    I just talked with our president, Mr. White. He was very happy with the <u>figures</u> ¹ our team achieved last quarter, <u>which</u> ² means our sales tactics are working. Therefore, to motivate our staff to keep on doing the great work, <u>each of our team members will get a three-day vacation</u> ³ as a reward. Not only that, all of us will get a <u>significant</u> ⁴ bonus by the end of this month. How does this sound? I know how I am going to use this extra money. I believe you <u>are</u> ⁵ too. Let's continue to work hard together to have a new record quarter.
Marketing Manager
Daniel Lord

收件人：全體職員

寄件人：Daniel Lord

主旨：傑出的銷售數字

    我剛才與總裁 White 先生談過了。他很滿意我們團隊在上一季所達到的銷售數字，這表示我們的銷售策略已經奏效。因此，為了激勵我們的職員繼續做出優秀的表現，我們每一位團隊成員將會獲得一個三天的假期，當作是一項獎勵。不僅如此，我們所有人將會在月底得到一筆大的獎金。這聽起來如何呢？我知道我該如何使用這筆額外的金錢。我相信你們也是的。讓我們繼續一起努力，再達到一個有全新紀錄的一季。

行銷經理

Daniel Lord

Q1　　*C*　　（A）grades（n. 分數）

（B）levels（n. 程度）

▶（C）figures（n. 數字）

（D）alphabets（n. 字母表）

▶解析　本句是說「總裁很滿意我們團隊在上一季所達到的銷售數字」，因此答案為（C）figures。

Q2　　*A*　▶（A）which

（B）that

（C）in which

（D）with whom

▶解析　"which means our sales tactics are working" 是用來形容 "He was very happy with the figures our team achieved last quarter"，是形容一整句話的形容詞子句，關係代名詞要用 which，因此答案為（A）witch。

Q3　　*A*　▶（A）each of our team members will get a three-day vacation（每一位團隊成員將會獲得一個三天的假期）

（B）participants will follow all the rules made by the team（參與者將會遵照團隊制定的所有規則）

（C）money can be earned through hard work（錢可以經由努力工作來賺取）

（D）planners should pay attention to all detailed regulations（籌畫者應該注意所有的細項規則）

▶解析　本句是說「為了激勵我們的職員做出優秀的表現，每一位團隊成員將會獲得一個三天的假期，當作是一項獎勵」，因此答案為（A）。

Q4　　*A*　▶（A）significant（adj. 重大的）

（B）miserable（adj. 悲慘的）

（C）digital（adj. 數位的）

（D）elegant（adj. 優雅的）

Q5　　*D*　　（A）do
　　　　　　　（B）can
　　　　　　　（C）did
►（D）are

解析 前句提到 "I am going to use this extra money." 後面要對應的就是 be 動詞 "I believe you are, too." 因此答案為（D）are。

UNIT 2　Study　8　來自媽媽的電子郵件

To: Tiffany<Tiffany2003@pchome.com.tw>
From: Nina<nina0936@yahoo.com.tw>
Re: Preparations

Dear,

　　I have to work late today, and I'm not sure what time I will get home from work [1]. I know we'll have a birthday party for you, so I've asked your brother to pick up the birthday cake at Happy Bakery, which is your favorite, isn't it? Make sure he's put it in the refrigerator [2]. I bought some juice and fruit yesterday, but I still need some condiments, therefore [3], please go to Jason Market to buy them when you are free. Remember to check the expiration date [4] because last time we bought something that isn't fresh. Oh, I almost forget to tell you that I also invited your uncles and aunts, and they all want to celebrate their niece's [5] 15-year-old birthday.

Love you,
Mom

收件人：Tiffany<Tiffany2003@pchome.com.tw>

寄件人：Nina<nina0936@yahoo.com.tw>

主旨：準備工作

親愛的，

　　今天我必須要加班，而我不確定何時我會從公司到家。我知道我們將會替你辦一場生日派對，所以我已經叫你弟弟到開心烘培坊拿取生日蛋糕，這是你的最愛，不是嗎？要確定他有將蛋糕放到冰箱裡。我昨天有買一些果汁與水果，但是我仍需要一些佐料，因此，當你有空請到 Jason 超市買它們。記得要檢查一下有效日期，因為上回我們有買到不新鮮的東西。喔，我差點忘記告訴你，我也邀約了你的叔叔、伯伯與阿姨、姑姑等人，而且他們都想要來慶祝他們姪女的十五歲生日。

愛你，

媽媽

Q1　___*B*___　（A）when am I going to come back

（我何時會回去）

► （B）what time I will get home from work

（何時我會從公司到家）

（C）how I can multi-task at the same time

（我能如何在同個時間多工作業）

（D）how many parties I have attended

（我參加過了多少場派對）

▶ 解析　本句是說「今天我必須要加班，而我不確定何時我會從公司到家。」在寫間接問句時，原本的問句的結構順序要改成一般直述句的順序，也就是先主詞、後動詞，因此答案為（B）。

223

Q2　*B*　（A）oven（n. 烤箱）
▶（B）refrigerator（n. 冰箱）
（C）furnace（n. 火爐）
（D）calculator（n. 計算機）

解析　本句是說「要確定弟弟有將蛋糕放到冰箱裡」，因此正確答案為（B）refrigerator。

Q3　*B*　（A）however　　　▶（B）therefore
（C）additionally　　（D）by contrast

解析　本句是說「我昨日有買一些果汁與水果，但是我仍需要一些佐料，因此，當你有空請到 Jason 超市買它們。」而空格處是兩句話的轉折詞，由此可知正確答案是（B）therefore。

Q4　*C*　（A）ornaments（n. 裝飾品）
（B）copyright（n. 著作權）
▶（C）expiration date（n. 到期日）
（D）state-of-the-art（adj. 最新進的）

解析　本句是說「記得要檢查一下有效日期，因為上回我們有買到不新鮮的東西。」，因此空格處要填入（C）expiration date。

Q5　*C*　（A）sister-in-law's　　　（B）cousin's
▶（C）niece's　　　　　　（D）nephew's

解析　本句是說「我也邀約了你的叔叔、伯伯與阿姨、姑姑等人，而且他們都想要來慶祝他們姪女的十五歲生日。」因此空格處要填入（C）niece's。

One of my reasons for **coming** [1] to Taiwan was to experience living in a different culture and to be exposed to new ways of thinking about life. A difference I have noticed **between** [2] Taiwanese women around my age who are also single and me is our understanding of independence. Although I would say that I have a good relationship with my parents, I have not lived with either of them since I was 17. And yet, a **majority** [3] of the single Taiwanese women in their late 20's or early 30's still live at home with their parents.

In North America, people might think that there is something wrong with a single woman of 30 who still lives at home. Here in Taiwan, **however** [4], it is expected that women stay at home until they marry unless their only option for work is to move to a different town. Even in that case, the preference is for the woman to live with her family. I think part of the reason for this is financial: it's expensive to live on your own. Aside from that, I think it would also be considered strange for a single woman to live alone in Taiwan when she has family nearby. They say that it would imply that she has some problems with her family.

Despite this, I wouldn't say that any of them are lacking in independence or in the ability to care for themselves. In fact, many of them shoulder huge responsibilities at home including contributing financially to the household, maintaining the home or caring for children and elderly relatives. In North America, we would say that the **measure** [5] of someone's independence is his or her ability to live away from family and survive. Yet many of us struggle for years to become financially independent and end up in dangerous or unsafe living environments to do this. Maybe there is something to be said for developing an independent identity within the family unit instead of having to cut yourself off from your family and rebuild your own life.

　　我**來**到台灣的原因之一是想要體驗在不同文化的生活，並接觸新的方式來思考人生。我查覺到和我差不多年紀、同樣是單身的台灣女性與我**之間**的不同之處，就是我們對於獨立自主的理解。儘管我會說，我跟我父母有不錯的關係，自從我十七歲的時候，我就沒有跟他們任何一位住在一起了。然而**大多數**的台灣單身女性在她們二十快三十歲、或三十歲出頭仍然跟她們的父母一起住在家裡。

　　在北美，人們可能會認為這樣一個三十幾歲的單身女性還住在父母的家中一定有什麼問題。**然而**在台灣這裡，除非她們唯一的工作選擇是要搬去一個不同的城鎮，否則女性直到結婚前都待在家裡的狀況是可以預期的。即使是那種情況，女性也比較喜歡跟家裡的人住在一起。我想造成這種情況的部分原因是因為經濟的關係：自己住的花費很高。除此之外，我想在台灣一個單身女子自己住而她有家人住在附近，會被認為是一件很奇怪的事。他們說這可能暗示著她跟自己的家人有一些問題。

　　儘管如此，我不會說她們任何一位缺少獨立自主的個性或是照顧她們自己的能力。事實上，許多女性在家裡都肩負著家裡龐大的責任，包括幫助家計、修繕房舍或是照顧小孩及年老的親戚們。在北美，我們會說**衡量**一個人的自主性，就是他或她離開家裡獨自生活及生存的能力。然而，我們很多人奮鬥好幾年才變得經濟獨立，最終卻是在危險而且不安全的生活環境做這件事。也許值得討論的是，在家庭單位裡發展出一個獨立的特性，而不是使自己脫離家庭再重建自己的生活。

Q1 ＿＿*C*＿＿　（A）come
　　　　　　（B）to come
　　► （C）coming
　　　　　　（D）came

解析 介系詞 "for" 之後要使用動名詞的形式，因此正確答案是（C）coming。

Q2 _*A*_ ▶（A）between
（B）in between
（C）from
（D）in

解析 "between...and..." 表示「在…和…之間」，因此正確答案是（A）between。

Q3 _*B*_ （A）major（adj. 主要的）
▶（B）majority（n. 多數）
（C）majorette（n. 樂隊的女隊長）
（D）minority（n. 少數）

解析 "a majority of" 指「多數的」，因此正確答案是（B）majority。

Q4 _*D*_ （A）and
（B）but
（C）in addition to
▶（D）however

解析 "however" 是表示「然而」的轉折詞。

Q5 _*C*_ （A）measurement（n. 尺寸大小）
（B）measuring（measure 的動名詞）
▶（C）measure（v. 測量 / n. 尺寸）
（D）measures（measure 是不可數名詞）

解析 "the measure of" 意為「判斷」，因此正確答案是（C）measure。

227

Many people study English for years and become functional [1] in daily life. They can survive talking to the occasional foreigner or get around with relative ease when they travel in English speaking countries. Nevertheless, there are still many people struggling to write clearly in English. This is where gaps in grammar comprehension and spelling become [2] glaringly obvious.

One great way to improve writing skills doesn't even involve holding a pen. It is enormously helpful just to read in English. This will help you become more familiar with common grammar structures and increase your vocabulary. It will also expose you to the spelling of words [3] that you have heard but have not seen spelled out. Writing is always easier when you have a model to draw on.

The other thing that it is essential to do is to write! Practice makes perfect, as [4] they say. Create for yourself a regular time for writing by taking a class, picking up a writing workbook, or trying to exchange English e-mail with friends. Practice explaining things or describing a scene. Then give your work to someone and ask for his or her opinion. Don't be afraid of criticism [5]. Having other people point out your weak areas is necessary if you want to correct problems. So if you want to write well, read and write as much as you can.

很多人學習英文很多年，並在日常生活中變得**實用**。當他們到英語系國家旅行時，他們可以跟偶爾碰面的外國人溝通，並相對容易到處去逛。儘管如此，仍然有很多人努力要寫出明確的英文，這就是文法理解與單字拼寫的差異變得格外明顯的地方。

　　一個提升寫作技巧的好方法甚至並不包含拿筆寫作。只是閱讀英文就有非常大的幫助。這將會幫助你對一些普遍的文法結構更加熟悉，並增加你的字彙量。這樣也能夠讓你接觸到那些曾經聽過但沒看過拼出來的單字拼法。當你有一個範本來取材時，寫作一直都比較容易。

　　另一件必定要做的事情就是去寫。正如人們所說的「熟能生巧」。透過選修一門課程、使用寫作練習簿或試著用英文電子郵件與朋友交流，來建立一個屬於你自己規律的寫作時間。練習表達某些事物，或是描述一個情境。接著將你的文章給某人過目，並詢問他或她的意見。不要害怕批評。如果你想要改正問題的話，讓其他人來指出你的弱點是必要的。所以如果你想要寫得好，盡可能地去讀、去寫。

Q1 ___D___ （A）function（n. 作用 / v. 工作）
　　　　　（B）functioning（function 的動名詞）
　　　　　（C）functions（function 的第三人稱單數）
　　　▶（D）functional（adj. 實用的）

　　▶解析　"become＋adj." 意為「變得…」，因此正確答案是（D）functional。

Q2 ___C___ （A）became
　　　　　（B）to become
　　　▶（C）become
　　　　　（D）have become

　　▶解析　空格處前後句子的時態皆為現在式，故要使用 "become" 使時態一致，因此正確答案是（C）become。

Q3 ___B___ （A）the word（單字）
　　　▶（B）words（word 的複數）
　　　　　（C）the vocabulary（字彙）
　　　　　（D）vocabularies（vocabulary 沒有複數型）

　　▶解析　"words" 是「單字」，"vocabulary" 則是「字彙」的意思，並且為集合名詞沒有複數型，此句強調多種單字，因此正確答案是（B）words。

Q4 ___A___ ► （A）as（conj. 如同）

（B）as if（猶如、好像）

（C）when（conj. 當）

（D）that（conj. 引導副詞子句，表「因為」）

▶解析　"as they say" 意為「如他們所說的」，因此正確答案為（A）as。

Q5 ___C___ （A）critics（n. 評論家）

（B）critiques（n. 評論文章）

► （C）criticism（n. 批評；批判）

（D）critters（n. 異常動物）

▶解析　"be afraid of＋N" 意為「害怕某事物」，而根據句意來看，正確答案為（C）criticism。

UNIT 3　Study　3　城市裡的狗

Some people are just crazy about their dogs. They refer [1] to their dogs as family members and buy presents for them on special occasions [2]. Some people even keep pictures of their dogs on their desks at work.

Unfortunately, many people who live in the city are inadvertently cruel to their dogs because they do not provide their beloved pets with [3] enough space to roam around. They buy their dogs as when they are tiny, adorable puppies and don't realize that as these dogs grow they will need more space than the average Taiwanese apartment will [4] allow. Often one can see horribly overfed and under-exercised dogs waddling pathetically [5] on the sidewalk or hear bored dogs barking all day long inside tiny apartments. People who really love dogs should make sure that they have the space to care for their dogs properly.

中
文
翻
譯

　　有些人就是對他們的小狗瘋狂著迷，他們將小狗稱為家中成員的一份子，而且在特別的時刻會買禮物給小狗。有些人甚至在辦公桌上擺放小狗的照片。

　　不幸的是，許多住在城市中的人在無意中會對他們的小狗殘忍，因為他們沒有用足夠的空間提供他們喜愛的寵物走動。他們當小狗還是嬌小、可愛的幼犬時買下牠們，而且沒有了解到當這些小狗長大以後，牠們會需要比台灣一般公寓會容許的範圍更大的活動空間。常常可以看到嚴重餵食過量和運動不足的狗，可憐兮兮地在人行道上蹣跚而行，或是聽到無聊的狗在狹小的公寓裡整天叫個不停。真正喜歡狗的人們，應該要確定他們有空間可以適當地照顧小狗。

Q1 ___*B*___　（A）prefer
　▶（B）refer
　　（C）call
　　（D）say

▶解析　　"refer to" 意為「稱為」，根據句意來看，正確答案是（B）refer。

Q2 ___*C*___　（A）occasionally
　　（B）occasioned
　▶（C）occasions
　　（D）occasion

▶解析　　"occasion" 意為「時刻」，是可數名詞，所以複數要加 s。

Q3 ___*D*___　（A）for
　　（B）not
　　（C）at
　▶（D）with

▶解析　　"provide sb with sth" 意為「提供某人某物」，根據句意來看，正確答案是（D）with。

$\mathcal{A}$ ► （A）will
（B）won't
（C）would
（D）willing

▶ 解析 本句前文為未來式，空格處應選擇 "will" 使前後時態一致，因此正確答案是（A）will。

Q5 $\mathcal{B}$ （A）pathetic（adj. 可憐的）
► （B）pathetically（adv. 可憐地）
（C）sympathetically（adv. 富有同情心地）
（D）pathos（n. 痛苦）

▶ 解析 "pathetically" 意為「可憐地」，修飾動名詞 "waddling"，根據句意來看，正確答案是（B）pathetically。

UNIT 3　Study　4　在台北的外國人

　　Traveling to foreign countries **requires** [1] a willingness to try things that are different. I believe this based on my current experiences as a foreigner working in Taipei and on the kinds of foreigners I meet from Western countries here. I would describe one kind as having successfully adapted and the others as not having successfully adapted **simply** [2] based on their willingness to try new things and, ultimately, their willing to be changed by the experience of living abroad.

　　The unsuccessful group wishes to duplicate their lives from home to Taipei, make a lot of money and then leave. This is of course impossible **because** [3] of the cultural, linguistic and culinary differences between the West and the East. As a result, they spend a lot of the money they intended to save <u>on</u> [4] Western luxuries, and they spend a great deal of their time being frustrated and unhappy.

The successful group is eager to try the unknown and acknowledges that living in a different country involves adopting a new <u>lifestyle</u> [5]. These people may have their frustrations or may develop dislikes about the new culture, but it is with the understanding that things here are "different," not "wrong." The successful group is often much more satisfied with their lives in Taipei, and I try hard to be part of this group.

中文翻譯

出國旅行**需要**有嘗試不同事物的意願,我相信這一點是根據最近我身為在台北工作的外國人的經驗,以及我在這裡遇見來自西方國家的外國人。我會說其中一群是適應成功的人,另一群是適應不成功的人,**僅僅是**根據他們嘗試新事物的意願,以及最後因異國生活的經驗而受改變的意願。

不成功的一群希望把他們的生活方式從家鄉複製到台北來,只想賺了大筆鈔票之後就離開。這當然是不可能的,**因為**東西方在文化、語言、烹飪方式上的不同。結果他們花費大筆原本打算要存下來的錢**在**西式的奢侈品上**面**,而且也用了大量的時間在沮喪和不開心之中。

適應成功的一群則渴望嘗試那些未知的事物,並且認知到住在一個不同的國家包含適應一個新的**生活方式**。這些人也許會感到沮喪,或是對這個新文化產生反感,但是他們會了解這些文化只是「不同」,而不是「錯誤的」。成功的一群常常對他們在台北的生活感到更滿意,我也努力試著成為這一群的一份子。

Q1 ___*A*___ ▶ (A) requires
　　　　　　(B) required
　　　　　　(C) requirement
　　　　　　(D) requiring

▶**解析** 主詞 "traveling" 為單數,因此空格處要填入動詞、時態為現在式,可知正確答案為(A)requires。

Q2 _C_ （A）simple（adj. 簡單的）

（B）sample（n. 樣品）

► （C）simply（adv. 簡單地；僅僅）

（D）sampled（sample 的過去式）

▶解析　"simply" 意為「簡單地」，在句中修飾分詞 "based"，可知正確答案為（C）simply。

Q3 _B_ （A）since

► （B）because

（C）when

（D）in effect

▶解析　"because of＋N" 表示「因為、由於」，選項中只有（B）because後面可以接介系詞 "of"。

Q4 _D_ （A）in

（B）by

（C）with

► （D）on

▶解析　"spend A on B" 意為「把 A 花費在 B 上面」，因此正確答案為（D）on。

Q5 _C_ （A）living（n. 生活）

（B）identity（n. 身分）

► （C）lifestyle（n. 生活方式）

（D）being（n. 生命）

▶解析　"a new lifestyle" 意為「新的生活方式」，可知符合句意的只有（C）lifestyle。

UNIT 3 Study 5 英文的重要性

English is an international language, for it is <u>widely</u> [1] used in the world. Over 800 million people are now users of English, and another 130 million <u>are leaning</u> [2] English in the classroom as a second or foreign language. English is important not only because it is a language of commerce, science and technology, <u>but also</u> [3] because it is an international language of communication. <u>So</u> [4] many new words are now becoming a part of the English vocabulary that English may be called "an <u>exploring</u> [5] language." That's what I realize about the importance of English.

英文是一個國際語言，因為它在世界各地被**廣泛地**使用，現今已經有超過八億的人口使用英文，另外有一點三億的人在課堂上**正在學習**英文作為第二或外國語言。英文是重要的，不只是因為它是商業、科學和科技上的一種語言，**還**因為它是國際上用以溝通的語言。現今有**這麼多**的新字成為英文字彙的一部分，英文可以被稱為是「**探索的語言**」了。那就是我所認知的英文重要性。

Q1 ___*B*___ （A）wide（adj. 廣泛的）
▶（B）widely（adv. 廣泛地）
（C）width（n. 寬度）
（D）wide（adj. 野生的）

▶ 解析 空格處後面為過去分詞 "used"，可知空格處應填入副詞來修飾分詞，因此正確答案是（B）widely。

Q2 ___*C*___ （A）is learned
（B）is learning
▶（C）are learning
（D）be learned

▶ 解析　空格處和前句一致使用現在進行式，主詞
"another 130 million (people)" 是複數，因此正確答案
是（C）are learning。

Q3 ___D___　（A）but only
　　　　　　（B）only also
　　　　　　（C）also
▶　　　　　　（D）but also

▶ 解析　"not only... but also..." 意為「不但…而
且…」，因此正確答案是（D）but also。

Q4 ___B___　（A）Such
▶　　　　　　（B）So
　　　　　　（C）So that
　　　　　　（D）Such as

▶ 解析　"so... that..." 表示「太…以致於…」，因此
正確答案是（B）So。

Q5 ___A___ ▶（A）exploring（adj. 探索的）
　　　　　　（B）experience（n. 經驗）
　　　　　　（C）export（v. 輸出）
　　　　　　（D）expert（n. 專家）

▶ 解析　"exploring" 意為「探索的」，形容空格處後
面的名詞 "language"，因此正確答案是（A）
exploring。

休閒類
生活類
書信類
應用類
記敘類
論說類
解答篇

Here are some tips on how to improve your writing. First, check that your writing makes sense! Here are some questions for you:

1. Is it correctly <u>organized</u>[1]?
2. Is your information presented clearly <u>in</u>[2] a logical order?
3. Have you put in all the information your reader needs?
4. Have you put in any unnecessary information?
5. Can you replace any words with more <u>precise</u>[3] vocabulary?
6. Have you checked the spelling and <u>punctuation</u>[4]?
7. Have you <u>made</u>[5] any grammatical mistakes?

Next time, when you write a composition, do not forget these points. Try them.

這裡有一些如何增進寫作技巧的技巧。首先，確定你的寫作是有意義的！有一些問題可供你思考：

1. 文章是否適當地**被組織**？
2. 你的資訊是否清楚地以合乎邏輯的順序呈現？
3. 你已經把讀者需要的所有資訊都放進文章中了嗎？
4. 你是否放進了任何不必要的資訊？
5. 你能否用更**精確**的字彙取代文章中的任何單字呢？
6. 你檢查過拼字和**標點符號**了嗎？
7. 你是否有**犯**任何的文法錯誤？

下一次當你需要寫一篇作文時，不要忘記這幾點，試試看吧。

Q1　　*B*　（A）organization
　　　▶（B）organized
　　　　（C）organize
　　　　（D）organizing
　　　▶解析　"organized" 意為「被組織」，是被動語態
　　　"be＋V-p.p." 的形式。

Q2　　*A*　▶（A）in
　　　　（B）for
　　　　（C）from
　　　　（D）off
　　　▶解析　"in a logical way" 意為「以一種合乎邏輯的
　　　方式」，因此正確答案是（A）in。

Q3　　*A*　▶（A）precise（adj. 精準的）
　　　　（B）predict（v. 預測）
　　　　（C）present（adj. 目前的）
　　　　（D）prepared（adj. 有準備的）
　　　▶解析　"precise" 意為「精準的」，形容後面的名詞
　　　"vocabulary"，因此正確答案是（A）precise。

Q4　　*A*　▶（A）punctuation（n. 標點符號）
　　　　（B）punctual（adj. 準時的）
　　　　（C）punch（v. 用拳猛擊）
　　　　（D）bunch（n. 一束）
　　　▶解析　"punctuation" 意為「標點符號」，是不可數
　　　名詞，而選項中只有（A）punctuation 符合句意。

Q5　　*A*　▶（A）correct（v. 改正）
　　　　（B）replace（v. 取代）
　　　　（C）retest（v. 再次測驗）
　　　　（D）value（v. 估價）
　　　▶解析　"to correct mistakes" 意為「改正錯誤」，因
　　　此正確答案是（A）correct。

There are some reasons for business diversification. Business' growth and diversification may be achieved both <u>internally</u> [1] and externally. For some activities, internal development may be advantageous. For others, careful analysis may reveal sound business reasons for external diversification.

<u>Factors</u> [2] that influence external growth and diversification through mergers and acquisitions include the following:

1. Some goals and objectives may be achieved more speedily through an external acquisition.
2. The cost of building an organization internally may <u>exceed</u> [3] the cost of an acquisition.
3. There may be <u>fewer</u> [4] risks, lower costs, or shorter time requirement involved in achieving an economically market share.
4. There may be tax advantages.
5. There may be opportunities to complement the capabilities of other units.

However, there are other things to be considered. Guidance may be obtained by answers to the following questions: Is there strength in the general management functions? Do the firm's financial planning and control effectiveness have broad application? Is the firm clear on both its strengths and its limitations? And in a world of continuing change, does management understand the company's missions <u>which</u> [5] is defined in terms of customer needs and wants, or in terms of problems to be solved? Please think about these questions.

企業多樣化有一些原因，企業的成長和多樣化可能在**內部**和外部實現。對有些活動而言，內部發展可能是有利的。對其他活動而言，謹慎的分析可能會顯示一個健全企業對外部多樣化經營的原因。

透過合併和收購來影響外部成長和多樣化經營的**因素**包括下列幾項：

1. 有些目標和目的藉由外部購併可能更快速地達成。

2. 建造內部組織的費用可能會**超過**購併的費用。

3. 達成廣大的市佔率可能含有**較少**的風險、較低的費用，或是較短的時間需求。

4. 可能有稅收優勢。

5. 可能有機會補充其他單位的能力。

不過，還有其他事項需要考慮。透過回答下列問題可能會獲得一些指引：一般管理職務是否有實力？公司的財務計畫和控制效力是否有廣泛運用？公司是否清楚本身的優勢與限制？而在這個瞬息萬變的世界裡，管理階層是否了解公司的任務**是**從客戶的需求和期望，或是就問題被解決來定義？請好好思考這些問題。

Q1 ___*D*___ （A）international（adj. 國際的）
　　　　（B）intend（v. 打算）
　　　　（C）interactively（adv. 互相作用地）
　► （D）internally（adv. 內部地）

　　▶解析　對等連接詞 "and" 的後面是副詞 "externally"，所以空格處應該選擇（D）internally。

Q2 ___*A*___ ►（A）Factors（n. 因素）
　　　　（B）Factories（n. 工廠）
　　　　（C）Face（v. 面對）
　　　　（D）Finally（adv. 最後）

　　▶解析　從 "that" 到 "acquisitions" 是形容詞子句，修飾先行詞，從選項可知只有（A）Factors 符合句意。

Q3 __A__ ▶（A）exceed（v. 超過）

（B）export（v. 出口）

（C）expert（n. 專家）

（D）especially（adv. 特別地）

▶解析 "exceed the cost"，意為「超過費用」，因此正確答案是（A）exceed。

Q4 __B__ （A）less（adj. 較少的，用在不可數名詞）

▶（B）fewer（adj. 較少的，用在可數名詞）

（C）more（adj. 較多的）

（D）the most（最多的）

▶解析 空格處的後面是可數名詞 "risks"，而 "fewer ＋可數名詞" 表示「較少的事物」，因此正確答案是（B）fewer。

Q5 __A__ ▶（A）which（關係代名詞，表「事物」）

（B）where（關係副詞，表「地點」）

（C）when（關係副詞，表「時間」）

（D）who（關係代名詞，表「人類」）

▶解析 "which" 引導後面的子句修飾事物名詞 "mission"，因此正確答案是（A）which。

UNIT 3 Study 8 學生與考試

Students are afraid of tests. **Whenever** [1] a test or an examination is approaching, they start to **become** [2] nervous. On the eve of their tests, they usually worry that they will fail **in** [3] their tests, so they burn the midnight oil in the hope that they will be able to get better grades. **As a matter of fact** [4], tests are part of a students' lives. Why should they be afraid?

As students, they ought to study hard and prepare for their future careers. So I think that a test is only used to test whether a student is <u>fully prepared</u> [5].

　　學生都害怕考試。**每當**接近考試或測驗的日子，他們就會開始**變得緊張**。在考試的前一天晚上，他們經常會擔心自己在測驗中失常，所以他們熬夜唸書，希望能獲得更好的成績。**事實上**，測驗是學生生活的一部分，為什麼他們要害怕考試呢？身為學生，他們應該是要用功讀書，並為自己將來的職業做準備。所以我認為測驗只是用來評量一個學生是**準備充足**罷了。

Q1　*B*　（A）Whatever（無論什麼）

　　　　▶（B）Whenever（無論何時；每當）

　　　　（C）Whichever（無論是哪一個）

　　　　（D）However（無論如何）

　　　▶**解析**　"whenever" 意為「每當」，所有選項中只有（B）Whenever 才是正確答案。

Q2　*D*　（A）getting

　　　　（B）get become

　　　　（C）becoming

　　　　▶（D）become

　　　▶**解析**　"to" 後面要加原形動詞，"become" 是「變得」的意思，因此正確答案是（D）become。

Q3　*B*　（A）to

　　　　▶（B）in

　　　　（C）out

　　　　（D）off

　　　▶**解析**　"fail in＋N"，意為「在某事上失敗」，因此正確答案是（B）in。

242

Q4 ___D___ （A）With（prep. 具有；隨著）
（B）However（adv. 然而）
（C）Nevertheless（adv. 儘管如此）
▶（D）As a matter of fact（phr. 事實上）

▶解析 片語 "as a matter of fact" 意為「事實上」，在句首修飾整個句子，因此正確答案是（D）As a matter of fact。

Q5 ___A___ ▶（A）fully prepared（準備充足）
（B）totally wanted（完全想要）
（C）absolutely（絕對有收穫）
（D）extremely scared（極度恐懼）

▶解析 "be fully prepared" 意為「準備充足」，所有選項中只有（A）fully prepared 才是正確答案。。

UNIT 3 Study 9 如何克服考試焦慮

Some people think high grades are not only obtained by burning the midnight oil on the eve of a test. In addition [1], the most effective way to learn is to ask your teacher to explain what you don't understand, to practice what you learn, and to put to use [2] what you acquire.

When you know that a test is approaching [3], you ought to relax. When you relax, you will be able to [4] develop your abilities and potential. You will find that it is very easy for you to answer all the questions on your test because relaxation can help you remember better. So nervousness during an examination can have a negative effect [5].

　　有些人認為高分不只是靠考前一晚熬夜唸書才獲得的。除此之外，最有效的學習方法就是去請老師解釋你不懂的地方、練習你所學習的東西，並且應用你所學到的。

　　當你知道考試快要接近時，你應該要放輕鬆。當你放輕鬆時，你將能夠發揮你的能力和潛能。你會發現對你而言，回答考試卷上的題目非常容易，因為放鬆能幫助你更順利記住。所以，緊張在考試期間可能會產生負面的效果。

Q1 ___*D*___　（A）In addition to（除此之外）
　　　　　　（B）Additional（adj. 附加的）
　　　　　　（C）Added（adj. 附加的）
▶　　　　　（D）In addition（另外）

　▶解析　"in addition" 意為「除此之外」，轉折詞的用法，而空格處在句首，因此正確答案是（D）In addition。

Q2 ___*A*___ ▶（A）put to use（應用）
　　　　　　（B）pull over（把～開到路邊）
　　　　　　（C）put out（撲滅）
　　　　　　（D）put on（穿上）

　▶解析　此句是說「應用你所學到的」，而 "put to use" 意為「應用」，因此正確答案是（A）put to use。

Q3 ___*B*___　（A）in the way（妨礙）
▶　　　　　（B）approaching（V-ing 接近）
　　　　　　（C）appreciating（appreciate「欣賞」的動名詞）
　　　　　　（D）application（n. 應用）

　▶解析　"be approaching" 表示某件事物的即將到來，因此正確答案是（B）approaching。

Q4   *A* ▶（A）will be able to

（B）can be able to

（C）may well be

（D）could be able to

▶ 解析   "be able to＋VR" 表示「能夠做某事」，未來式直接在前頭加上 will，而（B）、（C）、（D）選項皆是錯誤的，因此正確答案是（A）will be able to。

Q5   *C* （A）affect（v. 影響）

（B）affective（adj. 感情的）

▶（C）effect（n. 影響）

（D）enable（v. 賦予）

▶ 解析   空格處前有不定冠詞和形容詞，很明顯是要填入名詞，因此正確答案是（C）effect。

UNIT 3   Study 10   廣告

The most important purpose of advertising is to <u>inform</u> [1] customers of some products or services. The second purpose is to <u>sell</u> [2] products. The second purpose is utterly important to <u>manufacturers</u> [3]. <u>Due to</u> [4] advertisements, consumers think they really need something and will then buy it. After <u>buying</u> [5] the product, sometimes the consumers will complain to themselves, "Why do I need this?"

廣告最重要的目的在於告知消費者有某些產品與服務，第二個目的在於銷售產品。第二個目的對製造商來說是十分重要的，因為廣告，消費者覺得自己真的需要某項商品，接著會去購買。在購買商品之後，有時候消費者會埋怨自己：「為什麼我需要這個東西呢？」

Q1 ___*B*___ （A）information（n. 資訊）
► （B）inform（v. 告知）
（C）be informed（被告知）
（D）be acknowledged（被承認）

▶ 解析 "to inform sb of sth" = "to acknowledge sb of sth"，意為「告知某人某事」，空格處應填入主動語態的動詞，因此正確答案是（B）inform。

Q2 ___*D*___ （A）buy（v. 購買）
（B）send（v. 傳送）
（C）rent（v. 租）
► （D）sell（v. 販售）

▶ 解析 "sell products" 意為「販賣商品」，因此正確答案是（D）sell。

Q3 ___*A*___ ► （A）manufacturers（n. 製造商）
（B）customers（n. 顧客）
（C）consumers（n. 消費者）
（D）constructors（n. 營造商）

▶ 解析 此處必須根據上下文來選擇答案，空格處的下一句指出「消費者覺得自己真的需要某項商品」，因此可以推測出廣告對（A）manufacturers 很重要。

Q4 ___*C*___ （A）Because（conj. 因為）
（B）Now that（既然）
► （C）Due to（由於）
（D）As（conj. 當）

▶ 解析 "due to＋N" 意為「由於」，其他選項均為連接詞，後面要接子句，因此正確選項是（C）Due to。

Q5 ___*C*___ （A）bought
（B）buy
► （C）buying
（D）buyed

246

▶ 解析 空格處的原句應為 "After they bought" ，而省略動詞的句型變成 "After buying..." ，因此正確答案是（C）buying。

UNIT 3 Study 11 移民

There are a good number of immigrants all over the world. Immigrants move to other countries <u>for</u> ¹ different reasons. Wars, political and economic problems, or natural <u>disasters</u> ², like floods and earthquakes are all possible reasons. Of course, some people move to marry or to find better living conditions. When immigrants arrive in a new country, they often live in urban or suburban areas. <u>As a result of immigration</u> ³, many city neighborhoods change a lot. <u>For instance</u> ⁴, in San Francisco and Los Angeles, China towns are full of Chinese stores and restaurants. If you walk in China towns, you will just feel like walking in China, not the United States. Also, in Miami, you can find many Cuban stores and bakeries in some specific areas. People <u>living</u> ⁵ there can easily buy some special Cuban food and cuisines.

世界各地有大量的移民。移民因為不同的原因而移居其他的國家去。戰爭、政治和經濟的問題，或像是洪水和地震的自然災害，全都是可能的因素。當然，有些人移民是要去結婚，或是為了尋找更好的生活條件。當移民抵達一個新的國家時，他們通常住在城市的或是市郊的區域。由於移民的因素，很多城市的鄰近區域都有很多改變。舉例來說，在舊金山與洛杉磯，中國城內充滿了中國式的商店與餐廳。假如你走在中國城內，你將會感覺像是走進了中國，而不是美國。此外，在邁阿密，你可以在一些特定的區域找到許多古巴的商店與烘焙坊。住在那裡的人們可以很容易地買到特別的古巴食物與菜餚。

Q1 *A* ▶ （A）for
（B）by
（C）to
（D）on

▶️ 解析　本句是說「移民因為不同的原因而搬到其他的國家去」，"for some reasons" 是指「因為某些原因」，因此答案為（A）for。

Q2 *A* ▶ （A）disasters（n. 災難）
（B）warts（n. 疣）
（C）vacancies（n. 空缺）
（D）emergencies（n. 緊急事故）

▶️ 解析　本句是說「戰爭、政治或是經濟的問題，或像是洪水或地震的自然災害全都是可能的因素」，因此答案為（A）disasters。

Q3 *C* （A）In accordance with traditions（根據傳統）
（B）When it comes to immigration
（談到移民時）
▶ （C）As a result of immigration（由於移民的因素）
（D）In addition to living conditions
（除了生活條件之外）

▶️ 解析　本句是說「由於移民的因素，很多城市的鄰近區域都有很大的改變」，因此正確答案是（C）As a result of immigration。

Q4 *D* （A）On the contrary（正相反）
（B）To sum up（總而言之）
（C）Despite the fact that（儘管如此）
▶ （D）For instance（舉例而言）

▶解析 本句是說「舉例而言，在舊金山與洛杉磯，中國城內充滿了中國式的商店與餐廳」，因此答案為（D）For instance。

Q5 ___*C*___ （A）live
（B）to live
▶（C）living
（D）who living

▶解析 空格處原句的寫法是形容詞子句的結構，也就是 "People who live there ~ food and cuisines." 而 "who live there" 這句形容詞子句可以簡化成形容詞片語，即刪除關係代名詞 who 後，原來的動詞要改為現在分詞，因此答案為（C）living。

UNIT 3 Study 12 電視與電腦的發明

Television and computer are two important inventions that have a deep <u>influence</u> [1] on human beings all over the world. Television was invented in 1926 by John Logie Baird, a Scottish inventor. It was made of a box, knitting needles, a bicycle lamp, and a cake tin. Twenty years later, the first computer was built in 1946 by two American engineers. Later in 1972, the "microchip" was used, and small home computers were first <u>produced</u> [2] for personal use. That's <u>extremely</u> [3] different from the original one which was large enough to take an entire room. That's very hard to believe, <u>isn't it</u> [4]? Both of these inventions are imperative in the history. <u>People say</u>

that the more we have, the more we want. [5] That is to say, there must be more new inventions in this modern world in the near future.

中文翻譯

電視與電腦是兩項對世界各地的人類有深刻**影響**的重大發明。電視是在 1926 年被一名蘇格蘭的發明家 John Logie Baird 所發明的。它是用一個箱子、編織用的針、一個腳踏車燈以及一個蛋糕烤盤所製成。二十年後，第一台的電腦在 1946 年由兩位美國的工程師所製成。之後在 1972 年，「微晶片」開始被使用，而小型的家庭式電腦以個人用途首次**生產**。這和原本大到佔整個房間的電腦**非常**不同。那很難相信吧，**不是嗎**？這兩項發明都在歷史上非常重要。人們說：「擁有的愈多，想要的愈多。」也就是說，在不久的將來一定會有更多新的發明在這現代世界出現。

Q1 ___*C*___ （A）affection（n. 情感；影響）
　　　　（B）security（n. 安全）
　▶（C）influence（n. 影響）
　　　　（D）submission（n. 服從）

　▶解析　本句是說「電視與電腦是兩項對全世界的人類有深刻影響的重大發明」，因此答案為（C）influence。

Q2 ___*C*___ （A）product（n. 產品）
　　　　（B）production（n. 生產）
　▶（C）produced（V-p.p. 生產）
　　　　（D）productivity（n. 生產力）

　▶解析　本句是說「之後在 1972 年，微晶片開始被使用，而小型的家庭式電腦以個人用途首次生產。」其中 "produce" 為動詞，"were produced" 是被動語態，即「被生產」的意思，因此答案為（C）produced。

Q3 ___*C*___ （A）comfortably（adv. 舒適地）
　　　　（B）repetitively（adv. 重複地）

▶（C）extremely（adv. 非常）

（D）authentically（adv. 真實地）

▶解析　本句是說「這和原本大到佔整個房間的電腦非常不同」，因此正確答案為（C）extremely。

Q4　　*D*　　（A）doesn't it

（B）does it

（C）is it

▶（D）isn't it

▶解析　本句是說「那很難相信吧，不是嗎？」這題考的是附加問句的概念，"That's very hard to believe"是肯定句，因此要配否定的附加問句，"that"的代名詞為"it"，因此正確答案是（D）isn't it。

Q5　　*A*　▶（A）People say that the more we have, the more we want.（人們說：「擁有的愈多，想要的愈多。」）

（B）It is true that invention is not an easy thing.（發明並不是一件容易的事是真的。）

（C）Without a doubt, more people will put forth more advice.（無疑地，更多的人將提出更多的建議。）

（D）What we want to invest is more and more overwhelming.（我們想要投資的東西是越來越難以抗拒。）

▶解析　這題要根據前後文來作答，前句表示「兩項發明均是歷史上最重要的發明。」後句則說「換句話說，在不久的未來，一定會有更多新的發明在這現代世界出現」，因此正確答案是（A）People say that the more we have, the more we want。

251

Reading Articles

CHAPTER 5
閱讀理解

|最|常|考|生|活|情|境|題|型|

UNIT 1 生活休閒類

作答說明 本部份會有數段短文，每段短文後有 1-5 個相關問題。請就試題上 A、B、C、D 四個選項中，選出最合適者填入空格中。

Study 1 Kwanzaa

When the short days of winter begin, many cultural and religious groups celebrate holidays that incorporate the use of light to symbolize peace, love and togetherness. These celebrations often encourage people to look away from material concerns and spend time reflecting on what it means to be a good person. Jewish people celebrate Chanukah, Christians celebrate Christmas and Muslims, Ramadan.

Within the last few decades some African-Americans have begun to celebrate their culture. This holiday is known as Kwanzaa. Commonly believed by many to be based on an ancient African tradition, Kwanzaa was established in 1966 in the United States, though it does **draw on** several African traditions. It is celebrated from December 26th to January 1st every year.

Each of the days of Kwanzaa is acknowledged by the lighting of a candle. The candles are held in a special candle holder called a kinara. Each of the seven days also has a special theme around which **celebrants** can focus their reflections. These are: unity, self-determination, collective work and responsibility, cooperative economics, purpose, creativity, and faith.

Kwanzaa provides a time for African-Americans, who may come from many different faiths, to celebrate their shared history, struggles and successes. The universality of the seven daily themes bridges different belief systems, thus creating a holiday that shares the seasonal subjects of peace and togetherness while at the same time observing the uniqueness of African-American experiences.

Q1 _____ **Kwanzaa is** _____.

（A）an old African custom

（B）a holiday developed by African-Americans

（C）the African version of Chanukah

（D）a time of peace

Q2 _____ **The author says that it is important for the seven themes observed during Kwanzaa to be general because** _____.

（A）they need to compete with the other holidays at that time

（B）they are based on African traditions which are hard to translate

（C）it is celebrated by African Americans who come from many different religious backgrounds

（D）they need to be easier for children to understand

Q3 _____ **What does the holiday of Kwanzaa imply about African Americans?**

（A）That they have a unique history that is not adequately reflected in other American institutions.

（B）That they dislike non-African holidays.

（C）That none of them are Christian, Jewish or Muslim and thus need their own holiday.

（D）That African Americans don't agree with the way peace is expressed in other holidays.

Q4 _____ **In this passage, what does 'celebrants' mean?**

（A）A time to celebrate.

（B）A person who celebrates.

（C）Objects that one uses in a celebration.

（D）It's another word that also means celebration.

Q5 _____ **In this passage, what does 'draw on' mean?**

（A）To make a picture on a surface.

（B）To describe something.

（C）To borrow ideas.

（D）To get water.

Study 2 THANKSGIVING

If you notice foreigners in Taiwan hunting around for a turkey, then you can guess that it's probably time for Thanksgiving in North America. The arrival of Europeans to North America, or the "New World" as they called it, is **commemorated** by the festival of Thanksgiving, and it typically includes a turkey dinner. In Canada, this holiday is observed on the second weekend of October, and in the United States it is observed on the last weekend of November.

Of course, for the aboriginal people who were already living there when the Europeans arrived, North America was far from a new world. The conflicts between the European settlers who sought to **colonize** North America and the aboriginals who struggled to preserve their land and independence have made the idea of "celebrating" the arrival of Europeans distasteful for many. Some people choose to see Thanksgiving as a harvest holiday instead and prepare a large meal as a celebration of the bountifulness of the fall season.

Whatever their political leanings are, many people have fond memories of delicious meals shared with family. Their efforts in

Taiwan to find a turkey and acknowledge the holiday are, at heart, a way to enjoy something familiar in a foreign place.

Q1 _____ **What does the author suggest about the arrival of Europeans in North America?**

（A）That it was peaceful.

（B）That it was mutually beneficial for the aboriginal people and the new settlers.

（C）That few people can remember it, so no one wants to celebrate it.

（D）That it was marked by conflict.

Q2 _____ **For people who don't want to observe the coming of Europeans to North America, what is the other significance of Thanksgiving?**

（A）It is a time of the year to reflect on diversity.

（B）It is a time to celebrate the harvest.

（C）It is a time to celebrate aboriginal culture in North America.

（D）It is time to celebrate North American cuisine.

Q3 _____ **Why do people continue to observe Thanksgiving in spite of its contentious roots?**

（A）It has become a popular time of year for family to gather.

（B）North Americans just really love turkey.

（C）Turkey farmers aggressively promote the holiday all over the world.

（D）No one really knows why.

Q4 _____ **What does "commemorated" mean in this passage?**

（A）To remember friends.

（B）To honor something or someone with a ceremony.

（C）To have a party.

（D）To eat a meal with family.

Q5 _____ **What does "colonize" mean in this passage?**

（A）To build a home.

（B）To emigrate.

（C）To conquer people and take control of land.

（D）To leave a place.

Study 3 MINI-PICTURES

About ten years ago, if you looked closely at people's key chains or cell phones in Taipei, you might notice tiny, colorful photographs. The photographs typically depicted two or more people grinning madly or making silly faces at the camera. These pictures had bright backgrounds or messages framing the smiling faces.

These mini-pictures were enormously popular among teenagers at that time. Groups of teens out for a good time on a weekend evening might all pile into a picture booth to have some photos done. Sweethearts or best friends also had mini-photos taken as a memento of their relationship.

There were several things that made mini-photos so entertaining. The **atmosphere** in the photo booth was very lively and energetic. There was loud, pulsating pop music and everything was brightly lit. Another appealing aspect is that the photographs could be personalized or made unique for different occasions. The buyer could choose from a variety of backgrounds or holiday messages. In some cases, people wrote their own messages, such as "Together Forever" or "We're #1". Finally, the photos were inexpensive, so people could easily purchase many copies of different poses and could return many times.

Judging by the bustle of activity at any mini-photo shops, it seemed that the trend was thriving at that time. It was difficult to find room to pass on the sidewalk in front of one of these establishments. Although the mini-photos had their originality and affordability, their popularity faded after the emerging of smartphones.

Q1 _____ **Where did the author say people could find examples of mini-photos?**

（A）In photo booths.

（B）At night markets.

（C）On people's cell phones and key chains.

（D）In people's wallets.

Q2 _____ **Which kind of people would you most likely see at a mini-photo booth?**

（A）Close friends.

（B）Sweethearts.

（C）Classmates.

（D）Teenagers.

Q3 _____ **Why were mini-photos so popular at that time?**

（A）They were easy to make.

（B）They were cheap and can be made unique.

（C）The music played in the shops was pulsating.

（D）All the above are correct.

Q4 _____ **What does the author imply about the future popularity of mini-photos?**

（A）The trend may not be slowing down.

（B）Something else will take its place soon.

（C）There is no reason for its popularity to decrease.

（D）Teenagers are fickle and will soon be onto something new.

Q5 _____ **What does "atmosphere" mean in this passage?**

（A）The feeling and look of a place.

（B）The air.

（C）Outer space.

（D）The location.

Study 4 Blizzards

In Southeast Asia, people keep an eye out for the high wind and heavy rain of typhoons. In North America, blizzards are what cause trouble. From January to March, as winter tightens its hold on the central and eastern parts of the North American continent, the risk of blizzards is at the highest level. People living in these areas do what they can to prepare for these paralyzing storms.

A blizzard is characterized by winds of 55 kilometers per hour or more, snowfall of at least five centimeters an hour, temperatures near -20 degrees Celsius, and visibility of less than half a kilometer. They occur when warm air rises and pulls moisture from the Atlantic Ocean. The moisture moves inland and turns to snow as temperatures drop. It's the high wind and heavy snow that create chaos. People caught in a blizzard can be stranded during the storm, as well as after, as they struggle to clear the towering snowdrifts.

To prepare for the possibility of blizzards, many people living in central and eastern North America put emergency kits in their cars. During a blizzard, drivers are forced by the poor visibility to pull over and wait out the storm. Some of the things that people stock in the trunks of their cars are blankets, flashlights, batteries and **non-perishable** food. It's also considered a good idea to include a can and waterproof matches to melt snow for drinking in addition to a shovel, sand, a tow-rope, and jumper cables to help you get going again when the storm is over. These kinds of things don't take up much room and they become important for survival in case of an emergency. Thinking before blizzards come saves lives.

Q1 _____ **Where are blizzards a problem?**

（A）In the Atlantic Ocean.

（B）On the west coast of North America.

（C）In the central and eastern parts of North America.

（D）In Southeast Asia.

Q2 _____ **What makes blizzards so dangerous?**

（A）The rain freezes into ice as temperatures drop and the roads become slippery.

（B）People can be stranded because the limited visibility makes it impossible to travel.

（C）People can run out of supplies.

（D）People can freeze to death in the low temperatures.

Q3 _____ **What separates a blizzard from other storms?**

（A）The size of the snowdrifts.

（B）The geographic location.

（C）The speed of the wind, the amount of snowfall and the limited visibility.

（D）The wind comes from the east instead of the west.

Q4 _____ **What can people do to ensure that they survive a blizzard if they are trapped in their cars?**

（A）Keep a cell phone to call for help.

（B）Avoid traveling during blizzard warnings.

（C）Keep moving until they outrun the blizzard.

（D）Keep supplies in the trunks of their cars.

Q5 _____ **What does "non-perishable" mean in this passage?**

（A）Does not spoil easily.

（B）Light-weight.

（C）Not difficult to prepare.

（D）Packed in a can or plastic bag.

MISSION DOLORES, SAN FRANCISCO

One of the most interesting and historical tourist attractions in San Francisco is a building created to house the work of the missionaries who worked in the name of Saint Francis of Assisi. This saint is also the city's namesake. The original mission can still be viewed, and an educational museum has been founded to provide tourists with information.

Established in 1776, this is the oldest intact Mission of Saint Francis in the United States. Local aborigines who had been converted by the missionaries finished construction of the four-foot thick adobe walls in 1791. The priest who supervised the construction recorded that 36,000 adobe bricks were used to complete the structure. The original redwood logs used as support beams are still in place. In the present museum, there is a stunning photograph taken just after the earthquake that rocked San Francisco in 1906. In it, one can see that although the church immediately beside the mission building was completely destroyed, the mission itself stood strong. The photo is a **testament** to the solid construction of the building.

Some highlights of the self-guided tour that visitors can take are a diorama of the mission complex as it looked circa 1791; a series of drawings and photographs tracing the mission's history exhibited in a covered walkway, which includes images created in the 18th century; and the cemetery. The cemetery is a lovely garden that contains the graves of people buried from the beginning of the mission until the 1890s. It is a very peaceful place to spend a few minutes in quiet meditation at the end of the tour.

If you take the time to visit the Mission Delores while in San Francisco, you won't be disappointed.

Q1 _____ **What is the relationship between the Mission Delores and the city of San Francisco?**

（A）The mission serves in the name of the same saint that the city was named after.

（B）The mission was established by the city.

（C）The mission pre-dates the city.

（D）The city promotes the mission as a tourist attraction.

Q2 _____ **What makes the mission unique?**

（A）Its size.

（B）It was built by aboriginals.

（C）The original building is still standing.

（D）The design.

Q3 _____ **What can one see on a visit to the mission?**

（A）A memorial to those who died in the earthquake of 1906.

（B）A model showing how the mission was built.

（C）A tour guide who will show you around the museum.

（D）Drawings, photographs, a model of the original mission and the old cemetery.

Q4 _____ **What does the author imply about this tourist attraction?**

（A）That it is crowded and you will need a rest after seeing it.

（B）That it's something every visitor should see.

（C）That it is a little disappointing.

（D）That there is nothing unique about the building.

Q5 _____ **What does "testament" mean in this passage?**

（A）Evidence.

（B）An agreement.

（C）A document that details how a person's property will be settled after death.

（D）Either one of the two books of the Bible.

Study 6 CELINE DION

Celine Dion started performing as a singer at the age of 5 as part of a family music group in Charlemagne, Quebec in Canada. She was the youngest of fourteen children and music was a big part of her **upbringing**. Over the years, her fame has spread, and now people all over the world listen to the romantic ballads of this pop music superstar.

The pop music diva was born in 1968 and originally became popular in her home country, singing and recording in her mother tongue, French. In 1990, she took the risk of learning enough English to record an English CD, which was very successful in her home country and in the United States. She became an international sensation in 1996 after the release of her single, "Because You Loved Me," which was number one on music charts around the world. Later, she was under contract to perform at Caesars Palace in Las Vegas for three years and she also recorded some hit songs.

Q1 _____ **How did Celine Dion start her music career?**

（A）She was a music teacher.

（B）She sang in public with her family.

（C）She recorded an English CD.

（D）She traveled around the world with a singing group.

Q2 _____ What is Celine Dion's nationality?

（A）French.

（B）Quebecois.

（C）American.

（D）Canadian.

Q3 _____ What did she sign a contract to do for three years?

（A）To record more French CDs.

（B）To record only English CDs.

（C）To sing at Caesar's Palace.

（D）To make hit songs.

Q4 _____ For what kind of songs is she best known?

（A）The blues.

（B）Dance music.

（C）Love songs.

（D）Choral music.

Q5 _____ What does the word "upbringing" on line 4 mean?

（A）A period of studying English.

（B）A period of growing up.

（C）A period of being a mother.

（D）A period of learning singing.

Study 7 THAI FOOD

If you **have a penchant** for spicy dishes, Thai food is a must for you. Thai food can be so hot that travel guides recommend that travelers to Thailand learn how to say, "Mild, please," in the local language to avoid any bad experiences. The key to this flavorful cuisine is its incorporation of the freshest ingredients with generous use of garlic and red chilies. In addition to a reputation for being hot, Thai food has a characteristic tangy flavor derived from combinations of lime, lemongrass, and coriander. Other dishes have a uniquely salty flavor produced by special Thai fish sauces or shrimp paste.

Thai dishes are usually rice or noodle with meat, seafood, and vegetables and are typically ordered family-style so that diners can sample a variety of tastes. If you've never experienced Thai food, make a point of getting to a Thai restaurant soon. You won't regret it!

Q1 _____ **How does the author feel about Thai food?**
（A）It's too spicy.
（B）It's good, but you need to add extra garlic and chilies to give it flavor.
（C）It's really great food, but you have to travel to Thailand to get the best stuff.
（D）Anyone who likes spicy food should try Thai food.

Q2 _____ **If you have never eaten Thai food, what does the author recommend?**
（A）You should learn how to speak Thai first.
（B）You should to ask the cook to use only the freshest ingredients.
（C）You shouldn't delay going to a Thai restaurant.
（D）You should order some for your whole family.

Q3 _____ **According to the article, what kinds of flavors predominate in Thai cuisine?**
（A）Hot, spicy and tangy flavors.
（B）Sweet flavors.
（C）Sour, bitter tastes.
（D）Bland flavors.

Q4 _____ **What does the phrase "have a penchant" on the first line mean?**

（A）Dislike.

（B）Be fond.

（C）Have a hobby.

（D）Catch.

Study 8 DOGS AS FRIENDS

I like dogs very much because they are our best friends. Dogs have a close relationship with human beings. They are intelligent and loyal animals. They are human beings' companions, too. When we need them, they are beside us all the time.

Dogs are faithful to their masters. If their masters are attacked, they will bark at their masters' attackers loudly, and even attack them. **Dogs are by no means snobbish**. They never desert their masters because their masters are poor or sick. Some dogs even guard the tombs of their deceased masters until they die of **starvation**. So, we love them all the more for their loyalty.

Dogs are so useful. Basically, all dogs can watch our houses. Of course, for instance, they can help in hunting. They can also track down fugitives and detect drugs. They can sniff out whether there are survivors under the ruins.

No wonder so many people love to keep a dog as a pet. Dogs are really cute animals. I have had a cute dog for three years. We often play with each other and even sometimes I talk to the dog about my secrets.

Q1 _____ **What's the best title of the article?**

（A）Dogs are human beings' best friends.

（B）How to protect our dogs?

（C）Dogs and cats.

（D）How to raise dogs?

Q2 _____ **According to the article, what is not the main reason why dogs are useful?**

（A）Because they can watch our houses.

（B）Because they can find out the lives under the ruins.

（C）Because they can detect guns.

（D）Because they are faithful to their masters.

Q3 _____ **Which statement is not true?**

（A）Dogs have a close relationship with human beings.

（B）Dogs desert their masters because they're poor or sick.

（C）Some dogs even guard tombs of their deceased masters until they die for starvation.

（D）Dogs can help in hunting.

Q4 _____ **What does the sentence "Dogs are by no means snobbish" mean?**

（A）Dogs are not snobbish enough.

（B）Dogs are absolutely snobbish.

（C）Dogs are not snobbish at all.

（D）Dogs are snobbish sometimes.

Q5 _____ **The word "starvation" means?**

（A）very cold.

（B）very tired.

（C）very hungry.

（D）very sleepy.

UNIT 2　書信應用類

作答說明　本部份會有數段短文，每段短文後有 1-5 個相關問題。請就試題上 A、B、C、D 四個選項中，選出最合適者填入空格中。

Study 1　A sign

Restricted Area

Authorized Personnel Only
This area contains hazardous chemical materials.
Trespassers will be charged with mischief
and could be fined up to $25,000NT.

Q1 _____ **The sign warns people to stay out because _____.**
（A）the area has chemicals and other things that are dangerous
（B）this is a private home
（C）dangerous animals are being kept in the area
（D）secret research is being conducted here

Q2 _____ **People who sneak into the area will _____.**
（A）win some money
（B）be fined
（C）be beaten
（D）be hired by the company

Q3 _____ **You might see this warning sign** _____.

（A）in front of the White House

（B）by a dangerous river which runs extremely rapid

（C）in front of a chemical laboratory

（D）on the street where the traffic is really bad

Study 2 A notice

Notice:

If your appliance unexpectedly stops, turn it off, unplug it and wait five minutes for it to cool down. Then press the red "Reset" button on the safety plug until it clicks and your appliance will resume normal operation.

Q1 _____ **You need to wait for your appliance to cool down** _____.

（A）before unplugging it

（B）after each use

（C）if it turns itself off before you are finished using it

（D）when you hear it click

Q2 _____ **After you press the reset button, the appliance should** _____.

（A）start working again

（B）be repaired

（C）cool down for five minutes

（D）heat up

Study 3 A table

Triple 8 Long Distance Super Saver

Dial Triple 8 between October 1st and November 1st for big savings on overseas long distance rates.

Countries	Regular Rates	Super Saver Rates
Canada/USA	0.59 NTD / min	0.19 NTD / min
Singapore	1.3 NTD / min	0.59 NTD / min
Japan	1.3 NTD /min	0.59 NTD / min
Hong Kong	1.0 NTD / min	0.29 NTD / min

*Super Saver rates available from 8 a.m. to 8 p.m. on weekdays and all day long on weekends. For information on rates for other overseas locations, contact our customer service line.

Q1 _____ **When are the Super Saver discounts available?**

（A）From 8 a.m. to 8 p.m. every day.

（B）All day long, effective October 1st.

（C）For the month of October on weekends and from 8 a.m. to 8 p.m. on weekdays.

（D）Weekends only.

Q2 _____ **What countries are not included in the special?**

（A）European countries.

（B）Australia.

（C）Thailand.

（D）You need to call the company to find out.

INSTRUCTIONS FOR USE

Shake canister before using. Depress the nozzle and place an egg-sized amount of product in the palm of your hand. Spread evenly through slightly damp hair with your fingers and style as usual. For best results, don't this overuse product. If irritation occurs, discontinue use. For external use only. If product gets into eyes or mouth, rinse with water immediately.

Q1 _____ **What are these instructions most likely for?**
（A）Cooking oil.
（B）Hair-styling mousse.
（C）Skin cream.
（D）Medicated moisturizer.

Q2 _____ **If your skin gets red or sore from using this product, what should you do?**
（A）To use less.
（B）To see a doctor.
（C）To make sure that you are shaking the canister well enough.
（D）To stop using the product.

Q3 _____ **What should be done to achieve the best result when you use this product?**
（A）To depress the nozzle to squeeze as much amount as you can.
（B）To use it three times a day.
（C）To spread it evenly through wet hair.
（D）To mix it with an egg.

Study 5 A COVER LETTER

To whom it may concern,

In response to your advertisement, I am interested in applying to the Marketing Manager position you offer. I believe my qualifications as listed below meet your requirement.

* Master's degree in Business Administration,
* Managerial skills, leadership training and experience,
* Computer knowledge & foreign languages (English & French)
* Interpersonal skills and open-minded personality.

I am primarily task-oriented but relate well to people and have no problem working in one place for an extended period of time. I am very persistent and determined in achieving a challenging and rewarding career. I have an interest in finding a satisfying job, an openness to innovation, and a willingness to accept changes. I also possess a great deal of energy and enthusiasm and wish never to stop growing throughout my life. Whenever I observe opportunities to learn or perform, I won't give them up.

Enclosed please find a copy of my resume which describes my background and experience in detail for your reference. I should be glad to have an opportunity to talk with you in person to get your opinion on whether I am qualified for the position you offer. I look forward to hearing from you very soon.

Sincerely yours,

Jeff Chen

Q1 _____ **Which statement is wrong?**

（A）The writer got a master's degree in Business Administration.

（B）The writer has managerial skills, leadership training and experience.

（C）The writer has an interest in finding a satisfying job, is open to innovation, and is willing to accept changes.

（D）The writer has computer knowledge and is conversant in foreign languages, including English & Japanese.

Q2 _____ **What is the purpose of this letter?**

（A）Rent a house

（B）Look for a Marketing Manager

（C）Find out a job

（D）Make a friend

Q3 _____ **How did the writer know this chance?**

（A）From the Internet.

（B）Someone told him.

（C）From an advertisement.

（D）By chance.

Q4 _____ **What kind of attachment does the writer enclose?**

（A）A recommendation.

（B）An application form.

（C）An autobiography.

（D）A resume.

Study 6 RULES

Rules

1. **Always be punctual**.
2. Dress neatly.
3. Don't litter and eat inside.
4. Clean your desk before going home.
5. Never cheat.

Q1 _____ **Where might a person see this?**

（A）In an apartment.

（B）In a living room.

（C）In a dorm.

（D）In a classroom.

Q2 _____ **What does the sentence "Always be punctual." mean?**

（A）You should arrive on time every day.

（B）You should be quiet all the time.

（C）You can sometimes chat with others.

（D）You are permitted to be late.

Q3 _____ **According to these rules, which is incorrect?**

（A）You cannot wear slippers.

（B）You can going home leaving a mess on your desk.

（C）You cannot have your breakfast in the classroom.

（D）Cheating is not permitted.

Study 7 A MENU

MENU

Dinner Specials

Steak ·· NT $700
Pork ··· NT $500
Fish Sandwich ································· NT $340
Sweet & Sour Pork ······················· NT $450
Fresh Salad ····································· NT $300
Super Hamburger ·························· NT $220

Desserts and Drinks

Apple Pie ··· NT $120
Cheesecake ····································· NT $100
Ice Cream ·· NT $85
Coffee ·· NT $80
Soda ··· NT $80
Tea ··· NT $80
Milk ·· NT $75

Q1 _____ **What is not on the menu?**

（A）Hot chocolate.

（B）Salad.

（C）Seafood.

（D）Apple pie.

Q2 _____ **You order a steak, an apple pie, and a coffee. How much are you going to pay?**

（A）NT $700.

（B）NT $800.

（C）At least NT $900.

（D）At least NT $2000.

Q3 _____ **You don't like hamburgers, sandwiches and meat. Which dinner special will you order?**

（A）Sweet & Sour pork.

（B）Fish.

（C）Salad.

（D）Apple pie.

Q4 _____ **Which statement is not true?**

（A）You can eat some desserts here.

（B）All drinks are the same price.

（C）If you order 2 cups of ice cream, you have to pay $170.

（D）You can eat apple pie here.

Study 8 A NOTE ON A WALL

Lost Property Notice

1. Object lost: A Purse
2. Color: Stripped
3. Shape Round
4. Special features: With a bell
5. Things inside: Keys and checks
6. Place where the object was lost: In the fitting room
7. If found, please call: 0967-432-588

Q1 _____ **What is the purpose of the notice?**

（A）To find lost property.

（B）To find a lost pet.

（C）To find lost money.

（D）To find a lost relative.

生活類 休閒類 書信類 應用類 記敘類 論說類 雙篇類 文章類 解答篇

277

Q2 _____ **If you find the lost property, what should you do?**

（A）You should go to the front desk.

（B）You should call the phone numbers on the notice.

（C）You should give it to the police.

（D）You should throw it away.

Study 9 AN APPLICATION FORM

SPS Club Membership Application Form

Name: __William__   Sex: __Male__

Date of birth: __1973/6/27__   Age: __47__

Address: __3F, #23, Park Street, Taipei, Taiwan__

Telephone no.: __0983-564-856__

Occupation: __An English teacher__

Interests: __Swimming and SPA__

Signature: __William__

Date: __2021/6/6__

Q1 _____ **What information doesn't the form ask for?**

（A）birth date.

（B）Job.

（C）Hobby.

（D）Zodiac.

Q2 _____ **Where does the applicant live?**

（A）Los Angeles

（B）Kuala Lumpur

（C）Taipei

（D）Berlin

Study 10 AN IMPORTANT INSTRUCTION

Flight Safety Instruction

1. Please shut down your mobile phones when getting on the plane.
2. Please put your personal belongings in the higher compartment.
3. Please keep your seatbelt fastened when the captain turns on the seatbelt sign.
4. Please don't smoke on the plane.

Q1 _____ **Where might a person see this?**

（A）At school.

（B）In a mobile phone store.

（C）In the food stand.

（D）On the plane

Q2 _____ **When should you fasten your seatbelt?**

（A）After you get on the plane.

（B）When the captain turns on the seatbelt sign.

（C）Before you go to the restroom.

（D）There's no need to do it.

Study 11 TEXTBOOK INDEX

Index

Q1 _____ On which pages of the textbook would one find the information about the stockholders of a company?

（A）pp. 77-93

（B）pp. 26-28

（C）pp. 35-39

（D）pp. 151-154

Q2 _____ On which pages of the textbook would one find the information about a sharp rise of prices resulting from the too great expansion in paper money or bank credit?

（A）pp. 77-93

（B）pp. 26-28

（C）pp. 35-39

（D）pp. 151-154

Study 12 ADVERTISEMENT

Wanted

Good at English Language School
Since 1994

Position: A part-time English teacher

Qualification: Master's degree, major in English literature

Working hours: 7:00-10:00 p.m., Mon.-Fri.

Contact: call May at (02)2395-8592 or Fax: (02)2365-8599

Working Area: Near Taipei Train Station

Q1 _____ **What person might have an interest in this advertisement?**

（A）A person who is looking for a job as a full-time math teacher.

（B）A person who wants to learn English well.

（C）A person who likes to speak English.

（D）A person who wants to be a part-time English teacher.

Q2 _____ **Which statement is incorrect?**

（A）If you are interested in this position, you should call May.

（B）In case you get this job, you will probably work near the Taipei Railway Station.

（C）The total working hours are around 60 per month.

（D）The position offered asks the candidate to have at least a bachelor's degree.

Study 13 A LETTER OF COMPLAINT

Dear Mr. Wang,

I am writing this letter to tell you I just had a terrible trip in Bali. I booked my hotel room with your company. However, it was the worst holiday that I have ever had.

On July 10th, I went to your Taipei office. I booked my plane ticket there and paid all money in cash. I was shown some beautiful pictures of Palace Hotel. The hotel was so beautiful, and it had at least two swimming pools and four special restaurants. I was told to have my breakfast on the beach. That's really wonderful.

However, actually, when I arrived on August 2nd, there was nobody to pick me up at the airport. To my surprise, when I got to the hotel, it was not beautiful at all. On the contrary, it was old, dirty, and ugly. In the room, there was not enough space for me to hang up my clothes. There were electric wires coming out of the wall above the bed, and there were some spiders on the wall. That was disgusting.

So, frankly speaking, I am not happy with the trip you arranged for me. Your lies have forced me to ask for my money back.

Yours,

Terry Smith

Q1 _____ **What is the purpose of this letter?**

（A）To make a compliment.

（B）To give a congratulation on recovery.

（C）To wish someone well.

（D）To complain to someone.

Q2 _____ **Which statement is incorrect?**

（A）Terry booked the plane tickets to Bali on July 10th.

（B）The travel agent told Terry that the Palace Hotel was very beautiful.

（C）This letter to Mr. Wang is to protest what took place.

（D）Terry will sue Mr. Wang after he gets money back.

生活類
休閒類

書信
應用類

記敘論說類

雙篇
文章類

解答篇

UNIT 3 記敘論說類

作答說明 本部份會有數段短文，每段短文後有 1-5 個相關問題。請就試題冊上 A、B、C、D 四個選項中，選出最合適者填入空格中。

Study 1 DIFFERENCES

Modern times are very different from old ones. At this modern time, people like to watch TV. Television has many advantages. It keeps us informed of the latest news and also provides entertainment in the home. On the other hand, television has been blamed for the violent behavior of some young people and for encouraging children to sit at home, instead of getting exercise.

Additionally, a long time ago, most towns and villages were very small. The number of people who lived in every country was a lot smaller than it is today, too. There was no heavy industry, only agriculture, arts, and crafts, and these things weren't going to damage our environment. People did not use chemicals. There were no motor vehicles and no factories. There was, therefore, very little pollution. The lifestyles between modern times and old times are extremely different.

Q1 _____ **What advantages doesn't television have?**

（A）It keeps us informed of the latest news.

（B）It provides entertainment.

（C）It provides to get exercise.

（D）It gives us lots of fun.

283

Q2 _____ **Which statement is wrong?**

（A）The number of people who lived in every country was much bigger than its today.

（B）There were no motor vehicles. There were no factories. There was, therefore, very little pollution.

（C）Television has been blamed for the violent behavior of some young people.

（D）A long time ago, most towns and villages were very small.

Study 2 Mexico

Let me tell you something about Mexico. Mexico, the largest nation in Middle America, provides a good example of life in the region. Although Mexico is a large country, only 12% of its land can be used for farming. Another 40% is the grazing land, not for farming. The rest of the land is hills and mountains, dry, high plateaus, or wet coastal regions, and they are all not good for farming. The mountains are too steep to farm. The high plateau in the middle of Mexico would be good farmland if it had more water. However, actually, it doesn't. For all of these reasons, Mexicans must take care of the good farmland they have. Economy Mexico is also in a poor condition. It is said that's because the political condition seriously and deeply influenced the economy of Mexico.

Q1 _____ **What is the topic of this paragraph?**

（A）Mexico and Economics

（B）Mexico and its agriculture.

（C）Mexican farmers

（D）Waterlogged land

Q2 _____ **Why are the mountains in Mexico hard to farm?**

（A）Because they are too dry

（B）Because they are hills

（C）Because they are waterlogged

（D）Because they are too steep

Q3 _____ **Which statement is wrong?**

（A）Mexico is the largest nation in Middle America and provides a good example of life in the region.

（B）Although Mexico is a large country, only 12% of its land is good for farming.

（C）The high plateau in the middle of Mexico would be good farmland if it had more water.

（D）There is no need for Mexico to take care of the good farmland they have.

Study 3 Sports

Sport is good for both body and mind. A person who seldom exercises will not only get ill very easily but have slow reflexes as well. Frankly speaking, being ill is not fun at all, and having slow reflexes can be dangerous. An ill person can't study efficiently, let alone write and read effectively. A "slow motion" person has a hard time handling sudden changes. Therefore, sport is very necessary for anyone. I'm a sports fanatic. I enjoy playing baseball, basketball, table tennis and tennis. My favorite sport, however, is swimming. When you swim, you actually exercise almost every muscles in your body. Also, there are two great things that swimming can do for you. In summer, swimming can cool you, and in winter it helps you adjust to cold weather. So, why not come swim with me and I'll wait for you there by the swimming pool. Be sure to come!

Q1 _____ **What does the author imply us to do?**

（A）In summer, we can go to the beach with the author.

（B）We are all "slow motion" people.

（C）People feeling ill can work well.

（D）People who don't do exercises get ill more easily.

Q2 _____ **Which statement is wrong?**

（A）Sport is good for both body and mind.

（B）A "slow motion" person has a hard time handling sudden changes.

（C）An ill person can study efficiently, let alone write and read.

（D）Sport is very necessary for anyone.

Study 4 Soccer

Soccer is a sport loved by people all over the world. Many games are held in different places every year. The World Cup is the game that all the players want to play most. It is held every four years. Only the best team will win the final game.

The 2018 World Cup was over. Hundreds of thousands of people went to the games or watched them on TV day and night. They all got very excited and hoped their favorite team becoming the world's best team and winning the final game. In 2018, France won the championship. Actually, they won once in 1998.

Soccer is a team sport. There are eleven players in each team of a game. The earliest soccer games in England were not like what they are today. Games were played between two towns. Each team had more than five hundred players. Is that hard to believe? Anyway, take my words for it.

Q1 _____ **The next World Cup will be held in?**

（A）2021.

（B）2022.

（C）2023.

（D）1924.

Q2 _____ **When soccer was first played in England, around how many players in each team?**

（A）Around 5000.

（B）Around 500.

（C）Around 11.

（D）Around 111.

Q3 _____ **Why do hundreds of thousands of people go to the World Cup games?**

（A）They want to watch their favorite time win.

（B）They are the players of the games.

（C）They love to drink the world's best cup of tea.

（D）They become coaches for each team.

Q4 _____ **Which statement is true?**

（A）People go to the World Cup games every year.

（B）The best team in 2018 was England.

（C）To soccer players, World Cup games are more important than any other game.

（D）The worst team in 2018 was France.

Q5 _____ **Which statement is not true?**

（A）Soccer is a popular sport.

（B）The earliest soccer games in England are just like what they are today.

（C）Hundreds of thousands of people go to the games or watch them on TV day and night.

（D）Many soccer games are held in different places every year.

Study 5 ABOUT TESTS

When it comes to tests, I'll say that most students are afraid of tests. Whenever a test or an examination is approaching, they start to get nervous. On the eve of tests, they usually worry that they will fail their tests, so they **burn the midnight oil** in the hope that they will be able to get better grades. As a matter of fact, tests are a part of a student's life. As students, they ought to study hard and prepare for their future careers. Thus, I think that a test is only used to test whether a student is fully prepared.

In reality, student ought to at ordinary times listen carefully to what his teacher says in the classroom, and review his homework after school. Rome was not built in one day; high grades are not obtained by burning the midnight oil on the eve of a test. The most effective way to learn is to ask your teacher to explain what you don't understand, to practice what you learn, and to put to use what you acquire.

When you know that a test is on the way, you ought to relax. When you relax, you will be able to develop any kind of abilities and potential, and you will find that it is very easy for you to answer all the questions on your test sheets. Therefore, we just do our best to do it, everything will be all right. Anything can be achieved by diligence.

Q1 _____ **What does "burn the midnight oil" in the first paragraph mean?**

（A）Stay up late.

（B）Make a dinner.

（C）Fill up some gas

（D）Oil is lighter than water.

Q2 _____ **Why are students afraid of tests?**

（A）Because they have to pay more money for the tests.

（B）Because they may fail in passing the tests.

（C）Because they don't have much time to study at home.

（D）Because they don't like their teachers.

Q3 _____ **What is good for you to do when an exam is coming?**

（A）Relaxing.

（B）Cheating.

（C）Complaining.

（D）Doing nothing.

Q4 _____ **Which statement is not true?**

（A）High grades are not obtained by burning the midnight oil on the eve of a test.

（B）A test is only used to test whether a student is fully prepared.

（C）The most effective way to learn not to practice what you learn and not to put to use what you acquire.

（D）A student ought to pay attention to what his teacher says in the classroom, and review his homework after school.

Q5 _____ **What's the best title for the article?**

（A）Stop testing students as soon as possible.

（B）How to get good grades in your school.

（C）Students and tests.

（D）We should learn how to avoid tests.

AUNT AGATHA

Aunt Agatha almost ruined Tom and Mary's marriage. She arrived unexpectedly one spring day just after their 20th wedding anniversary. For Tom and Mary, that day was really a tragedy. Agatha announced that she wanted to visit for a week, but she stayed for the next 15 years. That's really a long time.

Agatha was bad-tempered and selfish. She wanted to watch "her" shows on TV and didn't let others watch theirs. She decided what they ate for meals. She complained about everything all the time. Eventually, after 15 years, she died. They buried her in the cemetery by the village church. After the funeral, Tom wrapped his arms around his wife and comforted her.

"I know you are upset, sweetheart," he said, "But try to **look on the bright side**. We can be alone again finally."

"I know, but I have a confession to make. I hated every day Agatha stayed with us. I only put up with her because she was your aunt" she said.

"My aunt?" yelled Tom. "I thought she was your aunt!"

Q1 _____ **What does "look on the bright side" in the third paragraph mean?**

（A）Be positive.

（B）Be nice to others.

（C）Be confident in everything.

（D）Be more passive.

Q2 _____ **How long did the aunt say she wanted to stay?**

（A）15 years.

（B）20 days.

（C）One week.

（D）50 days.

Q3 _____ **Where did they bury her?**

（A）In the church.

（B）In the temple.

（C）In the cemetery.

（D）In the front yard.

Q4 _____ **Which statement is not true?**

（A）Aunt Agatha almost ruined Tom and Mary's marriage.

（B）Aunt Agatha was bad-tempered and selfish.

（C）Aunt Agatha arrived unexpectedly one summer day just after their 20th wedding anniversary.

（D）Aunt Agatha died in the end.

Q5 _____ **What's the best title for the article?**

（A）A lovely aunt.

（B）An unexpected aunt.

（C）A terrific aunt.

（D）I forgot my aunt.

Study 7 EVERY WEEKEND

Every **weekend** is very important to the Chen family. During the week they don't have much time together, but they spend **a lot of** time together on the weekends.

Mr. Chen works at a bank during the week, but he doesn't work there on the weekends. Mrs. Chen works at a hospital, and she is an excellent doctor. Their children, Jennifer and John Chen, are elementary school students. They go to school during the weekdays, but they don't need to go there on the weekends.

On Saturday and Sunday, the Chens spend time together. On Saturday morning, they clean their house together. They work in the yard on Sunday afternoon, and sometimes they like to see a movie together on Sunday evening. The Chen family appreciate every weekend, and, of course, they appreciate the time they get together.

Q1 _____ **What does "weekends" mean?**

（A）Friday.

（B）Saturday and Sunday.

（C）From Monday to Friday.

（D）Friday and Saturday.

Q2 _____ **Why is every weekend important to the Chen family?**

（A）Because they can go to church together.

（B）Because they don't need to clean the house.

（C）Because they don't have much time to be together during the week.

（D）Because they have to clean their house.

Q3 _____ **When do they usually work in the garden?**

（A）Saturday morning.

（B）Sunday afternoon.

（C）Saturday afternoon.

（D）Friday evening.

Q4 _____ **Which statement is not true?**

（A）The Chen family is very happy.

（B）Mr. Chen is a banker.

（C）Mrs. Chen is a nurse in a hospital.

（D）The Chen family like to see a movie together on Sunday evening.

Q5 _____ **The phrase "a lot of" is equal to?**

（A）Little.

（B）The number of .

（C）Much.

（D）Fewer.

Study 8　GHOST

One day Mr. and Mrs. Collins spent a vacation in China. They stayed in an old hotel. The first day they arrived at the hotel, the clerk said to them, "I have to tell you that there is a ghost in the room which you are going to stay in. He was Chinese but loved English." It was terrible, but it was also too late to change to another room because all the rooms in the hotel were booked. Therefore, they had to sleep in the terrible room.

During the middle of the night, while sleeping, they heard some strange noise in the living room. Mr. Collins said to his wife, "The Chinese ghost must be there. Since your Chinese is better than mine, you go and tell him to leave here, OK?" "All right," answered his wife. She got out of bed and walked out of the bedroom. A few minutes later, she came back to her husband and said, "The Chinese ghost doesn't like talking with me in Chinese as much as practicing English with you. He wants you to talk with him."

Q1 _____ **Why didn't Mr. Collins change their room?**

（A）He didn't like to.

（B）No rooms were left.

（C）He wanted to know the ghost.

（D）Because everything was OK that night.

Q2 _____ **What did they hear in the midnight?**

（A）The clerk is talking to someone.

（B）Some strange noise.

（C）Some ghosts were talking.

（D）Nothing.

Q3 _____ **Which statement is not true?**

（A）Mr. and Mrs. Collins spent their vacation in China.

（B）The first day they arrived at the hotel, the clerk spoke to them.

（C）The ghost was very nice.

（D）During the middle night while sleeping, they heard some strange noise in the living room.

Q4 _____ **What was the mother language of the ghost?**

（A）English.

（B）Chinese.

（C）French.

（D）Italian.

UNIT 4　雙篇文章類

作答說明　本部分會有數段短文，每段短文後有 1-5 個相關問題。請就是題冊上 A、B、C、D 四個選項中，選出最合適者填入空格中。

Study 1　MENU AND ORDER　新題型

Pizza House Menu		
Pizza	Medium (3-5 people)	Large (6-8 people)
Pepperoni	$440	$660
Sausage	$450	$670
Cheese and Mushroom	$380	$580
Side Dishes		
Chicken Wings	$130 (5 pieces)	$180 (8 pieces)
Onion Rings	$50 (Medium)	$80 (Large)
French Fries	$40 (Medium)	$60 (Large)
Drinks	A can	a bottle
Soda or Tea	$20	$50

Pizza House Order Form

Name: Sandy Lord
Pizza: Large / Sausage
Sides: 5 pieces of chicken wings + Onion rings (Medium)
Drink: A bottle of soda
Delivery Fee: $0
VIP (90% of total cost): Yes

Order taken by *Carl Jones*

Q1 _____ **Who is Carl Jones?**
（A）An employee in Pizza House.
（B）A regular customer.
（C）A person who ordered pizza and side dishes.
（D）Sandy Lord's employer.

Q2 _____ **How much does the order cost?**
（A）900.
（B）810.
（C）670.
（D）850.

Q3 _____ **What kind of items CANNOT be ordered from the menu?**
（A）Soft drinks.
（B）Chicken.
（C）Seafood.
（D）Fries.

Study 2 ANOUNCEEMNT AND E-MAIL

Warm Breeze Department Store
Competition: Employee of the year

2019	2020	2021
Joan Rose	Ellie Wang	undecided
Men's Clothing Dept.	Women's Clothing Dept.	undecided

To: Laura Thomas, Diana Brown
From: Ali Huston
Subject: Employee of the year 2021

Dear fellow managers,

It's time for us to choose the employee of the year in Warm Breeze Department Store again. Do you have a particular ideal person in mind to recommend? Here are my two suggestions.

Joan Rose, of course, is always an awesome employee. Thanks to her hard work, the Men's Clothing Dept., indeed, made a record year once again. She certainly deserved to win the employee of the year one more. Should we let Joan win again, or encourage someone else this time? Another candidate is Lisa North in the Sporting Goods Dept. She is friendly and accommodating. She is never late or impatient to customers. She always goes the extra mile to help customers find something they want. What's more, she never says "No" when we ask her to work overtime during our anniversary.

Suppose that you agree with my two choices, do you prefer Joan Rose or Lisa North?

Looking forward to your feedback.

_____ **What is the Laura Thomas's position in Warm Breeze Department Store?**

（A）Custodian.

（B）Manager.

（C）Vice president.

（D）Consultant.

Q2 _____ **The phrase "suppose that" can be replaced by?**

（A）Although.

（B）If.

（C）While.

（D）As.

Q3 _____ **What can we know about Joan Rose?**

（A）She is an employee in the Women's Clothing Dept.

（B）Ellie Wang is her manager.

（C）She may win the second time competition.

（D）Diana Brown prefers her to be the employee of the year 2021.

Study 3 SCHEDULE AND LETTER 新題型

Charles's Itinerary
January 1st Tour in Taipei

9:00	Meet at Taipei Railway Station.
9:00-11:00	Take the MRT to Ximending and go window Shopping in Ximending.
11:00-12:00	Take the MRT to Longshan Temple and Visit the beautiful temple
12:00-14:00	Lunch Time in a Japanese food restaurant
14:00-17:00	Ride a minibus to visit National Palace Museum
17:00-19:00	Ride a minibus to take a hot spring in Yangmingshan
19:00-20:30	Dinner Time in a Japanese food restaurant
20:30-22:00	Ride a minibus to Taipei 101 and watch night views on the 89th floor

生活類

書信類

記敘類

雙篇

篇

休閒類

應用類

論說類

文章類

解答篇

Hi Lillian,

    I just got the itinerary planned by you. Thank you so much. I am so glad that I can finally have a holiday tour in Taipei City, which I've always wanted to visit. It seems so nice that I can visit the famous Longshan Temple and hang around the interesting area, Ximending. And I notice that you've arranged our lunch and dinner in Japanese restaurants. To tell the truth, I really want to try some local food, although I am Japanese. On January 1st, I will also have a meeting with my ex-coworker, so I am afraid I have to cancel the last activity. Once again, thank you so much for your arrangement and make this visit in Taipei City worthwhile. Please send me the updated itinerary again at your convenience.

Q1 _____ **What time is probably Charles's meeting with his ex-coworker?**

（A）9:00

（B）14:00

（C）19:30

（D）21:00

Q2 _____ **How will they go to Ximending?**

（A）On foot.

（B）By MRT.

（C）By bus.

（D）By taxi.

Q3 _____ **Which of the following statement is NOT true?**

（A）Lillian arranged the itinerary for Charles.

（B）They will have some time going shopping.

（C）Museum will be visited during the afternoon time.

（D）They will enjoy some Japanese food in Taipei.

To: Jeffrey Lin
From: Teacher Jose Su
Re: Improve your English ability

Dear Jeffrey,

　　As your English teacher, I advise you to take more English Classes. I have attached a schedule of classes from the International Village Institute. A number of your classmates have taken classes there, and it has a fine reputation. Take a look at the 101 courses. I think you should sign up for 101A. Even though you know how to use some English sentences to communicate with American people, it never hurts to start again from the beginning. Grammar courses would also be useful, and I think you are qualified for 102B course. Pronunciation course might be a good idea too, but there's no sense in overburdening yourself. In short, you can pick up the two kinds of courses in the beginning.

Teacher
Jose Su

International Village Institute
schedule of classes

Course #	Title	Hours / Tuition
101A	Basic Conversation	Mon. + Wed. 6:00 - 8:00PM /$3000
101B	Advanced Conversation	Tue. + Thur. 6:00 - 8:00PM /$3000
102A	Basic Grammar	Tue. + Thur. 8:00 - 10:00PM /$3500
102B	Advance Grammar	Mon. + Wed. 8:00 - 10:00PM /$3500
103	Pronunciation	Mon. +Wed. 8:00 - 10:00PM /$2500
104	Writing	Sat. 9:00 - 12:00PM /$2800

Q1 _____ **How many writing class in this institute?**

（A）One.

（B）Two.

（C）Three.

（D）Four.

Q2 _____ **How many days a week will Jeffrey have classes?**

（A）One day.

（B）Two days.

（C）Three days.

（D）Four days.

Q3 _____ **Which of the following statement is NOT correct?**

（A）Jose Su is Jeffrey Lin's teacher.

（B）International Village Institute has courses on weekdays and weekends.

（C）Jeffrey will follow Jose's advice to take a pronunciation course.

（D）The tuition Jeffrey has to pay for his courses is $6500.

Study 5 MEMO AND WORKING SCHEDULE

MEMO

To: All accounting personnel

Date: April 12th,2020.

Subject: New payroll system training

The management team has decided to replace the current type with a newer and more reliable set of the payroll system. The new kits are made by Apex Technology, which will be more user-friendly. They can also reduce the possibility of making errors. Apex will send two trainers to our accounting department to demonstrate how to use this new system. There will be two sessions. One is on May 2nd, from 2:00 PM to 5:00 PM. The other is on May 4th, from 9:00 AM to 12:00 PM. Please make sure each of you can attend at least one of these sessions. If you cannot come due to your work schedule, please feel free to contact me directly.

Brad Robinson

Head of Accounting

Accounting Personnel Work schedules
Day Shift (9:00 A.M. - 5:00 P.M.)
Evening Shift (2:00 P.M. - 10:00 P.M.)

Name	May 2	May 3	May 4
John	Day	OFF	Evening
Cynthia	OFF	Day	Evening
Mark	Evening	Day	OFF
Maria	Day	Evening	Day

Q1 _____ **What is the purpose of this memorandum?**

（A）To ask accounting personnel to change their shifts.

（B）To inform accounting staff about a recent workshop.

（C）To contact Apex Technology for further cooperation.

（D）To make sure that accounting staff keeps their original systems.

Q2 _____ **Who does most likely have to contact Brad Robinson?**

（A）John.

（B）Cynthia.

（C）Mark.

（D）Maria.

Q3 _____ **Which of the following statement is NOT correct?**

（A）Apex is a technology company.

（B）Maria has no day offs during these three days on schedule.

（C）Brad Robinson will be the trainer to teach the new system.

（D）On May 3rd, Mark will start his work at 9:00 AM

UNIT 1 Study 1 光扎節

When the short days of winter begin, many cultural and religious groups celebrate holidays that incorporate the use of light to symbolize peace, love and togetherness. These celebrations often encourage people to look away from material concerns and spend time reflecting on what it means to be a good person. Jewish people celebrate Chanukah, Christians celebrate Christmas and Muslims, Ramadan.

Within the last few decades some African-Americans have begun to celebrate their culture. This holiday is known as Kwanzaa. Commonly believed by many to be based on an ancient African tradition, Kwanzaa was established in 1966 in the United States, though it does **draw on** several African traditions. It is celebrated from December 26th to January 1st every year.

Each of the days of Kwanzaa is acknowledged by the lighting of a candle. The candles are held in a special candle holder called a kinara. Each of the seven days also has a special theme around which **celebrants** can focus their reflections. These are: unity, self-determination, collective work and responsibility, cooperative economics, purpose, creativity, and faith.

Kwanzaa provides a time for African-Americans, who may come from many different faiths, to celebrate their shared history, struggles and successes. The universality of the seven daily themes bridges different belief systems, thus creating a holiday that shares the seasonal subjects of peace and togetherness while at the same time observing the uniqueness of African-American experiences.

　　當冬季短晝開始時，許多文化與宗教團體會慶祝節日，包含使用火光來象徵和平、愛與團結。這些慶祝活動通常鼓勵人們不要注意物質的事物，並利用時間來反思身為一個好人的意義。猶太人慶祝光明節，基督徒慶祝聖誕節，而伊斯蘭教徒則是慶祝齋戒月。

　　在過去幾十年間，一些非裔美國人開始慶祝他們的文化。這個節日是人們所知的光扎節。許多人普遍認為這個節日是源於一個古老的非洲傳統，光扎節於 1966 年在美國成立，儘管它確實是吸收幾個非洲的傳統活動。這個節日是在每年 12 月 26 日到 1 月 1 日被慶祝。

　　在光扎節中的每一天都被認知要點燃一根蠟燭。而這些蠟燭會被擺放在一個稱為「kinara」的特別燭檯上。這七天的每一天也有一個特別的主題，慶祝節日的人們可以將他們的反省專注在這些主題上。這些主題是：團結、自我堅定、集體工作與責任、合作經濟、目的、創造力與信念。

　　光扎節提供這些可能來自許多不同信仰的非裔美國人一段時光，去慶祝他們所共同擁有的歷史、奮鬥與成功故事。在這七天中，每日主題的普遍性搭起了不同信仰體系之間的橋樑，因此建立起這樣的一個節日來分享和平與合群的週期性主題，同時也觀察到非裔美國人經歷的獨特性。

Q1 ＿＿＿*B*＿＿＿ **Kwanzaa is** ＿＿＿＿＿＿＿＿＿＿＿＿＿＿＿＿**.**
（光扎節是…。）
（A）an old African custom（一個古老的非洲習俗）
► （B）a holiday developed by African-Americans
　　　（一個由非裔美國人發展出來的節日）
（C）the African version of Chanukah
　　　（非洲版的光明節）
（D）a time of peace（一段和平的時光）

文章第二段提到「一些非裔美國人開始慶祝他們的文化。這個節日是人們所知的光扎節。」，因此符合敘述的答案是（B）。

Q2 ___C___ The author says that it is important for the seven themes observed during Kwanzaa to be general because _____.

（作者說光扎節慶祝七個主題的普遍性是重要的，因為…。）

（A）they need to compete with the other holidays at that time（它們需要與其他同時的節日競爭）

（B）they are based on African traditions which are hard to translate（它們基於難以說明的非洲傳統）

▶（C）it is celebrated by African Americans who come from many different religious backgrounds（它是由那些來自不同宗教背景的非裔美國人所慶祝的）

（D）they need to be easier for children to understand（它們需要對小孩而言更容易理解）

▶ 解析 文章第四段提到「光扎節提供來自不同信仰的非裔美國人一段時間，去慶祝共同擁有的歷史、奮鬥與成功」，因此符合敘述的答案是（C）。

Q3 ___A___ What does the holiday of Kwanzaa imply about African Americans?

（關於非裔美國人，光扎節暗指什麼？）

▶（A）That they have a unique history that is not adequately reflected in other American institutions.（他們有一段特殊的歷史，那是在其他美國習俗中無法充分反映出來的。）

（B）That they dislike non-African holidays.（他們不喜歡非非洲式的節日。）

（C）That none of them are Christian, Jewish or Muslim and thus need their own holiday.
（他們沒有一個人是基督徒、猶太人或是穆斯林，所以需要他們自己的假日。）

（D）That African Americans don't agree with the way peace is expressed in other holidays.
（非裔美國人不同意在其他節日中表達和平的方式。）

▶️解析　第四段最後一句提到「這個節日分享和平與合群的週期性主題，同時也觀察到非裔美國人經歷的獨特性。」，因此符合敘述的答案是（A）。

Q4 ___*B*___ **In this passage, what does "celebrants" mean?**
（在這段文章中，"celebrants" 指的是什麼？）

（A）A time to celebrate.（慶祝的時光。）

▶（B）A person who celebrates.（慶祝的人。）

（C）Objects that one uses in a celebration.
（某人用在慶祝活動的物品。）

（D）It's another word that also means celebration.
（另一個同樣意指慶祝的單字。）

▶️解析　"celebrant" 是指「慶祝的人」，因此正確答案是（B）。

Q5 ___*C*___ **In this passage, what does "draw on" mean?**
（在這篇文章中，"draw on" 指的是什麼？）

（A）To make a picture on a surface.
（在表面畫出圖案。）

（B）To describe something.（去描述某種東西。）

▶（C）To borrow ideas.（挪借其他想法。）

（D）To get water.（得到水。）

▶️解析　"draw on" 是指「使用一個人的想法」，因此正確答案是（C）。

If you notice foreigners in Taiwan hunting around for a turkey, then you can guess that it's probably time for Thanksgiving in North America. The arrival of Europeans to North America, or the "New World" as they called it, is **commemorated** by the festival of Thanksgiving, and it typically includes a turkey dinner. In Canada, this holiday is observed on the second weekend of October, and in the United States it is observed on the last weekend of November.

Of course, for the aboriginal people who were already living there when the Europeans arrived, North America was far from a new world. The conflicts between the European settlers who sought to **colonize** North America and the aboriginals who struggled to preserve their land and independence have made the idea of "celebrating" the arrival of Europeans distasteful for many. Some people choose to see Thanksgiving as a harvest holiday instead and prepare a large meal as a celebration of the bountifulness of the fall season.

Whatever their political leanings are, many people have fond memories of delicious meals shared with family. Their efforts in Taiwan to find a turkey and acknowledge the holiday are, at heart, a way to enjoy something familiar in a foreign place.

如果你察覺到在台灣的外國人開始到處尋找火雞，你可以猜測現在大概是北美感恩節的時間。歐洲人來到北美，或是他們稱作的「新世界」，是以感恩節的慶典被紀念的，而典型的感恩節包括一頓晚餐的火雞大餐。在加拿大，這個節日是在十月的第二個週末慶祝，而在美國則是在十一月的最後一個週末慶祝。

當然，對於當歐洲人到達時就住在那裡的原住民來說，北美根本不能算是一個新世界。這些尋求殖民北美的歐洲移民與那些奮力想要保護他們的土地及自主權的原住民之間的衝突，已經使得這種「慶祝」歐洲人到來的想法被很多人所厭惡。有些人反而選擇將感恩節看成是慶祝豐收的節日，並且準備一頓大餐作為秋季豐收的慶祝。

不管他們的政治傾向為何，許多人擁有跟家人分享美味大餐的美好回憶。他們在台灣找尋火雞以及感念這個節日所付出的努力，在本質上，是在異地享受熟悉事物的一種方法。

Q1 _____D_____ **What does the author suggest about the arrival of Europeans in North America?**

（作者暗示什麼有關歐洲人來到北美的情況？）

（A）That it was peaceful.（它是很和平的。）

（B）That it was mutually beneficial for the aboriginal people and the new settlers.

（它對於原住民跟新移民而言是互利的。）

（C）That few people can remember it, so no one wants to celebrate it.（很少人能記得這件事，所以沒有人想要去慶祝它。）

▶（D）That it was marked by conflict.

（它留下衝突的印記。）

▶ **解析** 文章第二段提到「尋求殖民北美的歐洲移民和當地原住民之間的衝突」，因此符合敘述的答案是（D）。

Q2 _____B_____ **For people who don't want to observe the coming of Europeans to North America, what is the other significance of Thanksgiving?**

（對於那些不想慶祝歐洲人來到北美洲的人，感恩節的另一個意義是什麼？）

（A）It is a time of the year to reflect on diversity.

（它是一年一次反映出多樣性的時光。）

▶（B）It is a time to celebrate the harvest.
（它是一個慶祝豐收的時光。）

（C）It is a time to celebrate aboriginal culture in North America.
（它是一段慶祝北美原住民文化的時光。）

（D）It is time to celebrate North American cuisine.
（它是一段慶祝北美佳餚的時光。）

🔊解析 文章第二段提到「有些人將感恩節看成是慶祝豐收的節日」，因此符合敘述的答案是（B）。

Q3 ___A___ **Why do people continue to observe Thanksgiving in spite of its contentious roots?**
（為什麼人們持續慶祝感恩節，儘管其爭議性的根源？）

▶（A）It has become a popular time of year for family to gather.（它已經變成了一段讓家人團聚的熱門時光。）

（B）North Americans just really love turkey.
（北美人只是很喜歡吃火雞。）

（C）Turkey farmers aggressively promote the holiday all over the world.（火雞雞農很積極地把這個節日推廣到世界各地去。）

（D）No one really knows why.
（沒有人真正知道為什麼。）

🔊解析 文章第三段提到「許多人擁有跟家人分享美味大餐的美好回憶」，因此符合敘述的答案是（A）。

Q4 ___B___ **What does "commemorated" mean in this passage?**
（在這篇文章中 "commemorated" 指的是什麼？）

（A）To remember friends.（紀念朋友們。）

► （B）To honor something or someone with a ceremony.（用儀式去紀念某事或某人。）

（C）To have a party.（舉行宴會。）

（D）To eat a meal with family.（跟家人聚餐。）

▶解析　"commemorate" 是「慶祝」的意思，因此正確答案是（B）。

Q5 ___ *C* ___ What does "colonize" mean in this passage?
（在這篇文章中 "colonize" 指的是什麼？）

（A）To build a home.（蓋一棟房子。）

（B）To emigrate.（移居國外。）

► （C）To conquer people and take control of land.
（征服一群人並且控制他們的土地。）

（D）To leave a place.（離開一個地方。）

▶解析　"colonize" 是「將⋯開拓為殖民地」的意思，因此正確答案是（C）。

UNIT 1 Study 3 迷你大頭貼

About ten years ago, if you looked closely at people's key chains or cell phones in Taipei, you might notice tiny, colorful photographs. The photographs typically depicted two or more people grinning madly or making silly faces at the camera. These pictures had bright backgrounds or messages framing the smiling faces.

These mini-pictures were enormously popular among teenagers at that time. Groups of teens out for a good time on a weekend evening might all pile into a picture booth to have some photos done. Sweethearts or best friends also had mini-photos taken as a memento of their relationship.

There were several things that made mini-photos so entertaining. The **atmosphere** in the photo booth was very lively and energetic. There was loud, pulsating pop music and everything was brightly lit. Another appealing aspect is that the photographs could be personalized or made unique for different occasions. The buyer could choose from a variety of backgrounds or holiday messages. In some cases, people wrote their own messages, such as "Together Forever" or "We're #1". Finally, the photos were inexpensive, so people could easily purchase many copies of different poses and could return many times.

Judging by the bustle of activity at any mini-photo shops, it seemed that the trend was thriving at that time. It was difficult to find room to pass on the sidewalk in front of one of these establishments. Although the mini-photos had their originality and affordability, their popularity faded after the emerging of smartphones.

中文翻譯

大約在十年前，如果你在台北仔細看人們的鑰匙圈或手機，你可能會注意到一些迷你且色彩鮮豔的照片。這些照片通常描繪了兩個或更多的人在鏡頭前面瘋狂大笑或做出很傻氣的表情。通常會有光鮮的背景或一些字句環繞這些笑臉。

這些迷你大頭貼當時在青少年之間非常受歡迎。一群在週末晚上到外面遊樂的青少年，可能會全部擠進一個拍攝大頭貼的亭子裡照幾張相片。戀人跟死黨們也常常去照一些迷你大頭貼來當作彼此情誼的見證。

有一些原因使得這些大頭貼如此有趣。在這些照相亭裡的氛圍充滿活力與朝氣。那裡有大聲、節奏性強的流行樂，每樣東西都閃著閃耀的光芒。另一項吸引人的層面就是這些照片可以為個人特製，或是為不同的時候做成特別的照片。購買者可以從各式各樣的背景或節日語句做選擇。在某些情況下，人們可以寫下他們自己的訊息，像是「永遠在一起」或「我們是最棒的」。最後，這些照片並不昂貴，所以人們可以輕易買下許多不同姿勢的照片，而且可以重拍很多次。

從這股在許多大頭貼店的狂熱活動來判斷，這股風潮似乎在當時很興盛。而要在這樣的一家店前的人行道上找路走通常是困難的。儘管迷你大頭貼有其原創性和易購性，它們的風潮在智慧型手機出現後就衰退了。

Q1 ___*C*___ **Where did the author say people could find examples of mini-photos?**

（作者提及在哪裡人們可以找到大頭貼的實例？）

（A）In photo booths.（在拍大頭貼的亭子內。）

（B）At night markets.（在夜市。）

▶（C）On people's cell phones and key chains.（在人們的手機上或鑰匙圈上。）

（D）In people's wallets.（在人們的皮夾裡。）

▶解析 文章第一段提到「人們的鑰匙圈或手機會掛著迷你大頭貼」，因此符合敘述的答案是（C）。

Q2 ___*D*___ **Which kind of people would you most likely see at a mini-photo booth?**

（當時你最有可能在大頭貼的亭子裡面看到哪一種人？）

（A）Close friends.（親近的朋友）

（B）Sweethearts.（戀人）

（C）Classmates.（同學）

▶（D）Teenagers.（青少年）

▶解析 文章第二段提到「迷你大頭貼在青少年間非常流行」，因此正確答案是（D）。

Q3 ___*D*___ **Why were mini-photos so popular at that time?**

（為什麼大頭貼在當時會這麼流行？）

（A）They were easy to make.（它們很容易製造。）

（B）They were cheap and can be made unique.（它們便宜而且具獨特性。）

（C）The music played in the shops was pulsating.（在大頭貼店裡面所放的音樂節奏性強。）

▶（D）All the above are correct.（以上皆是。）

▶解析 文章第二、三段皆有提到（A）、（B）、（C）三個敘述，因此正確答案是（D）以上皆是。

Q4 _____B_____ **What does the author imply about the future popularity of mini-photos?**

（作者暗示大頭貼未來的流行趨勢是什麼？）

（A）The trend may not be slowing down.

（這股風潮可能不會逐漸退燒。）

▶（B）Something else will take its place soon.

（其他的東西將很快地取代大頭貼。）

（C）There is no reason for its popularity to decrease.（沒有原因可以使這樣的流行消退。）

（D）Teenagers are fickle and will soon be onto something new.（年輕人是善變的，所以很快會迷上新事物。）

▶解析 第三段提到「智慧型手機出現後，迷你大頭貼就不流行了」，因此符合敘述的答案是（B）。

Q5 _____A_____ **What does "atmosphere" mean in this passage?**

（在這個文章中，"atmosphere" 指的是什麼？）

▶（A）The feeling and look of a place.

（一個地方的感覺與樣貌。）

（B）The air.（空氣。）

（C）Outer space.（外太空。）

（D）The location.（地點。）

▶解析 "atmosphere" 的意思是「大氣；氣氛」，因此正確答案是（A）。

In Southeast Asia, people keep an eye out for the high wind and heavy rain of typhoons. In North America, blizzards are what cause trouble. From January to March, as winter tightens its hold on the central and eastern parts of the North American continent, the risk of blizzards is at the highest level. People living in these areas do what they can to prepare for these paralyzing storms.

A blizzard is characterized by winds of 55 kilometers per hour or more, snowfall of at least five centimeters an hour, temperatures near -20 degrees Celsius, and visibility of less than half a kilometer. They occur when warm air rises and pulls moisture from the Atlantic Ocean. The moisture moves inland and turns to snow as temperatures drop. It's the high wind and heavy snow that create chaos. People caught in a blizzard can be stranded during the storm, as well as after, as they struggle to clear the towering snowdrifts.

To prepare for the possibility of blizzards, many people living in central and eastern North America put emergency kits in their cars. During a blizzard, drivers are forced by the poor visibility to pull over and wait out the storm. Some of the things that people stock in the trunks of their cars are blankets, flashlights, batteries and **non-perishable** food. It's also considered a good idea to include a can and waterproof matches to melt snow for drinking in addition to a shovel, sand, a tow-rope, and jumper cables to help you get going again when the storm is over. These kinds of things don't take up much room and they become important for survival in case of an emergency. Thinking before blizzards come saves lives.

在東南亞，人們關注颱風所帶來的強風豪雨。在北美，製造麻煩的則是暴風雪。從一月到三月，當冬天的威力掌控對北美大陸的中部和東部的影響，暴風雪的危機即在最高等級。住在這些地區的人們盡其所能的為這些可以使城鎮癱瘓的暴風雪做準備。

暴風雪的特徵包括時速 55 公里以上的風速，每小時至少 5 公分的降雪量，將近攝氏零下 20 度的低溫，以及能見度低於半公里。它們發生在暖空氣上升並將濕氣從大西洋拉進的時候。這些濕氣進入內陸，並在氣溫驟降時轉變成雪。這也是強風和大雪所造成的混亂。人們遇到暴風雪，可能會在暴風雪期間或之後受困，因為他們還要奮力地清除那些成堆的積雪。

為了對有可能到來的暴風雪作準備，許多住在北美中部和東部的人們在他們的車子裡都放置一個緊急工具箱。在暴風雪期間，駕駛們受低能見度所迫，必須把他們的車停在路邊，等待暴風雪結束。一些被人們貯存在他們後車廂的東西是毛毯、手電筒、電池跟可久存的食物。除了鐵鍬、一些沙子、一條拖曳纜繩及一些跨接線來幫助你在暴風雪過後繼續上路，能夠包含一個罐子跟一盒防潮火柴用來將雪融化作為飲用水，也會被認為是不錯的主意。這幾種物品並不會佔很多的空間，而且若有緊急狀況下他們就會變成生存的關鍵。在暴風雪來臨前先想好準備措施可以拯救很多生命。

Q1 ____*C*____ **Where are blizzards a problem?**
（暴風雪在哪裡會是個問題？）
（A）In the Atlantic Ocean.（在大西洋。）
（B）On the west coast of North America.
（在北美洲西岸。）
►（C）In the central and eastern parts of North America.（在北美洲中部跟東部。）
（D）In Southeast Asia.（在東南亞。）

▶ 解析　第一段提到「在北美，製造麻煩的則是暴風雪……當冬天的威力加強對北美大陸的中部和東部的影響」，因此符合敘述的答案是（C）。

Q2 ___*B*___ **What makes blizzards so dangerous?**

（是什麼使得暴風雪如此危險？）

（A）The rain freezes into ice as temperatures drop and the roads become slippery.

（當溫度降低時，雨會結凍成冰塊，然後路會變成濕滑。）

▶（B）People can be stranded because the limited visibility makes it impossible to travel.

（人們會被困住，因為有限的能見度使得通行變得不可能。）

（C）People can run out of supplies.

（人們可能會把生活必需品用完。）

（D）People can freeze to death in the low temperatures.（在低溫之下人們可能會被凍死。）

▶ 解析 文章第三段提到「暴風雪讓能見度降低，人們只能靠邊停等暴風雪結束」，因此符合敘述的答案是（B）。

Q3 ___*C*___ **What separates a blizzard from other storms?**

（是什麼讓暴風雪跟其他的暴風雨有所區別？）

（A）The size of the snowdrifts.（積雪的程度。）

（B）The geographic location.（地理位置。）

▶（C）The speed of the wind, the amount of snowfall and the limited visibility.

（風的速度、降雪量及有限的能見度。）

（D）The wind comes from the east instead of the west.（風來自東邊，而非西邊。）

▶ 解析 第二段提到「暴風雪的風速、降雪、低能見度」，因此符合敘述的答案是（C）。

Q4 _D_ **What can people do to ensure that they survive a blizzard if they are trapped in their cars?**

（被困在車內的時候，人們可以做什麼以確保他們從暴風雪倖存？）

（A）Keep a cell phone to call for help.

（留一支手機來打電話求救。）

（B）Avoid traveling during blizzard warnings.

（暴風雪的警告發布時避免出外旅行。）

（C）Keep moving until they outrun the blizzard.

（繼續開車直到他們脫離這場暴風雪。）

▶（D）Keep supplies in the trunks of their cars.

（在汽車後車廂中存放補給品。）

▶**解析** 第三段提到「要在車子後車廂放入緊急工具箱」，因此符合敘述的答案是（D）。

Q5 _A_ **What does "non-perishable" mean in this passage?**

（在這篇文章中， "non-perishable" 指的是什麼？）

▶（A）Does not spoil easily.（不容易腐壞。）

（B）Light-weight.（重量輕的。）

（C）Not difficult to prepare.（不難準備的。）

（D）Packed in a can or plastic bag.

（包在罐頭或塑膠袋裡面。）

▶**解析** "non-perishable" 的意思是「不易腐敗的」，因此正確答案是（A）。

UNIT 1 ⟨ Study ⟩ 5 舊金山都勒教會

休閒類 生活類

應用類 書信類

論說類 記敘類

文章類 雙篇類

解答篇

One of the most interesting and historical tourist attractions in San Francisco is a building created to house the work of the missionaries who worked in the name of Saint Francis of Assisi. This saint is also the city's namesake. The original mission can still be viewed, and an educational museum has been founded to provide tourists with information.

Established in 1776, this is the oldest intact Mission of Saint Francis in the United States. Local aborigines who had been converted by the missionaries finished construction of the four-foot thick adobe walls in 1791. The priest who supervised the construction recorded that 36,000 adobe bricks were used to complete the structure. The original redwood logs used as support beams are still in place. In the present museum, there is a stunning photograph taken just after the earthquake that rocked San Francisco in 1906. In it, one can see that although the church immediately beside the mission building was completely destroyed, the mission itself stood strong. The photo is a **testament** to the solid construction of the building.

Some highlights of the self-guided tour that visitors can take are a diorama of the mission complex as it looked circa 1791; a series of drawings and photographs tracing the mission's history exhibited in a covered walkway, which includes images created in the 18th century; and the cemetery. The cemetery is a lovely garden that contains the graves of people buried from the beginning of the mission until the 1890s. It is a very peaceful place to spend a few minutes in

319

quiet meditation at the end of the tour.

If you take the time to visit the Mission Delores while in San Francisco, you won't be disappointed.

中
文
翻
譯

舊金山最有趣且最有歷史意義的旅遊勝地之一，是一棟為了存放一群傳教士的作品而建造的建築物，這些傳教士以聖方濟各亞西西的名義傳道，而這座城市也是以這位聖徒命名。原來的教會還可供人觀賞，而一座教育博物館也已經建造以提供旅客資訊。

建於 1776 年，這是美國最古老且保存最完整的聖方濟各教會。受傳教士傳道而改變信仰的當地原住民，在 1791 年時完成了這棟建築四呎厚土磚牆的建造。而當時監工建造的神職人員記錄了，完成這棟建築物共用去 36,000 塊土磚。原本被用來當作支撐樑的紅杉木柱還是在原處。在現在的博物館裡，有一張拍攝於 1906 年舊金山大地震時令人震驚的照片。在這張照片中，我們可以看到雖然在這教會旁邊的教堂立刻就完全被摧毀了，教會本身卻依舊屹立不搖。這張照片就是這棟建築物堅固構造的證明。

遊客可以參加的自助導覽中有一些精采的亮點，就是一個看起來像大約在 1791 年時教會建築的仿真模型，一系列追溯教會歷史的畫作與照片被展覽於有頂的迴廊，其中還包含著 18 世紀時所創作的圖像，以及墓園。這座墓園是一個容納從教會開始到 1890 年代長眠於此的逝者的美麗花園。這是一個在導覽結束後可以花幾分鐘安靜沉思的祥和之地。

如果你在舊金山時，有時間來參觀都勒教會，你將不會失望。

Q1 ___*A*___ **What is the relationship between the Mission Delores and the city of San Francisco?**
（舊金山與都勒教會之間的關係是什麼？）

▶（A）The mission serves in the name of the same saint that the city was named after.
（這座城市是以這所教會所服事的相同的聖徒名字來命名。）

（B）The mission was established by the city.
（這所教會是由這座城市設立的。）

（C）The mission pre-dates the city.

（這所教會比這座城市早建立。）

（D）The city promotes the mission as a tourist attraction.

（這座城市推廣這所教會成為一個觀光景點。）

▶解析　文章第一段提到「教堂傳教士以聖徒方濟各的名義傳教，也是這座城市命名的方式」，因此符合敘述的答案是（A）。

Q2　__C__　**What makes the mission unique?**

（是什麼使這所教會獨特？）

（A）Its size.（它的規模。）

（B）It was built by aboriginals.

（它是由原住民建造的。）

▶（C）The original building is still standing.

（原本的建築仍然屹立不搖。）

（D）The design.（它的設計。）

▶解析　文章第二段提到「教堂在大地震仍屹立不搖」，因此符合敘述的答案是（C）。

Q3　__D__　**What can one see on a visit to the mission?**

（去參觀這所教會的人可以看到什麼？）

（A）A memorial to those who died in the earthquake of 1906.

（那些死於 1906 年大地震的逝者的紀念碑。）

（B）A model showing how the mission was built.

（一個展現這所教會如何被建造的模型。）

（C）A tour guide who will show you around the museum.

（一個可以帶你在這座博物館到處參觀的嚮導。）

▶（D）Drawings, photographs, a model of the original mission and the old cemetery.

（畫作、照片、一個原本教會的模型與古老的墓園。）

Q4　*B*　**What does the author imply about this tourist attraction?**

（關於這個觀光景點，作者暗示什麼？）

（A）That it is crowded and you will need a rest after seeing it.

（它是很擁擠，所以在你參觀完後將需要休息。）

► （B）That it's something every visitor should see.

（它是每一個觀光客一定要去的地方。）

（C）That it is a little disappointing.

（它有點令人失望。）

（D）That there is nothing unique about the building.

（這棟建築物沒有什麼獨特的地方。）

Q5　*A*　**What does "testament" mean in this passage?**

（在這篇文章中，"testament" 指的是什麼？）

► （A）Evidence.（證明。）

（B）An agreement.（一項協議。）

（C）A document that details how a person's property will be settled after death.

（一份詳述一個人的財產在他死後如何被安排的文件。）

（D）Either one of the two books of the Bible.

（舊約或新約聖經其中一本。）

UNIT 1 | **Study** | **6** | 席琳・狄翁

休閒類生活

應用類書信

論說類記敘

文章類雙篇

解答篇

Celine Dion started performing as a singer at the age of 5 as part of a family music group in Charlemagne, Quebec in Canada. She was the youngest of fourteen children and music was a big part of her **upbringing**. Over the years, her fame has spread, and now people all over the world listen to the romantic ballads of this pop music superstar.

The pop music diva was born in 1968 and originally became popular in her home country, singing and recording in her mother tongue, French. In 1990, she took the risk of learning enough English to record an English CD, which was very successful in her home country and in the United States. She became an international sensation in 1996 after the release of her single, "Because You Loved Me," which was number one on music charts around the world. Later, she was under contract to perform at Caesars Palace in Las Vegas for three years and she also recorded some hit songs.

席琳・狄翁在五歲時開始成為一名表演歌手,她是加拿大魁北克省查理曼市的家族樂團中的一份子。她是家中十四個小孩當中最年輕的,而音樂在她的成長過程中佔了很大的份量。幾年下來,她的名聲傳揚開來,而現在世界各地的人們都聆聽這位流行音樂天后所演唱的浪漫情歌。

這位流行音樂界的天后出生於 1968 年,一開始在她的家鄉以她的母語法文演唱和錄製歌曲而受到歡迎。1990 年,她冒險學習足夠的英語以錄製一張英文 CD,在她的母國和美國地區非常成功。她在發行蟬聯世界各地音樂排行榜第一名的單曲 "Because You Loved Me" 之後,在 1996 年便成為轟動全球的人物。之後,席琳・狄翁簽下契約,在拉斯維加斯的凱薩皇宮大飯店表演三年,她也錄製了一些暢銷歌曲。

Q1   *B*   **How did Celine Dion start her music career?**

（席琳・狄翁如何開始她的音樂生涯？）

（A）She was a music teacher.

    （她是一位音樂老師。）

►（B）She sang in public with her family.

    （她和家人在公開場合中演唱。）

（C）She recorded an English CD.

    （她錄製一張英文 CD。）

（D）She traveled around the world with a singing group.（她和演唱團體巡迴世界各地。）

▶️**解析** 文章第一段提到「席琳・狄翁是家族樂團的一份子」，因此符合敘述的答案是（B）。

Q2   *D*   **What is Celine Dion's nationality?**

（席琳・狄翁的國籍是什麼？）

（A）French.（法國人）

（B）Quebecois.（魁北克人）

（C）American.（美國人）

►（D）Canadian.（加拿大人）

▶️**解析** 第一段提到「席琳・狄翁來自加拿大」，而題目是問國籍，所以（B）是錯誤的，正確答案是（D）。

Q3   *C*   **What did she sign a contract to do for three years?**

（她簽的一份合約要在三年間要做什麼？）

（A）To record more French CDs.

    （錄製更多法文歌曲 CD。）

（B）To record only English CDs.

    （只錄製英文歌曲 CD。）

►（C）To sing at Caesar's Palace.

    （在凱薩皇宮大飯店演唱。）

（D）To make hit songs.

    （製作暢銷歌曲。）

解析 文章第二段提到「她在三年的合約中在凱薩皇宮大飯店演唱」，因此符合敘述的答案是（C）。

Q4 ___*C*___ **For what kind of songs is she best known?**

（她哪種類型的歌曲最為人熟知？）

（A）The blues.（藍調音樂）

（B）Dance music.（舞曲）

► （C）Love songs.（情歌）

（D）Choral music.（合唱音樂）

解析 文章第二段提到「 "Because you loved me" 是席琳・狄翁很紅的歌曲」，可以知道她最為人熟知的是情歌，因此正確答案是（C）。

Q5 ___*B*___ **What does the word "upbringing" on line 4 mean?**

（文中第四行的 "upbringing" 是什麼意思？）

（A）A period of studying English.

（讀英文的期間。）

► （B）A period of growing up.

（成長的期間。）

（C）A period of being a mother.

（成為一位母親的期間。）

（D）A period of learning singing.

（學習唱歌的期間。）

解析 "upbringing" 的意思是「養育」，因此正確答案是（B）。

UNIT 1 Study 7 泰國菜

If you **have a penchant** for spicy dishes, Thai food is a must for you. Thai food can be so hot that travel guides recommend that travelers to Thailand learn how to say, "Mild, please," in the local language to avoid any bad experiences. The key to this flavorful cuisine is its incorporation of the freshest ingredients with generous use of garlic and red chilies. In addition to a reputation for being hot, Thai food has a characteristic tangy flavor derived from combinations of lime, lemongrass, and coriander. Other dishes have a uniquely salty flavor produced by special Thai fish sauces or shrimp paste.

Thai dishes are usually rice or noodle with meat, seafood, and vegetables and are typically ordered family-style so that diners can sample a variety of tastes. If you've never experienced Thai food, make a point of getting to a Thai restaurant soon. You won't regret it!

如果你喜歡吃辣的料理，你一定要試試泰國菜。泰國菜可以辣到，旅遊指南甚至會建議到泰國的遊客學習如何用當地語言說：「麻煩味道淡一點。」來避免任何不好的經驗發生。這樣美味菜餚的關鍵在於，將最新鮮的食材加入大量的蒜頭和紅番椒。除了以辣度而出名之外，泰國菜擁有源自混合萊姆、檸檬香茅和芫荽特有的強烈味道。其他的菜餚有種特製魚醬或蝦醬的獨特鹹味。

泰式菜餚通常是米食或麵食搭配肉、海鮮以及蔬菜，而且經常是以傳統家庭用餐的方式供應，如此用餐的人可以品嚐多種的味道。如果你從未體驗過泰國菜，特地到泰國餐廳去吧，你不會後悔的！

Q1 ___*D*___ **How does the author feel about Thai food?**
（作者覺得泰國菜如何？）

（A）It's too spicy.（太辣了。）

（B）It's good, but you need to add extra garlic and chilies to give it flavor.
（還不錯，不過你必須多加一些大蒜和紅番椒來增添味道。）

（C）It's really great food, but you have to travel to Thailand to get the best stuff.

（真的是很棒的食物，不過你必須要到泰國去取得最好的食材。）

▶（D）Anyone who likes spicy food should try Thai food.

（任何喜歡辛辣食物的人應該嘗試泰國菜。）

▶解析 文章第一段提到「如果你喜歡吃辣，你一定要試試泰國菜」，因此符合敘述的答案是（D）。

Q2 ___C___ If you have never eaten Thai food, what does the author recommend?

（如果你從沒吃過泰國菜，作者建議些什麼？）

（A）You should learn how to speak Thai first.

（你應該要先學如何說泰語。）

（B）You should to ask the cook to use only the freshest ingredients.

（你應該要求廚師只使用最新鮮的食材。）

▶（C）You shouldn't delay going to a Thai restaurant.

（你不應該延緩去泰國餐廳用餐。）

（D）You should order some for your whole family.

（你應該為全家人點一些泰國菜。）

▶解析 文章第二段提到「如果你沒吃過泰國菜，你應該特地去泰國餐廳」，因此符合敘述的答案是（C）。

Q3 ___A___ According to the article, what kinds of flavors predominate in Thai cuisine?

（根據這篇文章，泰國菜主要的味道是什麼？）

▶（A）Hot, spicy and tangy flavors.

（辛辣且味道強烈。）

（B）Sweet flavors.（甜味。）

（C）Sour, bitter tastes.（酸、苦味。）

（D）Bland flavors.（淡而無味。）

Q4   *B*   **What does the phrase "have a penchant" on the first line mean?**

（第一行中的 "have a penchant" 指的是什麼？）

（A）Dislike.（不喜歡）

► （B）Be fond.（喜愛）

（C）Have a hobby.（有一個嗜好）

（D）Catch.（捉）

解析 "have a penchant" 是「喜愛」的意思，因此正確答案是（B）。

UNIT 1 Study 8 　與狗為友

I like dogs very much because they are our best friends. Dogs have a close relationship with human beings. They are intelligent and loyal animals. They are human beings' companions, too. When we need them, they are beside us all the time.

Dogs are faithful to their masters. If their masters are attacked, they will bark at their masters' attackers loudly, and even attack them. **Dogs are by no means snobbish**. They never desert their masters because their masters are poor or sick. Some dogs even guard the tombs of their deceased masters until they die of **starvation**. So, we love them all the more for their loyalty.

Dogs are so useful. Basically, all dogs can watch our houses. Of course, for instance, they can help in hunting. They can also track down fugitives and detect drugs. They can sniff out whether there are survivors under the ruins.

No wonder so many people love to keep a dog as a pet. Dogs are really cute animals. I have had a cute dog for three years. We often play with each other and even sometimes I talk to the dog about my secrets.

中文翻譯

　　我非常喜歡狗，因為牠們是我們最好的朋友。狗和人類有著親密的關係，牠們既聰明又忠心的動物，也是人類的夥伴。當我們需要牠們時，牠們總是在我們身邊。

　　狗對牠們的主人十分忠心，如果牠們的主人遭到襲擊，牠們會對襲擊者大聲吠叫，甚至還會攻擊他們。狗絕不是勢利的動物，牠們從不會在主人貧困或生病時離棄主人，有些狗甚至會守護亡主的墳墓，直到牠們自己飢餓而死。因此，我們因為狗的忠誠而更愛牠們。

　　狗是非常有用的動物，基本上，所有的狗都會看家。當然，舉例來說，狗能夠幫忙狩獵。牠們也能追蹤逃犯、緝毒。牠們能在事故現場嗅出是否有倖存者在斷垣殘壁下。

　　難怪有這麼多人喜歡養狗當作寵物，狗真的是很可愛的動物。我已經養一隻可愛的狗三年了，我們經常在一起玩，有時候我甚至會對牠說我的祕密。

Q1 ___A___ **What's the best title of the article?**

（這篇文章最適合的標題是什麼？）

▶（A）Dogs are human beings' best friends.

（狗是人類最好的朋友。）

（B）How to protect our dogs?

（如何保護我們的狗？）

（C）Dogs and cats.

（狗和貓。）

（D）How to raise dogs?

（如何飼養狗？）

▶ **解析** 文章第一段提到「狗是我們的好朋友」，因此符合敘述的答案是（A）。

Q2 ___C___ **According to the article, what is not the main reason why dogs are useful?**

（根據這篇文章，哪一點不是狗很有用的主要原因？）

（A）Because they can watch our houses.

（因為牠們可以看家。）

（B）Because they can find out the lives under the ruins.

（因為牠們可以在斷垣殘壁下找出倖存者。）

▶（C）Because they can detect guns.

（因為牠們能夠偵查槍械。）

（D）Because they are faithful to their masters.

（因為牠們對主人忠心耿耿。）

▶️解析 文章中沒有提到「狗會偵查槍械」，因此正確答案是（C）。

Q3 ___B___ **Which statement is not true?**

（哪一項敘述不是正確的？）

（A）Dogs have a close relationship with human beings.（狗和人類的關係親近。）

▶（B）Dogs desert their masters because they're poor or sick.

（狗因為主人貧窮或生病而離棄他們。）

（C）Some dogs even guard tombs of their deceased masters until they die for starvation.

（有些狗甚至會守護亡主的墳墓，直到牠們飢餓而死。）

（D）Dogs can help in hunting.（狗可以幫忙狩獵。）

▶️解析 文章第二段提到「狗不會因為主人貧窮或生病而離棄他們」，因此正確答案是（B）。

Q4 _C_ **What does the sentence "Dogs are by no means snobbish" mean?**

（「狗絕不是勢利的動物」這個句子是什麼意思？）

（A）Dogs are not snobbish enough.

（狗還不夠勢利。）

（B）Dogs are absolutely snobbish.

（狗絕對是勢利的。）

▶（C）Dogs are not snobbish at all.

（狗一點也不勢利。）

（D）Dogs are snobbish sometimes.

（狗有時候是勢利的。）

▶解析　"by no means" 的意思是「一點也不」，因此正確答案是（C）。

Q5 _C_ **The word "starvation" means?**

（"starvation" 這個單字指的是什麼？）

（A）very cold.（很冷）

（B）very tired.（很累）

▶（C）very hungry.（很餓）

（D）very sleepy.（很睏）

▶解析　"starvation" 意思是「飢餓」，因此正確答案是（C）。

<u>**Restricted Area**</u>
Authorized Personnel Only
This area contains hazardous chemical materials.
Trespassers will be charged with mischief
and could be fined up to $25,000NT.

管制地帶
未經授權不得進入
本區域存有危險化學材料，
侵入者將控以毀壞財物罪，
並最高可處新台幣 25,000 元的罰款。

Q1 _____A_____ **The sign warns people to stay out because**
_____.
（這個標示警告人們保持距離是因為…。）

► （A）the area has chemicals and other things that
are dangerous
（這個區域有危險的化學物質和其他物品。）

（B）this is a private home
（這是一個私人的住家。）

（C）dangerous animals are being kept in the area
（這個區域飼養危險的動物。）

（D）secret research is being conducted here
（此處正在進行祕密調查。）

解析 標示第二句提到「本區域存有危險的化學物
質」，因此符合敘述的答案是（A）。

Q2 _____B_____ **People who sneak into the area will _____.**
（溜進這個區域的人會…。）

（A）win some money（贏得一些金錢）

► （B）be fined（被罰款）

（C）be beaten（被咬）

（D）be hired by the company（被這間公司僱用）

▶️解析 標示最後一句提到「最高可處新台幣 25,000 元的罰款」，因此符合敘述的答案是（B）。

Q3 ___*C*___ **You might see this warning sign _____.**

（你可能會在…看到這個警告標示。）

（A）in front of the White House（在白宮前面。）

（B）by a dangerous river which runs extremely rapid（在水流湍急的危險河流。）

► （C）in front of a chemical laboratory

（在一間化學實驗室前面。）

（D）on the street where the traffic is really bad

（在交通很糟的街道上。）

▶️解析 標示提到「化學物質」，可能是在化學相關的場所，因此符合敘述的答案是（C）。

UNIT 2 Study 2 注意事項

Notice:

If your appliance unexpectedly stops, turn it off, unplug it and wait five minutes for it to cool down. Then press the red "Reset" button on the safety plug until it clicks and your appliance will resume normal operation.

注意事項：

如果您的設備意外停止運作，把電源關閉、拔掉插頭，並等待五分鐘使機器冷卻，接著按下在安全插座上面「重新啟動」的紅色按鈕，直到機器發出喀嗒聲響，您的機器就可以重新正常運作了。

Q1 _C_ **You need to wait for your appliance to cool down _____.**

（…您需要等待機器冷卻。）

（A）before unplugging it（在拔掉插頭之前）

（B）after each use（在每次使用之後）

▶（C）if it turns itself off before you are finished using it（如果在您還未使用完畢之前機器突然自動停止）

（D）when you hear it click

（當您聽到機器發出喀嗒聲響）

▶**解析** 注意事項第一句提到「如果設備意外停止運作，要關閉電源，並等機器冷卻」，因此符合敘述的答案是（C）。

Q2 _A_ **After you press the reset button, the appliance should _____.**

（您按下重新啟動的按鈕之後，機器應該會…）

▶（A）start working again（開始重新啟動）

（B）be repaired（被修理好）

（C）cool down for five minutes（冷卻五分鐘）

（D）heat up（發熱）

▶**解析** 注意事項後面提到「按下重新啟動的按鈕，機器會重新正常運作」，因此符合敘述的答案是（A）。

UNIT 2 [Study] 3 表格

Triple 8 Long Distance Super Saver

Dial Triple 8 between October 1st and November 1st for big savings on overseas long distance rates.

Countries	Regular Rates	Super Saver Rates
Canada/USA	0.59 NTD / min	0.19 NTD / min
Singapore	1.3 NTD / min	0.59 NTD / min
Japan	1.3 NTD /min	0.59 NTD / min
Hong Kong	1.0 NTD / min	0.29 NTD / min

*Super Saver rates available from 8 a.m. to 8 p.m. on weekdays and all day long on weekends. For information on rates for other overseas locations, contact our customer service line.

888 國際長途超省方案

10 月 1 日到 11 月 1 日期間撥打 888 國際長途電話，節省更多通話費。

國家	一般費率（新台幣）	超省方案費率（新台幣）
加拿大 / 美國	0.59 元 / 分鐘	0.19 元 / 分鐘
新加坡	1.3 元 / 分鐘	0.59 元 / 分鐘
日本	1.3 元 / 分鐘	0.59 元 / 分鐘
香港	1.0 元 / 分鐘	0.29 元 / 分鐘

＊「超省方案」費用優惠的時段為：平日早上 8 點到晚上 8 點，以及週末整天。欲知國外其他地區的費率，請與我們的客服專線聯絡。

Q1 _____*C*_____ **When are the Super Saver discounts available?**
（「超省方案」的折扣時間在何時？）

（A）From 8 a.m. to 8 p.m. every day.
（每天的早上 8 點到晚上 8 點。）

（B）All day long, effective October 1st.
（自 10 月 1 日起全天優惠。）

▶（C）For the month of October on weekends and from 8 a.m. to 8 p.m. on weekdays.
（10 月的週末與星期一到五的早上 8 點到晚上 8 點。）

（D）Weekends only.（只有週末。）

▶解析 表格第一句提到「10 月 1 日到 11 月 1 日」，最後提到「優惠時段為星期一到星期五早上 8 點到晚上 8 點」因此符合敘述的答案是（C）。

Q2 ___*D*___ **What countries are not included in the special?**
（有什麼國家不在特價方案之內？）
（A）European countries.（歐洲國家。）
（B）Australia.（澳洲。）
（C）Thailand.（泰國。）
▶（D）You need to call the company to find out.
（你必須自行電洽才能知道。）

▶解析 文章最後提到「欲知國外其他地區的費用，取與客服專線聯絡」，因此符合敘述的答案是（D）。

UNIT 2 | Study | 4 使用說明

Shake canister before using. Depress the nozzle and place an egg-sized amount of product in the palm of your hand. Spread evenly through slightly damp hair with your fingers and style as usual. For best results, don't overuse this product. If irritation occurs, discontinue use. For external use only. If product gets into eyes or mouth, rinse with water immediately.

 中文翻譯

　　使用前搖晃瓶身，按壓噴嘴，並在掌心擠出產品至一顆雞蛋大小的量，用手指均勻塗抹在微濕的頭髮上，再依習慣來做造型。為了達到最好的效果，不要過量使用這項產品。如有過敏現象發生，請停止使用。僅限外用，如果產品滲入眼睛或嘴巴，請立刻用清水沖洗。

Q1 _B_ **What are these instructions most likely for?**

（這可能是什麼產品的使用說明？）

（A）Cooking oil.（食用油）

▶（B）Hair-styling mousse.（頭髮造型慕絲）

（C）Skin cream.（潤膚乳液）

（D）Medicated moisturizer.（藥用潤膚霜）

▶**解析** 使用說明第二句提到「用手指均勻塗抹在微濕的頭髮上，再依習慣來做造型」，可以推測出這是和頭髮相關的商品，因此正確答案為（B）。

Q2 _D_ **If your skin gets red or sore from using this product, what should you do?**

（如果你的皮膚在使用這項產品之後紅腫發炎，你應該怎麼做？）

（A）To use less.（減少用量。）

（B）To see a doctor.（去看醫生。）

（C）To make sure that you are shaking the canister well enough.（確定你充分地搖晃瓶身。）

▶（D）To stop using the product.（停止使用產品。）

▶**解析** 使用說明最後提到「如有過敏現象發生請停止使用」，因此符合敘述的答案為（D）。

Q3 _C_ **What should be done to achieve the best result when you use this product?**

（使用本產品時，該怎麼做才能達到最好的效果？）

（A）To depress the nozzle to squeeze as much amount as you can.

（按壓噴嘴，盡量擠出多一點的量。）

（B）To use it three times a day.

（一天使用三次。）

▶（C）To spread it evenly through wet hair.

（均勻塗抹在濕髮上。）

（D）To mix it with an egg.

（將產品與雞蛋混和攪拌。）

▶ 解析　使用說明第二句提到「用手指均勻塗抹在微濕的頭髮上，再依習慣來做造型」，因此符合敘述的答案為（C）。

UNIT 2 Study 5 自我推薦信

To whom it may concern,

In response to your advertisement, I am interested in applying to the Marketing Manager position you offer. I believe my qualifications as listed below meet your requirement.

* Master's degree in Business Administration,
* Managerial skills, leadership training and experience,
* Computer knowledge & foreign languages (English & French)
* Interpersonal skills and open-minded personality.

I am primarily task-oriented but relate well to people and have no problem working in one place for an extended period of time. I am very persistent and determined in achieving a challenging and rewarding career. I have an interest in finding a satisfying job, an openness to innovation, and a willingness to accept changes. I also possess a great deal of energy and enthusiasm and wish never to stop growing throughout my life. Whenever I observe opportunities to learn or perform, I won't give them up.

Enclosed please find a copy of my resume which describes my background and experience in detail for your reference. I should be glad to have an opportunity to talk with

休閒類
生活類

應用類
書信類

論說類
記敘類

文章類
雙篇類

解答篇

you in person to get your opinion on whether I am qualified for the position you offer. I look forward to hearing from you very soon.

Sincerely yours,

Jeff Chen

敬啟者：

　　看了貴公司的徵才廣告，我對貴公司提供「行銷經理」一職很感興趣，我相信我於下方列出的能力符合貴公司的需求。

　　＊商業管理碩士學位

　　＊具備管理技巧、受過領導能力的訓練、有領導經驗

　　＊電腦知識及外語能力（英語及法語）

　　＊人際手腕及能接受新事物的人格特質

　　基本上我是個任務導向的人，不過和人們的關係良好，長時間在同一地點工作沒有問題。我對於從事一份有挑戰性且有益的職業非常堅持。我對於尋得一份令人滿意的工作有興趣、勇於創新，且樂於接受改變。我也精力充沛而且滿懷熱忱，從不希望在我的一生中停止成長。每當我看到有學習或表現的機會，我從不會放棄。

　　隨信附上個人履歷的副本，其中詳細描述我的背景和經驗以供您參考。期待有機會能夠個別和您面談，知悉您認為我是否能勝任這個職務的意見。希望很快能聽到您的回音。

謹啟

Jeff Chen

Q1 ___*D*___ **Which statement is wrong?**

（哪一項敘述是錯誤的？）

（A）The writer got a master's degree in Business Administration.（筆者取得商業管理的碩士學位。）

（B）The writer has managerial skills, leadership training and experience.

（筆者具有管理技巧、受過領導能力的訓練，並且有領導經驗。）

339

（C）The writer has an interest in finding a satisfying job, is open to innovation, and is willing to accept changes.

（筆者對於尋找一份滿意的工作有興趣，勇於創新，也樂於接受改變。）

▶（D）The writer has computer knowledge and is conversant in foreign languages, including English & Japanese.

（筆者具有電腦知識，而且精通外語能力，包含英語和日語。）

▶解析 筆者提到自己具備英語和法語的外語能力，因此錯誤的敘述是（D）。

Q2 ___C___ **What is the purpose of this letter?**

（這封信的目的是什麼？）

（A）Rent a house（租房子。）

（B）Look for a Marketing Manager

（徵求行銷經理。）

▶（C）Find out a job（找工作。）

（D）Make a friend（交朋友。）

▶解析 信件第一句提到「筆者對行銷經理一職感興趣」，因此符合敘述的答案是（C）。

Q3 ___C___ **How did the writer know this chance?**

（筆者如何得知這個機會？）

（A）From the Internet.（從網路得知。）

（B）Someone told him.（有人告訴他。）

▶（C）From an advertisement.（從廣告得知。）

（D）By chance.（偶然得知。）

▶解析 筆者提到自己在廣告上看到徵才訊息，因此符合敘述的答案是（C）。

Q4 _____ *D* **What kind of attachment does the writer enclose?**

（筆者會附上什麼樣的附件？）

（A）A recommendation.（推薦信）

（B）An application form.（申請表）

（C）An autobiography.（自傳）

► （D）A resume.（履歷表）

▶解析 在信件第三段提到「附上履歷表的副本」，因此正確答案是（D）。

UNIT 2 | Study | 6 | 規定

Rules

1. **Always be punctual**.
2. Dress neatly.
3. Don't litter and eat inside.
4. Clean your desk before going home.
5. Never cheat.

規定

1. 務必守時。
2. 衣著整潔。
3. 不要在裡面亂丟垃圾或吃東西。
4. 回家之前要先清理你的桌子。
5. 絕不作弊。

Q1 _____ *D* **Where might a person see this?**

（一個人可能會在哪裡看見這個規定？）

（A）In an apartment.（在公寓裡）

（B）In a living room.（在客廳裡）

（C）In a dorm.（在宿舍裡）

▶（D）In a classroom.（在教室裡）

🔊解析 規定中提到「要守時、衣著整齊、絕不作弊」，可推測是在教室裡，因此正確答案是（D）。

Q2 ___*A*___ **What does the sentence "Always be punctual." mean?**

（"Always be punctual." 這個句子是什麼意思？）

▶（A）You should arrive on time every day.
（你每天都要準時到場。）

（B）You should be quiet all the time.
（你應該一直保持安靜。）

（C）You can sometimes chat with others.
（你有時可以和其他人聊天。）

（D）You are permitted to be late.
（你被允許遲到。）

🔊解析 "punctual" 意思是「準時的」，因此符合敘述的答案是（A）。

Q3 ___*B*___ **According to these rules, which is incorrect?**

（根據這些規定，哪一項敘述是錯的？）

（A）You cannot wear slippers.（你不能穿拖鞋。）

▶（B）You can going home leaving a mess on your desk.（你可以在桌上留下一團髒亂就回家。）

（C）You cannot have your breakfast in the classroom.（你不能在教室內吃早餐。）

（D）Cheating is not permitted.（作弊是不允許的。）

🔊解析 規則 3 提到「保持桌面整潔」，因此（B）的敘述是錯誤的。

MENU

Dinner Specials

Steak ·· NT $700
Pork ·· NT $500
Fish Sandwich ·· NT $340
Sweet & Sour Pork·· NT $450
Fresh Salad ·· NT $300
Super Hamburger ·· NT $220

Desserts and Drinks

Apple Pie··· NT $120
Cheesecake ·· NT $100
Ice Cream ··· NT $85
Coffee·· NT $80
Soda··· NT $80
Tea··· NT $80
Milk··· NT $75

中文翻譯

菜單

晚餐特餐

牛排 ··· 700 元
豬肉 ··· 500 元
鮮魚三明治 ··· 340 元
糖醋豬肉 ··· 450 元
新鮮沙拉 ··· 300 元
超級漢堡 ··· 220 元

甜點和飲料

蘋果派 ··· 120 元
起司蛋糕 ··· 100 元

冰淇淋 ⋯⋯⋯⋯⋯⋯⋯⋯⋯⋯⋯⋯⋯⋯⋯⋯⋯⋯ 85 元

咖啡 ⋯⋯⋯⋯⋯⋯⋯⋯⋯⋯⋯⋯⋯⋯⋯⋯⋯⋯⋯ 80 元

汽水 ⋯⋯⋯⋯⋯⋯⋯⋯⋯⋯⋯⋯⋯⋯⋯⋯⋯⋯⋯ 80 元

茶 ⋯⋯⋯⋯⋯⋯⋯⋯⋯⋯⋯⋯⋯⋯⋯⋯⋯⋯⋯⋯ 80 元

牛奶 ⋯⋯⋯⋯⋯⋯⋯⋯⋯⋯⋯⋯⋯⋯⋯⋯⋯⋯⋯ 75 元

Q1 _A_ **What is not on the menu?**

（菜單上沒有哪一項？）

▶（A）Hot chocolate.（熱巧克力）

（B）Salad.（沙拉）

（C）Seafood.（海鮮）

（D）Apple pie.（蘋果派）

▶**解析** 菜單上沒有賣熱巧克力，因此正確答案是（A）。

Q2 _C_ **You order a steak, an apple pie, and a coffee. How much are you going to pay?**

（你點了一客牛排、一份蘋果派、一杯咖啡，要付多少錢？）

（A）NT $700.（700 元。）

（B）NT $800.（800 元。）

▶（C）At least NT $900.（至少 900 元。）

（D）At least NT $2000.（至少 2000 元。）

▶**解析** 牛排 700 元、蘋果派 120 元、咖啡 80 元，因此總共是 900 元，正確答案為（C）。

Q3 _C_ **You don't like hamburgers, sandwiches and meat. Which dinner special will you order?**

（你不喜歡漢堡、三明治和肉，你可以點哪一種晚餐特餐？）

（A）Sweet & sour pork.（糖醋豬肉）

（B）Fish.（魚）

▶（C）Salad.（沙拉）

（D）Apple pie.（蘋果派）

▶解析　在菜單中不符合這三項條件的餐點為沙拉，因此正確答案是（C）。

Q4 ___*B*___ **Which statement is not true?**

（哪一項敘述是錯的？）

（A）You can eat some desserts here.

（你可以在這裡吃一些甜點。）

▶（B）All drinks are the same price.

（所有飲料的價格都一樣。）

（C）If you order 2 cups of ice cream, you have to pay $170.

（如果你點兩份冰淇淋，必須付 170 元。）

（D）You can eat apple pie here.

（你可以在這裡吃蘋果派。）

▶解析　在菜單中牛奶的價格與其他飲料不同，因此（B）的敘述是錯誤的。

UNIT 2　Study　8　牆上的便條

Lost Property Notice

1. Object lost:	A Purse
2. Color:	Stripped
3. Shape	Round
4. Special features:	With a bell
5. Things inside:	Keys and checks
6. Place where the object was lost:	In the fitting room
7. If found, please call:	0967-432-588

尋找失物通知

1. 遺失物品：錢包
2. 顏色：條紋的
3. 形狀：圓形
4. 特徵：有吊一個鈴鐺
5. 內容物：鑰匙和支票
6. 物品遺失地點：試衣間
7. 如有尋獲，請電：0967-432-588

Q1 ___A___ **What is the purpose of the notice?**

（這個通知有什麼目的？）

▶（A）To find lost property. （尋找遺失物品。）

（B）To find a lost pet. （尋找遺失的寵物。）

（C）To find lost money. （尋找遺失的金錢。）

（D）To find a lost relative. （尋找失蹤的親戚。）

▶解析 通知標題為「尋找失物」，因此正確答案是（A）。

Q2 ___B___ **If you find the lost property, what should you do?**

（如果你找到這個遺失物，你應該怎麼做？）

（A）You should go to the front desk.

（你應該去櫃台。）

▶（B）You should call the phone numbers on the notice. （你應該撥打通知上的電話。）

（C）You should give it to the police.

（你應該把這件物品交給警察。）

（D）You should throw it away.

（你應該把它丟掉。）

▶解析 通知第 7 項提到「尋獲請打手機號碼」，因此符合敘述的答案是（B）。

SPS Club Membership Application Form

Name: ____William____　Sex:　Male
Date of birth: ____1973/6/27____　Age: ___47___
Address: ____3F, #23, Park Street, Taipei, Taiwan____
Telephone no.: ____0983-564-856____
Occupation: ____An English teacher____
Interests: ____Swimming and SPA____

Signature: ____William____
Date: ____2021/6/6____

中文翻譯

SPS 俱樂部會員申請表格

名字：____威廉____　性別：__男性__
生日：__1973/6/27__　年齡：___47___
住址：____臺灣臺北市公園路 23 號 3 樓____
電話號碼：____0938-564-856____
職業：____英文教師____
興趣：____游泳和水療____

簽名：__威廉__
日期：__2021/6/6__

Q1 ___D___ **What information doesn't the form ask for?**
（這份表格沒有要求哪些資訊？）
（A）Birth date.（出生日期）
（B）Job.（工作）
（C）Hobby.（嗜好）
▶（D）Zodiac.（星座）

▶解析　表格中並沒有星座的資訊，因此正確答案是（D）。

347

Q2 ___*C*___ **Where does the applicant live?**

（這位申請者住在哪裡呢？）

（A）Los Angeles（洛杉磯）

（B）Kuala Lumpur（吉隆坡）

► （C）Taipei（台北）

（D）Berlin（柏林）

▶ 解析　申請者的住址寫著臺灣臺北市，因此正確答案是（C）

UNIT 2　Study　10　重要指示

Flight Safety Instruction

1. Please shut down your mobile phones when getting on the plane.
2. Please put your personal belongings in the higher compartment.
3. Please keep your seatbelt fastened when the captain turns on the seatbelt sign.
4. Please don't smoke on the plane.

中文翻譯

航行安全指示

1. 登機時請將您的行動電話關機。

2. 請將您的隨身行李放置上方的隔層。

3. 機長亮起安全帶燈號時，請將安全帶繫緊。

4. 請勿在飛機上吸菸。

休閒類
生活類

應用類
書信類

論說類
記敘類

文章類
雙篇類

解答篇

Q1 _D_ **Where might a person see this?**

（哪裡可能會看到這個指示呢？）

（A）At school.（學校）

（B）In a mobile phone store.（手機銷售店）

（C）In the food stand.（路邊小吃攤）

► （D）On the plane.（在飛機上）

▶解析 標題寫著「飛機安全指示」，因此正確答案是（D）

Q2 _B_ **When should you fasten your seatbelt?**

（你應該在什麼時候繫緊安全帶？）

（A）After you get on the plane.

（在你登機之後。）

► （B）When the captain turns on the seatbelt sign.

（機長亮起安全燈號的時候。）

（C）Before you go to the restroom.

（在你去洗手間之前。）

（D）There's no need to do it.

（不需要這麼做。）

▶解析 指示第三項提到「機長亮起安全帶燈號時，請繫緊安全帶」，因此正確答案是（C）。

UNIT 2 Study 11 教科書索引

Index

Q1 ___*B*___ **On which pages of the textbook can one find the information about the stockholders of a company?**

（在教科書的哪一頁可以找到關於公司股東的資訊？）

（A）pp. 77-93

▶（B）pp. 26-28

（C）pp. 35-39

（D）pp. 151-154

▶解析 索引指出 pp. 26-28 是股東股利，因此正確答案是（B）。

Q2 ___*D*___ **On which pages of the textbook can one find the information about a sharp rise of prices resulting from the too great expansion in paper money or bank credit?**

（在教科書的哪幾頁可以找到因為紙幣和銀行信貸過度膨脹造成價格快速上漲的資訊？）

（A）pp. 77-93

（B）pp. 26-28

（C）pp. 35-39

▶（D）pp. 151-154

▶解析 索引指出 pp. 151-154 是通貨膨脹及失業，因此正確答案是（D）。

UNIT 2 **Study** 12 廣告

Wanted
Good at English Language School
Since 1994

Position: A part-time English teacher
Qualification: Master's degree, major in English literature
Working hours: 7:00-10:00 p.m., Mon.-Fri.
Contact: call May at (02)2395-8592 or Fax: (02)2365-8599
Working Area: Near Taipei Train Station

中文翻譯

徵才
好英語補習班
1994 年設立至今

職務：兼職英語教師

需求資格：碩士學位，主修英國文學

聯絡方式：請電洽 May (02)2395-8592 或傳真：(02)2365-8599

工作地區：鄰近台北火車站

Q1 ___*D*___ **What person might have an interest in this advertisement?**

（什麼人可能會對這則廣告有興趣？）

（A）A person who is looking for a job as a full-time math teacher.

（尋找全職數學教師工作的人。）

（B）A person who wants to learn English well.

（想要學好英文的人。）

（C）A person who likes to speak English.

（喜歡說英文的人。）

▶（D）A person who wants to be a part-time English teacher.（想要當兼職英文教師的人。）

⏵解析 此徵才廣告在徵求「兼職英語教師」，因此正確答案是（D）。

Q2 ___D___ **Which statement is incorrect?**
（哪一項敘述是錯的？）

（A）If you are interested in this position, you should call May.
（如果你對這項工作有興趣，你可以打電話給 May。）

（B）In case you get this job, you will probably work near the Taipei Railway Station.
（假如你獲得這份工作，你會在台北火車站附近工作。）

（C）The total working hours are around 60 per month.（總工作時數大約是一個月 60 小時。）

▶（D）The position offered asks the candidate to have at least a bachelor's degree.
（這份提供的職位要求應徵者至少要有學士學位。）

⏵解析 需求資格寫了碩士學位，因此（D）的敘述是錯誤的。

UNIT 2 Study 13 抱怨信函

Dear Mr. Wang,

I am writing this letter to tell you I just had a terrible trip in Bali. I booked my hotel room with your company. However, it was the worst holiday that I have ever had.

On July 10th, I went to your Taipei office. I booked my plane ticket there and paid all money in cash. I was shown

生活類
書信
記敘
雙篇
解答篇

休閒類
應用類
論說類
文章類

some beautiful pictures of Palace Hotel. The hotel was so beautiful, and it had at least two swimming pools and four special restaurants. I was told to have my breakfast on the beach. That's really wonderful.

However, actually, when I arrived on August 2nd, there was nobody to pick me up at the airport. To my surprise, when I got to the hotel, it was not beautiful at all. On the contrary, it was old, dirty, and ugly. In the room, there was not enough space for me to hang up my clothes. There were electric wires coming out of the wall above the bed, and there were some spiders on the wall. That was disgusting.

So, frankly speaking, I am not happy with the trip you arranged for me. Your lies have forced me to ask for my money back.

Yours,

Terry Smith

親愛的王先生：

我寫這封信是要告訴你，我剛在峇厘島經歷了一場糟糕的旅行。我在你的公司預訂飯店客房，但是那是我度過最糟糕的假期。

在七月十日，我到你在台北的辦公室。我在那裡預訂機票，而且所有費用都是以現金支付。有人讓我看了一些關於皇宮飯店的美麗照片，那間飯店很美，而且它至少有兩座游泳池和四間特色餐廳。我被告知會在海灘上吃早餐，那真是太棒了。

然而事實上，當我在八月二日抵達時，根本沒有人去機場接我。令我驚訝的是，當我走進飯店時，它一點也都不漂亮。相反地，它又舊、又髒、又醜。房間裡沒有足夠的空間讓我掛衣服，有些電線從床上的牆壁裸露出來，還有幾隻蜘蛛在牆上，真是噁心。

所以坦白說，我不滿意你為我安排的行程，你的謊言逼得我非得討回我的錢不可。

謹啟

Terry Smith

Q1 _____ **D** _____ **What is the purpose of this letter?**

（這封信的目的是什麼？）

（A）To make a compliment.

（提出讚美。）

（B）To give a congratulation on recovery.

（恭喜康復。）

（C）To wish someone well.

（向某人祝福。）

▶（D）To complain to someone.

（向某人抱怨。）

▶**解析** 信中第一行提到「要講述在峇厘島的糟糕經歷」，因此符合敘述的答案是（D）。

Q2 _____ **D** _____ **Which statement is incorrect?**

（哪一個敘述是不正確的？）

（A）Terry booked the plane tickets to Bali on July 10th.

（Terry 在七月十日預訂往峇厘島的機票。）

（B）The travel agent told Terry that the Palace Hotel was very beautiful.

（旅行社專員告訴 Terry 皇宮飯店很漂亮。）

（C）This letter to Mr. Wang is to protest what took place.

（這封給王先生的信是在抗議所發生的事情。）

▶（D）Terry will sue Mr. Wang after he gets money back.

（Terry 在要回他的錢之後會控告王先生。）

▶**解析** 信中沒有提到「拿到錢之後要控告王先生」，因此符合敘述的是（D）。

Modern times are very different from old ones. At this modern time, people like to watch TV. Television has many advantages. It keeps us informed of the latest news and also provides entertainment in the home. On the other hand, television has been blamed for the violent behavior of some young people and for encouraging children to sit at home, instead of getting exercise.

Additionally, a long time ago, most towns and villages were very small. The number of people who lived in every country was a lot smaller than it is today, too. There was no heavy industry, only agriculture, arts, and crafts, and these things weren't going to damage our environment. People did not use chemicals. There were no motor vehicles and no factories. There was, therefore, very little pollution. The lifestyles between modern times and old times are extremely different.

中文翻譯

　　現在的時代與舊時代有很大的不同，在現代，人們喜歡看電視。電視有很多優點，它告訴我們最近的新聞，也提供家中的娛樂。另一方面，人們把某些年輕人的暴行歸咎於電視，還指控電視鼓勵小孩子坐在家裡，而不是做運動。

　　除此之外，許久以前，大部分的城鎮和村莊都很小，每個國家的人口數也遠比今天要少得多。沒有重工業，只有農業、藝術和工藝，而這些事物都不會對環境造成破壞，人們不使用化學製品，沒有車輛、沒有工廠，因此污染也很少。現在與過去之間的生活型態是極度不同的。

Q1 ___C___ **What advantages doesn't television have?**

（電視所沒有的好處是什麼？）

（A）It keeps us informed of the latest news.

（持續提供我們最新的新聞。）

（B）It provides entertainment.（提供娛樂。）

▶（C）It provides to get exercise.（讓我們做運動。）

（D）It gives us lots of fun.（給我們許多樂趣。）

▶解析 文章第一段最後一句提到「電視鼓勵小孩坐在家裡，而不是做運動」，因此正確答案是（C）。

Q2 ___A___ **Which statement is wrong?**

（哪一個敘述是錯的？）

▶（A）The number of people who lived in every country was much bigger than its today.

（以前每個國家的人口數量比現在還多。）

（B）There were no motor vehicles and factories. Therefore, there was very little pollution.

（以前沒有車輛和工廠，因此污染也很少。）

（C）Television has been blamed for the violent behavior of some young people.

（人們把某些年輕人的暴行歸咎於電視。）

（D）A long time ago, most towns and villages were very small.

（許久以前，大多數的城鎮和鄉村都很小。）

▶解析 文章第二段提到「國家以前的人口數比現在還少」，因此正確答案是（A）。

UNIT 3 [Study] 2 墨西哥

Let me tell you something about Mexico. Mexico, the largest nation in Middle America, provides a good example of life in the region. Although Mexico is a large country, only 12% of its land can be used for farming. Another 40% is the grazing land, not for farming. The rest of the land is hills and mountains, dry, high plateaus, or wet coastal regions, and they are all not good for farming. The mountains are too steep to farm. The high plateau in the middle of Mexico would be good farmland if it had more water. However, actually, it doesn't. For all of these reasons, Mexicans must take care of the good farmland they have. Economy in Mexico is also in a poor condition. It is said that's because the political condition seriously and deeply influenced the economy of Mexico.

讓我告訴你一些有關墨西哥的事。墨西哥是中美洲最大的國家，提供該地區生活的最佳縮影。雖然墨西哥是一個大國家，但是只有 12% 的土地可用於農耕，另外 40% 則是放牧地，不可用於農耕。剩下的土地是山坡地和山地，乾燥聳峻的高原，或是潮濕的沿海地區，而它們皆不是良好的可耕地。山坡地勢太過陡峭而無法耕種；在墨西哥中部的高原如果有多一點水源的話，就會是很好的耕地，但事實上並沒有。基於這些所有的原因，墨西哥人民必須好好照顧他們所擁有的可耕地，墨西哥的經濟亦是在一個不好的狀況，據說是因為政治情況嚴重且深刻地影響到墨西哥的經濟。

Q1 _____ *B* **What is the topic of this paragraph?**
（這篇文章的標題是什麼？）
（A）Mexico and Economics.（墨西哥及其經濟。）
► （B）Mexico and its agriculture.
（墨西哥及其農業。）

（C）Mexican farmers.（墨西哥的農民。）

（D）Waterlogged land.（浸溼的土地。）

ℹ️**解析** 文章中間提到「墨西哥土地用於農耕的比例」，因此符合敘述的答案是（B）。

Q2　*D*　**Why are the mountains in Mexico hard to farm?**

（為什麼墨西哥的山地很難耕種？）

（A）Because they are too dry.

（因為它們太乾燥。）

（B）Because they are hills.

（因為它們是丘陵。）

（C）Because they are waterlogged.

（因為它們浸滿積水。）

▶（D）Because they are too steep.

（因為它們太陡峭。）

ℹ️**解析** 文章中提到「山坡太過陡峭而無法耕種」，因此正確答案是（D）。

Q3　*D*　**Which statement is wrong?**

（哪一個敘述是錯的？）

（A）Mexico is the largest nation in Middle America and provides a good example of life in the region.

（墨西哥是中美洲地區最大的國家，提供這個地區生活的最佳縮影。）

（B）Although Mexico is a large country, only 12% of its land is good for farming.

（雖然墨西哥是個大國，卻只有 12% 的土地適合耕作。）

（C）The high plateau in the middle of Mexico would be good farmland if it had more water.

（墨西哥中部的高原如果有更多水源，就會是很好的耕地。）

► （D） There is no need for Mexico to take care of the good farmland they have.

（墨西哥人不需要照顧好他們所擁有的良好耕地。）

▶ 解析 文章中提到「墨西哥人民因為種種原因需要照顧好現有的耕地」，因此（D）是錯誤的敘述。

UNIT 3 Study 3 運動

Sport is good for both body and mind. A person who seldom exercises will not only get ill very easily but have slow reflexes as well. Frankly speaking, being ill is not fun at all and having slow reflexes can be dangerous. An ill person can't study efficiently, let alone write and read effectively. A "slow motion" person has a hard time handling sudden changes. Therefore, sport is very necessary for anyone. I'm a sports fanatic. I enjoy playing baseball, basketball, table tennis and tennis. My favorite sport, however, is swimming. When you swim, you actually exercise almost every muscles in your body. Also, there are two great things that swimming can do for you. In summer, swimming can cool you, and in winter it helps you adjust to cold weather. So, why not come swim with me and I'll wait for you there by the swimming pool. Be sure to come!

中文翻譯

　　運動對身心都有益，不常運動的人不僅很容易生病，反應能力也會變慢。坦白說，生病一點都不好玩，而反應能力緩慢可能會有危險。生病的人無法有效率地讀書，更別說要有效地寫作和閱讀。「動作慢」的人難以應付突如其來的改變。因此，運動對任何人是十分必要的。我是個運動愛好者，我喜歡打棒球、籃球、桌球和網球。不過，我最愛的運動是游泳。當你在游泳的時候，你實際上幾乎運動到全身上下的肌肉。游泳還有可以為你帶來兩大好處。在夏天，游泳可以讓你涼爽，而在冬天，它幫助你適應寒冷的天氣。所以何不跟我一起去游泳，我會在游泳池畔等你，一定要來喔！

Q1 ___*D*___ **What does the author imply us to do?**
（作者暗示我們做什麼？）

（A）In summer, we can go to the beach with the author.
（夏天時我們可以跟作者一起去海邊。）

（B）We are all "slow motion" people.
（我們全都是「動作慢」的人。）

（C）people feeling ill can work well.
（感到不舒服的人可以做好工作。）

▶（D）People who don't do exercises get ill more easily.（不做運動的人容易生病。）

▶解析 文章第一句提到「不常運動的人容易生病」，因此正確答案是（D）。

Q2 ___*C*___ **Which statement is wrong?**
（哪一個敘述是錯誤的？）

（A）Sport is good for both body and mind.
（運動對身心都有益。）

（B）A "slow motion" person has a hard time handling sudden changes.
（「動作慢」的人難以應付突如其來的改變。）

▶（C）An ill person can study efficiently, let alone write and read.
（生病的人能夠有效率地讀書，更別提寫作和閱讀。）

（D）Sport is very necessary for anyone.
（運動對任何人而言都是十分必要的。）

▶解析 文章中提到「生病的人不能有效率地讀書、寫作和閱讀」，因此（C）的敘述是錯誤的。

UNIT 3 Study 4 足球

生活 休閒類

書信 應用類

記敘 論說類

雙篇 文章類

解答篇

Soccer is a sport loved by people all over the world. Many games are held in different places every year. The World Cup is the game that all the players want to play most. It is held every four years. Only the best team will win the final game.

The 2018 World Cup was over. Hundreds of thousands of people went to the games or watched them on TV day and night. They all got very excited and hoped their favorite team becoming the world's best team and winning the final game. In 2018, France won the championship. Actually, they won once in 1998.

Soccer is a team sport. There are eleven players in each team of a game. The earliest soccer games in England were not like what they are today. Games were played between two towns. Each team had more than five hundred players. Is that hard to believe? Anyway, take my words for it.

中文翻譯

　　足球是全世界的人都熱愛的一項運動，每年都在不同的地方舉辦許多比賽，世界盃是所有球員都想參加的比賽，每四年舉辦一次，只有最好的球隊將會在最後的決賽勝出。

　　2018 年的世界盃已經結束，成千上萬的人去現場觀看球賽，或是在家日夜觀看電視轉播。他們都變得很亢奮，希望自己最喜愛的球隊變成最棒的球隊，並贏得決賽，法國在 2018 年贏得冠軍，事實上，他們已經在 1998 年贏一次冠軍了。

　　足球是團體運動，一場球賽中各隊有十一名球員，最早在英國舉行的球賽不像今日的球賽，是在兩個城鎮之間比賽，每一個球隊有超過五百名球員，那樣很難相信吧？無論如何，請相信我說的。

Q1   _B_   **The next World Cup will be held in?**

（下一次的世界盃會在哪一年舉行？）

（A）2021.

► （B）2022.

（C）2023.

（D）1924.

▶ 解析 文章中提到「2018 的世界盃結束了」，可以推測出下次的世界盃在 2022，因此正確答案是（B）。

Q2   _B_   **When soccer was first played in England, around how many players in each team?**

（足球比賽首次在英國舉行時，每支球隊裡有多少球員？）

（A）Around 5000.

► （B）Around 500.

（C）Around 11.

（D）Around 111.

▶ 解析 文章中提到「最早在英國舉行的球賽每一隊超過 500 名球員」，因此正確答案是（B）。

Q3   _A_   **Why do hundreds of thousands of people go to the World Cup games?**

（為何成千上萬的人們去現場觀賞世界盃球賽？）

► （A）They want to watch their favorite time win.
（他們想要看自己最喜歡的球隊勝利。）

（B）They are the players of the games.
（他們是比賽的球員。）

（C）They love to drink the world's best cup of tea.
（他們喜歡喝世界最頂級的茶。）

（D）They become coaches for each team.
（他們成為每支球隊的教練。）

▶ 解析 文章第二段提到「人們觀看比賽是因為他們想要自己最喜歡的球隊勝利」，因此正確答案是（A）。

Q4 ____C____ **Which statement is true?**

（哪一項敘述是正確的？）

（A）People go to the World Cup games every year.（人們每年都會去現場觀看世界盃。）

（B）The best team in 2018 was England.

（2018 年最好的球隊是英國）

► （C）To soccer players, World Cup games are more important than any other game.

（對足球球員而言，世界盃比其他比賽都重要。）

（D）The worst team in 2018 was France.

（2018 年最差的球隊是法國。）

▶ 解析 第一段提到「每個球員都想參加世界盃」，因此符合敘述的答案是（C）。

Q5 ____B____ **Which statement is not true?**

（哪一項敘述不是正確的？）

（A）Soccer is a popular sport.

（足球是一種受歡迎的運動。）

► （B）The earliest soccer games in England are just like what they are today.

（最早在英國舉行的足球賽和今天的球賽是一樣的。）

（C）Hundreds of thousands of people go to the games or watch them on TV day and night.

（成千上萬的人去現場觀看球賽，或在家日夜觀看電視轉播。）

（D）Many soccer games are held in different places every year.

（每年有許多足球比賽在不同的地方舉行。）

▶ 解析 文章最後一段提到「早期在英國的比賽與現在不同」，因此（B）的敘述是錯誤的。

休閒類　生活類

應用類　書信類

論說類　記敘類

文章類　雙篇類

解答篇

363

When it comes to tests, I'll say that most students are afraid of tests. Whenever a test or an examination is approaching, they start to get nervous. On the eve of tests, they usually worry that they will fail their tests, so they **burn the midnight oil** in the hope that they will be able to get better grades. As a matter of fact, tests are a part of a student's life. As students, they ought to study hard and prepare for their future careers. Thus, I think that a test is only used to test whether a student is fully prepared.

In reality, student ought to at ordinary times listen carefully to what his teacher says in the classroom and review his homework after school. Rome was not built in one day; high grades are not obtained by burning the midnight oil on the eve of a test. The most effective way to learn is to ask your teacher to explain what you don't understand, to practice what you learn, and to put to use what you acquire.

When you know that a test is on the way, you ought to relax. When you relax, you will be able to develop any kind of abilities and potential, and you will find that it is very easy for you to answer all the questions on your test sheets. Therefore, we just do our best to do it, everything will be all right. Anything can be achieved by diligence.

談到考試時,我會說大多數的學生都害怕考試,每當接近考試或測驗的日子,他們就會開始緊張。在考試的前一天晚上,他們經常會擔心自己無法通過考試,所以他們會熬夜唸書,希望能獲得更好的成績。事實上,考試是學生生活的一部分。身為學生,他們應該要努力讀書,為自己將來的職業做準備。因此,我認為考試只是用來評量學生是否準備充足而已。

實際上，學生在平時就應該仔細聽老師在課堂上的講課，並在放學後複習他的功課。羅馬不是一天造成的；高分也不是靠考試前夕熬夜唸書就可以得到的。最有效率的學習方法就是請教老師解釋你不懂的地方、練習你的所學，並應用你獲得的知識。

在你知道接近考試的時候，你應該要放輕鬆。當你放輕鬆時，你將能夠發揮任何的能力和潛力，而你會發現，回答考試卷上所有的題目對你而言是這麼的容易，所以，我們只要盡力而為，一切都會沒問題的。任何事可以透過勤勉來達成。

Q1 ___*A*___ **What does "burn the midnight oil" in the first paragraph mean?**

（在第一段的 "burn the midnight oil" 是什麼意思？）

▶（A）Stay up late.（熬夜）

（B）Make a dinner.（做晚餐）

（C）Fill up some gas.（倒滿汽油）

（D）Oil is lighter than water.（油比水輕）

▶解析　"burn the midnight oil" 是「熬夜」的意思，因此正確答案是（A）。

Q2 ___*B*___ **Why are students afraid of tests?**

（為什麼學生害怕考試？）

（A）Because they have to pay more money for the tests.（因為他們必須要為考試多付一些錢。）

▶（B）Because they may fail in passing the tests.（因為他們可能無法通過考試。）

（C）Because they don't have much time to study at home.（因為他們在家沒有很多時間讀書。）

（D）Because they don't like their teachers.（因為他們不喜歡他們的老師。）

▶解析　文章第一段提到「學生在考試前一天害怕自己無法通過考試」，因此符合敘述的答案是（B）。

Q3 ___*A*___ **What is good for you to do when an exam is coming?**

（考試將至時，做什麼事情對你有益？）

► （A）Relaxing.（放鬆）

（B）Cheating.（作弊）

（C）Complaining.（抱怨）

（D）Doing nothing.（不做任何事）

▶解析 文章第三段提到「在你知道接近考試的時候，你應該要放輕鬆」，因此符合敘述的答案是（A）。

Q4 ___*C*___ **Which statement is not true?**

（哪一項敘述不是正確的？）

（A）High grades are not obtained by burning the midnight oil on the eve of a test.

（高分也不是靠考試前夕熬夜唸書就可以得到的。）

（B）A test is only used to test whether a student is fully prepared.

（考試只是用來測驗學生是否充分準備。）

► （C）The most effective way to learn not to practice what you learn and not to put to use what you acquire.

（最有效率的學習方法是不要練習你所學的，也不要應用你獲得的知識。）

（D）A student ought to pay attention to what his teacher says in the classroom, and review his homework after school.

（學生應該要仔細聽老師在課堂上的講課，放學後複習功課。）

▶解析 文章第二段提到「最有效率的學習方法就是……練習你的所學，並應用你獲得的知識」，因此（C）的敘述是錯誤的。

Q5 ___C___ **What's the best title for the article?**

（這篇文章最合適的標題是什麼？）

（A）Stop testing students as soon as possible.

（盡快停止讓學生做測驗。）

（B）How to get good grades in your school.

（如何在學校得到好成績。）

► （C）Students and tests.（學生與考試。）

（D）We should learn how to avoid tests.

（我們應該學習如何避免考試。）

▶ 解析 整篇文章都提到「學生與考試之間的關係」，因此符合敘述的答案是（C）。

UNIT 3 [Study] 6 Agatha 阿姨

Aunt Agatha almost ruined Tom and Mary's marriage. She arrived unexpectedly one spring day just after their 20th wedding anniversary. For Tom and Mary, that day was really a tragedy. Agatha announced that she wanted to visit for a week, but she stayed for the next 15 years. That's really a long time.

Agatha was bad-tempered and selfish. She wanted to watch "her" shows on TV and didn't let others watch theirs. She decided what they ate for meals. She complained about everything all the time. Eventually, after 15 years, she died. They buried her in the cemetery by the village church. After the funeral, Tom wrapped his arms around his wife and comforted her.

"I know you are upset, sweetheart," he said, "But try to **look on the bright side**. We can be alone again finally."

"I know, but I have a confession to make. I hated every day Agatha stayed with us. I only put up with her because she was your aunt" she said.

"My aunt?" yelled Tom. "I thought she was your aunt!"

Agatha 阿姨差點毀了 Tom 和 Mary 的婚姻。某個春天的某一天，她在他們結婚 20 年的慶祝之後意外地出現了。對 Tom 和 Mary 而言，那天實在是場慘劇。Agatha 阿姨聲稱她想要暫住一個禮拜，不過她在接下來的 15 年裡都住了下來，這實在是一段很長的時間。

Agatha 阿姨脾氣很糟、又很自私，她看「她想看的」電視節目，就不准別人看他們想看的，她決定他們餐點要吃什麼，她總是在抱怨每一件事。終於，在 15 年之後她死了，他們在村莊教堂旁邊的墓地埋葬了她。喪禮之後，Tom 雙手環抱著妻子、安慰她。

他說：「我知道妳很難過，親愛的，不過試著看好的一面，我們終於可以獨處了。」

她說：「我知道，不過我必須坦白，我討厭 Agatha 阿姨每天都纏著我們，我忍受她只因為她是你的阿姨。」

Tom 大叫：「我的阿姨？我以為那是妳的阿姨！」

Q1 ___A___ **What does "look on the bright side" in the third paragraph mean?**

（在第三段的 "look on the bright side" 指的是什麼？）

► （A）Be more positive.（正面一點。）

（B）Be nice to others.（對別人友善。）

（C）Be confident in everything.

（對每件事要有信心。）

（D）Be more passive.（消極一點。）

▶ 解析 "look on the bright side" 的意思是「持樂觀的態度」，因此正確答案是（A）。

368

Q2 ___C___ **How long did the aunt say she wanted to stay?**

（阿姨說她想要住多久？）

（A）15 years.（15 年）

（B）20 days.（20 天）

► （C）One week.（一個禮拜）

（D）50 days.（50 天）

▶ 解析 文章第一段提到「Agatha 阿姨說要暫住一個禮拜」，因此正確答案是（C）。

Q3 ___C___ **Where did they bury the aunt?**

（他們把她埋在哪裡？）

（A）In the church.（教堂）

（B）In the temple.（寺廟）

► （C）In the cemetery.（墓地）

（D）In the front yard.（前院）

▶ 解析 文章第二段提到「他們在教堂旁的墓地埋葬阿姨」，因此正確答案是（C）。

Q4 ___C___ **Which statement is not true?**

（哪一項敘述不是正確的？）

（A）Aunt Agatha almost ruined Tom and Mary's marriage.

（Agatha 阿姨差點毀了 Tom 和 Mary 的婚姻。）

（B）Aunt Agatha was bad-tempered and selfish.

（Agatha 阿姨脾氣糟又自私。）

► （C）Aunt Agatha arrived unexpectedly one summer day just after their 20th wedding anniversary.（Agatha 阿姨在夏天的某日突然拜訪，就在他們結婚 20 週年之後。）

（D）Aunt Agatha died in the end.

（Agatha 阿姨最後過世了。）

▶ 解析 文章第一段提到「Agatha 阿姨在春天的某一天出現」，因此（C）的敘述是錯誤的。

Q5 _____B_____ **What's the best title for the article?**

（這篇文章最合適的標題是什麼？）

（A）A lovely aunt.（可愛的阿姨。）

► （B）An unexpected aunt.（意外來訪的阿姨。）

（C）A terrific aunt.（很棒的阿姨。）

（D）I forgot my aunt.（我忘了我的阿姨。）

▶ 解析　全文提到「一位意外到訪就賴著不走的阿姨」，因此符合敘述的答案是（B）。

UNIT 3 [Study] 7 每個週末

Every **weekend** is very important to the Chen family. During the week they don't have much time together, but they spend **a lot of** time together on the weekends.

Mr. Chen works at a bank during the week, but he doesn't work there on the weekends. Mrs. Chen works at a hospital, and she is an excellent doctor. Their children, Jennifer and John Chen, are elementary school students. They go to school during the weekdays, but they don't need to go there on the weekends.

On Saturday and Sunday, the Chens spend time together. On Saturday morning, they clean their house together. They work in the yard on Sunday afternoon, and sometimes they like to see a movie together on Sunday evening. The Chen family appreciate every weekend, and, of course, they appreciate the time they get together.

中文翻譯

每個週末對陳家而言都是很重要的。星期一到五他們沒有時間聚在一起，不過他們週末花很多時間一起相處。

陳先生星期一到五在銀行工作，不過週末他不用上班。陳太太在醫院工作，她是一位很優秀的醫生。他們的孩子珍妮佛‧陳和約翰‧陳都是小學生，他們星期一到五要上學，不過他們週末不必上學。

在星期六和星期日，陳家人花許多時間聚在一起。星期六早上，他們一起清掃房子，星期日下午他們在庭院裡工作，有時他們喜歡在星期日晚上一起去看電影。陳家人珍惜每一個週末，當然，他們更珍惜家人相聚的時光。

Q1 _B_ **What does "weekends" mean?**

（在第一段的 "weekends" 指的是什麼？）

（A）Friday.（星期五）

▶（B）Saturday and Sunday.（星期六和星期日）

（C）From Monday to Friday.（從星期一到星期五）

（D）Friday and Saturday.（星期五和星期六）

▶解析　"weekend" 的意思是「週末」，也就是週六和週日，因此正確答案是（B）。

Q2 _C_ **Why is every weekend important to the Chen family?**

（為什麼每個週末對陳家而言是重要的？）

（A）Because they can go to church together.

（因為他們可以一起上教堂。）

（B）Because they don't need to clean the house.

（因為他們不需要清理房子。）

▶（C）Because they don't have much time to be together during the week.

（因為他們星期一到五沒有很多時間在一起。）

（D）Because they have to clean their house.

（因為他們必須清掃房子。）

▶解析　文章第一段提到「每個週末對陳家很重要，因為他們週一到週五沒有時間相處」，因此符合敘述的答案是（C）。

Q3 _B_ **When do they usually work in the garden?**
（他們通常什麼時候在花園工作？）
（A）Saturday morning.（週六早上）
▶（B）Sunday afternoon.（週日下午）
（C）Saturday afternoon.（週六下午）
（D）Friday evening.（週五晚上）

▶解析 文章第三段提到「週日下午他們會在庭院工作」，因此正確答案是（B）。

Q4 _C_ **Which statement is not true?**
（哪一項敘述是不正確的？）
（A）The Chen family is very happy.
（陳家人非常快樂。）
（B）Mr. Chen is a banker.
（陳先生是一位銀行行員。）
▶（C）Mrs. Chen is a nurse in a hospital.
（陳太太在醫院擔任護士。）
（D）The Chen family like to see a movie together on Sunday evening.
（陳家喜歡在星期日晚上去看電影。）

▶解析 文章第二段提到「陳太太在醫院工作，她是很棒的醫生」，因此（C）的敘述是錯誤的。

Q5 _C_ **The phrase "a lot of" in the first paragraph is equal to?**
（在第一段的 "a lot of" 這個片語指的是什麼？）
（A）Little.（很少）
（B）The number of.（…的數量）
▶（C）Much.（很多）
（D）Fewer.（很少）

▶解析　"a lot of" 的意思是「很多」，可用於可數、不可數名詞，因此正確答案是（C）。

UNIT 3　Study　8　鬼

One day Mr. and Mrs. Collins spent a vacation in China. They stayed in an old hotel. The first day they arrived at the hotel, the clerk said to them, "I have to tell you that there is a ghost in the room which you are going to stay in. He was a Chinese but loved English." It was terrible, but it was also too late to change to another room because all the rooms in the hotel were booked. Therefore, they had to sleep in the terrible room.

During the middle of the night while sleeping, they heard some strange noise in the living room. Mr. Collins said to his wife, "The Chinese ghost must be there. Since your Chinese is better than mine, you go and tell him to leave here, OK?" "All right," answered his wife. She got out of the bed, and walked out of the bedroom. A few minutes later, she came back to her husband and said, "The Chinese ghost doesn't like talking with me in Chinese as much as practicing English with you. He wants you to talk with him."

　　有一天 Collins 夫婦去中國度假，他們住在一間老舊的飯店。第一天到達旅社時，服務人員對他們說：「我必須要告訴你們，你們要住進去的那個房間裡有一個鬼，他是中國人，但是喜歡英文。」這樣很可怕，但是要換房間也已經太晚了，因為飯店的所有房間都被訂走了。於是，他們必須睡在這間可怕的房間裡。

　　半夜他們正在睡覺的時候，他們聽到客廳有一些奇怪的聲音。Collins 先生對他的太太說：「那個中國鬼一定在那裡。既然妳的中文比我好，妳去

373

請他離開好不好？」他太太回答：「好吧。」她起床走出臥室。幾分鐘之後，她回到丈夫身邊說：「那個中國鬼不喜歡跟我講中文，倒是比較喜歡跟你練習英文，他想要你去跟他說話。」

Q1 _B_ **Why didn't Mr. Collins change their room?**

（為什麼 Collins 先生不換房間？）

（A）He didn't like to.（他不喜歡換房間。）

▶（B）No rooms were left.（沒有空房間了。）

（C）He wanted to know the ghost.

（他想要認識那個鬼。）

（D）Because everything was OK that night.

（因為那天晚上一切都很好。）

🔊 解析　文章第一段提到「飯店的房間都訂走了」，因此符合敘述的答案是（B）。

Q2 _B_ **What did they hear in the midnight?**

（他們半夜聽到了什麼？）

（A）The clerk is talking to someone.

（服務人員在跟某個人說話。）

▶（B）Some strange noise.（一些奇怪的吵雜聲。）

（C）Some ghosts were talking.（有一些鬼在說話。）

（D）Nothing.（沒有什麼。）

🔊 解析　文章第二段提到「他們聽到客廳有奇怪的聲音」，因此符合敘述的答案是（B）。

Q3 _C_ **Which statement is not true?**

（哪一項敘述不是正確的？）

（A）Mr. and Mrs. Collins spent their vacation in China.（科林斯夫婦在中國度假。）

（B）The first day they arrived at the hotel, the clerk spoke to them.（他們第一天到達飯店時，服務人員就對他們說話。）

▶（C）The ghost was very nice.（那個鬼很親切。）

（D）During the middle night while sleeping, they heard some strange noise in the living room.

（睡到半夜，他們聽到客廳裡有一些怪聲。）

▶ 解析　文章中並沒有提到鬼是否很親切，因此（C）的敘述是不正確的。

Q4　＿＿＿*B*＿＿＿ **What was the mother language of the ghost?**

（這個鬼的母語是什麼？）

（A）English.（英文）

▶（B）Chinese.（中文）

（C）French.（法文）

（D）Italian.（義大利文）

▶ 解析　文章第二段提到「這個鬼來自中國」，可以得知他的母語是中文，因此正確答案是（B）。

UNIT 4　Study　1　菜單與訂單

Pizza House Menu		
Pizza	Medium (3-5 people)	Large (6-8 people)
Pepperoni	$440	$660
Sausage	$450	$670
Cheese and Mushroom	$380	$580
Side Dishes		
Chicken Wings	$130 (5 pieces)	$180 (8 pieces)
Onion Rings	$50 (Medium)	$80 (Large)
French Fries	$40 (Medium)	$60 (Large)
Drinks	A can	a bottle
Soda or Tea	$20	$50

Pizza House Order Form

Name: Sandy Lord
Pizza: Large / Sausage
Sides: 5 pieces of chicken wings + Onion rings (Medium)
Drink: A bottle of soda
Delivery Fee: $0
VIP (90% of total cost): Yes

Order taken by *Carl Jones*

比薩屋菜單

比薩	中（三～五人）	大（六～八人）
義大利辣腸	$440	$660
香腸	$450	$670
起司與洋菇	$380	$580

搭配附餐		
雞翅	$130（五塊）	$180（八塊）
洋蔥圈	$50（中份）	$80（大份）
薯條	$40（中份）	$60（大份）

飲料	一罐	一瓶
汽水或茶	$20	$50

比薩屋訂單

名字：Sandy Lord
比薩：大 / 香腸
附餐：五塊雞翅 + 中份洋蔥圈
飲料：一瓶汽水
運送費：$0
貴賓會員（所有費用打九折）：是

訂單紀錄者：Carl Jones

Q1 _____*A*_____ **Who is Carl Jones?**

（誰是 Carl Jones？）

▶（A）An employee in Pizza House.

（一位在比薩屋工作的員工。）

（B）A regular customer.（一位常客。）

（C）A person who ordered pizza and side dishes.

（點比薩與附餐的人。）

（D）Sandy Lord's employer.（Sandy Lord 的雇主。）

▶解析 從「訂單」的敘述中可以看到 Carl Jones 是填寫訂單的人，因此他應該是店內的員工，因此正確答案是（A）。

Q2 _____*B*_____ **How much does the order cost?**

（這份訂單多少錢？）

（A）900.

▶（B）810.

（C）670.

（D）850.

▶解析 訂單中的香腸大比薩要 670 元、五塊雞翅 130 元、中份洋蔥圈 50 元、一瓶汽水 50 元，加起來一共 900 元，由於貴賓會員可以打九折，因此一共要付 810 元，故答案選（B）。

Q3 _____*C*_____ **What kind of items CANNOT be ordered from the menu?**

（哪一項品項無法在菜單上被點到？）

（A）Soft drinks.（汽水。）

（B）Chicken.（雞肉。）

▶（C）Seafood.（海鮮。）

（D）Fries.（薯條。）

▶解析 本題是問「哪一個品項無法從菜單中點到？」除了海鮮的食品，其他選項都可以在菜單上看到，因此正確選項是（C）。

Warm Breeze Department Store
Competition: Employee of the year

2019	2020	2021
Joan Rose	Ellie Wang	undecided
Men's Clothing Dept.	Women's Clothing Dept.	undecided

To: Laura Thomas, Diana Brown
From: Ali Huston
Subject: Employee of the year 2021

Dear fellow managers,

　　It's time for us to choose the employee of the year in Warm Breeze Department Store again. Do you have a particular ideal person in mind to recommend? Here are my two suggestions.

　　Joan Rose, of course, is always an awesome employee. Thanks to her hard work, the Men's Clothing Dept., indeed, made a record year once again. She certainly deserved to win the employee of the year one more. Should we let Joan win again, or encourage someone else this time? Another candidate is Lisa North in the Sporting Goods Dept. She is friendly and accommodating. She is never late or impatient to customers. She always goes the extra mile to help customers find something they want. What's more, she never says "No" when we ask her to work overtime during our anniversary.

　　Suppose that you agree with my two choices, do you prefer Joan Rose or Lisa North?

　　Looking forward to your feedback.

休閒類
生活類

應用類
書信類

論說類
記敘類

文章類
雙篇類

解答篇

中文翻譯

溫暖微風百貨公司
競賽：年度最佳員工

2019	2020	2021
Joan Rose	Ellie Wang	未定
男裝部	女裝部	未定

收件人：Laura Thomas、Diana Brown

寄件人：Ali Huston

主旨：2021 年最佳員工

親愛的經理夥伴們，

　　又到了我們選擇溫暖微風百貨的 2021 年最佳員工的時間了。你們心目中有理想的特別人選要來推薦的嗎？我這裡有兩個建議。

　　Joan Rose，當然一直都是很棒的員工。多虧了她辛勤工作，男裝部門的確又再一次做出創紀錄的一年。她當然值得再次贏得年度最佳員工。我們應該讓 Joan 再次得獎，或是這一次我們應該鼓勵其他人呢？另一位人選是運動用品部門的 Lisa North。她很友善又隨和。她從不會遲到或對顧客不耐煩。她總是會多走幾步來幫助顧客找他們想要的東西。更重要的是，當我們要求她在周年慶加班時，她從不說「不」。

　　假如你們贊同我的兩個選擇，你們會比較偏好 Joan Rose 或是 Lisa North 呢？

　　期待你們的回應。

Q1 ___*B*___ **What is the Laura Thomas's position in Warm Breeze Department Store?**

（Laura Thomas 在溫暖微風百貨公司的職位是什麼？）

（A）Custodian.（管理員）

▶（B）Manager.（經理）

（C）Vice president.（副總裁）

（D）Consultant.（顧問）

解析 在信中 Ali Huston 稱 Laura Thomas 及 Diana Brown 為「親愛的經理夥伴們」，因此他們三位應該都是經理，因此正確答案是（B）。

Q2   *B*   **The phrase "suppose that" can be replaced by?**

（A）Although.（雖然）

▶（B）If.（如果）

（C）While.（當）

（D）As.（因為）

解析 本句是指「假如你們贊同我的兩個選擇，你們會比較偏好 Joan Rose 或是 Lisa North 呢？」所以 "suppose that" 是「假如」的意思，因此正確答案是（B）。

Q3   *C*   **What can we know about Joan Rose?**

（我們可以知道有關 Joan Rose 的什麼事？）

（A）She is an employee in the Women's Clothing Dept.（她是女裝部的員工。）

（B）Laura Brown is her manager.

（Laura Brown 是她的經理。）

▶（C）She may win the second time competition.

（她有可能第二次贏得競賽。）

（D）Diana Brown prefers her to be the employee of the year 2021.

（Diana Brown 比較偏好她成為 2021 年度最佳員工。）

解析 Joan Rose 不是女裝部門的員工，她是在男裝部工作；文中無法確認 Laura Brown 與 Joan Rose 之間的關係； Diana Brown 還沒有任何的回應。因此正確選項是（C），因為她可能繼 2019 年後在 2021 年再次獲得最佳員工獎。

Charles's Itinerary
January 1ˢᵗ Tour in Taipei

9:00	Meet at Taipei Railway Station.
9:00-11:00	Take the MRT to Ximending and go window Shopping in Ximending.
11:00-12:00	Take the MRT to Longshan Temple and Visit the beautiful temple
12:00-14:00	Lunch Time in a Japanese food restaurant
14:00-17:00	Ride a minibus to visit National Palace Museum
17:00-19:00	Ride a minibus to take a hot spring in Yangmingshan
19:00-20:30	Dinner Time in a Japanese food restaurant
20:30-22:00	Ride a minibus to Taipei 101 and watch night views on the 89ᵗʰ floor

Hi Lillian,

I just got the itinerary planned by you. Thank you so much. I am so glad that I can finally have a holiday tour in Taipei City, which I've always wanted to visit. It seems so nice that I can visit the famous Longshan Temple and hang around the interesting area, Ximending. And I notice that you've arranged our lunch and dinner in Japanese restaurants. To tell the truth, I really want to try some local food, although I am Japanese. On January 1ˢᵗ, I will also have a meeting with my ex-coworker, so I am afraid I have to cancel the last activity. Once again, thank you so much for your arrangement and make this visit in Taipei City worthwhile. Please send me the updated itinerary again at your convenience.

查爾斯的旅遊行程
一月一日台北之旅

9:00	台北車站會合
9:00 - 11:00	搭捷運到西門町 / 在西門町逛街購物
11:00 - 12:00	搭捷運到龍山寺 / 參訪美麗的寺廟
12:00 - 14:00	在一家日式料理餐廳吃午餐
14:00 - 17:00	搭小巴士到國立故宮博物院參觀
17:00 - 19:00	搭小巴士到陽明山泡溫泉
19:00 - 20:30	在一家日式料理餐廳吃晚餐
20:30 - 22:00	搭小巴士到台北 101 大樓 / 在 89 樓看夜景

Lillian 你好，

　　我剛才收到你規劃的旅遊計畫，非常感謝你。我很高興我終於能在台北市來一場假期旅行，這是我一直想拜訪的地方。似乎很棒的是，我能參訪有名的龍山寺，以及可以逛逛這個有趣的西門町區。而我有注意到你安排了我們的午餐與晚餐在日式料理餐廳。老實說，雖然我是日本人，但是我非常想嘗試一些本地的食物。在一月一日時，我也將與我之前的同事有約，所以我恐怕必須取消最後一個活動。再次非常感謝你的安排，讓這一趟台北行變得十分值得。請在你方便的時候，再寄一個更新的旅遊計畫給我。

Q1 ___*D*___ **What time is probably Charles's meeting with his ex-coworker?**

（Charles 和之前的同事可能在什麼時候見面？）

（A）9:00

（B）14:00

（C）19:30

▶（D）21:00

▶解析 在信件中提到「我與之前的同事有約，所以我

382

恐怕必須取消最後的一個活動。」預定行程最後一項是「20:30 - 22:00 搭小巴士到台北 101 大樓／在 89 樓看夜景」，因此可能的時間是（D）21:00。

Q2   ***B***   **How will they go to Ximending?**

（A）On foot.（走路）

▶（B）By MRT.（搭捷運）

（C）By bus.（搭公車）

（D）By taxi.（搭計程車）

▶解析   在行程中提到「9:00 - 11:00 搭捷運到西門町／在西門町逛街購物」，因此是搭捷運去，正確答案是（B）。

Q3   ***D***   **Which of the following statement is NOT true?**

（哪一項敘述不是正確的？）

（A）Lillian arranged the itinerary for Charles.

（Lillian 為 Charles 安排旅遊計畫。）

（B）They will have some time going shopping.

（他們將有些時間去購物。）

（C）Museum will be visited during the afternoon time.（博物館將在下午時段被參觀。）

▶（D）They will enjoy some Japanese food in Taipei.

（他們將在台北享受日式料理。）

▶解析   在信中提到「我有注意到你安排我們的午餐與晚餐在日式料理餐廳。老實說，雖然我是日本人，但是我想嘗試一下本地的食物。」因此他們應該是吃中式或台式的料理，因此（D）的敘述是錯誤的。

To: Jeffrey Lin
From: Teacher Jose Su
Re: Improve your English ability

Dear Jeffrey,

　　As your English teacher, I advise you to take more English Classes. I have attached a schedule of classes from the International Village Institute. A number of your classmates have taken classes there, and it has a fine reputation. Take a look at the 101 courses. I think you should sign up for 101A. Even though you know how to use some English sentences to communicate with American people, it never hurts to start again from the beginning. Grammar courses would also be useful, and I think you are qualified for 102B course. Pronunciation course might be a good idea too, but there's no sense in overburdening yourself. In short, you can pick up the two kinds of courses in the beginning.

Teacher
Jose Su

International Village Institute
schedule of classes

Course #	Title	Hours / Tuition
101A	Basic Conversation	Mon. + Wed. 6:00 - 8:00PM /$3000
101B	Advanced Conversation	Tue. + Thur. 6:00 - 8:00PM /$3000
102A	Basic Grammar	Tue. + Thur. 8:00 - 10:00PM /$3500
102B	Advance Grammar	Mon. + Wed. 8:00 - 10:00PM /$3500
103	Pronunciation	Mon. +Wed. 8:00 - 10:00PM /$2500
104	Writing	Sat. 9:00 - 12:00PM /$2800

收件人：Jeffrey Lin

寄件人：Jose Su 老師

回覆：改善你的英文能力

親愛的 Jeffrey，

　　身為你的英文老師，我建議你上更多英文課。我有附上來自國際村機構的課表。你有些同學已經在那裡上過課，而那裡的名聲很好。看一下 101 的課程，我想你應該報名 101A。即使你知道如何用一些英文句子與美國人溝通，但再次從基礎學起也無妨。文法課程也是十分有用的，我想你有上 102B 課程的資格。發音課程可能也是很好的主意，但是讓自己負擔過重也沒有意義。總之，你一開始可以先選這兩種課程就好。

老師

Jose Su

國際村機構課程時間表

課程編號	課程名稱	時段 / 學費
101A	基礎會話	星期一 + 星期三 晚上 6:00 - 8:00 /$3000
101B	進階會話	星期二 + 星期四 晚上 6:00 - 8:00 /$3000
102A	基礎文法	星期二 + 星期四 晚上 8:00 - 10:00 /$3500
102B	進階文法	星期一 + 星期三 晚上 8:00 - 10:00 /$3500
103	發音	星期一 + 星期三 晚上 8:00 - 10:00 /$2500
104	寫作	星期六 早上 9:00 - 12:00 /$2800

Q1 _*A*_ **How many writing class in this institute?**
（這間機構有幾堂寫作課？）

► （A）One.

（B）Two.

（C）Three.

（D）Four.

386

解析 在課表中只有一堂在周六早上的寫作課程，因此正確答案是（A）。

Q2   *B*   **How many days a week will Jeffrey have classes?**

（Jeffrey 一週有幾天要上課？）

（A）One day.

▶（B）Two days.

（C）Three days.

（D）Four days.

解析 在信中英文老師建議他選基礎會話課程101A，是週一與週三上課。另外還建議進階文法課程102B，也是週一與週三上課。所以一週總共有兩天要上課，因此正確答案是（B）。

Q3   *C*   **Which of the following statement is NOT correct?**

（哪一項敘述不是正確的？）

（A）Jose Su is Jeffrey Lin's teacher.

（Jose Su 是 Jeffrey Lin 的老師。）

（B）International Village Institute has courses on weekdays and weekends.

（國際村機構在平日和周末都有開課。）

▶（C）Jeffrey will follow Jose's advice to take a pronunciation course.

（Jeffrey 會遵照 Jose 的建議選擇發音課。）

（D）The tuition Jeffrey has to pay for his courses is $6500.（Jeffrey 必須要付 6500 元的學費。）

解析 在信中得知 Jose 是 Jeffrey 的老師；在課表中可知國際村機構有平日與週末的課程；Jeffrey 之後會上101A（3000 元）、102B（3500 元），總共要付 6500元；Jose 在信中提及不用上太多課，上兩種課即可，所以 Jeffrey 並沒有選發音課，（C）是錯誤的選項。

387

MEMO

To: All accounting personnel
Date: April 12th, 2020.
Subject: New payroll system training

The management team has decided to replace the current type with a newer and more reliable set of the payroll system. The new kits are made by Apex Technology, which will be more user-friendly. They can also reduce the possibility of making errors. Apex will send two trainers to our accounting department to demonstrate how to use this new system. There will be two sessions. One is on May 2nd, from 2:00 PM to 5:00 PM. The other is on May 4th, from 9:00 AM to 12:00 PM. Please make sure each of you can attend at least one of these sessions. If you cannot come due to your work schedule, please feel free to contact me directly.

Brad Robinson
Head of Accounting

Accounting Personnel Work schedules
Day Shift (9:00 A.M. - 5:00 P.M.)
Evening Shift (2:00 P.M. - 10:00 P.M.)

Name	May 2	May 3	May 4
John	Day	OFF	Evening
Cynthia	OFF	Day	Evening
Mark	Evening	Day	OFF
Maria	Day	Evening	Day

中
文
翻
譯

備忘錄

給：所有會計部的員工

日期：2020 年 4 月 12 日

主旨：新的薪資系統訓練

　　管理團隊已經決定將現有的薪資系統取代成一套更新、更可靠的薪資系統。這個新的成套工具是由 Apex 科技所製作，而它將會在使用上更友善。它們能夠降低犯錯的可能性。Apex 公司將會派兩名訓練人員到我們會計部門來展示如何操作這個新的系統。會有兩個場次的課程。一場是五月二日從下午兩點到五點。另一場則是五月四日早上九點到十二點。請確認你們每一位能夠參加至少一場次以上的訓練課程。假如你因為工作班表的安排而無法參與，請不要顧忌，直接與我聯繫。

Brad Robinson

會計主任

會計人員工作班表
日班（早上 9:00 - 下午 5:00）
晚班（下午 2:00 - 晚上 10:00）

姓名	五月二日	五月三日	五月四日
John	日班	休假	晚班
Cynthia	休假	日班	晚班
Mark	晚班	日班	休假
Maria	日班	晚班	日班

Q1　　___*B*___　**What is the purpose of this memorandum?**

（這封備忘錄的目的是什麼？）

（A）To ask accounting personnel to change their shifts.（要求會計人員更換班別。）

▶（B）To inform accounting staff about a recent workshop.

（告知會計人員近期的一場訓練課程。）

（C）To contact Apex Technology for further cooperation.

（聯絡 Apex 科技尋求進一步的合作。）

（D）To make sure that accounting staff keeps their original systems.

（確保會計人員維持原來的系統。）

▶ 解析 在備忘錄中提到「薪資系統將會換成 Apex 科技的系統，該公司會派兩位訓練人員來示範如何操作系統，一共有兩場課程。」因此正確答案是（B）。

Q2 _B_ **Who does most likely have to contact Brad Robinson?**

（誰最有可能必須和 Brad Robinson 聯絡？）

（A）John.

▶（B）Cynthia.

（C）Mark.

（D）Maria.

▶ 解析 在備忘錄中提到「假如你因為工作班表的安排而無法參與，與我直接聯繫。」而在班表可以得知 Cynthia 在五月二日休假，五月四日又是晚班。因此她兩場課程均無法參與，因此正確答案是（B）。

Q3 _C_ **Which of the following statement is NOT correct?**

（下列哪一項敘述不是正確的？）

（A）Apex is a technology company.

（Apex 是一間科技公司。）

（B）Maria has no day offs during these three days on schedule.

（Maria 在這三天的班表都沒有休假。）

▶（C）Brad Robinson will be the trainer to teach the new system.

（Brad Robinson 會是教學新系統的訓練人員。）

（D）On May 3rd, Mark will start his work at 9:00 AM.

（五月三日 Mark 將從早上九點開始他的工作。）

▶ 解析 在備忘錄中提到 Apex 科技會請兩位訓練人員教學新系統，Brad Robinson 則是通知訓練課程的人，因此（C）的敘述是錯誤的。

Reading Articles

CHAPTER 6
閱讀模擬試題

◎ UNIT 1 模擬試題

|閱|讀|模|擬|試|題|

UNIT 1 模擬試題

作答說明　本測驗分三部分全為四選一的選擇題，共 35 題，測驗時間為 45 分鐘。

第一部分：詞彙

共 10 題，每題含一個空格。請由試題冊上的四個選項中選出最適合題意的字或詞作答。

Q1　The restaurant is always _____ to choose a supplier in order to provide high-quality fresh foods.

（A）selective

（B）careful

（C）magnificent

（D）acceptable

Q2　Throughout his career, Tom has _____ the respect of his coworkers for his integrity and dedication.

（A）earned

（B）dumped

（C）modified

（D）reduced

Q3　How _____ can you wear that dress? It looks awful.

（A）at the place

（B）in the end

（C）on earth

（D）by no means

Q4　Mr. Lin _____ the seminar by half an hour so that he could cover all the topics he wanted to talk.

（A）appointed

（B）extended

（C）eliminated

（D）discovered

Q5 Family Grocery sells a great section of _____, including lettuce, carrots and mushrooms that comes directly from the local farms.

（A）machines   （B）furniture

（C）perspectives   （D）produce

Q6 The reduction of electricity consumption in our houses is one thing we can do to slow _____ warming.

（A）global   （B）modest

（C）unforgettable   （D）determined

Q7 My teacher told me to modify my report _____ due to the fact that I made so many spelling and grammatical mistakes.

（A）suddenly   （B）thoroughly

（C）absolutely   （D）accidentally

Q8 Carson Company _____ its gross income will double in the next quarter because of the technology they have recently improved.

（A）projects   （B）objects

（C）rejects   （D）injects

Q9 The university announced that it was doing more to _____ the regulations to ensure the campus safety.

（A）set up   （B）apply for

（C）give out   （D）look into

Q10 After watching a horror movie in the cinema, I thought I was going to _____ .

（A）keep on   （B）throw up

（C）fill out   （D）sign up

第二部分：段落填空

共 10 題，包括二個段落，每個段落個含 5 個空格。請由試題冊上四個選項中選出最適合題意的字或詞作答。

Questions 11-15

PLEASE NOTE

New Taipei City Library will be closed ___**11**___ September 6th, Mid-Autumn Festival. The library will be closed at 10:00 P.M. on September 5th, and will not ___**12**___ 8:00 A.M. of the morning of September 7th. We apologize to our regular patrons for any ___**13**___ caused by the closure. In any case, those wishing to ___**14**___ books during this period will still be able to do so. Patrons should simply use the drop-off slots next to the entrance to the library. Also, we would like to remind you that ___**15**___ around the library is for your benefits. Trash cans are located on each floor near the elevators. No littering. Thank you very much for your cooperation.

Have a nice holiday,
New Taipei City Library

Q11 _____ （A）on （B）in
　　　　　　（C）at （D）above

Q12 _____ （A）accept donations at
　　　　　　（B）reopen until
　　　　　　（C）close again from 7 A.M. to
　　　　　　（D）return to the check-in counter at

Q13 _____ （A）favor （B）suspense
　　　　　　（C）inconvenience （D）method

Q14 _____ （A）purchase （B）return
　　　　　　（C）withdraw （D）publish

Q15 _____ （A） keeping neat （B） keep neat
　　　　　　 （C） to keeping neat （D） kept neat

Questions 16-20

COMPUTER CLASSES FOR BIHU COMMUNITY

On October 31st, computer classes for residents of Bihu Community will __**16**__. Designed for all levels, from basic, intermediate through high advanced, each session will contain many computer skills for people to learn.

The classes will be held at the Bihu elementary school auditorium at 10:30 A.M. to 12:30 P.M. every Monday and Thursday for totally three months. Therefore, __**17**__. There is no charge to join, but __**18**__ should pre-register online first. For more information, please call 2458-8956 directly. __**19**__ people in each class will be limited to forty-five __**20**__ the limited computers which can be used. Thus, register your classes ASAP to secure your spots!

Q16 _____ （A） proceed （B） verify
　　　　　　 （C） diversify （D） tolerate

Q17 _____ （A） please pay your tuition on time
　　　　　　 （B） please remember to attend each class punctually
　　　　　　 （C） no people will be allowed to use the computers
　　　　　　 （D） please return your membership cards as you leave

Q18 _____ （A） passengers （B） participants
　　　　　　 （C） handlers （D） planners

Q19 _____ （A） A number of （B） The number of
　　　　　　 （C） A chuck of （D） The variety of

Q20 _____ （A） on the other hand （B） on account of
　　　　　　 （C） in order that （D） in spite of

第三部分：閱讀理解

共 15 題，包括 5 個題組，每個題組含 1 至 2 篇短文，與數個相關的四選一的選擇題。請由試題冊上的選項中選出最適合者作答。

Questions 21-23

Memo

To: All staff numbers
From: Tina Wang, Personnel Office
Subject: Dress Code

In response to a recent issue about staff members' attire, we have decided to hold a ballot. Please tell us your opinions. Give us your suggestions and feedback.

Question:
Should staff members be allowed to wear casual clothes on Friday?

○ Yes, **casual** clothes should be allowed.

○ No, uniforms only.

Please reply Yes or No. Just check one, and then send your choice through E-mail. My email address is: Tina_Wang@FlyAir.com.tw Thank you very much for your help!

Q21 _____ **What is the purpose of this memo?**

（A）Remind staff members of a new dress code.

（B）Do a survey regarding company's dress code.

（C）Recheck whether staff members follow the dress code or not.

（D）Hold a ballot to vote against the dress code.

Q22 _____ **How can staff members respond to this memo?**

（A）Make a phone call.

（B）E-mail back to the Personnel Office.

（C）Put it into a suggestion box.

（D）Hand in at the next meeting.

Q23 _____ **The word "casual" in the survey question can be replaced as:**

（A）informal

（B）inexpensive

（C）fancy

（D）unusual

Questions 24-26

Wonders in the world

Three famous and ancient wonders in the world are The Taj Mahal, The temple of Angkor Wat, and Machu Picchu. People who have been to these attractions say that they will never forget what they have seen. These three wonders attract millions of visitors every year and are considered the most precious architectures on earth.

The Taj Mahal

Constructed in India in the 17th century, The Taj Mahal was designed as a tomb for a king's wife. A white, magnificent, and unbelievable building now has become an important asset in this mysterious Asian country.

The Temple of Angkor Wat

Constructed in Cambodia in the 12th century, the temple of Angkor Wat was designed as a religious and honorable place. The design and the art of architecture have influenced deeply in this special Asian country. Today, the site is being repaired and preserved by the United Nations, an international organization.

Machu Picchu

Constructed high in the Andes Mountains of Peru by Incas. Experts believe that it was also built for religious purposes. People are amazed when they see the great architecture in such high mountains. As for today, still, no one can exactly tell how people in the ancient world climb up the steep mountain without any tools or equipment.

Q24 _____ **According to the article, which architecture was constructed by Incas?**
（A）The Taj Mahal
（B）The temple of Angkor Wat
（C）Machu Picchu
（D）All of them

Q25 _____ **Who might have the most interest in this article?**
（A）People who want to travel abroad and appreciate some wonders of the world.
（B）People who want to know about the history of Russia.
（C）People who are curious about different businesses' assets.
（D）People who feel bored with studying each country's architecture.

Q26 _____ **Which of the following statements is NOT true?**
（A）The temple of Angkor Wat was designed as a religious and honorable place.
（B）People are amazed when they see Machu Picchu in such high mountains.
（C）The temple of Angkor Wat is being repaired and preserved by the United States.
（D）The temple of Angkor Wat was constructed in Cambodia in the 12nd century.

Questions 27-29

New American Restaurant ~ TGG
Opens Downtown

Last week I went to a new American restaurant located in the center of Taipei City. It's on Zhongxiao East Road, Section 4th, near the Taipei City Hall Terminal. This is a cheerful and vivid fast food store with some friendly, confident, efficient, and helpful servers. All of the meals I ordered were ready **in a flash**. My favorite hamburger and my wife's fried rice were cooked just the way we liked them. It is pretty difficult for me to forget the first bite when I tasted that house salad for the first time. I really think it is out of this world! How appetizing! The only complaint about the restaurant is the background music. This loud heavy metal music really made me feel like a fish out of the water. But don't get me wrong. As a matter of fact, I love this place. I recommend to my friends and relatives that they should visit this charming one. If you are looking for a place for a quick bite to eat next time in the center of Taipei City, this new American restaurant is your ideal option.

Food quality ★★★★★
Service quality ★★★★★
Price ★★★★
Atmosphere ★★★★
Location ★★★★

Q27 _____ **What is the purpose of this article?**

（A）Complain about a new restaurant

（B）Review a fast food store

（C）Recommend a recipe

（D）Conduct a survey

Q28 _____ **What does the "in a flash" mean in the fourth line of this passage?**

（A）very fashionable

（B）very quickly

（C）very shining

（D）very indispensable

Q29 _____ **Which statement is correct?**

（A）The loud heavy metal music in the restaurant made the writer feel energetic.

（B）The servers in this restaurant need more training.

（C）The restaurant is located downtown.

（D）The writer is satisfied with the price the most in the restaurant.

Questions 30-32

Stress! Stress! Stress! Lots of people are talking about it. Do you hate your job? Do you always have no time to spend with your children? Balancing work and family can be tiring. If stress left your dreary feeling untreated, it can cause serious mental health problems. Moreover, mental problems might cause more physical problems. Do not wait anymore. Take the stress test NOW. At the Beautiful Heart Professional Health Services Center, we offer:

Family counseling

Stress management

Career counseling

Personality Test

Make an appointment anytime online.

beautifulheart@nphc.com

7:00 A.M. to 10:00 P.M. TEL: (02) 7676-8888

Counseling Follow-up

Name: Gina Chung

Patient's chief complaint:

(1) She has a bad relationship with her mother-in-law. Her husband's misunderstanding makes her feel depressed. She has trouble sleeping at night.

(2) She was under lots of pressure at work. She has too many jobs on hand. She works late almost every day, but still has no chance to get a promotion or pay raise.

Professional advice:

(1) The patient needs to face her family problem. Tell her husband what she likes and dislikes when dealing with her mother-in-law. Ask for her husband's support.

(2) She needs to ask for a raise directly and says "NO" to any additional work. Tell her boss about her feeling.

(3) She can take a sleeping pill at night until she has no trouble sleeping.

Date for re-appointment: March 10th, 2020.

Q30 _____ **Who will have the most interest in this advertisement?**

(A) Stress counselors

(B) Unemployed people

(C) Medical industry workers

(D) Working parents

Q31 _____ **What can be inferred about Gina Chung?**

(A) She is single and has a stressful job.

(B) She had complained about the doctor's advice.

(C) She did a personality test in the clinic.

(D) She will see the doctor again on March 10th, 2020.

Q32 _____ **What might Gina Chung do after receiving pieces of advice from the doctor?**

（A）Face the problem and quit taking sleeping pills.

（B）Talk with the manager and require a pay increase.

（C）Cut the relationship with her husband's mother.

（D）Resign from her job immediately.

Questions 33-35

Worldwide International, Inc.
Division Heads Conference
Wednesday, December 7th 3:30PM
Place: Company Meeting Room 5

AGENDA
1. Office supplies issues
2. Winter conference plans
3. The year-end banquet
4. New HR regulations
5. Review last year's performance
6. Budget Report

To: Anita Blair
From: Jasmine Rosemary
Re: Yesterday's conference

Dear Anita,

I am concerned about your sudden illness. Are you feeling better now? The conference yesterday went well, and it started on time. We rearranged the order of the agenda a bit. We talked about the fifth item first because we all thought that the last year's performance needed a quick review, and then we can go ahead for the coming year. The meeting lasted for 2 hours and we had no extra time to finish the sixth item. We set the date for the next month's conference, which should include the item we didn't discuss this time. It will be held on the 17th. Also, because some outside consultants will participate in the next meeting, we need a bigger room to make everyone more comfortable. I think Room 5 is too small. Either Room 1 or Room 3 will be a good choice.

Sincerely yours,
Jasmine

Q33 _____ **What item was discussed last?**

（A）Review last year's performance

（B）New HR regulations

（C）Office supplies issues

（D）Budget Report

Q34 _____ **What time did the meeting end?**

（A）3:30 P.M.

（B）5:30 P.M.

（C）4:30 P.M.

（D）2:30 P.M.

Q35 _____ **When is the next meeting?**

（A）December 17th

（B）January 17th

（C）December 7th

（D）January 7th

一、詞彙（共 10 題）

Q1 The restaurant is always _____*B*_____ to choose a supplier in order to provide high-quality fresh foods.

（這間餐廳總是謹慎的選擇它的供應者，為的是提供高品質的新鮮食材。）

（A）selective（adj. 選擇的）　▶（B）careful（adj. 謹慎的）

（C）magnificent（adj. 極好的）　（D）acceptable（adj. 可接受的）

▶解析　四個選項中，除了（B）careful 以外，其他選項的意思皆不符合題意。

Q2 Throughout his career, Tom has _____*A*_____ the respect of his coworkers for his integrity and dedication.

（在 Tom 的職涯中，因為他的正直與奉獻，贏得他同事們的敬重。）

▶（A）earned（V-p.p. 贏得）　　（B）dumped（V-p.p. 丟棄）

（C）modified（V-p.p. 修正）　（D）reduced（V-p.p. 減少）

▶解析　四個選項中，除了（A）earned 以外，其他選項的意思皆不符合題意。

Q3 How _____*C*_____ can you wear that dress? It looks awful.

（你究竟為什麼要穿那件洋裝？它看起來很糟。）

（A）at the place（在那個地方）　（B）in the end（最後）

▶（C）on earth（究竟；到底）　　（D）by no means（絕不）

▶解析　四個選項中，除了（C）on earth 以外，其他選項的意思皆不符合題意。

Q4 Mr. Lin ___*B*___ the seminar by half an hour so that he could cover all the topics he wanted to talk.

（林先生將研討會延長半個小時，因而他可以完成所有他想要講的主題。）

（A）appointed（v. 指派）　▶（B）extended（v. 延長）

（C）eliminated（v. 消除）　（D）discovered（v. 發現）

▶解析 四個選項中，除了（B）extended 以外，其他選項的意思皆不符合題意。

Q5 Family Grocery sells a great section of ___*D*___, including lettuce, carrots and mushrooms that comes directly from the local farms.

（家庭食品雜貨販賣多種選擇的農產品，包括萵苣、紅蘿蔔與蘑菇，這些均是直接從在地農場所取來的。）

（A）machines（n. 機器）　（B）furniture（n. 家具）

（C）perspectives（n. 展望）　▶（D）produce（n. 農產品）

▶解析 四個選項中，除了（D）produce 以外，其他選項的意思皆不符合題意。

Q6 The reduction of electricity consumption in our houses is one thing we can do to slow ___*A*___ warming.

（減少我們家中的電力消耗是一件我們可以做的事情，來減緩全球暖化。）

▶（A）global（adj. 全球的）

（B）modest（adj. 溫和的）

（C）unforgettable（adj. 難忘的）

（D）determined（adj. 有決心的）

▶解析 四個選項中，除了（A）global 以外，其他選項的意思皆不符合題意。

407

Q7 My teacher told me to modify my report ___*B*___ due to the fact that I made so many spelling and grammatical mistakes.

（我的老師要我徹底地修正我的報告，因為我有太多拼字和文法的錯誤。）

（A）suddenly（adv. 突然地） ► （B）thoroughly（adv. 徹底地）

（C）absolutely（adv. 絕對地） （D）accidentally（adv. 意外地）

▶解析 四個選項中，除了（B）thoroughly 以外，其他選項的意思皆不符合題意。

Q8 Carson Company ___*A*___ its gross income will double in the next quarter because of the technology they have recently improved.

（Carson 公司推測他們的總收入在下一個季度會增加雙倍，因為他們最近改善的技術所致。）

► （A）projects（v. 推測） （B）objects（v. 反對）

（C）rejects（v. 拒絕） （D）injects（v. 注射）

▶解析 四個選項中，除了（A）projects 以外，其他選項的意思皆不符合題意。

Q9 The university announced that it was doing more to ___*A*___ the regulations to ensure the campus safety.

（這間大學宣布他們要做更多事項來制定一些規範，以確保校園安全。）

► （A）set up（v. 制定） （B）apply for（v. 申請）

（C）give out（v. 分發） （D）look into（v. 調查）

▶解析 四個選項中，除了（A）set up 以外，其他選項的意思皆不符合題意。

Q10 After watching a horror movie in the cinema, I thought I was going to ___*B*___.

（在戲院看了一部恐怖電影之後，我想我快要嘔吐了。）

（A）keep on（v. 繼續） ► （B）throw up（v. 嘔吐）

（C）fill out（v. 填寫）　　　　　（D）sign up（v. 簽名）

▶解析　四個選項中，除了（B）throw up 以外，其他選項的意思皆不符合題意。

二、段落填空（共 10 題）

Questions 11-15

PLEASE NOTE

New Taipei City Library will be closed <u>on</u> September 6th, Mid-Autumn Festival. The library will be closed at 10:00 P.M. on September 5th, and will not <u>reopen until</u> 8:00 A.M. of the morning of September 7th. We apologize to our regular patrons for any <u>inconvenience</u> caused by the closure. In any case, those wishing to <u>return</u> books during this period will still be able to do so. Patrons should simply use the drop-off slots next to the entrance to the library. Also, we would like to remind you that <u>keeping neat</u> around the library is for your benefits. Trash cans are located on each floor near the elevators. No littering. Thank you very much for your cooperation.

Have a nice holiday,

New Taipei City Library

請注意

新北市圖書館將於九月六日中秋節當日休館。圖書館將於九月五日晚上十點閉館，直到九月七日早上八點才會再開放。對於固定來訪的讀者因為休館而造成的不便，我們感到很抱歉。無論如何，任何想要在這段時間還書的人，還是可以來還書，讀者只需要使用圖書館入口處旁的投書孔。此外，我們也想要提醒您，維持圖書館四周整潔也對您有益。垃圾桶位於每層樓的電梯旁。請勿亂丟垃圾。非常感謝您的合作。

祝您有美好的假期，

新北市圖書館

Q11 _A_ ► （A）on　　　　　　　（B）in
　　　　　（C）at　　　　　　　（D）above

▶解析　放置於日期（幾月幾號）前的介系詞為 on，因此答案為（A）on。

Q12 _B_ 　（A）accept donations at（在…接受捐款）
　　　► （B）reopen until（直到…再開放）
　　　　（C）close again from 7 A.M. to
　　　　　　（從 7 點到…再閉館）
　　　　（D）return to the check-in counter at
　　　　　　（在…歸還至報到櫃台）

▶解析　本句是指「圖書館將於九月五日晚上十點關閉，直到九月七日早上八點才會開放」，因此正確答案為（B）reopen until。

Q13 _C_ 　（A）favor（n. 幫助）
　　　　（B）suspense（n. 焦慮）
　　　► （C）inconvenience（n. 不方便）
　　　　（D）method（n. 方法）

▶解析　本句是指「對於固定的讀者因為休館而造成的不便，我們感到很抱歉。」，因此正確答案為（C）inconvenience。

Q14 _B_ 　（A）purchase（v. 購買）
　　　► （B）return（v. 歸還）
　　　　（C）withdraw（v. 抽回）
　　　　（D）publish（v. 出版）

▶解析　本句是指「任何想要在這段時間還書的人，還是可以來還書」，因此正確答案為（B）return。

Q15 _A_ ► （A）keeping neat
　　　　（B）keep neat
　　　　（C）to keeping neat
　　　　（D）kept neat

▶解析　本句是用動名詞（V-ing）來當主詞，因此正確答案為（A）keeping neat。

模擬試題

解答篇

COMPUTER CLASSES FOR BIHU COMMUNITY

On October 31ˢᵗ, computer classes for residents of Bihu Community will <u>proceed</u>. Designed for all levels, from basic, intermediate through high advanced, each session will contain many computer skills for people to learn.

The classes will be held at the Bihu elementary school auditorium at 10:30 A.M. to 12:30 P.M. every Monday and Thursday for totally three months. Therefore, <u>please remember to attend each class punctually</u>. There is no charge to join, but <u>paticipants</u> should pre-register online first. For more information, please call 2458-8956 directly. <u>The number of</u> people in each class will be limited to forty-five <u>on acconnt of</u> the limited computers which can be used. Thus, register your classes ASAP to secure your spots!

碧湖社區電腦課程

在十月三十一日，為碧湖社區居民開設的電腦課將要**進行**。課程設計包含所有程度，從基礎、中級到優級，每堂課都將包含許多電腦技巧提供人們學習。

這些課程會在碧湖國小的禮堂舉行，在每週一、四的早上 10:30 至中午 12:30，為期總共三個月。因此，**請記得準時來上每一堂課**。參加無須繳交費用，但是**參加者**應該要事先上網登記。若需要更多資訊，請直接來電 2458-8956。每堂課**的人數**會限制在 45 人，**因為**有限的電腦可被使用。因此，請盡快來登記您的課程，以確保您的位置！

Q16　　*A*　▶（A）proceed（v. 進行）
　　　　　　（B）verify（v. 證明）
　　　　　　（C）diversify（v. 多樣化）
　　　　　　（D）tolerate（v. 忍受）

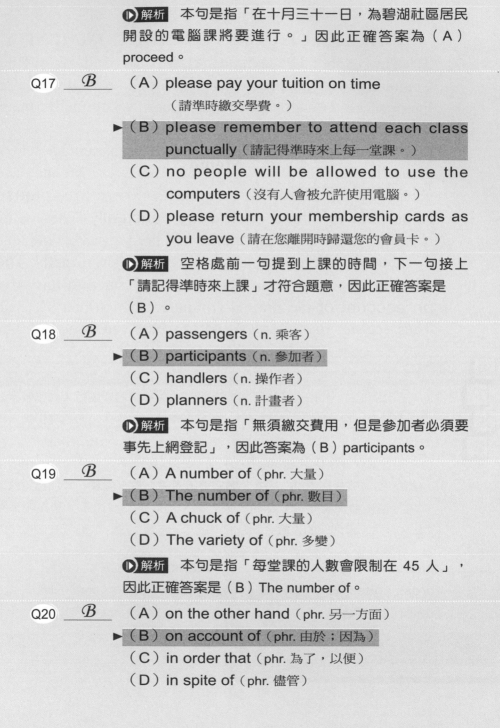

▶解析 本句是指「在十月三十一日，為碧湖社區居民開設的電腦課將要進行。」因此正確答案為（A）proceed。

Q17 ___*B*___ （A）please pay your tuition on time
（請準時繳交學費。）

▶（B）please remember to attend each class punctually（請記得準時來上每一堂課。）

（C）no people will be allowed to use the computers（沒有人會被允許使用電腦。）

（D）please return your membership cards as you leave（請在您離開時歸還您的會員卡。）

▶解析 空格處前一句提到上課的時間，下一句接上「請記得準時來上課」才符合題意，因此正確答案是（B）。

Q18 ___*B*___ （A）passengers（n. 乘客）

▶（B）participants（n. 參加者）

（C）handlers（n. 操作者）

（D）planners（n. 計畫者）

▶解析 本句是指「無須繳交費用，但是參加者必須要事先上網登記」，因此答案為（B）participants。

Q19 ___*B*___ （A）A number of（phr. 大量）

▶（B）The number of（phr. 數目）

（C）A chuck of（phr. 大量）

（D）The variety of（phr. 多變）

▶解析 本句是指「每堂課的人數會限制在 45 人」，因此正確答案是（B）The number of。

Q20 ___*B*___ （A）on the other hand（phr. 另一方面）

▶（B）on account of（phr. 由於；因為）

（C）in order that（phr. 為了，以便）

（D）in spite of（phr. 儘管）

▶解析 本句是指「每堂課的人數會限制在 45 人，因為有限的電腦可被使用。」，因此正確答案是（B）on account of。

三、閱讀理解（共 15 題）

Questions 21-23

Memo

To: All staff numbers
From: Tina Wang, Personnel Office
Subject: Dress Code

In response to a recent issue about staff members' attire, we have decided to hold a ballot. Please tell us your opinions. Give us your suggestions and feedback.

Question:

Should staff members be allowed to wear casual clothes on Friday?

○ Yes, **casual** clothes should be allowed.

○ No, uniforms only.

Please reply Yes or No. Just check one, and then send your choice through E-mail. My email address is: Tina_Wang@FlyAir.com.tw Thank you very much for your help!

單字解釋：

memo（n.）備忘錄

dress code（phr.）服裝規範

attire（n.）服飾

feedback（n.）回饋

subject（n.）主旨

in response to（phr.）回應

hold a ballot（phr.）進行投票

casual（adj.）休閒的

413

備忘錄

收件人：所有員工

寄件人：Tina Wang，人事處

主旨：服裝規範

　　回應最近有關員工服裝規範的事宜，我們已經決定要舉辦投票。請告訴我們您的意見。給我們您的建議與回饋。

問題：

員工是否應該被允許在週五穿著較休閒的服裝？

○是，休閒服裝應該被允許。

○否，只能穿制服。

　　請回答是或否。只需打勾一項，接著將您的選擇用電子郵件寄出。我的電子信箱是：Tina_Wang@FlyAir.com.tw 非常感謝您的協助！

Q21 ___*B*___ **What is the purpose of this memo?**

（這封備忘錄的目的是什麼？）

（A）Remind staff members of a new dress code.

（提醒員工新的服裝規範。）

▶（B）Do a survey regarding company's dress code.

（做一項有關公司服裝規範的意見調查。）

（C）Recheck whether staff members follow the dress code or not.

（再次確認員工是否有遵守服裝規範。）

（D）Hold a ballot to vote against the dress code.

（舉辦投票來反對服裝規範。）

▶ 解析　文中有提到「回應最近有關員工服裝規範的事宜，我們已經決定要舉辦投票。」，因此符合敘述的答案為（B）。

Q22 ___*B*___ **How can staff members respond to this memo?**

（員工可以如何回應這封備忘錄？）

（A）Make a phone call.（打一通電話。）

▶（B）E-mail back to the Personnel Office.

（用電子郵件回覆人事處。）

（C）Put it into a suggestion box.

（放入一個建議箱中。）

（D）Hand in at the next meeting.

（在下次會議時交出去。）

(▶)解析 文中有提到「將您的選擇用電子郵件寄出」，

而寄件人是來自人事處，因此符合敘述的答案為

（B）。

Q23 ___*A*___ **The word "casual" in the survey question can be replaced as:**

▶（A）informal（adj. 非正式的）

（B）inexpensive（adj. 不昂貴的）

（C）fancy（adj. 別緻的）

（D）unusual（adj. 不平常的）

(▶)解析 此處 "casual" 是指「不正式」的意思，而

（A）informal 與 casual 同義詞，因此正確答案是

（A）。

Questions 24-26

Wonders in the world

Three famous and ancient wonders in the world are The Taj Mahal, The temple of Angkor Wat, and Machu Picchu. People who have been to these attractions say that they will never forget what they have seen. These three wonders attract millions of visitors every year and are considered the most precious architectures on earth.

The Taj Mahal

Constructed in India in the 17th century, The Taj Mahal was designed as a tomb for a king's wife. A white, magnificent, and unbelievable building now has become an important asset in this mysterious Asian country.

The Temple of Angkor Wat

Constructed in Cambodia in the 12th century, the temple of Angkor Wat was designed as a religious and honorable place. The design and the art of architecture have influenced deeply in this special Asian country. Today, the site is being repaired and preserved by the United Nations, an international organization.

Machu Picchu

Constructed high in the Andes Mountains of Peru by Incas. Experts believe that it was also built for religious purposes. People are amazed when they see the great architecture in such high mountains. As for today, still, no one can exactly tell how people in the ancient world climb up the steep mountain without any tools or equipment.

單字解釋：

ancient（adj.）古老的　　　　wonder（n.）奇觀

attraction（n.）景點　　　　　precious（adj.）珍貴的

architecture（n.）建築　　　　magnificent（adj.）壯觀的

mysterious（adj.）神祕的　　　religious（adj.）宗教的

honorable（adj.）榮耀的　　　 expert（n.）專家

世界奇觀

　　世界上三個知名又古老的奇觀是泰姬瑪哈陵、吳哥窟與馬丘比丘。曾經去過這些奇觀的人們說，他們將永遠不會忘記他們看過的一切。這三個奇觀每年吸引了數百萬的旅客，也被認定為地球上最為珍貴的建築。

泰姬瑪哈陵

於十七世紀在印度建造，泰姬瑪哈陵被設計為一位國王妻子（皇后）的陵寢。白色、壯麗又非常驚人的建築，現在已經成為這個神祕的亞洲國家的重要資產。

吳哥窟

於十二世紀在柬埔寨建造，吳哥窟被設計為一個宗教與榮耀之地。此建築的設計與藝術已經深刻影響了這個特別的亞洲國家。今日，這個遺跡正被聯合國（國際組織）整修、保存。

馬丘比丘

由印加人在祕魯的安地斯山脈建造。專家相信這也是因為宗教的目的而被建成。當人們在高山之中看到這宏偉的建築物時，都感到十分驚奇。至於今日，仍然沒有人可以正確說出，在古代的人們要如何在沒有任何工具或設備的情形下，爬上陡峭的山。

Q24 ___C___ **According to the article, which architecture was constructed by Incas?**

（根據這篇文章，哪一個建築物是被印加人建造的？）

（A）The Taj Mahal（泰姬瑪哈陵）

（B）The temple of Angkor Wat（吳哥窟）

▶（C）Machu Picchu（馬丘比丘）

（D）All of them（以上皆是）

▶解析 文中有提到馬丘比丘是「由印加人在祕魯的安地斯高山上建造」，因此正確答案是（C）Machu Picchu。

Q25 ___A___ **Who might have the most interest in this article?**

（誰可能對這篇文章最感興趣？）

▶（A）People who want to travel abroad and appreciate some wonders of the world.

（想要出國旅遊並欣賞一些世界奇觀的人。）

（B）People who want to know about the history of Russia.

（想要知道俄羅斯歷史的人。）

（C）People who are curious about different businesses' assets.

（對不同企業資產好奇的人。）

（D）People who feel bored with studying each country's architecture.（對研究每個國家的建築感到無趣的人。）

▶解析 文中有提到三個世界奇觀，潛在的讀者應該會是熱愛在世界各地旅遊的人，因此正確答案是（A）。

Q26 ___C___ **Which of the following statements is NOT true?**

（下列哪一項敘述不是正確的？）

（A）The temple of Angkor Wat was designed as a religious and honorable place.

（吳哥窟被設計為一個宗教與榮耀之地。）

（B）People are amazed when they see Machu Picchu in such high mountains.

（當人們在高山之中看到馬丘比丘時，都感到十分驚奇。）

▶（C）The temple of Angkor Wat is being repaired and preserved by the United States.

（吳哥窟正由美國整修與保存。）

（D）The temple of Angkor Wat was constructed in Cambodia in the 12th century.

（吳哥窟於十二世紀在柬埔寨建造。）

▶解析 文中提到「今日，這個遺跡正被聯合國（國際組織）整修、保存」，因此不是被美國整修、保存，因此正確答案是（C）。

Questions 27-29

New American Restaurant ~ TGG Opens Downtown

Last week I went to a new American restaurant located in the center of Taipei City. It's on Zhongxiao East Road, Section 4th, near the Taipei City Hall Terminal. This is a cheerful and vivid fast food store with some friendly, confident, efficient, and helpful servers. All of the meals I ordered were ready **in a flash**. My favorite hamburger and my wife's fried rice were cooked just the way we liked them. It is pretty difficult for me to forget the first bite when I tasted that house salad for the first time. I really think it is out of this world! How appetizing! The only complaint about the restaurant is the background music. This loud heavy metal music really made me feel like a fish out of the water. But don't get me wrong. As a matter of fact, I love this place. I recommend to my friends and relatives that they should visit this charming one. If you are looking for a place for a quick bite to eat next time in the center of Taipei City, this new American restaurant is your ideal option.

Food quality ★★★★★
Service quality ★★★★★
Price ★★★★
Atmosphere ★★★★
Location ★★★★

單字解釋：

terminal（n.）車站；終點站　　　spiritual（adj.）精神的

vivid（adj.）活潑的　　　confident（adj.）自信的

efficient（adj.）有效率的　　　appetizing（adj.）開胃的

background music（phr.）背景音樂

heavy metal music（phr.）重金屬樂

fish out of the water（phr.）感到不自在

don't get me wrong 不要誤解我

as a matter of fact（phr.）事實上 relative（n.）親戚

ideal option（phr.）理想選擇　　atmosphere（n.）氣氛

新的美式餐廳～TGG 在市中心開幕了

　　上週我去了一家位於臺北市中心新開的美式餐廳。它在忠孝東路四段，靠近市府轉運站。這是一家令人愉悅又活潑的速食店，又有一些友善、自信、有效率又有幫助的服務生。所有我點的餐點一下子就都被準備好了。我最喜愛的漢堡與我太太的炒飯就是以我們所喜歡的方式來烹煮。當我第一次品嚐招牌沙拉時，對我來說真的很難忘記那第一口的滋味。我真的覺得它太美好了。多麼美味呀！對這間餐廳唯一的抱怨是背景音樂。這種大聲的重金屬樂真是讓我十分不自在。但是可別誤解我。事實上，我很愛這個地方。我推薦給我的朋友與親戚，他們應該拜訪這個迷人的餐廳。下次在臺北市中心，如果你正在找可以快速吃飯的地方時，這間新開的美式餐廳就是你理想的選擇。

食物品質　★★★★★

服務品質　★★★★★

價格　★★★★

氣氛　★★★★

位置　★★★★★

Q27　　*B*　　**What is the purpose of this article?**
（這篇文章的目的是什麼？）

（A）Complain about a new restaurant.
（抱怨一家新開的餐廳。）

► （B）Review a fast food store.
（評論一家新開的速食餐廳。）

（C）Recommend a recipe.（推薦一道食譜。）

（D）Conduct a survey.（做一項調查。）

▶解析 文末可見這間餐廳各項指標的評比等級，可知作者在評論這間店，因此正確的選項是（B）。

Q28 ___*B*___ **What does the "in a flash" mean in this passage?**
（在這篇文章的 "in a flash" 是什麼意思？）

（A）very fashionable（非常時尚）

▶（B）very quickly（非常快速）

（C）very shining（非常閃亮）

（D）very indispensable（非常不可或缺）

▶解析 在文中 "in a flash" 是指非常快速的意思，與其同義的是（B）very quickly。

Q29 ___*C*___ **Which statement is correct?**
（哪一項敘述是正確的？）

（A）The loud heavy metal music in the restaurant made the writer feel energetic.
（餐廳中大聲的重金屬樂讓作者覺得有精力充沛。）

（B）The servers in this restaurant need more training.（這家餐廳的服務生需要更多訓練。）

▶（C）The restaurant is located downtown.
（這家餐廳位於市中心。）

（D）The writer is satisfied with the price the most in the restaurant.
（作者對這家餐廳的價格最滿意。）

▶解析 文中提到「作者上週去一家位於市中心新開的美式餐廳」，因此正確答案是（C）。

Stress! Stress! Stress! Lots of people are talking about it. Do you hate your job? Do you always have no time to spend with your children? Balancing work and family can be tiring. If stress left your dreary feeling untreated, it can cause serious mental health problems. Moreover, mental problems might cause more physical problems. Do not wait anymore. Take the stress test NOW. At the Beautiful Heart Professional Health Services Center, we offer:

Family counseling
Stress management
Career counseling
Personality Test

Make an appointment anytime online.
beautifulheart@nphc.com
7:00 A.M. to 10:00 P.M. TEL: (02) 7676-8888

Counseling Follow-up

Name: Gina Chung

Patient's chief complaint:

(1) She has a bad relationship with her mother-in-law. Her husband's misunderstanding makes her feel depressed. She has trouble sleeping at night.

(2) She was under lots of pressure at work. She has too many jobs on hand. She works late almost every day, but still has no chance to get a promotion or pay raise.

Professional advice:

(1) The patient needs to face her family problem. Tell her husband what she likes and dislikes when dealing with her mother-in-law. Ask for her husband's support.

(2) She needs to ask for a raise directly and says "NO" to any additional work. Tell her boss about her feeling.

(3) She can take a sleeping pill at night until she has no trouble sleeping.

Date for re-appointment: March 10th, 2020.

單字解釋：

stress（n.）壓力

mental（adj.）心理的

follow-up（n.）後續事項

promotion（n.）升遷

professional advice（phr.）專業的建議

additional（adj.）額外的

dreary（adj.）沮喪的

counseling（n.）諮詢

misunderstanding（n.）誤解

pay raise（phr.）加薪

壓力！壓力！壓力！很多人都正在討論這件事。你討厭你的工作嗎？你總是沒時間陪伴你的孩子嗎？平衡工作與家庭可以是很累人的，如果你讓沉悶的感覺擱著不治療，這可能會造成嚴重的心理健康問題。更甚者，心理問題可能會造成更多身體的問題。千萬不要再等待了。「現在」就來做壓力測試吧！在 Beautiful Heart 專業健康服務中心，我們提供：

　　家庭諮詢

　　壓力管理

　　職涯諮詢

　　人格測試

可隨時線上預約。

beautifulheart@nphc.com

早上七點到晚上十點，電話：(02) 7676-8888

諮詢的後續事項

姓名：Gina Chung

病患主訴：

（1）她與婆婆感情不睦。丈夫的誤解讓她感到沮喪。她夜晚難以入睡。

（2）她在工作上承受許多壓力。她手上有太多工作、幾乎每天加班，但是仍沒有機會升遷或是加薪。

專業建議：

（1）這名病患需要面對她的家庭問題。告訴她的丈夫在她與婆婆相處時，喜歡或是不喜歡的地方，並尋求丈夫的支持。

（2）她需要直接要求加薪，並對額外的工作說「不」，告訴她的老闆關於她的感受。

（3）她可以每晚服用一錠安眠藥，直到沒有睡眠的問題為止。

複診日期：2020 年 3 月 10 日

Q30 _D_ **Who will have the most interest in this advertisement?**

（誰會對這則廣告最感興趣？）

（A）Stress counselors.（壓力顧問。）

（B）Unemployed people.（失業的人。）

（C）Medical industry workers.（醫療產業職員。）

▶（D）Working parents.（有工作的父母。）

▶解析 第一篇文章提到「你討厭你的工作嗎？你總是沒時間陪伴你的孩子嗎？」，因此符合敘述的答案是（D）。

Q31 _D_ **What can be inferred about Gina Chung?**

（可以推測出關於 Gina Chung 的什麼事情？）

（A）She is single and has a stressful job.

（她單身，而且有一份壓力大的工作。）

（B）She had complained about the doctor's advice.（她抱怨過醫生的建議。）

（C）She did a personality test in the clinic.
（她在這間診所做了一項人格測驗。）

► （D）She will see the doctor again on March 10th, 2020.
（她將在 2020 年 3 月 10 日再次與醫生見面。）

▶ 解析 第二篇文章提到「複診日期：2020 年 3 月 10 日」，因此符合敘述的答案是（D）。

Q32 ___B___ **What might Gina Chung do after receiving pieces of advice from the doctor?**
（收到醫生給的幾項建議後，Gina Chung 可能會做什麼？）

（A）Face the problem and quit taking sleeping pills.（面對問題並停止服用安眠藥。）

► （B）Talk with the manager and require a pay increase.（與經理談談並要求加薪。）

（C）Cut the relationship with her husband's mother.（切斷與丈夫母親的關係。）

（D）Resign from her job immediately.
（立刻辭去她的工作。）

▶ 解析 第二篇文章提到「直接要求加薪，並對額外的工作說『不』，告訴她的老闆關於她的感受」，因此符合敘述的答案是（B）。

Worldwide International, Inc.
Division Heads Conference
Wednesday, December 7th 3:30PM
Place: Company Meeting Room 5

AGENDA
1. Office supplies issues
2. Winter conference plans
3. The year-end banquet
4. New HR regulations
5. Review last year's performance
6. Budget Report

To: Anita Blair
From: Jasmine Rosemary
Re: Yesterday's conference

Dear Anita,

    I am concerned about your sudden illness. Are you feeling better now? The conference yesterday went well, and it started on time. We rearranged the order of the agenda a bit. We talked about the fifth item first because we all thought that the last year's performance needed a quick review, and then we can go ahead for the coming year. The meeting lasted for 2 hours and we had no extra time to finish the sixth item. We set the date for the next month's conference, which should include the item we didn't discuss this time. It will be held on the 17th. Also, because some outside consultants will participate in the next meeting, we need a bigger room to make everyone more comfortable. I think Room 5 is too small. Either Room 1 or Room 3 will be a good choice.

Sincerely yours,
Jasmine

單字解釋：

agenda（n.）議程

include（v.）包括

participate in（phr.）參與

rearrange（v.）壓力

consultant（n.）顧問

世界國際公司
部門主管會議
12 月 7 日，週三，下午 3:30
地點：公司五號會議室

議程
1. 辦公室用品議題
2. 冬季會議計畫
3. 尾牙宴會
4. 新的人事規範
5. 檢閱去年績效
6. 預算報告

収件人：Anita Blair
寄件人：Jasmine Rosemary
回覆：昨天的會議

親愛的 Anita，

　　我很擔心你突然生病了，你現在好多了嗎？昨天的會議進行順利，並且準時開始。我們稍微重新排列了一下議程順序。我們先討論了第五事項，因為我們全都認為去年的績效需要快速檢閱，接著我們才能為下一年繼續進行。這場會議持續了兩個小時，而我們沒有時間完成第六個事項。我們也訂好了下個月的開會時間，應該會包含我們這次未討論的事項，會在 17 日舉行。此外，因為有些外來的顧問會參加下次的會議，所以我們需要更大間的會議室，讓每個人更舒適。我覺得五號會議室太小，要麼一號或是三號會議室會是個好的選擇。
謹啟，

Jasmine

Q33 ___*B*___ **What item was discussed last?**
（哪一個項目是最後討論的？）
（A）Review last year's performance
（檢閱去年的績效）
▶（B）New HR regulations（新的人事規範）
（C）Office supplies issues（辦公室用品議題）
（D）Budget Report（預算報告）

▶解析　第二篇信件提到「我們先討論了第五項……這場會議持續了兩個小時，而我們沒有時間完成第六個事項」，因此第四項是這次最後討論的議程，再看到第一篇議程表可以得知第四項議題為「新的人事規範」，因此正確答案是（B）。

Q34 ___*B*___ **What time did the meeting end?**

（這場會議在幾點結束？）

（A）3:30 P.M.

▶（B）5:30 P.M.

（C）4:30 P.M.

（D）2:30 P.M.

▶解析 第二封信件提到「這場會議持續兩個小時」，再看第一篇議程可以知道會議室在「下午三點半」開始，因此正確答案是（B）。

Q35 ___*B*___ **When is the next meeting?**

（下次會議的時間是何時？）

（A）December 17th

▶（B）January 17th

（C）December 7th

（D）January 7th

▶解析 第二封信件提到「我們也訂好了下個月的開會時間……會在 17 日舉行」，再看到第一篇議程可以知道這場會議是 12 月 7 日，下個月是 1 月，因此正確答案是（B）。

新制多益

考前衝刺拿高分！
聽力、閱讀、單字全面提升

百萬考生唯一推薦的新制多益單字書！

不管題型如何變化，持續更新內容，準確度最高！

依 2018 年最新改版多益題型整理編排，滿足各種程度需求，學習更有效率！

定價：499 元

全新收錄完整 10 回聽力測驗試題

「題目本＋解析本」雙書裝、3 版本 MP3，做模擬測驗、複習單題、記單字，都好用！讓最強多益破解機構 Hackers Academia 帶你快速提升解題能力、穩穩拿到黃金證書！

定價：880 元

全新收錄完整 10 回閱讀測驗

「題目本＋解析本」雙書裝、單字總整理線上音檔，精準模擬實際測驗、解答詳盡清楚！讓最強多益破解機構 Hackers Academia 帶你快速提升解題能力、穩穩拿到黃金證書！

定價：880 元

台灣廣廈 國際出版集團
Taiwan Mansion International Group

國家圖書館出版品預行編目（CIP）資料

新制全民英檢中級閱讀測驗必考題型 / 陳頎著.
-- 初版. -- 新北市：國際學村, 2021.02
　面；　公分
　ISBN 978-986-454-149-2（平裝）
　1.英語　2.讀本

805.1892　　　　　　　　　　　110000565

🌐 國際學村

NEW GEPT 新制全民英檢中級閱讀測驗必考題型
按照最出題趨勢系統性分析閱讀考題，只看幾個關鍵字就能寫出正確答案！

作　　　者／陳頎	編輯中心編輯長／伍峻宏・編輯／陳怡樺
監　　　修／國際語言中心委員會	封面設計／何偉凱・內頁排版／菩薩蠻數位文化有限公司
	製版・印刷・裝訂／東豪・紘億・秉成

行企研發中心總監／陳冠蒨　　　　媒體公關組／陳柔彣
　　　　　　　　　　　　　　　　綜合業務組／何欣穎

發　行　人／江媛珍
法 律 顧 問／第一國際法律事務所 余淑杏律師・北辰著作權事務所 蕭雄淋律師
出　　　版／國際學村
發　　　行／台灣廣廈有聲圖書有限公司
　　　　　　地址：新北市235中和區中山路二段359巷7號2樓
　　　　　　電話：（886）2-2225-5777・傳真：（886）2-2225-8052

代理印務・全球總經銷／知遠文化事業有限公司
　　　　　　地址：新北市222深坑區北深路三段155巷25號5樓
　　　　　　電話：（886）2-2664-8800・傳真：（886）2-2664-8801
郵 政 劃 撥／劃撥帳號：18836722
　　　　　　劃撥戶名：知遠文化事業有限公司（※單次購書金額未滿1000元需另付郵資70元。）

■ 出版日期：2021年02月　　　　ISBN：978-986-454-149-2
　　　　　　2023年08月3刷　　　　版權所有，未經同意不得重製、轉載、翻印。